# Under His Wings Trilogy

The Sparrow
Book 1

The Hawk
Book 2

The Eagle
Book 3

by

Ronna Bacon

The Sparrow
Book 1

Laycee Bradley has been targeted by an unknown assailant and comes to rely on an old friend, Joshua Logan, to help.   When both Laycee and Joshua disappear under mysterious circumstances, it is up to Joshua's brother, Police Chief Caleb Logan, and Laycee's brothers, Liam and Leith, to race against time to solve the mystery before it's too late. Laycee comes to realize that she really more important in God's eyes than the lowly sparrow.

The Hawk
Book 2

Leith Bradley is a tile setter targeted by a smuggler. Regan Evans' family owns the tile shop and she becomes a target, too, because of her connection to Leith. Leith and Regan are faced with kidnappings, murders, and the unknown as they and their families race to find the smuggler before murder raises its very ugly head in the Bradley family. Leith, like the hawk, watches out for his family in a silent steady manner.   He learns through his trials that God provides a strong tower for him in times of trouble.

The Eagle
Book 3

Liam Bradley, eldest in the Bradley family, has seen his sister and brother settle with God-chosen life mates. Through no fault of his own, he stumbles onto a package that people will kill to get back. Ashling Downie, new to Riverville, saves Liam's life and becomes a target as well. To keep themselves safe and help solve the mystery, Ashling takes them to her friends on the street. Liam's family and the police are hot on the trail. Liam's nickname on the street is the eagle. He is the protector of his family. He learns that God is the source of his strength at all times.

Psalm 91:4.   He will cover you with his feathers,
and under his wings you will find refuge; his
faithfulness will be your shield and rampart.

Psalm 17:8.   Keep me as the apple of your eye; hide
me in the shadow of your wings.

(KJV)

The Sparrow

Under His Wings Trilogy
Book 1

by

Ronna Bacon

The Dedication

To my Mother, Helen Marie Jackson Bacon, who instilled in me a love of reading and challenged me to follow my dream of writing a novel with the words "Why don't you?". Mom, this is for you. Wish you were here today.

Verses to Remember

Matthew 10:31   "So do not fear; you are more valuable than many sparrows."

Luke 12:6 "Are not five sparrows sold for two cents? Yet not one of them is forgotten before God."

Table of Contents

THE SPARROW

Prologue

A black-clothed form snuck down the hallway of the seniors' home. He peered around a corner, making sure the nurses and other staff were busy. Seeing his way clear, he rounded the corner, making for Room 1121.

He stopped at the door and listened. Silence met his ear. He softly opened the door and slipped through, a dark shadow in the dim light. He stopped and stooped over the form in the bed. Good, she was asleep. Let's just hope she stays that way, he thought, and that the drawers don't creak.

He crept on silent rubber-shod feet to the table in the corner. Carefully opening the drawer, he felt around. Drawing out the papers, he flipped through them. Yes—here was the financial information he needed. Another quick search found a signature. He quickly stuffed the papers in his pocket, stilling at movement from the bed. He slanted his eyes that way. She was still asleep.

Creeping from the room, he managed to make his way back out without being seen. He had the information he needed. Now he could complete his work for the Mastermind.

He slid into his car and started it, creeping away at low speed. He didn't want to get stopped for speeding. He sent a quick text that he had what he needed and sent it the Boss.

Once he was at the bed and breakfast, he pulled out the papers. Something was missing. He frantically searched for the encrypted message. It was not there. His mind raced, trying to figure where he had lost it and couldn't. The Mastermind would not be pleased, but he would make sure the Mastermind never found out.

Now to get to work. He would have to leave for a few days but he would be back. What he needed was at his own place in the nearby city.

Chapter 1

The rain was slanted sideways and cold as it hit her face. She shivered and ducked her head lower but it didn't make any difference. She was soaked. And cold. And was sure she heard footsteps behind her. It would do no good to turn—she couldn't see anything for the rain and the darkness.

She reached for the door and then screamed as a hand came out of the darkness and took hold of the handle. She jumped back and looked up. It was a stranger, but she felt she knew him. She darted through the door and into the dining room and then through to a private dining room. She was scared. Too many things had been happening lately for her not to be.

She kept going through into the kitchen, past the staff busy with the meals for the evening diners and then to the back door. Opening it slowly, she looked around. It seemed clear. So far, so good. Now she just had to make it out of town and she hoped to be safe.

She splashed through the rain and puddles to her truck, hitting the lock just as she reached it. Scrambling inside, her hands shaking so badly she could hardly fit the key into the ignition, she fired up the engine and then put the truck into gear. She drove forward, desperately looking around for anyone who didn't belong.

She screamed and hit the brakes as a figure stepped into her path. She twisted the wheel and then hit the accelerator, the truck fishtailing in the wet. It was not the same man who had been in the restaurant but she was too scared to stop. Panicked, she drove through the barrier and then onto the road. Lights appeared in her rearview mirror.

Swerving on to the road, she sped through town, turning right and left, hoping that whoever was behind her was totally lost. There were no more lights in her mirror. She took the next right and hit the highway out of town. The rain was still coming down in torrents and she could tell the temperature was dropping. Without taking her eyes off the road, she reached over and hit the heater switch, flooding the cab with welcome warmth.

She slowed and then made a left turn. She had to be careful. The road was slick with mud and fallen leaves and it would take just one brief falter in her attention to the it and she would be off into the woods. She crept along as fast as she dared, checking frequently in her mirror for lights.

Then, it happened. She saw a flash of light in front of her and without thinking hit the brakes. The truck fishtailed and then slid off into the deep ditch. She tried frantically to bring the truck under control but it was too late. She felt the crunch of the truck hitting thick trees, the feel of the airbags going off and then nothing.

****

Joshua Logan picked himself up out of the puddles and shook his hands to rid them of the water. He ran for his SUV, digging his keys out and unlocking the vehicle as he slid to a stop. Yanking open the door, he slid in and once the motor was running, spun out of his parking slot and out on the road. He caught a glimpse of red lights and raced towards them. He had to admire Laycee Bradley. She sure seemed to know what she was doing. Wipers working at full speed, he followed her, far enough back that he wouldn't alarm her. He had a pretty good idea where she was headed and though he wouldn't get ahead of her to cut her off, he could follow her. He knew there was a cottage close that the Bradley family used. No many people knew about it.

He turned on to the same winding narrow track that Laycee had taken. Suddenly he slammed on his brakes. Yes - there were tail lights in the ditch. Defensive driving took over and he was able to stop safely. He leapt from his vehicle and ran to her door. Wrenching it open, he noticed she was not moving. He reached across her and undid her seat belt and then checked her for injuries. Her face had redness and bruising and he knew she had to be in some pain from the seat belt. No bleeding. No broken bones. God looked after her, he thought. He carefully lifted her out and headed to his SUV. By the time they were there, Laycee was soaked. He grabbed a blanket from the back seat and wrapped her snuggly in it, set her on the seat and fastened her in with the seat belt.

Laycee Bradley stirred. Something wasn't right, she thought. She tried to move but couldn't. She could hear a voice beside her. Opening her eyes, she struggled to focus. Joshua's face came into focus.

"Joshua," she whispered. "It's you. I thought it was someone else after me."

"There is," he replied. "We need to get you out of here. Is there anything in your truck you need? Anything hidden anywhere in it? I know how you like to hide things to keep them safe."

She thought and then said, "I have a bag behind the seat. Under my seat, tucked up, there's a brown envelope. Make sure you get that. I can't think…" Her voice faded and her eyes closed.

Joshua took a look at her and then shut the door as softly as he could. He ran back to the truck, fished around under the driver's seat and found the envelope. He pulled out the bag she mentioned, took the keys and made sure nothing else was left. He knew he would have to call his brother, the police chief for the area, but that could wait until they were safe.

He headed his truck away from the site, knowing the rain would wash away any evidence of another vehicle. Laycee was being chased, followed by who knows who, and he didn't want anyone knowing where she was until he could make sure she was safe.

Joshua reached up into the kitchen cupboard and pulled out his favourite mug, filling it with fresh coffee. After adding cream and sugar to how he liked it, he wrapped his fingers around it, relishing the heat. It may be September on the calendar but it was cold and dreary, with a dampness that went to the bones. He stopped and touched the pictures of his family on the wall in the sunroom — his parents, his brother and his family. How was he ever going to explain what he had gotten himself into when he didn't even know himself?

Leaving the kitchen, he wandered through his home to the living room. The only real light came from the fireplace that was spreading warmth and comfort. He stopped to check the logs; no, he didn't need to add one yet. He straightened the pictures on the mantle. He knew he was just putting in time, time that neither he nor Laycee had, he felt.

He turned and halted beside the couch, looking down at Laycee still sleeping. She had not stirred at all when he laid her there, still bundled up in the blanket from the truck. He nudged the blanket up a bit higher around her neck, brushing the black curls away from her face as he did so. The bruises on her face were more prominent now. What have you gotten into, Laycee? He asked himself. And how can I help? You don't like to have help, but you are so far over your head right now you need it.

He continued his path to the large picture window at the front of the house, standing to the side and pulling the drapes back a bit to see out. It was still pitch black and raining. He couldn't tell if anyone was out there, but he still felt uncomfortable, as if someone knew where they were and was just waiting for the right time.

Turning, he returned to the chair he had been sitting in before he went to refill his coffee. Setting the large brown ironstone mug on the table, he settled further back in his favourite chair. It wasn't much to look at but it was old and comfortable. It had been his grandfather's chair and many memories were associated with it. The best memories were the Bible stories and verses his grandfather had shared and the prayers he had put to heaven for his family. Joshua so wished his grandfather was still there to pray for them now. He really needed the prayers of a warrior to get through what he feared was coming.

Picking up his Bible, he spent time in reading and prayer, seeking for wisdom and courage. He needed this time to prepare, but what was he preparing for?

He tugged out a pad of paper and pen from the table drawer and started to list what he knew. He was a carpenter not a detective but knew facts were what mattered. He liked facts. Now to start — where?

****

"I paid you to find her and bring her to me." The voice on the phone was shaking in rage. "What went wrong?"

Tom Brown ran his hand through what hair he had and wished for the hundredth time he had never heard this voice. He had no idea who it was; contact was always by phone and untraceable for him.

"She was spooked. She couldn't have seen us, but she ran. She must have had help, she has totally disappeared. No sign of her or her truck."

"Find her!" Tom shuddered at the venom in the voice. "If you fail, you will be the next statistic and I will find someone else."

The phone clicked off angrily in his ear. Tom blew out a breath and then looked at his brother Andy, who was staring at the floor, watching ants move across the stickiness. They weren't cleaners and really didn't care about the mess and garbage strewn through the house. They weren't home much, any way.

"Any ideas?" Andy asked.

"No!" Tom was short with his brother. He didn't like the situation. They were small time crooks, into break and enters and shop lifting. How had they been found and why had he ever agreed? Money—that had to be it. They needed money to live.

Tom suddenly spun and pointed at Andy. "Who was that guy that followed her? Maybe he has her. Did you get a glimpse of his vehicle?"

Andy shrugged, not really caring about anything at the moment. He had done a lot of drinking when they came back after their failed attempt and his brain just didn't want to work. "No, unless it's someone related to her."

"We need to find out." Tom angrily threw a bottle across the room, watching it shatter on the wall. "We will have to stake out her brothers and see if they lead us anywhere. I'm not ready to die for this yet."

Tom slammed the door on his way to his car. It was an old rusty car and just barely ran but it was all he could afford. Shutting the door took effort as the hinges weren't great. He picked up the papers sitting on the passenger seat and thumbed through them. Yep, he thought, one of the brothers, but which

one? He turned the key and the motor reluctantly
came to life. He pulled away from the curb, leaving a
trail of black smoke and headed for one of the
brothers' homes. Now came the part he hated —
being patient.

Chapter 3

Joshua tapped the end of the pen on the tablet, then stopped, glancing over at Laycee to make sure the slight noise had not awakened her. It hadn't.

He started his list:

Lacyee is running — why?

Who is after her?

Is it work or personal?

Is it because of someone else?

He flipped the page and started describing the scene from the night before and what all he could remember of the men and the vehicle. It wasn't much. The weather had made it very difficult to see much and he had been more focused on making sure Laycee was fine.

He dropped the tablet to his knee, acknowledging he knew very little. Leaning his head back, he uttered a prayer for wisdom and guidance. Opening his eyes, he glanced over to the couch. Laycee was stirring.

Laycee slowly twisted under the blankets. She was stirring, in that state between sleep and being awake. She was sore all over and when she felt her face, it hurt. Her eyes didn't want to open but she managed to crack them. A fire flickered in her vision. Where was she? She wondered. It was not her home — she didn't have a fireplace.

Movement came into her line of sight and she shoved herself backwards, stopping when she ran out of room. Her eyes flew open. Who was that? Surely not one of the men who had dogged her steps for the last three weeks, showing up wherever she was, following her vehicle.   She felt the panic rising within her, and she desperately searched for a way to escape.

Joshua crouched down into her line of sight. He waited for her to speak, but he could see the panic and fear welling up in her.

"It's okay, Laycee." He spoke in a soft voice. "You're safe. I won't let anyone hurt you."

Laycee focused her eyes. "Joshua? It's you?" Her voice was incredulous.   "How did I get here? And just where is here?"

"I found you and brought you here. It's my place. Tell you what. Why don't you have a shower and get yourself sorted out? It's late but I can get you something to at least eat and drink if you want."

He reached out a hand to help her up. She hesitated and then took his hand. Gently, he raised her to a sitting position

"Take your time.   You'll be dizzy for a bit. There's no rush," he added as she tried to stand.

Dizziness was there and she felt so off balance.   She waited for a few minutes and then struggled to her feet. Standing was not a good idea and if it hadn't been for Joshua's strong hands, she would have fallen.

Once she felt steady, he let go of her hands, hovering to make sure she didn't fall.

"The bathroom is just down the hall.   There are some samples of shampoo and soap well as a new toothbrush and toothpaste. Towels are on the counter. I also left some clean clothes for you."

She glared at him.

"It's okay. When Caleb and Hannah and the kids come out, sometimes it's really late when they go to leave and the kids are already asleep. Hannah leaves stuff here so they have clean clothes for the next morning. The clothes are hers. She would want you to use them. I think they're about the right size."

Laycee closed her eyes and then apologized. Her mind was not functioning at its usual speed. She knew Hannah from her Bible study group and felt sure Joshua was right.   Clothes were clothes and meant to be worn.   The whole Logan family were givers, albeit in a quiet, inconspicuous manner.

She untangled her feet from the blanket. Still somewhat unsteady, she managed to make her way to the bathroom. Once inside the room, she was startled when she caught her image in the mirror. Bruises and burns. She could feel the pain from the bruising from the seat belts.

After showering and dressing, she noticed Joshua had left some cream and ibuprofen tablets. Using the cream on her face hurt but then it soothed. She downed a couple of ibuprofen, hoping they would work. She stood for a moment, head down, lost in thought. Why was Joshua helping her? Who was after her? The biggest question was why?

Joshua heard the click of the bathroom door and turned to face the kitchen doorway. His Golden Retriever, Blues, pushed against him, and he absently rubbed his ears. His mind was racing as to the whys and hows. Somehow, he had to convince Laycee to let him help, keep her brothers updated and out of danger, and find out what was actually going on.

Laycee appeared in the doorway, hesitant about entering. She gave a little half-smile to him. Blues decided it was his turn to take over. He moved over in front of Laycee, sat and then leaned against her. Eyes turned up to her face, a look of absolute adoration planted itself on his face. Laycee laughed and then reached out a hand for Blues to sniff. He licked instead, firmly establishing that Laycee was just all right in his books. She bent and hugged him, so desperate to hug her own dog, a tricoloured Shetland Sheepdog named Defiant. She also so wanted to cuddle with her tuxedo cat, Terror.

"Feeling better?" Joshua asked, as he reached for a mug to pour her a coffee. He handed it to her and indicated where the cream and sugar was.

"I am. Thank you." Laycee pulled out a chair at the round oak table and sat. She played with the edge of the placemat, not sure what to say or if to say anything at all.

"What would you like, Laycee, some toast or something different?" Joshua kept a sideways watch on her, not sure either if he should be saying anything about what happened.

"Toast is fine. Do you have whole wheat or a grain bread?"

"I do. One or two pieces?"

"One I think for now."

After he had the piece of toast on a plate and in front of her, with a selection of butter, jam, cheese spread and peanut butter, he refilled his coffee cup and took a seat at the opposite side of the table from her.

Laycee avoided his eyes, instead glancing around the kitchen. She liked the off white cabinets, the mottled brown and cream countertop. White appliances, she thought—nice. I like that. There was not a lot of clutter on the countertop, but she could tell the kitchen was well used and often. Apparently Joshua liked to cook.

"Laycee," Joshua spoke in a soft voice, "we need to talk about what happened."

Laycee shot a look at him and then turned her attention to her toast. Blues leaned hard against her leg, chin on her thigh. She looked down at him and laughed. He was drooling, wanting some of her toast. She didn't know if he was allowed some, so she ignored him.

"What do we need to talk about?" she asked, delaying the inevitable questions and thoughts she wanted to avoid.

"First, why were you being chased? Who is after you?"

"I don't know," she replied. "I really don't know. I'm a secretary, not working on some big hush-hush project. I'm not in law enforcement so that someone would be after me because of that. I don't know." Her voice rose as she spoke, showing how much it had affected her.

"Okay." Joshua watched her, noting the way she avoided his eyes, the way she ran her fingers through her shoulder-length black curls. He reigned in his thought of how he would like to do the same. "So we need to figure this out."

"We?" she cried. "No, I can't let you. I just can't let anyone else get hurt." Her face paled in fright as she imagined what could happen. "I don't know. I am just so afraid. I can't think of who would be after me."

Dropping her piece of toast, she jumped from the table and almost ran into the living room. Joshua dropped his head into his hands and breathed a quick prayer for guidance. God knew what was happening; they had to trust Him at a time when trust seemed to hard.

Following at a slower pace, Joshua entered the room to see Laycee standing staring at the fire. One hand gripped the mantle so tight her knuckles were white. What had scared her so bad? What was it or who was it?

The sudden, unexpected trilling of music startled both. Laycee jerked, her hand knocking over pictures on the mantle. Joshua reached to steady her, then withdrew his hand.

"That's my phone! That's Liam's ring tone. Where's my phone?" Laycee's eyes searched for her bag, wanting so much to speak with her older brother. He could be a pain at time, too protective, but he was always there when she needed him. And this was one time she really needed him.

"Here's your knapsack." Joshua handed her the bag he had retrieved from her truck.

Her hands shaking, Laycee unzipped the bag and felt for her phone. It had stopped ringing by the time she found it. She saw that a voice mail had come through and dialled her number. It was Liam.

"Where are you, Laycee? Why don't you answer?" She could hear almost panic in her brother's normally calm voice. "You're not home. The police have called. There was a break-in at your house and it has been trashed. Call me. Let me know you're okay."

The phone rang again and she almost dropped it. She answered and breathed a sigh of relief when she heard Liam's voice.

"Laycee - where are you? Are you okay?"

"Liam, I had an accident…"

"An accident? Where are you? Which hospital? I am on my way!" She could hear his keys hitting the door as he headed for his vehicle.

"No, Liam, don't. I'm okay. I'm not in a hospital. A friend found me and is looking after me."

"A friend?" Liam's voice rose to a shout. "Who and where? I'm coming to find you."

"Liam, no. It's not safe. Someone is after me and I don't know who." At this point, her voice was breaking and she could feel tears in the back of her throat. She angrily swiped at her eyes.

Joshua watched, compassion and caring in his gaze. He knew how it would feel if it was his sister.

"Laycee, I don't care. Tell me where you are."

"No, I won't!"

Joshua reached and took her phone, then pushed her gently down into his chair.

"Liam," he spoke into the phone. "It's Joshua Logan. I found Laycee and she's with me. Someone is really after her and she is afraid they may be looking for her through you and Leith."

"Joshua - what, why, how? Okay, let me get this straight. Laycee is running, has an accident, and you just happen to find her? Where is she?"

"She's with me, I said. We need to meet somewhere to talk, but it has to be somewhere safe. I am not sure where, though."

Joshua looked over at Laycee, who was vigorously shaking her head.

"Can I get back to you with a place, Liam? Laycee's safe for now. I think I know of somewhere but I need to check first. You need to be thinking of a place as well. This may come back on you and Leith, so make sure he's in the loop."

There was silence on the phone. Then Liam spoke, his voice more subdued, "It's that bad? I didn't know. I...I...I just want to make sure Laycee's safe. It scared me when the police called and said her place had been trashed and she was nowhere around."

"Give me 30 minutes and I'll call you back."

Joshua clicked off the phone, then stared at it as he turned it over and over in his hand, a thoughtful look on his face. He could feel the palpable fear and anger coming from Laycee. Where to go and who to trust?

Laycee stomped over to the window and cracked open the heavy, floor to window, dark blue drapes. She knew Joshua lived out in the boonies, as she called it, but didn't realize how open around the house it was. Brush was cleared back far from the house, as best she could see in the dark. There were motion sensor lights up and from what he had said in the past, a really good security system. She figured something in his past had dictated this but she didn't know him well enough to ask. Was now the time to do so?

Joshua looked up from his phone and watched Laycee. There was so much he wanted to say. He had been a silent observer for years, wanting to get to know her better, but not sure how to. He felt he knew so little about her other than she had a strong faith in God. Would that faith hold? He knew his would be tested over and over during the next few days, at least, he hoped it would be days, not weeks. Hours would be even better.

"Laycee. We need to come up with a plan. We can't wing it any more. Whoever is after you will be following Liam and Leith. They may even be outside if they happened to see my SUV."

Laycee shook her head. "No, I can't meet them. I can't bring danger to them."

"Laycee, it's already there. They were probably watching your place and saw Liam there. They probably already know you have two brothers and know their activities and schedules. What we need to do is try and figure out who and why."

Laycee turned to face him, letting the drapes fall back in to place. Her eyes were shining with tears and traces of tears tracked across her cheeks. She drew in a shaky breath.

"All right, then, what do you suggest? And just because you suggest it, doesn't mean it happens." Joshua grinned at her feistiness. "And wipe that grin off your face, buster."

Now that was the Laycee he knew— ready to face the world and conquer it.

"First, we pray." He reached out a hand and she hesitantly took it. His warm firm grasp helped to steady her.

"Father, You know what's going on. You know the fear Laycee is facing. You are in control. Lead us with Your wisdom. Help us to plan and follow You. Remind us that we are more important to You than a sparrow. Give us the strength we need. Provide protection for those we love and for ourselves. Amen."

Laycee stood for a minute, wrapped in the knowledge that God was in control and that He really did care what happened. She raised her eyes, meeting Joshua's. She hesitated, trying to figure out the look in his eyes.

"Where do we go from here?" She asked.

"First, we have to have something more to eat. Who knows when we well next eat. I also want to pack up some food and drinks to take with us. Then I need to get Blues ready to go. We may need him."

"I can look after the food. Do what you need to do." Laycee turned and headed for the kitchen.

Joshua looked after her for a minute, shook his head and headed for his bedroom. A quick shower, change of clothes, a packsack stuffed with what he needed from there, and he was ready to go. He stopped in the hallway, dropped his pack, and pulled out the saddlebags he used for Blues. He made sure the supplies were still there: maps, flashlight, batteries, first aid kit, whatever he needed on his search and rescue treks.

He stopped at the pantry and filled another pack with food and water bottles as well as the collapsible dishes for Blues. When he turned to the kitchen, he saw that Laycee had made sandwiches, pulled out apples and oranges, and water and juice, and was stuffing another pack with them. She was also pulling out spare clear bags and markers and stuffing them in too.

"Why the bags and markers?" he asked.

"Evidence. If we find anything, we need to put it in something," she replied, not looking up from her task.

"But we're not the police. It won't be accepted as evidence."

"I don't care. I need to do this. If we find something, we'll call in the police, but I am not sure who I can trust."

"We can call Caleb. He's the law, he can help."

"Sure, but if we can't reach him, then what?" Laycee argued back.

"We'll keep trying. We'll figure it out." Joshua cocked his head to the right and studied her. She was too calm, taking it too silently. She was ready to break and he knew it was coming. What would be the tipoff?

Laycee's hands stilled. She dropped the snacks she was holding and her hands flew to her mouth. Tears welled in her eyes.

"Defiant. Terror. Where are they? Are they all right? I have to get home. I have to find them. I need them. They need me!" Her voice rose with each word, fear evident in her voice. She turned for the door, then stopped. She ran at Joshua, pounding at him. "You need to take me home. I need to go home. I need to find them!"

Joshua gripped her upper arms, trying to stop her fists. When that didn't work, he simply wrapped his arms around her and held her. Her fists stopped and her fingers clutched into his plaid work shirt, tightening until the knuckles were white. He could feel the dampness on his shirt. He didn't care. She needed the tears, she needed the hug.

When her shaking had stopped and he could hear just broken breaths, he set her back from him and dipping his head, looked into her eyes.

"We'll find them. Let me call Liam and see where they are. He'll know. He was at your home with the police." He waited until she finally gave a small nod, then reached for his phone.

Dialling Liam's number, he asked as soon as Liam answered, "Laycee needs to know where her pets are. She's starting to panic."

"Leith has them. He's taking them to Doc Victor. Doc was willing to open up his office to check them out, then Leith was going to take them with him. They seem fine, just real clingy, more than usual." Joshua could hear the eye roll in that sentence. He knew from Liam that Laycee and her animals were inseparable, that where one was in the house, they all were. It would have been devastating to Laycee if something happened to either one. "I found Terror tucked away in a corner of the closet. She wasn't too happy about me digging her out. Defiant was still in his crate. Laycee always covers it part way, so the vandals may not have seen him, or else decided he didn't matter."

Joshua tilted the phone away from his mouth and reassured Laycee that the pets were fine, that her brother had them and was taking care of them.

Putting the phone back to his mouth, he asked, "Have you come up with a spot to meet yet? We're getting ready to leave and need to know where to find you."

"There's an old hunt camp back a ways from your place. Here are the directions. Laycee knows where it is, if she can keep her head straight." Joshua snickered, knowing that Liam was being sarcastic. Of all of them, Laycee was the one with the best memory, who could always be depended on to keep everyone and everything straight and in line. "Make sure you're not followed. Turn off your location on both your phones before you leave. I'm doing the same. Not sure if the goons after Laycee have our numbers but chances are they do, having tossed her place."

"We'll do that. Leaving soon. If something happens, I'll send a text."

Joshua touched his phone and turned off the location application. He then reached for Laycee's and did the same. She watched in silence, emotions spent.

"All right, let's hit the road," Joshua scooped up backpacks and Blues' leash. Blues headed for the door. Turning off lights on the way to the door, he stopped and keyed in his password for the security system. He put a hand out to Laycee to keep her inside.

"Wait. I'll put the stuff and Blues in first and then come back." Quickly following through on his word, he came back, took Laycee's hand, rekeyed in his password and locked the door. He helped Laycee in the SUV and then keyed the motor to life. He took a look around in the dark, wondering if they were being watched, and also wondering when he would see his place again. Work could wait. He was held up anyway on his renovation job right now waiting for material and trim. The customer was understanding, and Joshua had looked at this time as a short vacation. Vacation it was not, but friends were more important.

Liam tapped his fingers on the steering wheel, deep in thought. Who was after his sister? She was a secretary, did volunteer work in a senior's home, and didn't have any enemies, at least none that he knew of. It was just too bizarre. He knew her employer, a physician, who was an upstanding member of the community and of their church. Nothing about him screamed problem or danger. His own work as a landscaper certainly didn't bring danger to either Laycee or Leith and Leith was a tile setter; nothing there seemed out of place. Joshua—he knew him, not well, but enough to know that he was a compassionate, caring person. Leith likely knew him better, having worked on Joshua's renovation projects.

He picked up his phone and dialled Leith's number.

When Leith answered, his first question was about Laycee's animals.

"Doc Victor says they're okay.   Shaken, scared, but not hurt in any way.   Defiant will be sticking a lot closer to Laycee now though, given the separation anxiety Shelties are known for. Terror is Terror—she'll be okay as well."

"That's a relief.   Laycee just about lost it, Joshua said, when she remembered they were home when the break-in happened."

"Did Caleb say if anything was missing that he could see?"

"Not that he knew of, but then, it would take Laycee to know. She knows exactly where everything in and if someone has touched something of hers."

"That she does. Remember all those times we messed with her, moving or just touching something?"

"Yeah. I can remember Mom lighting into us for that. It was fun, though, at the time." Liam sighed. "I just wish I knew what was going on right now, what Laycee had gotten mixed up in."

"Me, too. That's our sister that they're after. I want a piece of them. I can't think of anything that she's mentioned lately that might be a clue."

"Nor me. I.." Liam's voice trailed away.

"What? Did you think of something?"

"Yeah. She mentioned about six weeks ago that something seemed wrong with the lady she was visiting with. Defiant wanted to really snuggle up and cling to her, almost as if he sensed something. Laycee just shrugged it off. Apparently, the lady died a week or so later, and Laycee though Defiant had picked up on that."

"That's worth mentioning to Caleb. Do you know the name?"

"No, but I'm to meet Laycee and Joshua in a bit. I won't tell you where, but I will call once we're together and we can think it through, all four of us. Let Caleb know that Laycee is safe, but not where she is."

"Will do. Be careful, brother. In my prayers. This is when I wish Mom and Dad were still here, our prayer warriors."

"I know. I miss that. Sometimes, I really need their prayers."

Liam clicked off his phone, and then turned off the location app. He didn't think he was being followed but took a circuitous route to the hunt camp.

Dawn was breaking as he turned into the narrow, tree-canopied lane. Undergrowth brushed against his truck as he crept down towards the camp. He peered through the windshield. No tracks. Good. That must mean that he was first or that no one knew where they were.

He parked before he reached the camp and turning off the vehicle, he stepped out and closed the door, locking it before he did so. He didn't want the sound of the key fob beep to alert anyone around.

He stepped carefully forward, making sure of what was under each foot before he set his weight on it. When he spied the camp, he stopped at the edge of the woods and looked around. It seemed okay, but he waited. No movement at all.

He then proceeded across the short distance to the back door. Unlocking it, he swung the door open and stepped to one side. Nothing. He stepped inside. It was the same as when he was last there about six weeks ago. Good. Now to wait for Laycee and Joshua. He refused to light a fire—it would be a dead giveaway that someone was there.

A slight noise sent him to the side of the door. He waited. Hushed footsteps approached, two people by the sound of it. The footsteps stopped. He waited. Then a form entered the room. He waited. When the light hit, he breathed easier and spoke.

"Joshua."

Joshua spun around in surprise.

"Liam. You're here."

"Where's Laycee?"

Laycee stepped through the door and into her big brother's embrace. His bear hug was tight and her arms clasped him just as tight. Moments passed before they moved back and looked into each other's faces.

"Ouch." Liam's fingers traced the bruises and redness on her face.

Laycee smacked his arm. "Is that all you can say, ouch?"

Liam smirked. "Well, yeah! What else do you want me to say?"

Laycee huffed and turned her back on him. Joshua caught the look on her face and the tears in her eyes and exchanged a look with Liam.

Liam placed his hands on her shoulders. "I'm glad you're okay. You had me worried."

Laycee stood still for a moment and then moved away to stand at the desk in the corner of the room.

"Do you remember Grand-dad working here? He always would stop and spend time with us, no matter how busy he was with the books and records."

Liam knew she was avoiding the questions he wanted to ask, buying time to get her emotions back in control.

"I do. Both sets of grandparents always had time for us. They helped mold us to who we are today."

"That they did."

Laycee turned, eyes flying around the room, taking in everything. Everything looked the same, but she wasn't. The night had changed her and not for the good, she thought. She moved from desk to table to kitchen to fireplace to bookshelf.

At the bookshelf, she stopped. Something was different. Someone had been here and moved books around. Who would have been here?

"Liam, did you move the books around when you were here last?" she asked.

Liam's look changed and he strode across the room to stand beside her. Laycee was tall for a woman, 5'8" but Liam seemed to tower over her tonight, his 6'2" frame lean and strong.

"No, I didn't. What's different about the shelf?"

Joshua was beside the siblings, taking in their looks. Both were tall and lithe. Black hair was curly and he knew both had brown eyes. Their facial features were so similar, anyone would know they were brother and sister, and he knew Leith looked like them, except for having hazel eyes. This could be a problem. They were a close knit family and if you hurt one, you hurt all three.

"The books have been moved. I though we were the only ones who had keys to the place now."

"We are."

Liam strode to the doors and took a look at the locks. Nothing seemed odd about them, no scratches or signs that they had been broken into. Windows were the same. Strange.

Lacyee moved the books back to where they should be. She stopped with the last book in her hand. Something made her open it. Inside was an envelope that had not been there the last time she read it.

Her eyes flew up, meeting Joshua's and then moving to Liam. She tilted the book and showed them. Both men moved towards her and Liam reached for the book.

The long white envelope was not marked in any way. From the medicine cabinet in the bathroom, Joshua dug out some tweezers, then used them to pick up the envelope. Placing it on the table, he checked out the front and then flipped it over. It wasn't sealed. He pulled back the flap and then pulled out the folded sheet of paper inside. Just an ordinary sheet of copy paper, it seemed.

He unfolded it and then stopped. Laycee and Liam crowded around him, reading the numbers. Eyes flew to each other's. What had they stepped into?

Joshua pulled out his phone and took a picture of the letter. He then sent an email to his brother, Caleb, with the photo attached. Caleb needed to know. No matter what Laycee said, law enforcement had to now get involved.

Caleb Logan closed his Bible and rubbed his hand across the worn leather cover, deep in thought. His mind sometimes had trouble grasping the concept that God cared so much, when he saw so much destruction in his career. Being a police officer had gotten more and more difficult and dangerous. He picked up his mug of tea and wandered over to the French door overlooking the backyard. Liam had done a wonderful job on it; the mixtures of flowers and hard surfaces were amazing. He could faintly hear the tinkle of the waterfall through the glass.

He felt a hand on his side and reached around to hug his wife, Hannah, to him. He was blessed. He was blessed with such a sweet wife who understood how important he felt his work was and with two sons who loved him and couldn't wait to share their adventures with him. Steam rising from her flavoured coffee mixed with the scent of his herbal tea. They stood for a while, just enjoying the early morning and being together. All too soon, he would be off and she would be busy with the rambunctious preschoolers they called their sons.

Caleb's phone vibrated and he sighed. All too early, someone was looking for him. Hannah took his mug as he reached for his phone.

"It's from Joshua," he stated. "Now I wonder what's up. Liam seemed to think he and Laycee were in some sort of trouble last night."

"I hope he's okay," Hannah responded, a worried look creeping into her eyes.

Caleb brought up the text Joshua and sent and read it. He tensed and then read through the text again. Just what have you gotten into, Joshua, he wondered. How deep in this going to get?

"Is everything okay?" He faintly heard Hannah's voice.

Dragging his thoughts back from the text, he nodded. "I think so. Just keep us in prayer. I don't know where Joshua is right now, but he certainly need protection. He seems to have gotten into something that I don't like and I don't know where he is right now."

Giving Hannah a quick kiss goodbye, Caleb strode for the door and to his unmarked SUV. His mind kept replaying the text message.

Once at his office, he greeted those officers already there on his way to his office. He searched the room and then beckoned at Ben Johnson who was the head of the detective branch of the department. The gray-haired Ben made his way over and joined Caleb.

"Close the door, Ben." Once the door was closed and they were seated, Caleb pulled out his phone. He read the text again and then passed his phone to Ben.

Ben read over and over. His gray eyes was puzzled when he looked up.

"What is this? And why has Joshua sent it to you?"

Caleb ran his fingers through his blond hair and sighed. "Laycee Bradley was targeted by someone last night and Joshua was there. She was in an accident and he has taken her to a safe place until we can figure out who and why."

"That's why she wasn't in her truck when the patrol found it. They have been searching the woods but haven't had any luck."

"Yeah. We need to call them in." He picked up his phone and let the dispatcher know to do just that.

"So now we need to figure out what this is and what it means."

Using his Bluetooth connection, Caleb sent the text to his computer. Ben rose and watched over his shoulder as he brought it up. It seemed even more chilling in larger print:

26 12 12 15

19 15

19 7 7 23 12 25 1 1 22

4 19 16 26

1 10 12

26 1 10 15 24

15 11 12 8 22 19 14

10 1 1 10

Caleb read the figures again, trying to make sense of them. They didn't.

"What on earth?" Ben asked. "What is this all about?"

"I don't know. Unless……". He grabbed his phone and sent a quick text, fingers tapping on the desk.

The phone jingled with the incoming text.

He looked at it and sighed. Things had gotten only muddier.

"They don't have any idea what this is, either. Some kind of code but what's the key?"

Ben threw a glance at Caleb, back to the phone, and then leaned back against the wall, letting his weight rest on it. "Well, that does it."

Caleb snorted, but he agreed with sentiment. This just got a whole lot bigger than someone after Laycee. What had she stumbled upon?

"So, Caleb, how did that note get into that book in the first place?"

Caleb stilled. A horrifying thought crossed his mind. It had to be someone who knew Laycee, someone who had been at the cabin. He closed his eyes in a silent prayer of protection for the ones there and then picked up his pen, beginning to devise a plan on how to proceed. For once he agreed with Ben—lists were good.

Liam brought over a fresh cup of coffee and sat at the table across from Joshua. He looked worn. He picked up the plastic bag with the note in and read it once again. It didn't make sense. Just a bunch of numbers.

Joshua looked up from his note pad and then shoved it across the table to Liam, nodding for him to look.   He had been listing ideas and people he suspected.

Liam turned it so he could read it. Maybe Joshua had an idea. He was lost. He wanted to protect his sister but against an unknown enemy, how could he?

"I like some of these ideas," he said, "but how do we prove any of them? Laycee hasn't said she has noticed anything out of the ordinary."

"No. I think she has. She just doesn't know it. Something is off, someone is off, and we'll figure it out."

"It had better be before anyone gets hurt." Liam felt himself get more and more angrier. His stomach burned at the thought of his sister being in someone's crosshairs.

The page of numbers sat between the two men, taunting them.

Liam sighed. "It's 6. I need to get going. I have to be on the job today; I can't leave it to my foreman. This client is way too big a deal." He was torn—needing to get to work and needing to stay.

Joshua looked with compassion at his friend. They had known each other pretty well before but this had just added a new dimension to their friendship. He knew Leith was champing at the bit to be with them, but he was out of town today, sourcing material for a renovation he was working on. He wouldn't be back until tomorrow. That meant Joshua would be the one Laycee would have to depend upon, and at the moment, he just wasn't confident that he could protect her against the unknown.

Liam rose and put his mug in the sink. He stepped over the couch where Laycee had stretched out and was asleep. He stood for a few minutes, staring down at her, then reached and tugged the blanket up around her neck. She didn't stir, one hand tucked under the pillow and the other hand curled up under her chin. The bruises were darker, dark in comparison to her ivory skin. He leant over and dropped a quick kiss on her hair and then turned. Lifting a hand to Joshua, he walked out the door and to his vehicle, not knowing what would be coming and not knowing if he would see Laycee that night. He could only leave her with the Lord.

Joshua lifted the paper with the numbers on it again. He knew there was a code but he was too tired to figure it out. His eyes drooped closed and he laid his head on his outstretched arms. Soon the cabin was quiet, except for the click of Blues' nails as he patrolled.

A couple of hours later, Laycee stirred, grimacing at the pain she felt. Her eyelids fluttered as she roused. A rough tongue swiped across her hand and she jumped. Eyes open, she found herself eye to eye with Blues.

He sat, then laid his chin on the couch, almost nose to nose with her. A tongue came out and swiped across her face, catching her mouth. Then he grinned, tongue lolling off to one side, and brown eyes fixed on her.

"Yuck! You just had to do that, didn't you, big boy?" Laycee wiped off her mouth. Blues' head tilted to the side as he listened to her.

Laycee's eyes searched the room, taking in the wide logs of the wall, the worn wide plank flooring, the worn but comfortable furnishings. Many a vacation had been spent here. She remembered her parents and the way they had raised them, the way they made sure there was fun to their lives.

Her eyes continued to move and stopped on Joshua. His head was still on his arms and she could tell he was sound asleep. Moving quietly, she threw back the blanket and sat up.

"That wasn't such a good idea," she said to Blues, as her head spun. Waiting until the world stopped spinning, she stood and made her way to the bathroom. Splashing water on her face, she studied herself in the mirror. She sure wouldn't win any beauty contests, she thought, but then life was more important than that. She looked down, darks thoughts crossing her mind. She just couldn't understand what was happening. Why her?

She stepped quietly back into the kitchen area and moved to make a new pot of coffee. Perhaps that would help to clear her mind, it felt so foggy. She grabbed an apple out of the pack they had brought and turned to the table.

Joshua had awakened and was watching her.

"Feel any better?"

"Some. I think the nap helped." She poured them both fresh mugs of coffee and then sat at the table. She pulled over the note she had found and studied it once again. "Did you and Liam make any headway on this?"

Joshua shook his head. "No. Liam had to leave anyway. He said he would call or text." He looked at Blues who was snuggled in tight to Laycee, head on her knees, eyes closed in sheer delight as she rubbed his ears. "I think I've lost a dog."

Laycee looked down and then grinned. "I always seem to attract dogs. They follow me all over."

Joshua laughed and then looked at the clock.

"Were you to be at the seniors' home today?"

She shook her head. "Not today. I have had to take a break after Mrs. Lang passed away. She was just so special. Do you know if Leith is bringing me my pets?"

It was Joshua's turn to shake his head. "He's out of town today. Liam said they were at his place, but he didn't think we should go there. He figures both their places are being watched."

Laycee closed her eyes in pain. She missed her pets. Defiant was just so much a part of her, she swore he could read her mind. Even with the mischief he got into, the pens and paper he chewed up and spit out, the toys strewn all over the house, he was just too lovable. She needed to hug him and bury her face in his fur. She needed to laugh at Terror, at the way she threw herself around, at her musical trill of a meow/purr combination, her deer-in-the-headlight stare. Soon, she promised, very soon she would be back with them.

Chapter 10

Caleb stared once again at the note. His mind spinning at the possibilities, he was suddenly afraid.

Ben moved to take a seat in one of the arm chairs at the front of his desk, picking up a pad of paper and pen.

"Time to brainstorm. What do we know and what do we suspect?"

Caleb stared across the room at the framed diplomas, commendations and awards. He didn't see them. Hannah had had them framed and hung on the pale cream walls. The dark wood frames matched the trim and wainscoting of his office, which set off the mixed brown carpeting. There was no window, but she had made sure he had good lighting, knowing how many hours he spent there.

Caleb drew his gaze back to Ben His mind was starting to process what was happening, and he didn't like it one bit. That was his brother who was involved in who knew what.

"There are just too many things it can be," he replied. "Laycee seems to the one everything hinges on, or is that the way we are meant to think?" He spoke slowly as new ideas raised their heads.

Ben started to make a list. He loved lists. He loved to plot scenarios and cross off the ones that didn't work. Caleb had always told him he would have made a good screenwriter but Ben just laughed. He was where he wanted to be and doing what he loved.

"Okay - so here goes: grandparent scam, drug theft, drug dealing, elder abuse, mediation mixups, employee problems…I guess you're right on this one. We don't have enough information to made a clear decision as to what it is. We need to talk to Laycee."

"I agree but I don't think we'll get her anywhere near us right now. She's running scared, and I can't say I blame her."

"Has Joshua ever said anything in the past about Laycee? I know he volunteers with the search and rescue but does she? Or one of her brothers?"

"That's a good thought. Maybe it has nothing to do with the seniors' home."

Caleb threw his pen down in frustration and leaned back in chair, the black leather creaking. He ran his hands through his hair, his gaze once again going across the room. There had to be something. What were they missing?

Ben took another look at the message. Then he straightened. "You know what this is, don't you?"

Caleb shook his head.

"It's a cryptogram. Letter substitution, I bet. Each number would be a letter." Ben's mind was racing faster than he could speak. "If we can figure out the code, then we might be able to figure out what it is." He jumped to his feet and headed for the door. "I'll let you old folks sit around while us young folks work on it."

Caleb laughed and tossed a balled up piece of paper after him, bouncing it off the closing door. Ben might just be right. He picked up his phone and sent a text to Joshua, asking him if they had thought of that.

Then, looking at his desk, he sighed. There was other investigations he needed to work on. He would let the "young folks" struggle with the numbers, he would be busy elsewhere. He shook his head at Ben's joking. Ben was an old-timer on the force and knew when a bit of levity helped. He had a lot to learn and he hoped Ben stayed around while he did.

Bending his head over his paperwork, he become engrossed in it. Time passed. He looked up, startled at the passing of time, when he heard a tap at his door. He stood, opened the door, and faced Liam Bradley. Moving aside, he motioned Liam in and shut the door.

Liam stood and stared at him, sitting when Caleb asked him to have a seat.

"What's going on, Caleb? What do you know?"

Caleb was silent for a moment, then knowing he could be honest with his friend, stated, "I wish I knew, Liam. I really wish I knew. Ben is working on the text; he has an idea it's a cryptogram, but other than that, I really don't know. There are so many possibilities, and I have a couple of detectives tracing Laycee's last few weeks to see if something stands out."

Liam's gaze never left his face. "So we really are at a loss, is that what you're saying?"

"Right now, I would. But I am confident we'll find something soon and be able to unravel the puzzle."

"I hope so." Both men became silent, lost in their thoughts.

****

"What do you mean, you can't find the paper?" The voice hissed through the phone, its very tone sending shivers of fear down the listener's spine.

"I can't. I have no idea where it is. I don't have it. I never had it," he protested.

"Find it. If you don't….." The voice died away with the threat.

Tom shuddered, not wanting to think about what the threat implied. He knew he had to find that paper. If not, he knew he would pay the price.

Andy looked at him and shrugged as if it were not a big deal. Andy had no idea of that was going down. As long as he had a bottle or a fix, he was fine.

The phone clicked angrily in Tom's ear. He threw his at the couch. Now what? He had to find Laycee, but she seemed to have disappeared off the face of the earth.

He grabbed his phone and his keys and jerked his brother to his feet, pushing him out the door ahead of him and to his car. Shoving Andy into the passenger seat, he climbed into the driver's side and started the car.

"Where're we going, Tom?" Andy's words were slurred. Tom knew that he was a liability but he was still his brother. He would need his help at some point, just needed to get him sober.

Tom's car peeled away from the curb and shot out of the subdivision. He drove around aimlessly for a while then decided to park down the street from Laycee's house. Maybe someone would come and he could follow them. At this point, that was all he had, the possibility someone would lead him to her.

****

Ben shoved the door open in excitement, stopping when he saw Liam.

Caleb waved him in. "At this point, Ben, we might as well let Liam know what we know. He's not going anywhere until he does know."

Ben nodded. "I think I've got it figured out. It's a straight substitution, letter for number. Very elementary, in fact. I would think that whoever made it knew it had to be simple."

Caleb's eyes never left Ben's face. "So, what did you come up with?"

Ben sat down in the chair beside Liam. "I am not sure how much you know about cryptogram puzzles, but there is a simple substitution of letter for letter. Say, you want an "A" so you put in "X" as the letter "A". In this case, they have put in numbers for the letters. Once I figured out the vowels, it was easy. Usually once you solve the vowels or common letters, you can figure out what the rest is."

"Okay," Liam said. "That's easy to understand. Now, what does the note say?"

Both men leaned closer to Ben as he pulled out the sheet he had been working on.

"It took me a while to figure out the vowels. I finally got that 19 is A, which meant it had to be a short word, to make any sense; 15 became T. I substituted the 19s and 15s. Then I worked on the numbers that were the same and side by side.

"This is what I got: Meet at Applewood Farm, one month Tuesday, noon."

Caleb sat back. Applewood Farm was just outside town. Contrary to its name, there were no apple trees on it. The name was just something a long-ago owner made up, to spite the fact that apple trees couldn't grow on the land for some reason. Today it was a thriving bed and breakfast inn, which catered to a very select clientele, and offered special deals for events.

"But what Tuesday?" Liam felt like he was asking an overly obvious question.

Ben looked grim. "That's what we need to figure out. And I don't think the owners of the Farm are involved. They've been part of the community and church for years."

Laycee was tired. She was tired of hurting. She was tired of not being at home. She was tired of hiding. She was just plain tired. She shoved back her chair and stood. Her hand on the door, she stopped. "I'm going outside. I need air. And I don't care if anyone is out there who wants to hurt me. They can't make it any worse." The door slammed behind her.

Joshua jumped at the loud bang. He rose, opened the door, and sent Blues out with her. Blues would alert if anyone was around. He considered Laycee part of his family now and his drive was to protect his own.

Joshua headed back into the kitchen. They needed to eat and soup and sandwiches would be an easy fix. The soup would stay hot until Laycee came back in.

The trilling of his phone caught his attention. Tilting it to look at it, he answered, "Caleb. What have you got?"

"Ben solved the puzzle. What do you know about Applewood Farm? And what does Laycee know?"

Joshua's body stilled. Now it was beginning to make some sense. He had to find Laycee. But where outside was she?

"I'll call you back." Hanging up on Caleb's protest, Joshua headed for the door.

Blues was barking, his angry bark that denoted strangers. Joshua hit the outside in a full run, looking for Laycee and Blues. Around the corner of the cabin, he found Laycee on the ground, not moving. Blues was huddled beside her, not barking now and chin on her back. Joshua hit the ground as a bullet hit the log of the cabin near his head. Somehow, someone had found them. He quickly dialled Caleb's number.

"Caleb, Laycee's down and someone is shooting at us. We're pinned outside the cabin."

Joshua raised his head and looked around. He couldn't see or hear anything. He dragged himself over to Laycee and reached for her. She was breathing. He couldn't see if she was hurt and Blues wouldn't move. Joshua shoved his dog away and then hugged Laycee under one of his arms. If they could make it back into the cabin, they could hide. There was an underground cellar not many people knew. He began to crawl towards the back of the cabin, moving cautiously and stopping every few feet, listening for approaching footsteps or more bullets. Blues crept on his belly beside him and helped to pull Laycee with them. Once they made the back of the cabin, Joshua moved faster. The door was just ahead.

They had made it back inside. He couldn't stop to check on Laycee yet, they had to get to the secret room. He grabbed their backpacks and the letter, snagging their phones too. Everything got stuffed in one of the packs. He reached for the wall, hitting the spot Laycee had told him about. The section of wall moved.

"In you go, Blues." Blues looked at him as if he was nuts and then entered the dark dusty space. Joshua threw in the packs and then turned. He locked the doors and then stooped, gathering Laycee in his arms. He tilted his head. Yes, there were footsteps outside, making their way around the cabin. He stepped into the room after Blues and shoved the wall section back in place. He prayed fervently that whoever was out there either couldn't make it into the cabin or had no idea of a secret room.

****

Caleb sprang to his feet and raced for the door, Ben and Liam on his heels. Barking orders, he ran for the door and his car. He could hear footsteps behind him—Ben and Liam headed for his car, patrol officers headed for their cruisers.

"Give me the address for the cabin," he barked at Liam.

Liam stared at him.

"The address. What is it?"

Liam stuttered as he gave it, his mind going to his sister. He vaguely heard Caleb on his radio giving the address and directing the patrols.

Lights and sirens on, Caleb sped through town, leading a convoy of cruisers. Both Ben and Liam grabbed for support as the car rocketed down the road and around corners.

Caleb sent up prayers, hoping that they would be in time, that both Joshua and Laycee would be safe. He didn't want to face Hannah if something happened to Joshua; Joshua was the brother Hannah had never had and had always wanted. His widow could accept the dangers of his job, but Joshua shouldn't be facing those dangers.

Liam closed his eyes. He couldn't bear to think of what they might face.

Caleb's phone rang. He dug it out and tossed it to Ben, so that he could keep his attention on the road.

"It's Joshua," Ben stated. "A text - they're in a hidden room?" He turned and shot a look at Liam, nodding when Liam's eyes found his and then slid shut. "So far, he says they're safe but Laycee is hurt. He can't see how bad. He doesn't want to put on any light in case someone is in the cabin."

"Get paramedics on the way. When we get there, Liam, you stay back. I don't need you getting the way until we have the situation locked down and safe." Caleb barely spared a glance at his friend as Liam acknowledged this.

Caleb slowed as he neared the turn to the cabin and silenced the siren and turned off the lights. He parked and got out, as did Ben. Liam stood near the cruiser, face drawn and hands clasped.

Caleb drew his men around him and sent them, some to watch the road, others to circle around the cabin. He turned to Ben and motioned him to follow. They disappeared from Liam's sight.

Liam's phone chimed, and he looked down. Leith.

"Hi, Leith."

"Liam, what's up? Something is, I can tell from your voice."

"There is. Ben solved the cryptogram Laycee found. But there's been a shooting at the cabin and we don't know what all is going on. Joshua got them into the room and now Caleb and his men are on their way in. Joshua said something about Laycee being hurt but I don't know what he means." Liam's voice was breaking and tears gathered in his eyes.

Leith was silent, then "I'm on my way. I'm in town and will be there in 10 minutes."

"Be careful, Leith. We don't know yet who is involved. I feel like I can't trust anyone."

"I hear you." The phone clicked off.

Liam turned his phone over and over in his hands, ready to pitch it at the nearest tree. He wanted, no needed, to be there at the cabin, but knew he had to wait. It wasn't fair. First, their parents were taken far too soon and now Laycee.

Chapter 12

Liam heard a vehicle behind him and a door slam. He turned. Leith had been stopped by a young officer. He jogged over.

"He's my brother. Let him through."

"I'm sorry, sir. I can't do that."

"I'll take the responsibility. That's his sister in that cabin." Liam reached over and pulled Leith to his side. The patrol officer made a move to stop them, then halted at the look on Liam's face. As they walked back to Caleb's car, the officer was on their heels.

"Any word yet?" Leith's face reflected his own, showing the fear, worry and anxiety they both felt.

Liam shook his head and then brought Leith up to date on what they had discovered so far.

Leith looked thoughtful as he stared at Liam, then looked down the lane towards the cabin.

Liam cocked his head and raised an eyebrow. Leith looked at him and then shook his head.

"I'm thinking."

"I know. I can smell the smoke." This was a longstanding joke between the brothers.

"Yeah, right. That's not my brain cells burning, that's yours." He started to say something, then stopped as Liam took a look at the officer standing near them, intently listening to their conversation. "Later."

The brothers stood shoulder to shoulder, side by side, watching for word, almost identical in looks and colouring. The Irish in their ancestry showed through in their colouring. Liam's eyes were brown, Leith's hazel. Both stood over 6', with just a mere fraction of an inch between their heights. Concern was etched on their faces. Their phones both vibrated in their pockets, and after a quick peek, they returned them. Right now, what was important was down that little, narrow, tree-shaded lane that had undergrowth into the track in spaces. Texts and voice mail could wait.

Ben appeared from the trees and beckoned them forward. The young officer jogged ahead and spoke with him, gesturing towards Leith. Ben shot a look at the brothers, then said something to the officer, who in turn jogged back to his car.

Ben waited for the brothers and then spoke.

"It was kids. They thought Blues was a wild dog and they were shooting at him, just for fun." Ben's face showed his anger and frustration. "Caleb needs you to show him the panel to get in. Joshua isn't answering his phone."

The brothers broke into a run and headed for the family cabin. Caleb stood in the doorway, watching as his officers dealt with the youths and searched for evidence. He looked up as the two approached.

"I need to know where the door is. We need to make sure they're okay."

****

Laycee stirred in Joshua's arm. Her eyes opened. She felt safe. But it was so dark. Had she been unconscious for that long? Was she blind? Panic started to rise and she fought to get loose.

Joshua let her go and heard her stumble to her feet, Blues tight to her.

"Laycee, it's okay. We're safe."

"Where are we?"

"Do you remember telling Liam telling me about that secret panel one day we were talking about renegades and the underground railway?" At her nod, he continued, "We're in there. You had gone outside and I heard shooting. I found you and now we're in here until Caleb comes."

"But Caleb won't know where the panel is. How will we know when it's safe?

"Caleb might not know but your brothers do. He'll find out from them."

Laycee moved back toward the sound of his voice and touched his arm. He snugged her up against him under his left arm, leaving the knotted fist of his right hand free. He would do his best to protect her, someone who was becoming very dear to him. He didn't know how she felt, but he wanted to pursue this once events had finished and she was once again safe from the unknown.

"Do you know how long we've been in here?" Her voice was unsteady. He could hear and feel her fear.

"Not sure, but not long. I was able to get a call to Caleb, so he's likely out there now. We can't open the door until we know he's there, and I have set my phone to silent."

She gave a little laugh. "Good thinking. No use warning everyone where we're hidden."

A sound at the wall stopped them and they shrank as far back as they could. A hand on Blues' neck showed his hackles raised.   A low growl rumbled from deep within him.

A crack of light showed and then widened as the panel opened. It blinded them. They could hear voices but for a minute couldn't make out the words.

Blues snarled and barked.

"Call off your dog, Joshua."   Joshua's eyes slid closed in relief as he heard Caleb.

"Blues, down."   Blues moved and then stopped growling. His tail brushed against the wall, giving whispers of sound.

"You can come out now. It's safe. It was kids. They thought Blues was a wild dog and starting shooting at him. Are you both okay?"

"We are." Joshua took Laycee's hand and led her out of the room. They both stopped to let their eyes adjust back to the sunlight and then looked around.

Laycee sprang towards her brothers, who enveloped her in a huge hugs.   Shudders and suppressed sobs shook her. Liam's eyes raised, to stare first at Caleb and then Joshua.

"We need to get her away from her and somewhere safe." He felt like he was stating the obvious.

"No, Liam." Laycee pulled back. "I'm not running. I can't. I have to work Tuesday and there is no way I'm not."

"Laycee, it's not safe. We don't know yet who's after you or why."

Laycee stood back from her brothers, hands on hips, and glared at them. "Stop playing the oldest brother card, Liam. It won't work. You know right well I have to work. Being the only secretary means that I do.”

The three siblings debated this, at times with voices raised. Caleb looked at Joshua, who just shrugged, a smile on his face. Caleb shook his head and then turned to the door when Ben appeared, beckoning him outside.

Caleb and Ben walked towards the water and then stopped.

“What do you have?”

“Something interesting. I don’t know how it connects, but one of those boys is the son of an accountant in town.”

Caleb shared a look with Ben, then turned to where the youths were standing, handcuffed and waiting to be taken into town. “We need to process them. We’re not letting them off. But we need to make sure that no one but you and I know the connection to Laycee. This is just getting too bizarre for words.” Caleb rubbed the back of his neck, lost in thought. How much deeper was it going to get? “Take them into town and start processing them. They’re over 18 so we don’t need to call their parents. Make sure to do everything by the book, and I mean everything.”

Ben nodded, then glanced at the cabin. “They’re ok? It sounded like it.”

“Yeah. So far. We need to meet somewhere and come up with a plan to end this. It’s getting to the point that something bad is going to happen and we won’t be able to prevent it because we haven’t a clue.   Call me when you’re done with those over there. I’ll try and figure out what and where.”

Ben took a step away and then turned. “Annie said she was getting together with Hannah and some ladies from the church to go over to Laycee's house and try and clean it up for her. Is that safe?"

Caleb's gaze met Ben's. "I guess it's as safe as anywhere. But hold her off for a few hours. I want Laycee to walk back through her house and see if anything is missing. Knowing her, she'll know as soon as she walks in."

Ben shook his head. "More than likely." With a wave, he strode over to the youths and all had soon disappeared down the lane.

Chapter 13

Caleb stepped back into the cabin

"Still at it, are they?" He asked Joshua.

Joshua laughed. "You got it. I think Laycee is winning."

Caleb smiled. "I think you're right. Those two are just so happy she's safe, I think they'll let her." He paused. "Laycee needs to go back to her house." As Joshua started to shake his head, Caleb continued, "She needs to see if anything is missing. No one else knows what she has in her house, only she does. She's determined to go back to work on Tuesday and it will take the next couple of days to get everything sorted around. You can bet those two won't let her stay on her own."

Joshua's gaze went to Laycee. She was becoming so important to him now and he didn't think he could handle anything else happening. "Yeah, you're right. Are we done here now?"

Caleb nodded, then strode over to where the three Bradley siblings were still locked in a heated battle of words.

"Okay, you three. Enough!" The firmness of his voice cut through the words and all three turned in surprise to stare at him. "We're done here. Laycee, we need you to go back through your house and see if anything is missing. Let me have the original of that document, show me where it was found, and then we're gone."

Laycee complied. Walking back down the lane in single file, Laycee kept very close to Joshua, with Blues tight to her side.

"You can have your dog back, Joshua. I'm going to find mine."

Joshua laughed. "Not happening. I think he's adopted you. You're part of his family now."

They sorted out themselves into vehicles. Laycee refused to go with either one of her brothers, causing raised eyebrows and questioning looks. She just stuck her nose up in the air and climbed into the vehicle with Joshua.

No words were exchanged on the drive to her house. They weren't needed.   Joshua reached for Laycee's hand and held it. She looked at their hands, looked at him, gave a small smile, and then stared out the window. He was becoming important to her and she wasn't sure how she felt or if she even wanted him to be.

Joshua pulled into her driveway and parked. Stopping her from getting out, he caught her eyes.

"Let Caleb go through the house again. Let him make sure it's okay. You don't have to do this on your own. We're here for you."

Laycee swallowed hard, emotions mixed, but anger and fear predominant. Who had been in her house? And why? She was a secretary, not into crime, and she felt confident that her boss, a prominent physician, was the same. Now what? She knew she had to go in but she was just so hesitant.

She stepped out of the vehicle and stood watching as Caleb entered. Leith jogged over and draped his arm around her shoulders.

"Cheer up, hun. Caleb will make sure it's okay for you to go in. You know that."

Laycee laid her head on her brother's shoulder and drew in a shaky breath. When she left late yesterday afternoon (and was it not even 24 hours?)

she didn't know she would be returning home to this. She never imagined she would be running for her life.

Liam's gaze wandered all over the neighbourhood, taking in vehicles parked on the street. He stopped by Laycee and asked, "Do you see any vehicles that don't belong?"

She looked around and shook her head.

Caleb appeared on her front porch and beckoned them forward. Laycee hesitated. She was not ready to do this. She was not ready to see what destruction was there.

Caleb came down the steps and stopped in front of her, bending so he could look into her downcast eyes. "It's not nice, Laycee. I won't lie to you. There doesn't look to be a lot of damage, just stuff tossed around."

Laycee looked up at him and nodded. Liam and Leith each took a hand and the three walked forward. Caleb glanced at Joshua, and then his gaze stopped at the look on his brother's face. He nodded. Yep, he thought, he has it bad and I can remember that feeling.

Caleb came up behind them. "I'm sorry, Laycee. I know it's a mess from the crime tech crew. We'll get it cleaned up for you." He stopped and pulled out his phone. It was Ben and it looked as if he was needed back at the office. He took his leave, promising to have Hannah come by to help Laycee clean.

Laycee took a deep breath and stepped into her home. Tears filled her eyes as she looked at the destruction in her living room. Pictures were off the wall, frames and glass broken. Pillows and seat cushions from her couch and chairs were slashed and the stuff spread around. The few knick knacks she allowed herself were in pieces. She walked through into the dining room and then the kitchen. The kitchen was the worse, with everything from her cupboard pulled out and broken and spilt. The same went for the fridge. She turned and headed down the hall to the bedrooms. It was the same.

She sank to the floor and cradled her head on her knees as sobs wracked her body. She had been through so much in the last few hours. When would it end?

An arm came around her shoulders and a head was laid on hers. She knew it was Joshua. He said nothing, simply sat and held her until the sobs stopped. She could hear her brothers gathering up the broken glass and broken pieces of her life. She raised her head and stared ahead.

Joshua saw the change that came across her face. It was not a nice change. She was deeply angry and ready to fight back, but he was afraid for her. He didn't know if she would win or lose and he didn't want to take the chance that she would be gone from his life. He gently brushed back her hair and tried to get her to look at him.

Laycee shook off Joshua's arm and sprang to her feet. She was mad and you didn't make a Bradley mad. Her anger she would work off in cleaning and tidying up her home but it would also be directed at finding the culprits.

Later that afternoon, when her house was back to as normal as it could be and the broken and destroyed furniture removed, Laycee wandered through her house. Leith had gone to get her pets at her insistence. She needed them.

Now, she needed her laptop. It was gone. She looked around and made sure. Then as the two men watched, she stomped across the dining room to the built-in cabinet and pulled out an ornamental leaf. A section moved and a safe appeared. She punched in the code and pulled out a black box.

"What's that?" Liam asked.

"It's my backup. I always store everything to an external hard drive—there is nothing stored on the laptop so when they took it they got nothing. Though why they would think there is something on it I don't know. I don't have work stuff on it. Nothing. It's like a brand-new computer. It also has a really good password, one that would be really hard to break."

Ben looked up as Caleb walked by him and then at his nod followed him into his office, closing the door behind him. Both men sat. Caleb took a sip of the tea he had picked up on his way in. It was getting late and he needed to get home.

"What do you have?"

"Something interesting. Those young fellows are mixed up in something big. They're scared right now and not saying much. They haven't asked for lawyers yet so I'm hoping a night in jail will make them talk." Ben thought for a minute. "One of them is related to the accountant. I think we need to do some more research on them. I am still trying to figure out the Applewood Farm connection."

"I agree. Who's good at research that we can bring on board, who we can absolutely trust? I don't want too many involved as yet, but I know talk is going to get around about what happened today. Were we able to keep it quiet about why Laycee was there?"

"I think so. As far as it goes, Laycee was there with Joshua for a day away from town. That's what I've put out. I don't like not telling the truth but in this case we need to protect Laycee. Try Annie - she's really good at sourcing information."

"Most definitely. All right, Ben, wrap it up for the day and head home. I'm going soon."

"See you tomorrow. Make sure you get some down time. I am pretty sure it's going to get very interesting very soon."

"You know, I hate it when you're right."

Ben laughed, closing the door behind him. Caleb worked for a while longer and then headed home to his wife and boys. He needed to be with them.

****

Laycee dug her fingers into Defiant's fur as he lay curled up tight to her on the couch Liam had brought over for her. Her couch and some other furniture would need to be replaced as would picture frames. She was tired just thinking about it. It helped to have Defiant next to her. He had gone wild when Leith brought him back late that afternoon, barking, jumping, doing his Sheltie spins and dances. When she sank to the floor, he had been all over her —kisses, on her knee, away and then back for her hugs. Terror, when let out of her crate, had taken one look, nose in the air, and then meandered over to the laundry room where Laycee kept her food dish up on the dryer. When she had inspected her domain, she returned and rubbed up against her, back arched and her tail doing its quiver that she gave when she was content and eager to please.

Laycee's head went back on the couch and her eyes sank closed. She was tired and needed some sleep. Liam had insisted he was staying the night and at the moment, was out on her back deck. She knew he had a cup of coffee with him—he never seemed to be without one. She hated that he and Leith and Joshua had gotten so involved in what was happening, whatever that was. She had sent Leith and Joshua home about an hour ago.

Liam came in, shutting and locking the back door, and setting her alarm.

"We need to look at better locks for you."

Laycee snorted. "Like that will help? They managed to disarm the alarm system by cutting the

74

cable and then breaking in. I don't think better locks
will make any difference."

"Maybe not."

Laycee rose, cutting off his next words. She
had a pretty good idea of what was coming and was
in no mood to listen. "I'm heading for bed. See you
in the morning."

Liam stopped her with a hand to her arm.
"I'm glad you're okay. God was watching out for
you. I just want you around for a few more years."

Laycee dropped a quick kiss on his forehead.
"I know. I've got a few years of bugging you left to
do."

Liam laughed. "Night, hun."

****

Tom was running scared. Somehow he had
heard what had happened at the Bradley cottage.
Word had gotten around among some of his friends.
He had no idea where Andy was but he could only
hope Andy was not one of the punks who had shut up
the cottage, aiming at a dog. It would be like him to
have that happen.

The trilling of his phone startled him. He took
a quick look. It was the Boss. He threw his phone
across the room, breaking it. He was done. He
grabbed a duffel bag from the closet and stuffed it
full of his and Andy's clothing. That was all that they
had that was theirs in this rundown trailer. He was
out of here. He would try and find Andy and barring
that, he was out of town tonight. He had no idea
where he was headed but it was far from here.

He didn't bother locking the door—there was
nothing to steal. He jumped in his vehicle, keyed it
to life and burnt rubber as he left the park. After
driving around for a while, he headed out of town.

No, Andy was underground somewhere or else he had messed up and was in jail. He would try and find him once he got settled in a new town. Maybe he should just get a job and stay away from crime. Crime certainly wasn't working for him right now.

****

The Boss cursed. That no-good punk was not answering his phone. He slammed his glass down on the desk, spilling his drink. His employer was coming down on him to find the information and he had had to hire two low-downs to try and find it. They messed up, which meant he had messed up. Mistakes were not permissible. His life was now on the line and he intended to make Laycee pay when he got his hands on her and got the information he needed.

His phone rang, stilling his inner raging. It was her, the Mastermind. He didn't know what he was going to say, how he was going to explain that he no longer had control of the two he had hired and that he was no closer to finding what she wanted. She wouldn't take it well. Failure was not an option. It was life or death for him, his life or his death. He had money squirrelled away in banks overseas that no one knew about. He intended to live and live well once he got out of the country.

The Sunday morning sun peeked over the horizon. Laycee's eyes opened. She knew sleep was over, and it was only 5 a.m. She reached over and hugged Defiant, sleeping tight to her, and then reached for Terror, sleeping perched on her as she lay on her side. Terror's purrs started and she licked Laycee's arm.

Laycee shoved Defiant enough that he jumped off the bed, followed by Terror. The two were inseparable, not typical for cat and dog. Laycee grabbed her mint green terrycloth robe and shoved her arms into it. She headed for the back door to let the dog out and then reached for the animals' food dishes for their breakfast. She filled their water bowls, one in the kitchen, the other in the living room. Stretching, she looked around her house. It looked empty but the sunny yellow of the walls, the dark laminate flooring and the cream trim and ceiling always perked her spirits. Today it didn't. She still felt violated at the intrusion into her home. She lifted her heart to God, asking for protection and peace.

When she turned back to the kitchen, Liam was standing at her island. She loved that kitchen— the off-white cabinets, solid brown countertop and polished bronze fixtures. A little oak island in the middle was all she needed. The kitchen wasn't big enough for a table but she had a dining room; that's all she needed.

"So," Liam asked. "How are you? And what mischief do you plan on getting into today?"

Laycee swatted him on the way by. "I'm fine, and the mischief was not of my making." Nose in the air, she made her way to the fridge, then realized she didn't have much in the way of groceries to make breakfast, thanks to the intruders yesterday.

"Go, get yourself ready. We'll go out for breakfast. It's almost 7 now. Deb will have the cafe open."

"If it's your treat?"

"It is. Get going. I'll make sure the animals are taken care of."

Laycee stepped out of her house and looked around. It seemed normal, but she was nervous. She felt like there were eyes boring into her back, watching every move she was taking away from her safe spot. She quickly jumped into Liam's vehicle.

"Laycee, Caleb is meeting us. He called when you were getting ready. Just us three. He needs to run something by you."

Laycee turned her head to look at her brother, shrugged, and then turned her gaze back out the window. She didn't notice that Liam's eyes kept going to the rearview mirror. He thought they were being followed but wasn't sure. He wasn't the police, so he really didn't know how to tell.

Caleb was waiting for them in a back booth at the Crazy Quilt Cafe. Deb Saunders, the owner, loved quilting almost as much as she loved to cook and had decided this was the perfect name for her place. Liam let Laycee slide onto the black vinyl bench seat and then slid in beside her.

Caleb waited until they had placed their orders and then looked at Laycee.

"Laycee, we have some things to go over. I have some questions to ask as well." He stopped speaking as their food was placed in front of them and Liam offered a quick prayer of thanks.

"Caleb, I would rather not answer anything right now, not here." Laycee gaze shot around the cafe. She felt eyes on her but who? Everyone in the cafe at that point she knew from town. It was not a large town, small town in fact, but right now, she wished to be in a huge city where anonymity was the norm.

Caleb nodded. "That we can do. Somewhere else. So tell me, Liam, how's work?"

Liam's fork stopped halfway to his mouth and then he laughed. "Quick change of subject, there, my friend. Work is going well. How are your gardens?"

The two men's conversation drifted off into mundane, every day topics. Caleb dropped money on the table for their meal and then stood.

Laycee and Liam followed him from the cafe.

Caleb stood by his personal truck, eyes searching the area. He too felt uncomfortable, a sense of danger, and he had learned to never ignore his gut feelings. "Okay. Let's take my vehicle. We need to talk and it's probably the best not to talk in public."

Once they were seated in Caleb's truck, he hesitated. "We need to go back over the whole timeline again." At Laycee's startled look, he continued, "We don't have your statement. I want you to walk me back over everything that you can remember. Here, dictate into this and I can have it transcribed for you to sign." He handed her a small dictator.

She looked at it and then him. "Dark ages still, Caleb?"

He shrugged and then laughed. "It works."

Laycee directed him to the restaurant where it all started on Friday night, going over each step she had taken, who she could remember seeing there, to the point where she had fled. He drove to where her truck had gone off the road. She shuddered as she looked at the area, knowing it was only God's hand that kept her from serious injury.

He then drove to the Bradley cabin and parked in front of it. He turned off the vehicle, then laid a hand on her arm.

"We're going to go in, Laycee. We need to search this place as well to see if there is anything else here. Someone was in here and left that envelop. There may have been more than one occasion that happened."

Laycee shuddered at the thought. "Did you ever figure out what the paper said?"

Caleb was silent long enough that Laycee turned to look at him. He nodded. "I am not going to tell you until after your statement is finished and signed."

They searched the cabin. Nothing was found. Laycee looked around, then stepped outside, a thoughtful look on her face. Where would someone hide something?

Liam came up behind her. "Still thinking?"

"Yeah. Where would you hide something if you wanted to make sure no one else found it?"

Brother and sister looked at the out buildings, and then at each other. Both raced for the boat house. Caleb followed them, knowing they were on to something, or at least he hoped they were.

Liam reached up under the eaves above the entrance door. He felt something.

"Caleb, I think you need to pull this out. I don't think it's something we left from years ago."

Caleb took Liam's place and reached up to the small area. He felt a small paper package. He sighed. Sunday or not, his crime evidences team would be back. He knew they had searched the boathouse the day before but whether they had looked up at the eaves or not was another matter. Or else someone had been here since and placed this. He pulled out his phone, called for the team, and then hesitated. Phone slipped back into his jacket pocket, he turned to Liam and Laycee

"We might as well get comfortable in the cabin. Do you have any tea, Laycee?"

Laycee gave a small smile. "We do. A real variety. Which do you prefer?"

As Laycee and Caleb walked ahead of him, discussing the merits of various teas, Liam followed more slowly, deep in thought. This was getting out of hand. Who and what and why? His mind drifted to the Applewood Farm B&B. A thought made him turn and look across the small lake. It was what he thought.   The B&B was directly across the lake. Now it was making sense. He quickened his steps to catch up with the others and let Caleb know what he had discovered. Caleb took a step back and looked across the lake, then looked at Liam and nodded. Yes - things were beginning to make sense, but what kind of sense?

The Mastermind was very angry. Someone had failed. Someone had messed up weeks and months of careful planning. It had come down to one person who had chosen wrongly. She stomped around her office, footsteps deadened by the plush cream carpet. Her gaze shot around the room but didn't take in the beautiful wood furniture, the dark wainscoting and trim, the maroon velvet drapes at the windows, or the cream wallpaper. She strode back to her desk and dropped into the luxurious desk chair. No expense had been spared in her office, although the rest of the house was not decorated to the degree this was.

She stabbed the number for the Boss. He was not answering. Her anger level continued to climb. Someone was going to pay for this. And that would start with that little brat, Laycee Bradley. It was her fault. Somehow, she had to have found out what was going on.

A knock at the door startled her. She was a master at concealing her emotions and quickly pulled a bland face over the anger.

"Come in."

Her housekeeper entered, handing her the morning mail, and then left.

The Mastermind flipped through the mail and stopped at an envelope that had just her name on it, not that of her organization. The return address was from Oak City, just the street address, no name.

Picking up her letter opener, she quickly slit open the envelope and withdrew the typed page. Her features darkened again in anger. How dare he?

How dare he threaten to take away what she had accumulated? He would pay. Just as soon as she finished here.

****

Caleb watched his team pack up and leave. They had taken the package with them and would open it in the lab. A call would come to him once that was done. He scrubbed his hands down his face and then through his hair. It was going to be a long day. It was Sunday and he had planned to be at church with Hannah and their boys. He pulled out his phone and gave her a quick call, letting her know he might not make it.

Liam approached him, uncertainty in his steps and gaze. Caleb sighed. Whatever was going on just got a whole lot bigger and he still had to figure out how Laycee was involved.

A sound of an approaching vehicle caught his attention. It stopped and both Joshua and Leith stepped out. Liam must have called Leith. Now that the whole gang was here, maybe they could get some answers.

"Liam, why don't you see if you and Laycee can rustle up some coffee and tea and maybe something to eat? It's been a while since our breakfast and I could use something to fuel the brain cells."

Liam grinned. "That's all you think of, isn't it? You haven't changed. Sure, I'll get right on it."

Caleb smiled, shaking his finger at his friend. They had been in the same class at high school, but it was just over the last few years that their friendship had grown close. They were in a small men's Bible study group and often met for a quick coffee or lunch when they could swing it.

Joshua headed for the cabin as Leith approached Caleb. Leith's face was grim, making him seem so much older.

"What's going on, Caleb? We saw the team leaving."

Caleb hesitated, then indicated the cabin. "Let's go inside. We need to talk. I had the team sweep for bugs, so I know the place is clean."

"Bugs - as in…" Leith's voice trailed off.

Caleb nodded as they headed for the cabin. Laycee had made both coffee and tea and had mugs poured for all. She hadn't found much to prepare to eat but had found some soup and crackers that were still fresh.

Gathering around the table, Caleb took a sip of his tea and then, setting the mug back down, wrapped his hands around it. He closed his eyes and offered a quick prayer for wisdom and guidance. Looking around he searched the faces of the other four.

Liam was simmering with anger. The big brother in him was frankly showing on his face. His knuckles were white as he gripped his mug.

Next to him, Leith's face had become unreadable. There was rage palpating from him, nevertheless. His eyes were fixed on Laycee and Caleb found them shuttered. Leith had always been one who was very open with his emotions. Not any more.

His brother was next. Joshua sat beside Laycee, his eyes glued to her. Caleb knew his brother well. Joshua was in love and the woman he loved was in danger. Anger was there but determination was as well. Joshua was going to solve this, no matter the cost.

Caleb's gaze travelled back over the three men before resting on Laycee. Her eyes were down, looking at her clasped hands. They were loosely clasped, not clenched as he thought they would be. There was a look of peace on her face, strangely not fear or anger. He tilted his head as he contemplated what was going on with her. A few hours earlier, she had been afraid and terrorized. Not any more.

Caleb looked down, then looked once more at Laycee. He pulled over the tablet of paper and pen she had left on the table. Laycee had turned on a radio and soft music played in the background. He caught the song that was playing and nodded. Now he knew why she was calm. She had turned it over to God and He had put peace in her.

The Boss had gone into hiding. He knew the Mastermind was after him. He had failed and failed mightily. His life was now in danger. He had packed up what he could and abandoned his apartment. He was hoping that they had found the parcel he left at the cabin. He knew the hiding place of the Bradley siblings. He had heard them talking about it in the past, back when they were all kids playing around the lake. He had withdrawn as much money as he could, had his passport in his fake name, and was just waiting for dark to get away. He had had enough. It wasn't worth it any more. Tickets were booked on a flight out of the country for tonight. He hoped he made it to the airport in Oak City.

Looking back, he regretted a lot. He didn't regret the wealth he had accumulated, but he did regret the danger he had put friends into.

A noise at the door of the abandoned house startled him. A shape appeared, a shot rang out, and he cried out in pain. As darkness closed in on him, he knew he had lost. He had played the game and the cards were no longer in his favour. He sank to the ground and the darkness overcame his sight. Empty hands stretched out. The form stood over him, then picked up his duffel bag. This is what his life had come to—dying in an abandoned house, alone, a victim of his own making.

****

The Mastermind grimaced at what she had had to do, but then smiled. One less person to worry about. She was taking control. She would be the one doing everything now. She had a source she could go to for information and that was what she intended to do. No one suspected who was in her pocket and deep in her pocket at that. She just needed to tidy up a few loose ends that the Boss had left. Time to search out those two losers he had hired. The boss may have once been from this area but he had been gone for years. No one would know he was missing. No one would know he was gone.

She turned and crept back through the woods. She hated the woods. She hated the bugs and animals. She hated the smell of the woods. She hated everything about them. Yet here she was stuck in one because the Boss messed up big time. He had paid. Now she would make the others pay for her discomfort.

****

Caleb cleared his throat; the three men's eyes shot to his face. He kept his eyes on Laycee. She seemed detached, lost in thought.

"Laycee." He began, then stopped as his phone rang. He stepped outside to take his call and then returned, looking down at a text he had just received. Yes, things were progressing, and this text just made something a little bit clearer.

Joshua reached over and gripped Laycee's hand. It was cold. She looked up at him from under her eyelashes and they shared a long look. She sighed and then looked at her brothers. She could feel their emotions and wished she had never been the one to bring that to them, whatever "that" was.

Caleb seated himself again and hesitated before he spoke. "Laycee, I know we have gone over just about everything and that your statement is now ready to sign. However…" His voice trailed away as he sought for the words he needed to proceed. It was not going to be easy. It was actually going to be really difficult and he expected a fight from her.

"Laycee, that package was actually another note. We're working on finding out who the sender is, but it is someone who knows you and knows you fairly well. We need to be looking at your friends and those you have worked with, including those you volunteer with."

Laycee's eyes grew in size as he spoke, then slid close. It was what she had feared. Someone was after her. SHE had brought this danger to herself and her family and friends.

"Who and why?"

Caleb pulled up the text on his phone.

He read it silently to himself and then showed her:

Laycee

You are in danger. Someone wants you dead. You have something they want and unless you turn it over you won't be safe.

Turn it over and you just might live.

A Friend

Laycee gasped. What was going on? Who was doing this? As she grappled with this, Caleb shared the text with the other three. Glances were shared, plans were made with those glances, and Laycee's freedom to move around on her own just shrank.

"Do you have any idea?"

She shook her head. "I don't. I know just about everyone in town, mostly because of my job, and I can't say anything about that because of confidentiality. I can't think of anyone who stands out."

Caleb nodded. It was what he had suspected. Laycee was trusting and giving. She was loved by those she worked with and by her friends. Ben had checked and she was one of the volunteers the residents of the home looked forward to seeing the most. It would be difficult to determine who the person was, but he would do it. Joshua's face said the same.

Joshua abruptly shoved back his chair and lifted Laycee to her feet. "We're out of here. We'll meet you at your office." Clasping her hand he led her from the cabin, shoved her into his truck, and drove away.

The three remaining stared at the door, then at each other.

"He's got it bad." Leith snickered, bringing some levity to the moment.

"Yes, he has." Liam agreed. "Let's get this cleaned up. Caleb, we can manage. Head back into Riverville. Leith and I will do some brainstorming. You don't need all of us there. Just keep us as updated as you can."

"Will do. Thanks, guys. I hope and pray this is over in the next day or so, but I am thinking it won't be."

Laycee was silent as they drove back to Riverville, silent as Joshua stopped and got her a coffee from her favourite coffee shop, silent as he pulled up and parked at the police station, silent as they entered and waited to be cleared to go through, silent as he led her to Caleb's office, silent as she sat. He was getting worried. She was shutting him out and he didn't like it.

Caleb entered, Ben behind him, and shut the door. He didn't go behind his desk, instead perched on the edge near Laycee.

"Laycee, we have your statement here. We just need to have you proofread it and sign it that it's correct. Then we need to talk."

Laycee nodded woodenly, taking the file and pen she was handed. She quickly read her statement and then scrawled her signature.

She stood, hesitated and then headed for the door and was gone before anyone could stop her. This had surprised them. Joshua ran after her but she was already gone. He headed out the door and there was no sign of her. Caleb and Ben were at his heels. Caleb had suspected this. There were not a lot of places she could go to and he would look at each one. He sent a quick message to Liam.

Liam and Leith headed for Laycee's, knowing she would want her Sheltie and cat. They were her comfort.

Laycee had not shown up. Liam searched outside as Leith searched inside. He let Defiant out of his crate and into the backyard. Defiant followed Liam everywhere as he took in every aspect of the yard. Things seemed normal. Leith exited the back door, shaking his head at Liam's questioning look. Where was she?

Joshua's heart raced. Laycee had to be close. He frantically searched around his vehicle, around the station and then the surrounding blocks. She had totally disappeared. He asked anyone he came across. Laycee had not been seen.

Caleb sent Ben back in to alert the patrol officers to watch for Laycee. He had a bad feeling. She had moved so quick, they had not had time to react. Now they were behind and had to pick up the pieces and find her.

Hours later, they regrouped at Laycee's house. Leith carried Terror around; she needed that contact.

Caleb looked up from the papers he had in his hand. "No sign of her. Either she's very good at hiding or someone has her. I'm afraid my gut says it's the latter."

They nodded. A command centre had now been set up in Laycee's dining room. Liam slammed his fist on the wall and then left to the back yard. Defiant crept close to him as he sat down on the steps. Hugging his sister's dog, he bowed his head and prayed. A fervent prayer that his sister would be found.

It was a long night. No word. No sleep. By morning, they just knew something was wrong.

Liam's phone vibrated. He pulled it out and stared at it. Laycee had sent a text.

"I'm fine. Had to think. Home soon. Feed Defiance and Kat for me." He stilled.

"Caleb, look at this." He handed him his phone.

"She's fine and on her way home?"

Leith and Joshua stood staring at them. All this for nothing?

Liam shook his head. "It's not her. She would never mix up the name of her dog and she never calls Terror Kat."

Caleb looked grim. Issuing orders, steps were set in process to track her phone.

Officers had spoken to Laycee's employer, her friends, the therapy pet organization, nurses and staff at the seniors' home. Nothing stood out. But there was something there, something off, that Caleb couldn't put his finger on.

An officer entered and spoke quietly with Caleb. He searched the room and beckoned Ben over. They spoke for a few minutes and then Ben left.

Caleb approached Liam and Leith. "No word yet. Ben had to leave for something else. We'll find her."

Liam's grim gaze met Caleb, a challenge in the eyes. "So far, we haven't. Each moment it takes makes it more dangerous for her."

Leith stood shoulder to shoulder with Liam, united in their search.

"Look. I need to leave for a while. I'll be back. Officers are speaking with her neighbours again. There were some who were away over the weekend. I take it you'll both be staying here?" At their nods, he turned and left.

****

Joshua sat at his kitchen island, absently rubbing the soft golden fur around Blues' ears. Chin on Joshua's leg, Blues sighed in contentment and closed his eyes. Joshua took a swig of water and then pulled his tablet over. Touching it, he brought up a word processing program and starting listing: dates, events, friends he had, friends Laycee had, groups she was part of that he knew about. There was just too much information.

He rose and moved into the living room, parting the drapes to look out. A cruiser sat in front of his house; Caleb was being thorough. Joshua let the drapes fall back into place and turned. He knew how to do renovations, not how to plan a crime and institute it or to take it apart and understand the mentality behind it. He stopped, an idea crossing his mind. He needed his computer, not his tablet this time. He booted up the computer and started. It made sense to think through this by first deconstructing what had happened and then following the pieces.

Hours later, he rubbed his eyes. He was tired, his eyes closing on him. He thought he had something and looked at the clock. He couldn't call anyone at 3 a.m. He would have to wait. He saved what he was working on and headed for bed. He needed some sleep. Maybe it would be clearer to his muddled mind in the morning.

A couple of hours later, Joshua stirred. Blues was up and moving around, unusual for him at night. Joshua quickly dressed and crept down his stairs. Blues was at the back door, woofing quietly. Joshua peeked through the blinds and saw nothing. He unlocked the door and let Blues out. The dog streaked for the back of the yard, quiet barks floating back. The barks stopped abruptly. Joshua stepped out on the deck, calling for Blues. He stepped down the few steps and onto the flag stones. He moved toward the back of the yard, intent on finding Blues. A whisper of a sound came too late. He felt a crushing blow and then blackness overcame him. He didn't feel the hands that picked him up roughly and slung him over a shoulder, didn't feel the pain of being thrown into the back seat of a pickup, didn't feel the jouncing. Hands dragged him out of the truck eventually, carried him to a building and then let him fall to the cold damp dirt. He didn't hear the clicking of a padlock nor feel the silence and darkness around him.

****

Leith and Liam stretched out on the blankets on the Laycee's living room floor. Defiant curled up tight to Liam, and Terror had plopped herself atop Leith. They needed to be comforted as well as give comfort.

"Where do you think she is?" Leith's voice was quiet and sad.

There was silence, then "I wish I knew. She disappeared so fast. Joshua said he was out the door in just minutes and she was gone. She had no vehicle; she had to get a ride with someone."

"Sure but why isn't she here? She would be even if she had gotten a ride."

"I know. Mom would say pray about it and leave it with God. He's in control and cares more about us than anything. I just wish she and Dad were here right now to pray."

Leith nodded, even though Liam couldn't see him. The silence grew, soon broken by the men's soft snores. Terror rose, stretched and jumped off Leith, making her way to the front window and ducking in behind the drapes. Plopping herself down on the windowsill, she watched the car sitting in front of the house, no lights, no movement from it. Unblinking, she watched, head moving to follow it as it pulled away. Tail lights didn't appear until it was around the corner. Who was watching, she would have asked if she was human. She lifted her paw and started washing the black and white fur, interest lost in the outdoors.

Leith started at the sound of a door closing. He jumped and looked around him. Then he remembered where he was. Liam was still sound asleep, Defiant still curled up tight to him, but brown eyes open and watchful.

Leith rose and moved to the window. Opening the drapes, he saw Caleb making his way to the door. Checking his watch, he was surprised that it was after 8. They must have been tired. He would soon need to drop by his office to see if the material had arrived and he knew Liam needed to get to his job site. He walked over and gave Liam a nudge with his foot. "Caleb's here. Come on, sunshine. Time to rise and shine."

Liam grunted and then sat up as Leith opened the door. Caleb handed him a takeout tray of coffee, snagging his own cup of tea, and the bag of biscuits and bagels he had picked up.

"Any word?" Liam asked.

Caleb grunted, then motioned with the bag. "First, we eat. Then we talk. It's gonna be a long day."

Caleb was right. It was a long day that worked its way to another and another. They were growing tired, with little sleep and little food and little news. Caleb had had an officer stationed outside during the night until he had been needed in another area of town.

Chapter 19

"Ben!" Caleb yelled for him as he headed for the door and his vehicle.

Ben looked up and then followed. "What's up?"

"A couple of hunters were out checking out their blinds and cabins, to see what repairs they needed to make before fall. I know, it's only September but you know Earl and Henry. They like everything in order. Apparently they stumbled upon a body in an abandoned cabin near Logan Lake."

Ben froze, then looked over. "Joshua!"

Caleb shrugged. "It doesn't fit the description of what he was wearing and the responding officer said the man's build was wrong. I want you to take a look at this and see if it fits in with Laycee's case." He slammed his open hand on the steering wheel. "I just wish I knew where those two were."

"I know, I know." Ben agreed. "I've working on the lists with Liam and Leith. We've been able to eliminate quite a few people. There are some names we're not sure of, so I'm doing further checking."

"Let's meet later today and go over everything then. Maybe we'll have an ID on the body by then."

Caleb pulled to a stop near the coroner's van and got out. He headed over to the detective who was heading up the investigation.

Jim Townsend looked up at Caleb and shook his head. Caleb's eyes shut in relief. It wasn't Joshua.

"Who do we have?"

"I have no idea why he would be out here or why he was shot, but it's Peter Adams."

Caleb and Ben shot a look at each other. "Peter Adams. Now that rings a bell. Wasn't he the forger we were looking for, last from Oak City?"

"That he was. I gather that's who you've found?"

Jim nodded. "It looks as if he's been here for four days or so. The coroner will know more once he's done the autopsy. He still had his wallet and all his ID. Looks like one bullet to the head."

"Execution style. That just adds a whole new case to our overloaded books. We're going to be looking for who hired him."

Jim looked at Caleb, hesitated, and then said, "He's around the same age as Laycee and Joshua. In fact, I think I saw he was in Laycee's high school class."

Caleb shot Jim a look. What would a forger have in common with Laycee?

****

Joshua roused, prying open his eyes. Blackness swirled in front of him and his eyelids slid closed. Later, he opened his eyes again, and the world stood still. He moved cautiously rolling over onto his back. He felt lightheaded but there was no more blackness. He turned his head, taking in where he was. It was an old boat house, he thought, as he could hear water nearby. He sat up and regretted it as the world spun and nausea rose. Fighting back against both, he stumbled to his feet swaying for a minute. He shivered, feeling the dampness and the coldness, yet burning up at the same time. He focused on the door and inched his way over, his head pounding with each step. He pulled on the door and yanked it open. Sudden sunlight tortured him. His eyes closed, he dropped to his knees and then fell forward, blackness once again closing in.

The sudden noise of a door being pulled open stopped the officers at the cabin. Ben spun, looked at Caleb, and then drew his weapon as he headed for the noise. Caleb, weapon in hand, followed as did some of the other officers. They halted at the edge of a clearing, ensuring it was safe.

"Caleb. Over there at the boat house? Is that a body?"

Caleb squinted against the bright sun and nodded. They cautiously made their way across the small clearing, trusting in the officers behind them to keep them safe. They stopped just short of the boat house and looked around.

Caleb squatted down and reached for the body. He felt the movement of the back and knew the man was alive. He holstered his weapon and turned the man over

"Joshua!" he cried. He could hear Ben in the background yelling to get an ambulance. He quickly felt over Joshua's body for wounds, stopping at the back of his head. There was a nasty lump there. Caleb knew he had to leave his brother lay still until the paramedics had assessed him and could move him safely. "Ben, get blankets. We need to get him warm."

Ben raced for the vehicles and returned as quickly as he could. Tucking the blankets around Joshua, he laid a hand on Caleb's shoulders and then moved away. He stepped into the boat house and looked around. It was empty, except for some skittering of little feet and cobwebs. He shuddered, thinking of how Joshua had laid there for overnight.

Caleb watched as the paramedics worked on his brother and then moved him to a stretcher. He followed behind. Ben stopped him with a hand on his arm.

"Call Hannah. Then go with him. I'll process this and catch up with you. Davis will drive you." He motioned to one of the young officers standing nearby. "Drive Caleb to this hospital and then go get his wife, Hannah."

Davis nodded and reached for Caleb's keys. Caleb handed them over almost without thought.

Hannah raced into the Emergency Department, frantically searching for her husband among the people waiting. She saw him turned and slammed her body into his.

"It's really Joshua?" she asked. At his nod, she continued, "How is he?"

"Dr. Young is with him now. They're running tests and he said something about an X-Ray or a CT of the head. Joshua was knocked out and it looks like he was unconscious for a time. They need to make sure there is no damage. We have to wait until we speak with him to find out how long he was out there." Caleb's voice broke.

Hannah drew him over to a chair and pulled him down with her. She looked up as their pastor and his wife approached. "Sweetheart, Pastor Bob and Sue are here. Let's pray."

Gathering around them, the pastor led them in prayer, bringing Joshua to the Lord for healing and also for Laycee to be found. The room silenced around them, hushed at the solemnity and seriousness of the moment.

Dr. Young emerged from the exam rooms and looked for Caleb. Hannah touched his arm and pointed. Caleb rose as the physician approached

"Good news, Caleb. Good news. Looks like a concussion but nothing more serious. He's been in the elements, though, and we'll need to keep him for a day or so to make sure nothing comes of that."

Caleb's eyes slid shut and then reopened. He shook the physician's hand and thanked him.

As he turned, he say Liam and Leith hovering near the door. He spoke to Hannah and then preached them.

"We heard," Liam said. "Is he okay?"

Caleb nodded. "Concussion. Exposure but Dr. Young thinks he's okay."

Leith's hands clenched into fists. "Any idea of why or who?"

Caleb shook his head. "Too soon. Ben's working the area and will let me know what he finds. As soon as I can, I'm headed back to talk with Joshua."

"My gut says it's related to Laycee. I spoke with Ben. He said you found the body of a forger in the woods nearby. Any relation to this?"

Caleb was silent, trying to come up with the words that would dispel their fear and worry without being overheard in a room full of listeners.

He nodded to the outside door and they stepped through it.

"I think somehow it is. It is starting to make sense. I need to speak with the police department in Oak City to see what they have and then track his steps. I want Laycee found too."

"We know you do." Leith's voice was taut with worry. It had been four days since Laycee was seen and he felt they were no closer to finding her or what had happened to her. "I need to go. I'll talk to you later." He spun on his heel and rushed away.

They watched him go. Liam's voice reached to Caleb, "He's worried and he wants to help, just doesn't know how. What can I do?"

"You're not a police officer, Liam, but I could use your help. I want to stay and see Joshua as soon as he's back in a room. Then let's meet. Hopefully Ben will be back in town and has some answers."

Liam nodded and watched as his friend trudged back through the doors. This was wearing everyone down, but Caleb seemed to be hit the worst at the moment. Finding his brother alive would help but they still needed answers. He raised his eyes to the sky and sent up a silent prayer, once again pleading for his sister.

****

Five hours later, the four men sat around the kitchen table in Caleb's home. Papers and files were stacked on the table. Hannah moved around, making sure they had their food and drinks and then, dropping a kiss on Caleb's cheek, left the room to spend time with her sons.

"Ben, let's start with prayer. Humanly, we're doing everything I think we can. We could sure use some divine intervention right now."

Ben led them in prayer, pleading for Laycee, asking for healing for Joshua, and for wisdom and strength for themselves. He reminded the Lord that they were the apple of His eye and that He cared for sparrows, much more so for them.

There was silence, then paper rustling as Caleb sorted through what he had and what he could share with the two Bradley men. He had spoken to the mayor and the police board and knew they were on board with them being involved. Being upright and honest men in the community helped.

The silence continued as they read their material. Liam, always needs a visual thanks to his landscaping skills, reached for a tablet of paper and a pen to start charting ideas.

Caleb rose and made fresh tea for himself and a pot of coffee for the others, refilling their mugs when it was brewed. He stretched and looked at the clock. It was late.

He studied the other three and paced through the house and up the stairs. Stopping at his boys' room, he entered. They were sound asleep. He pulled the covers up more tightly on them and dropped a kiss on each of the heads.

He left and turned towards his own bedroom. Hannah was still up, curled up in a blanket in her favourite chair, a light on low, and her Bible on her knee. He crouched down beside her and she drew him into a hug.

"How's it going?" She asked.

"We're not getting far. I just know we're missing something but I don't know what." He sighed. "It would be nice if you can up with an idea. You always have great ideas."

"Well, thank you." She kissed him and then drew back. "I do have an idea but I didn't want to influence you."

He cocked his head and waited. He knew she was searching for words, something she would do when she wanted to explain something and wasn't sure how to proceed.

"You think it is something Laycee is involved in?" At his nod, she continued, "Okay. She has her friends, her church, her work, and her volunteer duties. You have pretty much eliminated her friends, her work and her church. That leaves her volunteer duties. About all I know she is involved with is the Take-A-Lick Pet Therapy. It's run by an accountant in town, Joy Smith. I don't think you'll find anything with the Applebys from Applewood Farm. I have known Doris and George for years. What you would likely find is that someone stayed there, contacted someone here and it went from there."

Caleb stared at her, amazed at how succinct an explanation she had just given. She was right. They had eliminated just about everything else.

"Hannah, you're wonderful. No wonder I love you so much." He kissed her, spun and raced out of the room.

Hannah touched her mouth and smiled. Yes, Caleb was now on a hunt. Thank the Lord that He had given her those thoughts tonight.

Caleb's phone rang as he descended the stairs. It was the hospital, letting him know that Joshua had been awake, talking but had drifted off to a normal sleep. That buoyed his steps even more.

The three men looked up as he sat back down. He looked around at them.

"Hannah, bless her, has had a suggestion. What do you know about Take-A-Lick Pet Therapy and its founder, Joy Smith?"

Ben's pen dropped. "That's it. That's what has been bugging me. Rumours are that Joy is in financial difficulty. You know she does a lot of freebie work at the seniors' home. Worth a looksee at her."

Liam and Leith's eyes snapped between the two officers. Were they finally getting somewhere?

"Okay, it's getting late. Let's pick it up in the morning. Ben, I want you to go through her financials. Get a court order if you have too. Get

Lucy to take a look at the seniors' home, match up any deaths with the residents Laycee has recently visited."

"Leith, Liam, what do you know about Peter Adams?"

Leith's eyes met Liam, then shot to Caleb.

"Peter was in some of Laycee's classes. He tried hard to get her to go out with him, but she wouldn't. She would never tell us why, other than he wasn't her type. I always thought there was more."

Liam picked up the thread. "He's Joy Smith's son, you know. Dad had heard rumours that he was just a hair away from being in trouble with the law. Laycee said he could copy his Mom's signature and was always signing excuses to get out of school."

Ben and Caleb shared a glance. It was closing in on Joy Smith. They needed more information and proof.

****

The next morning, he was met in his office by the three men. Ben looked excited, so Caleb knew he had some information.

Leith spoke. "Mrs. Appleby called last night, asking about Laycee. We know them from the years at the lake. She said she hadn't seen Joy for a couple of years, that they had used her for their accounts, but in the last couple of years, she was really pushing them to invest in funds she controlled. They weren't comfortable with that and changed their accountant."

Ben was nodding. "That's what I've been hearing, too. She's pushing for investments. Some of the seniors at the home were approached and refused. Interestingly, there were about three or four who said no, but when the family checked their accounts after they died, it showed investment withdrawals. They weren't aware of this. I'm having Annie track these down."

Liam was silent. "So it's all about money? Is that why Laycee was chased and has now disappeared?"

"We don't know for sure, Liam, but I will have traces put on Joy's business and personal accounts and have an unmarked car follow her. We'll also find out if that forger from Oak City had contact with her. What I was hearing is that Joy and Peter were estranged. The police detective last involved in his case is investigating that now and will email his findings. He hoped to have something solid by noon."

Anger simmered just below the surface. Joshua had been injured and Laycee was missing. This drew them together closer than any blood ties.

A tap came at the door, and Annie appeared at Caleb's invitation to enter. She handed him a folder and before releasing it, sent him a look. He studied her and then nodded. Yes, she had come through. He wanted to go through the information first, then with Ben before he shared it any further.

After the men had left, Caleb headed over to the hospital to see Joshua. Entering his room, he found him sitting on the side of the bed, dressed.

"Where do you think you are going?"

Squinting at him, Joshua replied, "To find Laycee."

"No. You're hurt and you're not steady on your feet. I'm taking you to Hannah. Fill me in on what happened."

"I don't know. I remember sitting there, Blues wanting out, not getting Blues to come back. I stepped out and that's the last I remember. How long was I gone?"

Caleb figured it would be this way but still had had to ask. "Let's get you home. And you were gone for about 12-18 hours. Do you remember what you are doing last?"

Joshua sighed, his headache making thinking difficult and blurring his vision. "I was working on trying to sort out a timeline and people and had gone to bed. Blues alerted and I followed him outside. That's the last I remember. If I can get to my computer, I need to show you something. I think it's tied to the therapy group and seniors. At least that's what I thought."

Caleb nodded, helped Joshua to a wheel chair and pushed him outside. The sun caused Joshua to blink and cringe at the renewed headache. "I think you're on to something. That's what we've figured out too."

As Caleb drove towards his home (Joshua would be spending time with them), he continued, "Tell me what you know about Peter Adams?"

"Peter?" Joshua's brow crinkled in thought. "I haven't heard of him in years, since before I finished high school. He had left town about the time his Mom remarried. He didn't like the guy. He wouldn't even come back after Joy divorced him. I don't think Joy and Peter got along all that well. Come to think of it, I remember now that he wasn't her son, just her step son."

Caleb absorbed the new information, adding layers to what they knew and adding questions that needed to be answered.

The Mastermind was livid. The forger she had hired was dead. That no-good step son of hers had outlived his usefulness. It seemed though that he had tried to throw a monkey wrench into her plans. Look where it landed him! Good riddance! Joshua Logan had been found. It was all falling apart. Her scheme to get rich was in ruins, thanks to that Laycee Bradley. She was ready to kill her, if only she could find her. Where had she run to?

A knock at her business office door startled her. Pulling her face back into the impassive look she always had, she acknowledged her secretary. Behind the woman, Caleb and Ben loomed. A flicker of anger flashed through her eyes and was gone.

Caleb entered, followed by Ben. He said nothing, just stared at her. She stared back, not giving anything away.

"Why, Joy? Why did you do it? Was it the money? Was it the thrill of fooling people?" Caleb's voice had unleashed anger.

She was suddenly afraid. "I don't know what you're talking about. And close the door on your way out. I have a teleconference in 10 minutes."

"No, you don't. You have a conference with us, at the police station. Stand up."

She sat there staring at him. "What?"

"You heard me. Stand up. You're under arrest. Cuff her, Ben." Caleb turned as a heavy glass paperweight hit the door frame. "Add assaulting a police officer to the charge," he told Ben, hearing him read her her rights.

Caleb sighed. They knew why and how Joy had been swindling the elderly and others who weren't so alert. She had made millions in a phoney investment scam. That was now in the hands of seasoned investigators and financial people, who were hopeful to return much of the money she had scammed.

Joshua was safe. Now he had to find Laycee

****

Laycee stirred, feeling the warmth of the sun on her face. She felt wood underneath her. It wasn't the same feeling she had had for days. At least she thought it was days. She opened her eyes and closed them just as quickly. The sun was bright. She gradually opened them and just laid there, relishing the warmth after the coldness she had felt. She glanced around. She was free. There were no walls. No windows. No doors.

She sat up and looked around again. She was back to where it had almost started days ago. She was on the dock at the cabin. Her phone was laying beside her.

She picked up the phone and looked at it. It was charged. Very strange.

Hand shaking, she flipped through her contacts and found Liam. She punching in his number hoping he answered and it didn't go to voice mail.

"Hi, you've reached Liam. Leave your name and number."

Laycee sobbed, wanting to speak with him. She tried Leith and got his voice mail too.

She looked up and then once again down at her phone. Trembling she searched and found the number she was looking for.

"Hello?"   She heard the warm tenor voice answer.

"Joshua?"

She heard the pause, then "Laycee?   Is that you? Where are you? I'm coming."

"Joshua, I'm at the cabin. Come get me. I can't reach Liam or Leith."

"Honey, I'm on my way!" Joshua almost sang the words. He clicked off and then dialled Liam's.

As Liam answered, Joshua was yelling, "She's safe, Liam. She's at the cottage. I'm on my way."

Joshua heard a Praise the Lord and then silence. He knew Liam would be calling Leith.

He dialled Caleb.   "Caleb, Laycee called. She's at the cabin. I'm on my way there."

Caleb was yelling at him not to go. With no response from Joshua, he ran from the station, Ben on his heels, barking orders for patrol officers, investigators and paramedics to get there.

The paramedics surrounded Laycee, much to the consternation of her brothers. Joshua paced off to the side.   Caleb stood and watched as the investigators probed the area and bagged what might be evidence.   The senior paramedic stood and beckoned Caleb over.

Caleb stood at the side of the stretcher, his hand on Laycee's arm. She opened her eyes, and then drifted off.   He nodded for them to leave, knowing that the three men who waited would be right behind them. He would get her story later. He looked up, gave a prayer of thanks, and pulled out his phone to call his wife with the good news.

Laycee looked around her living room. It seemed to be filled with people, all thankful she was safe.

Caleb sat down beside her. "Okay, Laycee, give. What happened?"

"I really don't know. I came out of the police station that day and that's the last I really remember until today. I vaguely remember someone speaking to me and that's it."

"What we figure happened is that Joy Smith had you grabbed. She was behind it all. She had set up phoney investments and she thought you had found out about it from one of the seniors. We found the man who was forging documents for her. She removed him once she had no need for him. The two men who ransacked your house—no word on them but I hope they are still alive somewhere and are a lot smarter than they were. The forger had stayed at the Applewood Farm, which is the note you found directing him to go there."

"I guess I'll never really know, will I?"

Ben, who had been on his phone, spoke up. "We do. Joy's estranged step son had found out what she was up to. He knew the violence his mother was capable of and didn't want to see you hurt."

Laycee's eyes studied Ben. "I don't remember her having a step-son."

Ben shook his head. "Peter Adams." Laycee's eyes brightened as she recalled Peter now. "He's been away from here for many years. He had taken to forging documents and from what I am hearing had done a very good job, almost undetectable from the original.

"Joy Smith had set up a scam involving the seniors at the home you volunteered at. She somehow thought you had found out and were gathering documentation to prove it. She had your house ransacked. Peter had stayed at Applewood Farm and had wandered over to your cabin to put in time. He was pretty good at picking locks. Somehow he placed that envelop in that book and moved the books around. That's what you found."

Laycee shook her head. "All this for something I had no idea about? People are strange." Laycee stopped. "Where's my backpack? That brown envelop. I found in it Ella Lang's room one day. She didn't want it, said it wasn't hers. I took it and never looked at it. I actually forgot about sticking it up under the truck seat.

Caleb reached for it and opened it, spending out the documents. They all crowded around him and looked. It was the evidence they needed to seal Joy Smith's doom. There were original documents of Ella's as well as papers showing the attempt to forge her signature. There was also instructions from Joy to Peter on how he was to proceed and what Joy needed in order to set up her scam and gain control of Ella's finances. They had found much more incriminating evidence with the search of Joy's home and office and her financial accounts.

"How did you get these?" Liam asked.

Laycee stared at the papers. "Ella told me to take them. The cleaners found them on the floor in her room. She was adamant they weren't hers. I took a peek and had planned to turn them in. I stuck them under my truck seat and then forgot about them until the accident."

"Why the cryptogram?" Joshua asked.

Ben spoke up. "It really wasn't meant to be one but when Peter lost that envelop that Laycee found in Ella's room, Joy decided that everything thing should be coded. Because she's an accountant, numbers came naturally to her."

"Why was Joshua taken?" Leith wondered.

"No particular reason, other than he was always with Laycee over those days, and they couldn't be sure what he knew. They also couldn't get to Laycee if he was around. They had apparently hired two men to track her and get the documents. We have one of them in jail on unrelated drinking charges and he talked before he was totally sober. His brother has left town."

Laycee sat back down and cuddled Terror in her arms. She sighed, "All this because of money. All this because someone got greedy." She stopped. "But who set me free? Who took me from Ella's house where she had me locked up in a bedroom to the dock at the cabin?"

The men stopped and looked at each other and then at her. That was a good question

"I promise we'll find out," Joshua said, eyes focused on the woman he loved. "The main thing is that God spared you and sent someone."

Ben spoke up. "I did find out. Joy's housekeeper was terrified of Joy, but when she locked Laycee up in the bedroom, she had to do something. She knew Joy's step-son was on to Joy and wanted to help Laycee. She had her husband help Peter move Laycee to the cabin, figuring we would find her, when Joy was arrested."

Liam and Leith shared a glance, then Liam spoke. "You know what Mom and Dad would have said? God is in control. We may never know the full extent of what you went through or were spared, but God values you more than a sparrow."

"What happens with the therapy group now?" Leith asked.

Caleb responded, "The board will be meeting and setting up new officers and new protocols. It will continue."

Laycee nodded, then spoke, "Okay everyone out. I want some me time with Defiant and Terror. Party next week."

"Can't you name that cat anything but Terror?" Leith complained. "She certainly isn't a terror." He ducked the cushion flying at his head as the room emptied to laughter.

Joshua took a look at her, dropped a kiss on her head and left, promising to come back the next day.

Laycee stretched out on the couch, Defiant curled up behind her knees, and Terror perched on top of her. She was home and safe.

Epilogue

Two months later, it seemed a dream what she had gone through. Laycee wandered through her house and then stepped out the back door to stand on her deck. The breeze was still warm, for November.

Defiant curled up on her feet, his tri-coloured coat glistening in the sun. Terror perched on her shoulder. She heard the door close behind her and strong arms came around her. She leaned back against Joshua. He had become an almost daily visitor, one she depended on.

Terror decided that Joshua's shoulder made a better perch, higher up, and climbed up on him. She gave his ear a thorough washing and then sat looking around her domain.

"Your cat just washed my ear, you know."

Laycee grinned and nodded.

"Your cat is now talking to me."

Laycee snickered, knowing what was coming.

"Your cat is singing. Singing, do you hear?" Joshua's voice was incredulous. He had never heard a cat sing. Laughter erupted and shook his body.

Terror shot off his shoulder, claws digging in, with a loud meow. The sparrows in the yard scattered. Defiant took off after them, barking, Blues on his heels, with Terror speeding along in a black and white flash.

"Your dog is herding the birds."

Laycee started to laugh, finding it difficult to stop. "He's a Sheltie, a herding dog. Herding dogs herd. He's only doing what comes naturally."

Joshua joined in her laughter. Then, as the evening light dimmed, he sobered.

"Laycee, I am so glad you are safe. You have come to mean the world to me."

She turned to look up at him. "Okay, let's go steady."

He laughed and looked down at her, hugging her close. "You've got it. Going steady, I like that. We'll see where it goes. With you, I know it will be an adventure."

She hugged him. "With you, I know it will be too. With God on our side, we'll make it through."

They stood there for a few minutes, then Laycee spoke. "Ok, we've gone steady. Let's get engaged."

Joshua's laugh echoed through the yard. The two dogs and the cat came back and sat looking up at them. They were certain their humans had just lost it.

Joshua looked down at Laycee, met her eyes, and kissed the woman he had come to love dearly. "I can see it will be a life-long adventure. Can we keep our secret for a while?"

Her brown eyes sparkled as she gazed up at him and hugged him. "Sure, for a day or two." She stood in silence, then said, "God really does care, doesn't He? I look at a sparrow now and remember that He loves and cares for me so much more than one of them. We are His. He has had to teach me that over and over, but during this time especially, it really did make sense."

"That we are, my love. That He does."

Dear Readers:

Thank you for taking the time to read my very first, debut novel.   This novel has been bouncing around in my head for years.   The first few paragraphs of Chapter 1, where Laycee is pursued and then crashes her truck, are literally taken step by step from a dream. My dreams are suspense novels and I have often woken up scared, but wondering how the story turns out, and sometimes with a scream in my throat. I am an avid reader. The love of books was instilled in me as a child by my Mother, who loved to read, and always gifted books at Christmas, birthdays, and sometimes just because. As an adult, we would race to be the first to read a novel by a favourite author, but ended up taking turns. On the day she graduated to heaven, she literally had a book in her hands just minutes before she was called Home.

I live in a house with three Shetland Sheepdogs, a sable girl named Emma, a tricoloured boy named Liam, and a tricoloured girl named Natalie. They are my world. They add so much enrichment and enjoyment to my life. Of course, a Sheltie had to make his way into the book. Defiant is loosely based on my Liam. Liam really does herd the birds, including the seagulls that fly in from Lake Erie. Added to the mix are two rescue cats. Ceilidh (pronounced Kaylee) is a gray tabby the dogs' breeder found on a highway and saved. I fell in love with this little kitty, who loves to curl up and cuddle. Ciara (pronounced Keera) is a little tuxedo rescue. Terror in the book is based on her. She really does chirp and sing and romp her way through the days, often sleeping on top of me at night. Of course, these two cats are convinced they are Shelties. A man's house is said to be his castle; mine is more a circus at times, but it is my home and sanctuary.

I would like to thank a couple of friends who have taken the time to read through the drafts. Jean West, author in her own right, has read and critiqued my novel and offered valuable support and advice. Thank you, Jean. I enjoy the entertainment that your three Shelties bring to your life. And another dear friend and sister in Christ, Faye Silvestro Kubassek. Thank you, Faye, for being a friend and support over the years and believing in my dream and taking the time to read through the manuscript as well. You are a treasure in my life.

My Mother challenged me one day when I shared about two years before she left us in 2010 that I wanted to write a novel. Her response was "Why don't you". Mom, here's the novel. I just wish you were here today so I could put the very first copy of my very first book in your hands. My Father was quiet but we knew he supported us in our endeavours. I can hear his "You did a wonderful job" in my ear as I write. They were the prayer warriors of our family. That is missed. Cherish the time with your parents and family. It is too short.

We sometimes look at the big picture of life and end up overwhelmed. That is not how God expects us to think. Take a look at the lowly sparrow, despised by many, living through all kinds of conditions. God cares for these sparrows. Yet in His word, it is very clearly stated that we are so much more to Him. Trust Him in your daily walk. You're never alone.

Once again, thank you. Enjoy the adventures of Laycee and Joshua. I used to snicker when authors would comment on how the plot changed and characters would enter a book and take over. Not any more. That is exactly what happened. The plot of the book is not what I started out with. Caleb was to be a minor character but law enforcement ended up needings a strong person. Characters changed from villain to friend. The constant was God's caring.

As I end, I can hear Liam and Leith clamouring in the background, demanding that their stories be told, and so, the adventure will continue with the Bradley siblings.

The Hawk

Under His Wings Trilogy
Book 2

by

Ronna Bacon

Dedication

The story of The Hawk, Leith Bradley, is lovingly dedicated to my father, Ronald Bradley Bacon, a carpenter by trade. Some of his actual words to me are contained in the book. As I sit here and contemplate this story, I can hear his words to me, that he so often repeated during the last year of his life, "You did a wonderful job." Dad, for you. Luv you lots and miss you.

Verses to Remember

Job 39:26
"Is it by your understanding that the hawk soars,
Stretching his wings toward the south?

Psalms 61:3
"For You have been a refuge for me, A tower of
strength against the enemy.

Proverbs 18:10
The name of the Lord is a strong tower, the righteous
run to it and are safe.

Table of Contents

Dear Readers

Prologue

Moving stealthily, the black form inched his way through the building, searching for the crates he needed. Using the flashlight he carried sparingly, he checked the labels. The crates were there, just as promised. He opened them as quietly as he could, checking around frequently for the security guard. He had no desire to be found.

The packets placed as far down as he could reach, he tapped the lids back on. A noise to his left stopped him and he crouched, clicking off his light. The security guard's large light flashed around and then moved on.

He slipped back out as quickly and as silently as he could. The alarm here was a joke, easy to disarm and easy to arm again. He laughed to himself as he looked around outside the building and then slid easily around the locked gate. The packets would leave the factory tomorrow and then he'd would pick them up once they got where they were headed.

Leith Bradley slowed his pickup and then turned into the parking lot for Sullivan's Tiles. It was a small family-owned store, a bit more expensive than the larger stores, but he would have to drive further and was not guaranteed the selection they had here. John Sullivan went out of his way to have quality tile, marble, and granite, and had a selection not available in most stores.

Leith parked and then headed into the store. John wasn't out front but Leith knew where the dolly was and soon had found the thin-set, tiles, and grout he wanted. Wheeling the loaded dolly over to the counter, he waited. This was so unlike John. He always was around, hearing the door chime even in the warehouse at the back.

Leith looked around, then stepped behind the counter. Something felt off.

"John, are you here?" he called, walking back into the warehouse. Pallets lined the walkways and shelving was interspersed as well.

"John?" he called again. It was darker here than he expected, darker then usual. Lights seemed to be out.

Leith continued towards the back, not finding anyone around. Then the merest whisper of sound found him. He turned but not quick enough. A hard fist connected with his jaw, sending him backwards and into crates of tiles. His head slammed back and he crumpled to the floor.

The figure, clad in jeans and a hoodie, stood over him. He brought his foot back and kicked Leith in the ribs. Leith lay unmoving, oblivious to the world around him. Blood trickled slowly from the cut on his jaw.

The figure crouched down and then stood. He looked around, not finding what he wanted. The crates were to be here. His contact had told him which ones he needed and they were missing. He cursed, then kicked at Leith again.

Sound from the front of the store brought his head around. His gaze shot through the warehouse and he slipped silently to the door. He would be back.

****

Regan Evans hummed softly to herself as she juggled a cardboard tray of coffees, a bag of muffins, tile catalogues, and her keys. She touched the door and found it unlocked. Guess Uncle John beat me this morning, she thought. He must be feeling better. Regan had returned to her hometown, to help her uncle manage the tile store while her parents had taken a well-deserved month-long vacation. She hadn't heard from them in a couple of days, but she figured she would soon.

Setting the tray of coffees on the counter, she dropped the bag of muffins to answer the phone. This was not her most favourite part of the business —dealing with the customers. She much preferred to be laying the tiles herself. After hanging up the phone, she shrugged out of her jacket and gathered up her purse to take back to the office.

She looked at the loaded dolly and wondered. Uncle John must have been working on an order for a customer.

"Uncle John," she called, "I have your coffee," as she headed back to the office just off the showroom. That's strange, she thought. The door is closed. It's never closed when we're open.

She turned the knob and stepped in. Her purse and coat hit the floor as she dropped down by her uncle. He looked to be asleep. She reached out a shaking hand and felt. Yes, he had a pulse. She trembled as she snagged the phone and called 911.

Soon, the place was filled with police personnel and paramedics. She watched as they worked on her uncle and then loaded the stretcher into the ambulance. She was torn. She felt she needed to stay but needed to go. Ben Johnson nodded at her and sent her with her uncle.

Caleb Logan strode through the door of the store and looked around, keen eyes taking in everything. Ben moved towards him just a shout came from the warehouse area. Caleb and Ben hit the warehouse floor in full run, almost plowing down a young newly recruited officer.

The officer's pale face indicated something else was going on. Caleb shot him a swift glance. First time for a body, he thought. He jerked his head for the officer to go past him.

Ben knelt beside the crumpled body. Feeling for a pulse, he breathed a sigh of relief. "We'll need another ambulance."

"Get us some more light." Caleb crouched beside Ben. "Wonder who we have. Regan didn't think anything was disturbed but she found it strange there was the loaded dolly at the front and no customer."

Ben nodded. "That is strange. I wouldn't think a tile company had much to steal, other than their cash for a day, and I know for a fact John and Joseph do a deposit every night, keeping just enough out for a day's float."

Caleb turned at the noise behind him and then stood to let the paramedics have his place. He stepped away with Ben, discussing possibilities, when the senior paramedic called to him.

"Caleb, can you come here?"

"What do you have?"

"It's Leith Bradley. He's been pretty beaten up."

Caleb stopped, stunned at the development. What was Leith doing back here? He spun on his heel and stared towards the front of the store. That would be his dolly. Leith was a tile setter and almost exclusively used the Sullivan's stock. He turned back.

"How is he?"

"Not great. He's had a pretty good blow to the face and it looks as if his head hit the crates there."

Caleb watched as they worked on his friend and then rushed him out the door. Ben's hand on his shoulder startled him and he looked around.

"Call Liam. Go. I'll work this."

Caleb thanked the older man and pulling out his phone, headed for his vehicle. This was not a call he wanted to make but Leith was alive. He stopped and looked up at the sullen sky, still with drips of the rain/snow mix coming down. This is not how he planned his day.

Worried, he walked into the Emergency Department of their local hospital. Two victims and he had no idea why. He sighed. He just hoped Leith hadn't gotten mixed up in something like his sister, Laycee, had about six months ago. That adventure had almost cost Caleb his brother and Leith and Liam their sister. The accountant who had masterminded the financial fraud was awaiting trial and he hoped she went away for a long time. Adding the murder of her step-son to the charges just might make it happen.

Caleb headed to the registration desk and then back into the examination area.

"Caleb."

He turned. Liam Bradley was headed towards him. No Laycee but he knew that Joshua and Laycee had had plans to spend the day in a nearby town. Joshua had taken a rare day off from his renovation business.

"What happened? How's Leith?"

Caleb stopped his friend with a hand on his shoulder. "I'm headed back there now. He was unconscious when we found him. He looked like he had taken a beating."

Liam's brown eyes bored into Caleb's. "How does a person get beat up at a tile store?"

Caleb stared back. "That's what I want to know and I intend to find out."

Dr. Young stood next to them as they turned. "Liam, you can go back with Leith for now, but we'll be taking him down shortly for some imaging—X-Rays and a possible CT scan."

Liam nodded and then turned to the room where his brother lay.

The two men watched him go, then Caleb spoke, voice controlled and professional.

"How is he, really?"

Dr. Young pulled off his glasses and scrubbed a hand over his eyes. I'm getting too old for working here all night, he thought. "He's still unconscious. He has at least a concussion, a nasty blow to the jaw that needed stitches. The blow to the back of the head is what concerns me. He also looks as if he was kicked in the ribs."

Caleb's head raised. "So, you knock a man out and then kick when he's down? Unbelievable! How is John?"

"He's fine. He's awake. He said he had been feeling faint this morning and figures he passed out. His blood pressure was high and so was his blood sugar. I'll keep him in for a couple of days to sort it all out." Dr. Young hesitated as if to say more, then shook his head. He couldn't breach the confidence his patients had in him keeping their privacy.

Caleb nodded, then watched as Liam stepped back out of the room as they wheeled Leith away.

Liam's shoulders slumped and he leaned against the wall. How was he supposed to be the head of the family and protect them when they kept getting into situations he couldn't control? At least Laycee was out of town today. He would need to call her. He pulled out his phone and turned it over and over.

Caleb stopped beside him and leant against the wall beside him. "You're bearing those burdens again, Liam."

Liam nodded. Without taking his eyes off his phone, he asked, "Who did this and why?"

"Early stages yet, Liam. The crew is still gathering the evidence. We'll sort it out."

Liam snorted. "Sort it out is right." His eyes raised and there was an angry hard look in them. "You'd better before anything else happens to him."

Caleb took the measure of his friend, knowing his anger was not directed at him. "We will. We will. Call your sister." He turned and walked away, heading back out into the fray, but his heart was heavy. What was happening in his town?

Liam sighed, then punched in his sister's speed dial number. At her answer, he could hear the happiness in her voice. He so hated to destroy that. "Laycee, I need you back here. It's Leith." His voice broke and he swallowed the lump in his throat. "He's been hurt pretty bad."

Laycee gasped and then he heard Joshua speaking with her. He knew they would be back without any further questions and without any hesitation. The three Bradley siblings were close and you didn't strike one but you struck all three.

Regan stood at her uncle's bedside and grasped his hand. "I thought I was going to lose you."

"Not yet, sweetheart. I've got too much living to do." John looked at his niece. "It'll be up to you to run the store, you know. You're capable and I'm only a phone call away. At least for a couple of days. I can work in the office tomorrow or the next day."

Regan gave an unladylike snort at that. "I know I can, I just don't want to. That's not what I expected when I came back home. I know you can and you no doubt will. You need to listen to the doctor."

John smiled. "The Good Lord has a habit of changing our expectations, throwing in those curve balls. We'll get there. Just lock the door and put a note on it if you have to. People in this town understand and I can bet there'll be ladies and gentlemen from the church dropping by just to help out. It's what we do."

Regan nodded. She knew that. That was small town life. She had run from that 10 years ago. She just wasn't used to it any more, having lived in a large city for so many years. She really didn't know if she was that ready to have the town that involved in her life again.

"Go. Find out how our friend, Leith, is. Caleb wouldn't say."

She nodded. "I will. I feel bad that I didn't know he was there."

"How could you? There was the loaded dolly but I could have been gathering an order."

Regan agreed. "It's still not right. Why would someone attack him and in our store?"

"Leave it to Caleb and his men. Now, go. Do what I asked." John paused. "Regan, make sure that order gets over to Leith's job site. It's important."

Regan dropped a kiss on her uncle's cheek, and then turned. She hesitated as if to say something, then moved to the door, leaving her uncle on his own. He leaned back on his pillows, face drawn and pale. He had hidden how he was feeling until she left but he felt rough. He knew his heart was wearing out. He was ready to join his wife, Maggie, in heaven. His mind drifted into well-remembered Bible verses and then into prayer.

****

Liam stood at the foot of his brother's bed, eyes fixed on him. His hands grasped the foot board, warming the cold metal. His mind was racing as he watched, trying to figure it out. Leith had no enemies. He was the one who watched out for everyone, young and old. Leith lay still, not moving even in pain. A dark purple bruise coloured the left side of his face under the white bandage; he had needed four stitches to close the wound. It was the lump on the back of his head that had the physicians worried. He hadn't woken up or moved since he was brought in hours ago. He knew the concerns the physicians didn't voice. He prayed for his brother to awaken as he dropped his head and closed his eyes in exhaustion. Laycee had been there but Joshua had convinced her to go home for a while and sleep. She hadn't wanted to but it said something about the love she shared with Joshua that she let him overrule her natural instinct to stay with her family.

There was a soft tap and the door and it cracked open letting in a narrow band of light. Liam turned and watched as a young woman entered, the light showing auburn hair.

She stepped forward hesitantly. "Dr. Young said it was okay to come. I just wanted to see how he is," as she nodded at the bed.

Liam remained silent, eyes watching carefully. She looked familiar but he couldn't put a name to her face.

Regan stepped forward, as silently as her boots would let her. Liam looked down as he heard the dull thuds. Interesting, he thought, work boots. A pretty lady like that in work boots.

Regan stopped near the end of the bed as Liam turned once more to his vigil. "Here," she said, as she shoved a cup of coffee towards him. "Dr. Young said to bring this to you and that he would be along shortly.

Surprise had Liam's hand going out for the cup. Now what was going on? he wondered.

Regan studied Leith's still form. She remembered him for their school days and to see him like this was disconcerting, especially as he had been hurt on their property.

"Uncle John wanted to know how Leith was. He sent me up."

Liam turned, silent, as he once again studied her and then nodded. "You're John's niece, Joseph and Rebecca's daughter." At her nod, he continued, "I had heard rumours you were back in town to help your uncle. How is he?"

Regan drew in a deep breath. How many more people would remember how she had run? "He's going home tomorrow. The doctors have adjusted his medications. He hadn't been feeling well and that's what happened to him." She grew silent, and then turned. "I am praying for Leith." She turned and almost ran from the room.

Liam watched her leave, surprised at the tears he had seen in her gray eyes. As the door clicked shut behind him, movement from the bed caught his attention. Setting down the coffee cup, he moved to the head of the bed, placing a hand on Leith's shoulder. Leith was moving restlessly now, head turning. His face grimaced with pain, and then his eyes flickered open, not focusing on anything.

"Hey, Leith, come on, wake up, brother." Liam reached for the call button for the nurse as he continued to study his brother's face. Eyes opening and shutting, Leith was rousing. It had been a long day and Liam was exhausted, but the exhaustion was quickly fleeing.

The nurse entered on silent rubber-shod feet and watched for a minute, then moved to check his vitals. She gave Liam a quick smile and nodded. "He's waking up. Dr. Young is still here, he's been in Emergency all day. I'll page him."

Leith's eyes opened once again and he frowned as he struggled to focus. His mouth was dry as he tried to form words. Someone held a straw to his mouth and he greedily sucked in water. "Where am I? What happened?"

"We were hoping you could tell us. Right now you're in the Riverville Hospital." Dr. Young spoke, then examined Leith. "Well, that hard Bradley head is at work again. You have a concussion and will need to take it easy for a few days. We'll see how you are tomorrow." He spoke over his shoulder,

"I need to go see some people who may actually be sick."

Liam smiled. Dr. Young and his wife had been good friends with his parents before they lost both of them, one to an accident and one to heart disease.

Leith stared at the door and then at his brother. "What happened?"

Liam sighed and then spoke, "I wish I knew. You were found beat up and unconscious at the Sullivan's. Had you gone there for more tile?"

"I don't remember. If there's where I was found, then I guess I did. I know I needed to get more of the one tile for that tile work in the kitchen on that house. I also needed some of that special grout and thin-set mortar." Leith's eyes slid closed and his breathing deepened.

Liam settled himself in for the night. He was going nowhere. Someone had attacked his brother and he wasn't letting him face them alone.

****

Regan headed for her car. It was late and she needed to be at the store early tomorrow to meet the cleaning crew. She wanted it back up and running right away. She thought about what had happened that day and drew in a shaky breath.

Looking at the sky, she paused as she unlocked her car door. "Thank you, Lord, for protection. Send healing to Uncle John and Leith and help the police to find out who did this and why. Let us never take for granted Your protection."

She spun at a sound near her but saw nothing. Sliding behind the wheel, she locked her doors before starting the motor and leaving.

She didn't see the dark form rise from behind a car two vehicles over from where she had parked or the fists clenched in anger. The Jester had missed. The King would not be happy. Cursing at his luck, he turned and headed back to the street to his truck. He ignored the ringing phone. He knew who it was and he was not ready to answer. Soon, he would have to. If he only knew who had hired him to find those packets. He had lingered outside Leith Bradley's room and learned he didn't remember much. That was good because if he did he would need to be dealt with.

****

The King stared out the window, hands clenched together behind his back. Things were not going as he expected. His henchman, the Jester, had failed to abduct that girl. At least Leith was still unconscious. He would be dealt with summarily if he ever remembered anything. He had to find those packets. He had promises to keep and those promises were not in his greedy hands. He turned and stormed around the small office, narrowly missing furniture and file folders. Someone had his packets and when he found them, that person would pay and pay handsomely and not with money.

He pulled out the phone he used to called the Jester. No, that idiot had not called back yet. The clock was ticking and soon his time would be over.

Leith dug his fingers into the side of the bed, fighting to keep his balance through the dizziness and nausea plaguing him. Laycee stood in front of him, hands planted on her hips, and a frown on her face.

"You are not going home," she decided. "You can hardly stay upright as it is."

"Laycee, leave it." Leith squinted up at her. "I'm going. The paperwork is filled out. The doctor said I need to take it easy but I can go home."

"That's not exactly what he said," Liam spoke up. "He said you could go home if you had someone with you for a few days. And definitely no work."

Leith shrugged, trying to hide the flicker of pain that crossed his face. Okay, so he wasn't doing as well as he thought. The headache was intense, intense enough it hurt to open his eyes. He couldn't afford to be off work. He had a deadline for the tiles being done and there was little grace time in it. He would manage. He groaned as Liam helped him into a wheelchair and then pushed him towards the elevator. Yeah, maybe he would take today off.

Liam shook his head as he wound their way to the door and helped Leith up into his truck. Leith leaned back, eyes closed, his face pale and strained. It took a lot out of him, just that move from the hospital. There was no way he would be ready to work again this week and it was only Tuesday. Liam prepared himself for the argument to follow.

Laycee waved as she pulled away from near them. She would be headed to Leith's house and be planning to stay for a long while, if he knew her. Even Joshua couldn't dissuade her.

Liam stole a quick glance at his brother and then concentrated on the drive. He watched his rearview mirror. There was a small, rusted car sticking really close to his bumper. He turned into the pharmacy and stopped; the car had followed him in and parked down the ways. No one exited it. Taking out his phone, he snapped a quick photo of it and tried to get the license, or what part of the license plate he could through the rust.

Leith's breathing was even and quiet. Liam figured he had fallen asleep and would stay that way for the few minutes he was in the pharmacy. Returning quickly, he scanned the parking lot. The car had left, but he had a bad feeling. Pulling out his phone he sent a quick text with the pictures to Caleb and to Ben. There, it was done—they would look into it.

"Wake up, buddy." Liam carefully shook Leith's shoulder as he stood at the open truck door. Leith stirred but didn't open his eyes. "You're home, Leith. Time to rise and shine."

"Go away. I want to sleep."

Liam grinned, then nudged Leith again. "That you may wish, brother, but if you want to sleep I think a bed might be a bit more comfortable than my truck."

Leith looked around with blurring eyes, then accepted Liam's help to enter his home. He dropped on his couch, put his feet up and dropped out of the world again. Laycee came up beside Liam and wrapped an arm around him as they stood staring at their brother.

“What happened to him, Liam?”

Liam hesitated, then spoke. “Caleb has some ideas but he hasn’t said much yet. I think Leith was in the wrong spot at the wrong time. You’re staying for a while?”

Laycee nodded.

Liam hugged her, dropped a kiss on her hair, and then headed for the door. “I’ll be back around 5 or so. I’ll stay the night.”

“Thanks, Liam. I’ll have supper ready. I’m just glad I can work from home now. Heading up that therapy group is a lot of work but it gives me the most flexibility of us all.”

Laycee locked the door, then grabbing a blanket from the closet, draped it over her brother. She undid his sneakers and pulled them off. Liam hadn’t bothered with Leith’s jacket, so she didn’t have to worry about that. She dropped into the easy chair across from him and studied him. Tears were near the surface at the thought that Leith could easily have died. Her anguish turned to prayers and she felt herself calming back down.

****

Regan pulled folders from the supply cupboard and headed back to the counter at the front. Uncle John was right—people from the church had shown up, cleaned up the place and even now a couple of the men his age were working away in the back. The place was tidy, clean and everything that had a place was in its place. She hesitated as she saw a woman leaning on the counter looking out the front.

“Can I help you?”

The woman turned, a big smile on her face. “No, I’ve come to help you. I’m Hannah Logan, Caleb’s wife.”

Regan frowned. "I don't know what you can help me with, but go ahead."

Hannah laughed. "Your parents talked a lot about you and how proud they were of you." Regan stared at her, not believing her. "They maintained that you could lay tile with the best of them, that you had apprenticed and were working for a company that did renovations of older homes that needed precise tiling done. So, here's the thing. I'm really good at sales and people stuff. You need help here. You're really good at tiling. Leith will need more help than he's willing to accept. This is what I propose: I work here and you go work for Leith."

Regan's eyes never left Hannah's face. Just where did she come up with that? And how on earth did she ever figure Leith would let her anywhere near the place he was working?

"I think that is a very sound idea." Uncle John spoke from behind her. "Leith can use the help and I know you are just as finicky as he is."

"Uncle John, that's not nice." Regan spun around to take him on, then noticed her cousin, David, hovering behind him. Cousins or not, she had never liked nor trusted him. His scruffy appearance didn't win her over now either. He only came around when he wanted something or needed something.

"Yes, it is. And starting tomorrow, I'm sending you over to his job site. He's shown me the plans. You can handle it."

"Yeah, and who will handle him, or for that matter, you?" Chin tilted, Regan tried her best to stare him down but knew it was a losing battle.

"Liam will." Her uncle grinned at her, knowing she was giving in. "I've seen your work. I've seen his work. Your styles are so close, it's scary. That is rare in this business. Pietro trained you both well."

Regan stared at her uncle. "Pietro trained him?"

Her uncle nodded as Hannah spoke up behind her. "I know Laycee and Joshua will help as will Caleb. Go. You'll enjoy working on that house."

A movement from her cousin caught her eye. Slanting a glance a him, she shuddered. A look of evil had crossed his face and just as quickly disappeared. What was it?

Her eyes moved back and forth between her uncle and Hannah. Now she placed Hannah, a woman slightly older than herself but who had been in clubs at school with her. She sighed. She really did miss the feel of the tiles and the thin-set mortar and the grout, the feeling of pride in laying the tiles and finishing off the pattern. She wasn't all that happy in the store, even though she did love the customers and could put up with answering questions and sharing her knowledge.

"All right, I give." A quick smile from Hannah and a hug from her uncle showed she had made the right decision. "Now, how do I get into the house?"

"I have the keys." A male voice brought her head up. Liam now stood by Hannah.

"Now that's a set-up if I ever saw one!" Regan exclaimed.

"Yes, I guess you could say it was. Why don't we head over to the house and I can show you what Leith has been working on."

Once in the truck, Regan shot Liam a glance. "How is Leith? And bigger question, how is he going to take this?"

"He was sleeping when I left him at home this morning. Yes, he insisted on going home. Laycee's with him. She can work flexible hours so it helps. No matter what he says, he will not be ready to work the heavy full days that he has been lately. He did say he needed to hire but he didn't know of anyone in town who was trained and he didn't have the time to train." Liam looked over at Regan. She was staring out the side window, a shuttered look on her face. "I don't know why you left all those years ago, but I do know that God has brought you back here for just this time. John and your Dad have often spoken, with pride I might add, about your work. You're a natural."

Regan was silent. "I can't talk about why I left. Others are involved. I just had to get away. I just don't like going behind Leith's back" She stopped speaking. "I miss that work. Dad wasn't happy at first that I moved away and had gone into a construction-type of work. He didn't want me working on jobs with the rough and tough men of construction, but Pietro was good. He made sure I was never alone. He treated me like a granddaughter. His sons and grandsons just opened their homes to me. I miss them." She blinked away tears, then looked at Liam. "One thing—if Leith strongly objects, I'm out of there. I won't be put in the middle of a family fight over this."

Liam smiled. Lord, I just think You brought Leith a real friend that he needs. She won't take his nonsense. He needs that.

"I'll handle him. Right now, he's not moving well at all. Dr. Young wants him off work to heal. But he's stressed about this job. He's been behind waiting on the tile and now that he has some of them, he said it would take about a month to finish. I don't understand the tile trade. Ask me about gardens or landscaping, I can help you with that."

Regan looked at him in silence, then turned to stare at the house where Liam had stopped. She knew this house, has loved it since she was a child. It was over one hundred years old she knew, with porches and gingerbread and all the architectural details that fit the age and style. She had never been inside but had always wanted to. It had been the second home for a prominent doctor from Oak City and had recently been sold. She was going to enjoy working here, that is, provided Leith let her.

Liam stood beside his truck, keys in hand, watching Regan's face. He knew they had made the right decision in asking her to help. Now he had to convince Leith that it would work. And he wasn't all that confident he could.

Regan wandered through the house, just enjoying the renovations that were happening, taking the look of the house back to when it was built. The renovator was a master craftsman, she could tell, who loved his work. She looked down at the marble in the main foyer and then made her way through to the kitchen. Here, work was still in progress. She reached out to touch the colourful backsplash. The mixture of colours was true to the palette of one hundred years ago. Tiles from outside the country, she knew from what she had been told. The work was precise and very detailed. She looked down at the plans Leith had laying on the covered countertops. Yes, it was very detailed, but she knew she could handle it. She could see Pietro's influence there.

She turned to Liam and nodded. He breathed a sigh of relief, came over and hugged her.

Surprised, she stepped back, looking up at him in shock.

"You'll do," Liam said. "Now I have to beard the lion in his den."

"Can you get me a set of keys and take me back to my truck? Seeing as Hannah has kicked me out, I'll start today."

"That I can do." And thank you, Lord, Liam breathed a small sigh of relief.

"Who's the renovator, Liam? He's doing good work."

Liam stopped in surprise. "It's Joshua Logan, Caleb's brother. He has a real talent for fixing up these older homes."

Regan nodded. "He always was interested in that."

Ben knocked and then entered Caleb's office. He dropped down in the chair in front of the desk, a discouraged look on his face. This was unusual for Ben.

"What do you have?" Caleb studied the older officer. He could see the fatigue in his face. Ben had been working hard to try and find the culprits of the break-in but he had run out of leads.

"Nothing. There was no evidence that the team could find. I just don't know, Caleb. Something is there." Running his hand through his gray hair, he continued, "It's not like other break-ins we have had. Nothing was taken. No property damage done. If Leith hadn't been there at the wrong time, he wouldn't have been hurt. Something smells, though. Just like last time. This isn't the first time John has mentioned someone searching their warehouse."

Caleb leaned back in his chair. "I know. There's something there." He leaned forward again and resting his elbows on his desk, he said, "Get the information from John about their suppliers. Maybe there's a link there somewhere we don't know about."

Ben's keen eyes looked up and studied Caleb. "You're thinking smuggling or something along that line?"

Caleb hesitated, then nodded. "And don't tell me that hasn't crossed your mind. We have a lot of leg work to do."

Ben snorted. "You mean I do. I hear John's niece is going to be working with Leith. How's that going?"

Caleb shook his head. It was amazing to him how Ben knew his town and what was happening. Over the years, he had formed a link of friends and contacts who shared information with him. He laughed. "Liam was breaking the news. I'm glad it's not me. Hannah is going to help out in the store while the boys are at preschool. I'm okay with that. We just need to find the culprit."

"And with that being said, I'll just toddle off and see what I can find out." Ben shut the door behind him.

Caleb sat in deep thought. What was happening in his town? First the accountant with her financial schemes and murders and now this. Was it just that Leith was in the wrong place at the wrong time? Was is just a simple break-in or as he suspected something much deeper and more sinister? He would let Ben puzzle it out for a while. Ben loved digging into these mysteries. Caleb knew he wouldn't rest until he came to the right conclusion, whatever that might be.

****

The Jester finally answered the King's call.

"What happened? Why did you attack Leith? You have brought attention to us that shouldn't be."

The Jester could feel the fury vibrating through the phone.

"He saw me. He was right where the crates were supposed to be."

"You idiot! Now the police are involved. They won't stop looking. You have may just blown up something I have had going for a long time. Handle it."

The Jester winced as the called ended in an abrupt manner. Yes, he would have to handle it. That Innocent had been wrong. He had given him the wrong information. He would track him down and he would pay. Then he would have to find those crates and those packets. His own life very likely depended on that fact. He ran his hand through his shortly cropped light brown hair. He had a sudden thought. If he could get close to Regan, maybe she could lead him to the crates. His face brightened. It wouldn't be a hardship getting to know this beautiful lady.

****

Leith stirred, grimacing at the pain in his head at the movement. His eyes opened, shut and then openly slowly again as he adjusted to the light. He heard movement in front of him and saw Laycee sitting on the edge of her chair across from him, head tilted to the side so she could look at him.

"How's the head?"

"How do you think it is? It hurts."

Laycee gave a soft laugh. "Of course it does, brother, of course it does. You have a concussion. Now, do you want something to drink or eat?"

Leith laid there, then slowly sat up, fighting the spinning of the room and the nausea. He did feel better upright. Now he just needed to make his way for a shower and he might feel more human. As his hands rubbed his face, he added a shave to that. His fingers stopped at the bandage and he fingered it.

151

"You had four stitches there in case you forgot."

"Like I remember that."

Laycee laughed again. "The ladies will love your battle scars, you know."

Leith whipped a pillow at her, then regretted it. Laycee's face crunched up as she shared his pain. A movement to his side showed Joshua coming in from the kitchen, Liam on his heels.

"Good to see you upright," Joshua said, as he perched on the chair arm beside Laycee.

Leith squinted at them, then moved to stand. He was shaky. He felt like he had been run over and tossed out with the trash. Not a good feeling. The dizziness and nausea were there but not as bad as they had been when he stood in the hospital room. What day was it any way?

"It's Thursday," Liam commented. Leith glared at him. "I knew you would want to know. Now let's get you looking more human. I'm glad you put in that guest suite downstairs. You won't be climbing stairs for a while."

Leith stopped once he entered the bathroom and stared at his reflection. He looked as bad as he felt. Maybe the shower and shave would help.

Liam propped a shoulder against the door frame and watched his brother, frown in place. Their eyes met in the mirror. They would talk soon and not in front of Laycee if they could help it. She would want to know every detail of what happened and would go charging in to try and help. Leith did not want that. Not knowing what or who was horrible.

"We'll talk once Laycee goes home. Are you going to manage okay?"

Leith looked around and sighed. "I think so. No tub side to crawl over so that helps. Just stick around close in case I need help."

Liam nodded, closing the door to the room. He wandered over to the window and moved the blind slats to look out. The guest room faced the side street. His gaze took in everything, then stopped. There was that rusted car again. Who was it? He made a note to call Caleb or Ben. Someone was following one of them and he wanted to know who.

Leith stepped from the bathroom, looking much more like himself, but still shaky. He sat on the bed as Liam approached. Looking up, he asked, "Has Laycee gone?"

Liam nodded. "Joshua took her home. She left some soup and fresh bread. Feel like something to eat?"

"Yeah, I think so. Just give me a minute. This feels worse than when I took that hit playing football in high school."

"It was worse, much worse. Someone tried to kill you." Leith's eyes flew to his brother's. "Come on. Let's get some food into you and I'll tell you what's been happening."

An hour later, Leith was back on the couch, coffee mug in hand. He looked around the room. It was bare. It needed something but he had no idea what. He should think about a dog, he thought, but with his work so busy and putting in so many hours, it wouldn't be fair. He really needed to try and find someone to hire. Maybe Pietro would have a lead on someone he had trained who was looking for a move to a smaller town. He would call him in the next couple of days and asked. He really didn't know how he was going to finish the Bell House job.

Liam had finished cleaning the kitchen and sat in one of the recliners while Leith was lost in thought. He watched his brother carefully, noting that he was not as cautious in his movement, but he could tell the headache was still there. He stood and went to find some painkillers. He handed them to Leith. Leith took them without comment so Liam knew he was hurting. Sitting back down, he sipped at his own coffee and waited. He had great patience, but Leith had even more. It was sometimes a competition between the two as to who gave in first.

"Okay, Liam. Tell me. I don't remember anything from that morning. The night before I had made plans to go get more supplies. You tell me it looks as if I did. Fill me in."

Liam looked at his hands. He sighed, set his coffee mug on the table beside him and then leaned forward. "What I am telling you is what Caleb and Ben have deduced. You had gone to the store, not found anyone out front and loaded up your dolly. You went looking for John and happened on a thief. He knocked you out. When he hit you, you slammed back into some crates and that's how you ended up with the concussion. John's niece came in, found him and then left with the ambulance to take him to the hospital. Officers were searching the warehouse and found you. The young officer that found you— he thought you were dead. It was not a pretty scene for him. They didn't realize at first it was you."

Leith shuddered. He didn't remember but maybe it was a good thing. "So what happened with John?

"I guess he hadn't been feeling well and passed out. He's back at work."

"Work." Leith grimaced. "I need to get back there tomorrow. There's that timeline I need to meet.

Other trades are depending on me finishing when scheduled."

Liam shook his head. "You're not ready."

"I don't have a choice. There's only me."

"Then maybe it's time you found someone to hire."

Leith looked at his brother, and thought that he had read his mind. "I know. I just don't have the time to interview and hire. It's not like hiring a labourer. This is detailed work that needs skilled hands."

Liam looked at his brother and then his gaze looked past him. Leith's eyes narrowed. Yes, he thought. Liam has done something and just doesn't know how to tell me.

"What did you do?"

Liam looked guilty. "John knew of someone Pietro trained that was in the area on a temporary basis. He says he's seen this person's work and he found it really hard to tell it from yours. I spoke with Pietro. This person has been highly trained by him and was working with him up until about six weeks ago before asking for a temporary leave of absence to come back to this area."

"Liam, why? Why? Why go behind my back?" Leith stood and paced.

"Leith, stop and think about it. You're not able to. You have said that Pietro is the best, that you would willingly hire anyone he trained. We'll go over tomorrow and see. If you don't like it, then I will personally tear out the work done and redo it under your supervision."

Leith was frustrated and hurting. He bit his tongue before he said something he would regret.

Finally, he gave a short nod and sat back down. His head dropped on the back of the couch.

"I'm frustrated."   He stated the obvious. "Why did this happen?"

Liam watched his brother, assessing his mood. "I don't know, Leith. I don't have the answers for you. I have watched you over the years. You are the watcher in our family. You watch over us all and step in without a word. Someone like that has difficulty asking or accepting help."   He paused, then continued, "When I look at you, I think of how God has provided a strong tower for us to run to and be safe. You are like a hawk perched on that tower, watchful and ready. It is time you yourself run for that tower."

Leith's body movements stilled as he thought over his brother's words. Liam had him pegged. Liam knew both he and Laycee well. Laycee was really like the sparrow—she had had a poor self image for years until she went through all the stuff last year and realized that God really did count her more important than this lowly bird.

He sighed, and raised his head to look across the room. Liam's eyes were closed and Leith knew he was in prayer. He cleared his throat and Liam's eyes opened.

Leith said nothing, just rose from the couch, and stopped beside his brother. He hesitated, then gripped his brother's shoulder, and made his way to his bedroom. He needed sleep if he was to work tomorrow.

****

The Jester watched the lights go out at Leith's home. He waited. He would probably need to find another vehicle. If they got sight of this one, they would remember it. He keyed the vehicle to life and headed out. Small towns were good but they could be bad too. He headed for a larger town and drifted around, looking at the malls and bars. He finally found what he wanted. He ditched the rusted vehicle he had been driving and slipped behind the wheel of the nice new extended cab pickup. Now he had height, muscle and metal. He would win this fight.

Driving back to his home, he parked where the vehicle could not catch any eyes and headed for bed. Tomorrow would be here soon, and he needed to search. If only the Innocent had not screwed up. He would have to be dealt with and would once the Jester had what the King wanted. He wondered what was in the packets. Maybe he would take a peek if he could get a chance.

Leith struggled the next morning. The headache was better but his body was aching all over. He dressed and slowly climbed down the stairs. He could hear Liam moving around in the kitchen and headed that way. Liam turned to look at him and then handed him his painkillers. Leith shook his head but Liam's hand shoved the bottle back. Glaring at him, he snatched the bottle and downed the medication.

"I'm sorry, Liam. That was uncalled for."

"No problems. Let's head for SueEllen's for breakfast. You need food."

Leith gave a small laugh. Yes, he definitely felt like eating.

At the local cafe they liked, Leith held the door for a young woman exiting. She glanced up and gave a word of thanks, gray eyes widening slightly when she saw him. Auburn hair was caught back in a pony tail under a baseball cap. Leith smiled, then frowned. He should know her. He watched her walk away, then entered at a push from behind. Liam had been standing there. Liam snickered. He had recognized Regan.

"There's Caleb. Let's join him." Liam lifted a hand to SueEllen and she nodded. Their usual breakfast would be on the way.

Sliding into chairs at Caleb's table, they greeted one another as mugs of coffee were set in front of them.

Once their meals had arrived and they had each asked the blessing on their food, Leith looked at Caleb.

"Tell me what you have. Who did this?"

Caleb's hand hesitated as he raised a forkful of eggs to his mouth. He chewed and then swallowed. Wiping his mouth, he sought for words. "We don't have a lot, Leith. There was not a lot of evidence there."

Leith's mouth hardened into a straight line. "Break-ins don't happen at tile stores. Other than the day's receipts, they don't have material that someone can easily haul away and sell on the black market." He worked his way through his breakfast, the food helping to clear the fog he was working under.

Liam's eyes travelled between his brother and his friend. There was something that was going on and it was causing undercurrents there. He hesitated to speak but he knew he had to.

"Where does John and Joseph get their supplies from? Is there something in one of the shipments that someone was looking for?"

Leith's eyes shot to him, shocked at the thought. Smuggling? No way. John and Joseph wouldn't be involved in that.

Caleb reached for his mug, took a swallow, and then looked around the cafe. There were no customers close enough to hear what he was about to say.

He still hesitated. The investigation was still in early stages and he didn't have a lot he could share at the moment. He finally nodded and looked at his two friends.

"That's what we're thinking." He raised a hand as Leith opened his mouth to speak. "We don't suspect either John or Joseph. They're not the ones we're focusing on. We have to trace the shipments back to the factory and then follow them to here. It's not a quick process. We are working with authorities in other countries. We will also likely have to involve federal authorities here in this country if contraband has crossed the border. Be patient." He stopped and pulled out his cell phone. "I need to go. Are we still on for dinner on Sunday?"

Liam nodded, then looked at Leith. "I am. I don't know about him though."

Leith punched his brother in the arm, then regretted at the discomfort moving through his body. He hauled his body up and headed for the door, knowing Liam had stopped to pay for their meals.

Liam parked before the house. He turned off the ignition, then reached across the cab and caught Leith's arm. "Before you go in, Leith, listen for a minute. I'm sorry. I should have waited and asked you. I know it's your business and I interfered. I shouldn't have. But I really do think you'll be happy. Before you blow it off, listen and look. I was here yesterday and saw the work. It's really good."

Leith stared out the windshield, thinking about his brother had said. They were close and Liam knew him well. He would listen and look but the final decision would be his. He gave a short nod, then shoved open the truck door. He stood for a minute to get his balance. A truck parked in the driveway caught his attention, a little green Ford Ranger. A memory tugged at him but he couldn't draw it to the foreground of his mind. Someone he knew had always wanted a truck like that. He shrugged. It would come.

He stared up at the house. This house had taken a lot from him but had taught him to reach inside, to grow, to expand. He figured part of that was learning to trust others but more so to put his trust fully in God. That was the tough part.

He headed up the walk and the front steps. It had dried so he could step in with his boots on. He noticed that craft paper had been laid over the tile for protection. He hadn't done that, so the new tile setter must have. Strange. Most guys wouldn't think to do that.

He found his way back to the kitchen and stopped. The kitchen was cleaned and as ready to be cooked in as he had ever found a kitchen, minus the appliances. His gaze went around. The floor was finished. He stepped over to the counter and looked. The backsplash was also finished. He reached out and touched it. He loved the colours and the way they played of the light oak cabinets and the off-white countertop. He looked closer at the backsplash, looking for issues, mistakes, anything that stood out. There was nothing. What Pietro had told Liam was the truth. This guy was good. He had doubted but okay, now he was convinced.

He turned to find Liam still standing in the foyer, fingering his keys. Leith stalked over to him and stood in silence. He saw small smile playing around Liam's mouth before he looked up.

"Okay, you were right. This guy's good. Now I have to find him and tell him he has a job."

Liam still had that bit of a smirk on his face. He nodded at the stairs. Liam looked, groaned and knew he had to walk up them, sore body or not.

Stepping onto the floor in the upper hall, he noted the house was almost completed trimmed out, painted, and wallpaper up. Just maybe Joshua would make his deadline. He was doing his best to help his friend. They had had just a few months to do the complete renovation and they were pushing to finish.

There was not a lot left but it was time consuming work.

Liam could hear soft humming from ahead of him. He tilted his head. That didn't sound like a man's voice. He listened again. No, definitely female. He looked behind him for Liam. Not there. Traitor, he thought.

He followed the humming down the hall to the master suite and then through it to the open bathroom doorway. He stopped. A slim figure was crouched in the shower, working her way up the wall with the tile, preciseness in every movement. He tilted his head and watched. She was good. He took a look at the worker again—auburn hair, plaid shirt, jeans. She was the woman from the cafe. He still felt he knew her but his mind was not functioning well today and he couldn't put a name to her. He waited until she sat back on her heels and then cleared his throat.

Regan closed her eyes. Leith was here. Well, it had been fun while it lasted. She mentally prepared herself to go back to selling tiles in the tile store. She turned and looked up at him.

Leith studied her. He still couldn't place her but he knew her.

"You're good. Liam said Pietro trained you."

"He did. I worked for him for years until I came back here."

Leith moved closer to the large shower area. She must have started early today, a lot of tile was laid already. She would pretty much be finished with the tiling by tomorrow and then would be doing the grouting.

He looked down at her upturned face. "Want a job? I'm hiring. I have more work than I can really manage on my own." He watched as her eyes slid closed and then opened again.

"If you really mean that, then yes." She stood and offered him her hand.

"We can do the paperwork later. Come with me. I need to go let Liam gloat and say I told you so. I just need your name to start with."

She stared at him. He really didn't know. "It's Regan Evans."

Leith spun from where he was walking ahead of her and stepped back to stop in front of her, causing her to take a step backwards. "That's why I know you. Regan. I often wondered where you were. Your parents and uncle sometimes spoke of you but never where you were working. Welcome home."

Regan stared up at him, shaken at his response. Being welcomed back into her hometown was not what she had expected. But then again, not many people knew why she had left, not even her parents. That was a secret she hadn't shared with them, but sighing inside, she knew she would have to.

She followed Leith down the stairs to where Liam was standing. Liam smiled and held out a hand to welcome her. She smiled back. Just maybe this was going to work out after all.

Liam left and Leith turned to Regan, motioning her to the kitchen. She trailed after him, not knowing what he was going to say, even though he had told her he was hired. She stopped in the door.

Leith stood leaning against the counter and spoke. "Come here, Regan." As she moved forward, he spoke, "You're very good. I can't really tell where you left off or I did. That is great. Thank you."

Regan breathed a sigh of relief and then nodded. "I need to get back to the tiles upstairs. Anything else?"

He shook his head. "Just make sure you leave by 5 tonight. It's Friday. We shut down by 5 and don't work the weekends. We need those breaks."

She was surprised, knowing he was pushing, but agreed.

****

The Jester said in his stolen truck across from the house and waited. How long would it be before they left and he could follow them?

The flash of lights in his mirror startled him. A police cruiser was headed down the street. He pulled away from the curb, taking care not to draw attention to himself. Someone might have reported him. As he turned a corner, he breathed a sigh of relief. No, not spotted. It must just be a routine patrol. He would be back. First, he had to find the Innocent. He was hiding but he would be found.

Leith sank back into Laycee's couch. It was comfortable. He rubbed a hand along the leather. It was not what he had expected her to get after her furniture had been destroyed in the break-in last fall, but he could see Joshua's hand in that. He was good for his sister. He sank his head back and closed his eyes, starting as he felt a warm body crawl into his lap. He looked down - Defiant, Laycee's sheltie, had decided he needed to be comforted. He rubbed the black and tan fur on the dog, then the white ruff. Defiant leaned harder into him, content, the reached up to lick at the wound on his jaw.

Leith pushed his head away, telling him it was healing and he didn't need his licking to help.

Hannah Logan sat down at the other end of the couch. He slanted a look at her and saw her smile. "How much trouble am I in?" She asked, eyes sparkling with mirth.

"Plenty. I'm going to tell the police on you." She laughed. "Actually, I need to say thank you. You pushed as did Liam. Regan is really good. I hope she'll stay around."

"Good. I'm glad that worked out. She was a really great kid, and I suspect has turned into a wonderful young lady."

"You knew her well from before?"

Hannah shook her head. "We were in some of the same clubs, but she really didn't let anyone close.

Then as soon as she graduated, she took off. No one ever said why. Maybe she'll open up with you."

Leith shook his head. "No. Not interested, Hannah."

Hannah laughed. "We'll see. But there is something I should warn you about. I have talked to Caleb and he said to let you in on it. Regan's cousin, David, is back. I caught some looks and undertones between the two of them the other day. It wasn't pleasant. David's look was that typical if looks could kill, you'd be dead look. John hasn't said much, but I get the impression he's not happy with David."

Leith thought about her words. "Thanks. I wouldn't pry but I'll see if she says anything. If you hear anything, let me know."

"I will." Hannah laid her hand on his arm. "I am so glad you're getting better. I was really scared when I heard."

Leith smiled as she arose and went to find her sons. He stood and then moved to the door. It was time he left. Tomorrow would be here soon and it would be a long day.

****

Regan muttered to herself as she drove to the job site. Why had she let them talk her into this? She knew better. She had had a crush on Leith Bradley all during high school. Now she had to keep herself in line so he didn't guess she still liked him. Maybe he would work in another part of the house all day and they won't cross paths. Yeah, right, like that will happen, she murmured. As she stopped in the driveway, Leith's truck was already there. She was surprised he was driving but then again, he wouldn't let anyone smother him with care. That was not him.

She grabbed her knapsack out of the truck and the kit she used to carry her tools. Pietro had given her some and she had accumulated the rest over the years. She headed for the door and heard her name called. She turned to see Leith striding across the driveway, headed for her. He reached for her kit and took it. Surprise had her releasing it. That was something they were going to have to talk about. She carried her own weight and that meant her own kit.

"Good morning." Leith smiled at her. "I've been inside. I see you finished the tiling in the bathroom. You came back on the weekend!" He accused.

She shrugged. "It needed to be done. We were down two or three days. Today I can finish it and move on."

Leith held the door for her and then stopped her with a hand on her arm. "I meant what I said, Regan. Work stops at 5 on Fridays and doesn't get picked up again until Mondays. In this job, we need that break. You have to learn to pace yourself. I know Pietro worked all kinds of hours but I don't. I have other things outside of work to do."

She looked down at her feet. She had been wrong, no matter how much she had wanted to please him. "I'm sorry. I'll remember." She grabbed her kit and climbed the stairs. Today had gotten off to a bad start and it was her fault.

Leith watched her climb the steps. He ran a hand through his black hair and frowned. That didn't go as he had planned. He would talk to her again at lunch.

Leith appeared at the doorway of one of the guest suites four hours later. "Regan, it's lunch time. Come on down to the kitchen."

"Be there shortly."

Leith headed back to the kitchen. He had found out from John what Regan's favourite meal was at the cafe and had talked SueEllen into doing up take out for him. She didn't often do a take out order but she liked both Regan and him. Secretly, she wanted to help along a romance and thought they were suited to each other.

Regan appeared in the doorway, nose twitching. Leith had set up a small folding table and brought in some folding chairs. He looked up at her.

"I dislike sitting on the floor to eat. There are part of the tools of my trade." He had spread out their meal and it smelled wonderful. "I needed to apologize to you. Thought lunch would help."

Regan's fingers went to her lips and her eyes brimmed with laughter. She tried hard but the snicker would out. "You told SueEllen you had to eat some crow. This is what she provided?"

Leith looked down at the fried chicken dinners and laughed. "I'd rather eat chicken than crow. Come on and sit."

They were about half-way through their meal when Leith stopped and wiped his mouth and then his fingers on the paper napkin. He gathered his thoughts and then spoke, "I did you a disservice, Regan. As a man in construction, I dislike seeing women working in the trades." He held up his hand as she went to speak. "Please, let me finish. Not all job sites are great. In fact, most of them have rough and tumble men on them who are not pleasant to women. There's a lot of talk and such that goes on that I wouldn't want a woman exposed to. Besides, it can be really heavy work and a woman's body is put together different from a man's. Women aren't meant to do the heavy work a man is—they're not built that way. It is hard enough on a man's body. Having said that, I know how Pietro and his family protected you.

That's how it will be with me. I'll pull you off a job if I think you need to be pulled off from it, and please don't protest against it. A lot of the time we're on our own or there are a few others working on site. I like working on Joshua's renovations. He has a really good clean crew working for him. He has also chosen well the sub-contractors he hires. I know you would be okay around them."

"Thank you, Leith. I will be my best." She pushed her meal container aside and propped her chin in her hands. "How long do you figure for this job, and what do you have coming up next?"

Talk went to the tiling work that was going on. Leith liked the input that Regan offered. She did have some good ideas.

Later that day, Regan started down the stairs. She heard muffled noise from the back and headed that way. She needed to talk to Leith about an issue that had come up.

She stepped through the kitchen to the back porch where Leith had stored the tiles. A black form spun at she stepped through and charged at her, knocking her back against the door. She screamed and the intruder disappeared out the back door.

Leith slammed his truck into park at the sight of a black figure racing around from the back of the house. He jumped from his vehicle but his body was too beaten up at this point to chase. Pulling out his phone, he called the emergency services and then ran for the house. Regan. Was she okay? He took the stairs two at a time and searched the upstairs, opening closets and doors. She wasn't there.

He called for her as he sped back down the stairs and thought he heard a voice from the kitchen. Reaching the kitchen, he saw Regan on her feet, leaning against the wall, hand on her back. He stopped in front of her.

"Are you okay?" He led her to a chair and pushed her down, noting her grimace as he did so.

She nodded. "Just had the wind knocked out of me." She took a deep breath. "Who was that?"

Leith shook his head. " I don't know. I couldn't chase but the police are on their way. Where was he?"

"In the back, at the crates of tiles. I came looking for you and found him instead." She stood and headed to the back porch. "What was he after?"

Leith's hand came out and he stopped her. "No, we can't go out there. We have to leave it. I guess it's now what you call a crime scene."

Regan's eyes slid shut. He was right. Another crime scene. What was this guy after or who was he after?

****

Ben found them an hour later. Regan had returned to her work in the upstairs. Leith had hovered for a while, then gone to see what was happening in the back porch. He had returned shortly before Ben came up the stairs and had pulled Regan from her work, telling her to wrap it up for the day. Regan had gone to stand at the window, watching the activity below, Leith standing in the middle of the room, hand on his head, lost in thought.

"Leith, Regan." Ben spoke from the doorway. Both turned at the sound of his voice. "We need you to come down stairs for a minute." At the sober look on his face, they exchanged glances, then followed him down the stairs.

Caleb stood at the kitchen counter, notebook out as he scrawled in it. He glanced up, then added more details to what he was writing. He stopped, leaning both hands on the counter. Looking up, he stared at them. Leith stared back, but Regan dropped her eyes.

Caleb nodded to the doorway and led them out to the back porch. Crates of the tiles were broken open, with some of the tiles shattered. Leith groaned. He didn't need this. He was so close to finishing. He prayed he had enough tile so that he could actually finish on time.

Ben spoke from behind them. "We think it was the same one who broke into the store. There's not a lot of evidence. Did you see his face, Regan?"

"No. All I saw was a black form coming at me. He had on a hoodie that blocked most of his face but I really didn't get a chance to see even that. It was just too fast." She stopped, remembering something. "I did see something. A tattoo or birth mark or something on a hand."

Caleb and Ben exchanged glances. "Which one?"

Regan held both of her hands out in front of her, frowning. She spun to face the doorway and held her hands up as if to push at someone. "The left one. On the inside of the wrist. Black and green and some blue, I think. I really don't know what the shape was, though. It's just kind of mingled together."

Caleb nodded. "That's more than what we had before. If you remember anything more, let me know. Now, to the crates. Leith, were they all opened?"

Leith shook his head. "No, we only open them as we need to, unless there is a great mismatch in colour. These ones have been great. I haven't had to open any more one or two at a time." He looked around at the opened crates and destruction. "What was he looking for?"

Caleb and Ben were silent. Leith looked at them. "All right, give. You have suspicions. This now involves me more than just being in the wrong place at the wrong time."

Ben spoke, "We suspect there has been contraband of some kind shipping from the factory or inserted into the crates at some stage on the delivery route. We have had rumours of this for a while, but nothing concrete that we can fix on. That has changed."

Regan drew in a sharp breath. "You don't suspect my Dad or Uncle, do you? They would never do that."

Caleb shook his head. "No, we don't. We think that the break-ins and missing material your uncle has been tracking are what has held the contraband. We don't know yet what it is." His keen glance speared both of them with a stern look. "We need you to both be very careful. You have had contact with the thief. If they suspect you can identify them, they may come looking for you." He ran a hand through his hair and continued, "We need you to keep on as you have been. Don't let them suspect."

Leith looked at Regan, seeing the whiteness and fear on her face. It seemed more than just what Caleb had said. He would find time to talk with her at some point.

****

The King was once again furious. The Jester had once again failed to find the packets. Just how hard was that task? He would need to be looking for new help or else he would need to pack up and move, and he wasn't about to do that. He had a nice little business going here—the contraband was a side business that brought in lots of money for him.

He turned at the sound of a bell, the mask falling back into place. He stepped through from the back of his store and greeted his customer, smoothness filling his voice. Tonight he would take steps. He was aware of who the Jester had hired and that person had screwed up. He had a feeling in his gut that he was being watched and that time was running out.

Chapter 7

Leith stood in the back porch after the police had left. He ran his hands through his hair and then scrubbed them down his face. What was going on, he wondered?

He turned as he sensed Regan at the door. He had become more and more aware of her presence around him as the day passed. They had moved past the difficult moments of their first few hours together and the way she had come on the job. She was a good fit for him at work, almost reading his mind. A stray thought crossed his mind that she would be a good fit for him, period. A good fit in his personal life as well.

Regan approached, watching him and then looking down. She had a broom in her hand. Sadness crossed her face at the destruction she saw.

She handed him the broom. "Here. I'll go get the garbage can. Or two. Or three."

"Thanks. Regan." She turned to him as he spoke. "I'm glad you weren't down here when he did this. I wouldn't want you hurt."

She gave him a searching glance, nodded and turned away. He watched her, knowing at some point, he would meddle and poke and prod to find out her history.

Together they worked at cleaning up the mess. Leith stretched. They had been able to salvage a lot of whole tiles. Some of the broken ones they had set aside as possibilities for small areas.

"Do you think you'll have enough?" Regan soft voice sounded from behind him. She was kneeling on the floor, stacking the last few tiles.

"I think so. If not, I'll see if John has more. He did have extras earlier and said he would set them aside for me." Leith carried out the garbage and returned. "Come on, Regan. Let's call it a day. We can finish up tomorrow."

"Okay." Regan's voice was distracted. "Leith, can you get me a flashlight, please? I need some more light."

He handed her his phone with the flashlight icon on. He watched as she reached down into a large crevice between the room floor and the wall. She pulled out a small brown envelope that had worked its way down.

"I don't know what this is, but I don't think it belongs here. It's too new to have been here long." She looked up at him. "We need to get this to Caleb and Ben."

Leith reached out and took the packet. It was slim but he could feel lumps through the paper. "It feels like pebbles or something." He tucked it in his pocket, then held out his hand for Regan.

She stood, deep in thought. "Pebbles." Her eyes flew to Leith. "Do you know where Caleb is right now?"

He shrugged. "I would imagine at home."

"Okay. You lead and I'll follow. This needs to go to him tonight."

Leith stared at her, puzzled. She pushed at him. "Go. Turn off the lights, lock up and let's go."

Caleb held his mug of tea, glad for the warmth on his hands. He was tired. He was tired some days of crime. He was tired of it affecting his family and friends. God was his strength, though, his strong tower. He loved the verses that talked of that. He watched as Hannah moved around the kitchen, cleaning and tidying it up from the meal and readying it for morning. The boys were asleep. He was home early today and had been able to spend time with them.

He reached for Hannah's hand and led her to the living room and together, they sank to the couch. He draped his arm around her and held her close.

Head on his shoulder, Hannah sighed. "I know you, Caleb. What's bugging you?"

He tightened his arm, giving thanks for the wife God had provided. "Nothing here at home. I'm just frustrated at the slowness of finding out what happened, at the block in the investigation."

Hannah went to speak, then stopped as the doorbell rang. It was not usual they had company during the week after supper. Friends knew to give Caleb time with his family.

Caleb sighed, set down his mug of tea, and went to the door. Peeking out, he saw Leith and Regan. He opened the door, greeting them and then indicating the living room. Hannah greeted them and started to rise.

"Please, Hannah, don't leave." Regan asked as she sat beside her.

"What brings you two by?" Caleb glanced between them, picking up on tension.

Leith hesitated, then reached for his pocket. "We were cleaning up and sorting through tiles after you all had left. Regan found this, dropped down in a crevice by the wall." He handed Caleb the packet.

Caleb looked at it, then shot a glance at Leith. Snagging a piece of paper from the office, he laid it on the coffee table. Carefully, he worked to open the sealed envelope. This may be what he had been looking for, the answer to what was going on. Upending it, he shook it slightly.

Hannah and Regan both gasped.

Leith swallowed hard, and then asked, "Is that what I think it is?"

Caleb used his pen to move around the pebbles. He nodded. "They're not pebbles, that's for sure. I will need to send them to the lab, but I suspect they are uncut diamonds. You have may found what the thief was after." He stopped, then continued, "Did you find any other packets?"

Leith shook his head. "That's the only one."

Caleb left, returned with a kraft envelope. He carefully inserted everything in it, sealed it and labeled it. "I'll get this sent off tomorrow. We have an answer in a few days." He caught their eyes with a piercing glance. "I don't need to tell you to be very careful. Smugglers play for keeps."

Regan shivered as she nodded. Why did she feel like the past was catching up with her?

Leith stopped Regan as she was getting in her truck. "I'll follow you home, just to make sure you get there. If you need me, call me."

She nodded. She had hoped that things would be different but it seemed like yesterday all over again. When would it stop?

****

The Jester was not amused. The Innocent had screwed up once again. Those two would not have rushed over here if they hadn't found something.

Now the Innocent would need to be dealt with. He wouldn't be able to retrieve that packet, if that's what Caleb had. Caleb was too wary and too smart. The King would be livid. He needed to deal with the issue before he found out and could only hope he didn't lose his own life in the process. The King would consider him dispensable.

Caleb strode into the station in the morning, eyes searching for Ben. He found him at the coffee station.

"Bring your mug. I have some news." Caleb spoke quietly.

Ben looked, then followed Caleb.

"Shut the door and sit." Caleb dropped into his chair and pulled the envelope from his pocket. "Leith and Regan brought this to me last night. Regan found it when they were cleaning up the mess. It contains what I think are raw diamonds. You were on the money about contraband. I need you to take this Oak City to the lab, but I don't want a big deal made of it. You need a day off, don't you? Take Marg and head into the city. Make a day of it."

Ben nodded. "Sure, that's what they were looking for. Put small packets in the crate, mark the crate and then retrieve them. Only somehow this time, something got mixed up. I wonder how much we've missed."

Caleb nodded. "That's my fear. I also suspect that it is only going to get worse. I can't put a tail on Regan and Leith. I don't have enough to support that. If I say anything to Liam, he'll smother Leith and that will go over like a lead balloon." He pointed to the packet. "Go. Spend some time with Marg. You've been putting in some long hours." He stopped and watched as his friend tucked away the packet. It wasn't the first time Ben had made a run like that. "Ben." Ben looked up. "I want you to consider something. We have the funding to set up for more training and I would like to see more training in evidence recovery and tracking evidence. I would appreciate it if you could give it some thought. You have the experience and the knowledge. You are also a born teacher. I've seen you work at church. I've seen you work with the young officers here."

Ben stilled. This had been a dream of his. "I'll pray about it and talk it over with Marg."

"Thanks. Not get out of here."

A few hours later, Caleb looked up at a tap at his open door. Liam stood there. He beckoned him in.

Liam shut the door behind him and then sat, staring at him in silence.

Caleb stared back, waiting for Liam to speak.

"Leith called me. Are those really uncut stones?"

Caleb hesitated. "They may be. We need to wait for the lab report."

Liam stood and paced. The anger was palpable. "This is my brother we're talking about. Someone tried to kill him. Are they going to try again?"

Caleb let him speak, knowing he had to vent. "I don't know, Liam. We still need to do a lot of leg work."

Liam looked at him, spun and headed for the door. He stopped, hand on the knob. "Let me know what you find out. I don't want another family member in the same situation Laycee ended up in."

"Liam." Caleb waited but Liam didn't turn. "I will do my best. My department will do their best to keep him and Regan safe. You know that. But you also know that when we are dealing with smugglers and contraband, it is very difficult."

Liam gave a curt nod and then left.

Caleb looked down at the work on his desk and sighed. He had pushed up through the ranks at a rapid pace, always wanting to the chief. When the chief had retired, he has tapped to take over at a young age. Today, he wished someone else had the responsibility. Paperwork had to be done, regardless of what was going one, and so he bent to the task.

****

Joshua and Leith stood together in what would have one time been the front parlour of the house. Looking around, they both looked pleased.

Joshua had a huge smile on his face. "We did it, Leith. We made the deadline early and stayed within budget. God has been good."

Leith smiled and agreed. "That He was. We wouldn't have though if it hadn't been for Regan. She's amazing with the tile work."

Joshua shot his friend a glance and nodded. Yes, he thought. Finally someone who interests Leith and shares a passion with him about his work.

Regan stepped in the room and stopped when she saw the two men, hesitating in a nervous manner. Joshua studied her. There was something she was holding back but what?

Leith turned and have her a smile. "Well done, Regan. You have helped us succeed."

Noise at the door drew their attention as Caleb, Hannah, and Liam entered. There would be a quick run-through the house with family and then in about an hour, the homeowners would walk through. Joshua and Leith knew they would be pleased. The house had good bones and had been a pleasure to restore.

"What do you say, shall we gather for dinner at the cafe?" Caleb asked. They agreed and made plans to meet later.

****

The Innocent stood in front of the Jester, shaking. He knew he had really screwed up this time. He thought he had found all the packets, only to find he had missed one. The King was very angry, he was told. This mistake on his part would cost dearly.

The Jester watched as the fear mounted in the young man. He could smell the fear. This young punk had served his time. It was time to remove the problem. His hand raised, he saw the Innocent's eyes widen. It was too late. A single sound and the Innocent was on the ground, never to rise again.

The Jester swept a look around to make sure he had left nothing to identify him and then turned, walking away from the body and the old abandoned factory. Justice, in his eyes, was done. Now he just had to save his own skin.

****

Leith stood by his truck in the parking lot and waited for Regan to step out of hers. He approached her and stood looking down at her. Her gray eyes met his. She was hesitant again in her manner and he wondered why. He reached for her hand, but she stuck hers in her pocket. Okay, he thought, too soon.

"I usually take a couple of days off after a job is finished and just wander through some towns, taking in the architecture and the sights. Would you like to join me tomorrow on a journey?"

Regan studied him, head tilted to the side. She gave a big sigh and said, "You're not making it easy working for you, you know." At his look, she shook her head. "Never mind."

She headed for the restaurant, Leith on her heels. "You never answered me."

She spun. "Would that trek be in the manner of a date or just two workers out searching for new ideas? It would never work, me dating the boss."

Leith threw his head back and laughed. "Okay, no date. Just two friends out enjoying a day together."

She thought, and then nodded. "All right. What time?"

"I'll pick you up at 8."

Sudden pinging broke through their conversation. Leith leapt for Regan and sweeping her into his arms, dodged behind a truck. He slid to the ground, cradling her and covering her with his body. He knew it wasn't hail and it wasn't a gravel parking lot for stones to be thrown up from tires. That had to be bullets.

The sound of sirens filled the area and red and blue lights reflected from the windows of the parked vehicles and the stores. Officers shoved open their doors and crouched behind them, revolvers at the ready, and searched the area.

There were no more shots. The shooter had accomplished his goal, gathered his evidence and left.

Caleb stepped from the cafe, revolver in hand, and headed for the patrol cars. He quickly sent officers to search the area. Ben approached.

"What happened here?"

Caleb's keen eyes turned on him as he holstered his revolver. "That's what I want to know. We're fortunate there wasn't anyone out here. But what was he shooting at?"

A sudden call caught his attention and he turned. An officer was waving him over towards a truck. Caleb and Ben ran towards him, hearts in mouth. Did they have a victim anyway?

Caleb slid to a halt as he rounded the front of the truck. Leith was on the ground, propped up against a tire, with an unmoving Regan in his arms. Caleb approached slowly and squatted down beside him.

"Leith." He waited. "Leith. Look at me."

Leith's eyes were fixed and staring. Even when Caleb touched his arm, he didn't move. Caleb scanned them both. There was blood on Regan's shoulder but he couldn't tell how bad the wound was, and Leith was not letting her go.

He stood and looked around. Spotting a senior officer, he waved him over and then sent him to the cafe. He would find Liam and bring him out.

"Ben, get the paramedics here. Bring them in on the grass behind the truck."

Ben looked at him. "No sign of the shooter." He sighed. "I guess we aren't done yet, are we?"

"No, my friend. I don't think we are." Caleb stood looking down at Leith. "I want to know which one of these he was after. They've now become targets and we'll need to arrange protection. Talk to Eddie and see what you can arrange. I'm authorizing overtime on this."

Ben nodded, then touched Caleb's arm. Liam stood a vehicle away, a pale and drawn look on his face. Leith and Regan hadn't made it to the cafe, and he had a bad feeling in his gut as Caleb moved towards him, a stern look on his face.

"Caleb..."

"Leith is not hurt, but I can't get his attention. Regan has been wounded. Leith must have taken her down and now I can't get him to release her so I can get her treated. Maybe you can get through to him."

Liam's eyes slid shut. Relief that his brother was okay slid through him, but worry also for the woman who was becoming a real part of their family. "Let me talk to him."

Liam squatted down by his brother, heart in mouth at the look on his face. He didn't remember ever seeing such a look. He placed a hand on Leith's arm.

"Leith." He waited and then spoke his brother's name again. "Let me have Regan. She needs help."

Leith stirred and his arms loosened on Regan. Liam lifted her away from his brother and handed her to Caleb. Quickly the paramedics moved in and took over her care.

"Leith. Come on, buddy, let's get you up." Liam pulled his brother to his feet.

Leith staggered and then caught his balance. The glazed look was fading.

"What happened?" He was finally able to get words out of his throat.

"There was a shooting, Leith. Regan got grazed." Leith's eyes shot past Caleb to the ambulance pulling away. "I need to get your statement but first Liam is going to take you to Emergency to get checked out."

Leith shrugged off their hands. "I'm fine."

"No. You are going and that's that." Liam pulled out the oldest brother card that he seldom had to use. "Caleb. Can you let Laycee know?"

Caleb nodded, and then motioned Eddie over. "Eddie will take you to the hospital. You can't have your vehicles yet until we release the scene."

Leith paced the waiting room at the hospital. He wasn't family and couldn't be with her. It frustrated him. They had tried to find her Uncle John and then her parents, with no success.

Caleb and Ben entered the hospital and headed back into the Emergency Department, stern looks on their faces. Leith exchanged a look with Liam and Laycee. Something was up.

Laycee grasped her brothers' hands and tugged. "Come, sit down. We need to pray. God knows what's happening."

Leith sank on the edge of a chair and half listened to his brother and sister in prayer. His mind was too numb and too muddled to form words, but he knew that God heard even a half-formed whisper. His eyes never left the door behind where he knew Regan was.

He started as an arm slid around him. Laycee had reached out to her brother. He shut his eyes and leaned back. Why did he feel it wasn't over yet?

Chapter 9

Ben came back through the waiting room, phone to his ear, almost on a run. The three Bradleys shared a glance. What was happening?

Caleb came out, hand under Regan's arm. She was pale and unsteady on her feet. He held up a hand to stop them from approaching and turned to Regan. They could see them arguing, Regan shaking her head in an adamant manner. Caleb didn't seem to be giving in though. Bringing Regan with him, he approached.

"Leith and Regan, someone is after one of you," he stated. "Until we can figure out who, we are going to be upping your protection."

Regan jerked her arm back from Caleb's grasp and stomped away. Before they could stop her, she was out the door. Leith moved to follow, but stopped at Caleb's grip. He turned to look at Caleb.

Caleb was shaking his head. "No. You're not going out there. You're a target. I have an officer out there watching for Regan. I figured she'd do this." He looked at Laycee and Liam. "Right now, my main concern is to get these two to safety. Ben was working on a place but got called to another situation. Neither of these two are going home."

Leith was shaking his head. "No, Caleb. I'm not putting anyone else at risk. If whoever it is wants to come after me, let them." He too broke from the group and was gone before anyone could make a move.

Liam headed after his brother on a run. Leith was gone as was Regan. How did they disappear so quickly? Liam heard a noise and looked to his left. He saw Regan and Leith standing with some officers. Good, he thought. Caleb pegged them right.

"They just had to try it, didn't they?" Caleb voice spoke from behind him.

Liam snorted and agreed. "So now what, Caleb? How do we keep them safe? Where to we tuck them? We can't put them out of circulation for months."

Caleb searched his friend's face. "I know. I just wish…" He pulled out his phone and looked. "I need to take this."

Liam walked toward Leith, who refused to meet his eyes. What was he going to do with him?

****

The King turned cold eyes on the Jester, who was sweating profusely even though the air was cold. He didn't speak, just watched in silence as the underling squirmed.

He turned and paced the room and paced back, once more stopping in front of the Jester. A hand reached out and the sound of flesh hitting flesh rang through the room.

"You have cost me a great deal, not just in money," the King stated. "From now on, you are not on your own. You make no decisions except what I tell you. These two gentleman behind you will be with you 24/7 from now on. They will be introduced as your relatives from outside the area, come to visit you."

He paused, stepped away and then came back. "If you step out of line even the tiniest bit, they will deal with you in a manner I doubt you will enjoy.

These are my Knights, who defend me and my property. Take care you do not offend."

The Jester could feel the chills running up and down his spine. He had really screwed things up. At a gesture, one of the Knights touched his shoulder and indicated he was to leave. They followed him. They would be his shadow from now on.

The King waited until he heard the outside door close and then in a fit of rage, flung his glass at the wall. It shattered, and liquid slowly flowed down to pool on the floor. If he couldn't get things under control, he was ruined. He needed to find the rest of those packets, and that fool of a Jester had taken away the only real chance he had.

****

Caleb climbed from his vehicle and stared at the house. He shook his head. There just didn't seem to be any way they could catch a break. He breathed a prayer for wisdom and guidance. He certainly had desire to cross that threshold of that home.

Ben came down the steps and stopped beside him, standing in silence, staring across the street. He shook his hand and then looked down at his hands.

Caleb leaned against his cruiser. "What do we have, Ben? Is it John Sullivan?"

Ben nodded. "It is. The paramedics called it when they came. They suspect it was his heart. We're waiting for the coroner."

Caleb's eyes slid shut. Another link in the chain but how did it fit in? "Any chance it's not natural?"

Ben turned his head, then shook it. "I doubt it. John's had bad health for years. He just never said much to anyone. We've been friends since grade school."

Caleb looked up at the house. "Have a team go through it any way. I would rather be sure than have to have them come back." He stopped. "Have you been able to reach Joseph and Rebecca?"

Ben shook his head. "I've tried. I reached their voice mail. Maybe Regan will have a better idea of where they are. They should be home soon. When they left, they were only planning on being gone a month and it's coming up to six weeks. But then, too, they have never taken a vacation." He stopped and swallowed hard. "This is not what they should be coming home to."

Caleb looked up at the sky. The sun was heading down and he had many hours left to get through. He wouldn't be making it home for his boys this night.

He turned, hand on Ben's shoulder. He went to say something and stopped. He tapped his hand a couple of times and then headed back around to the driver's door. "Did you come up with a safe place to stick Leith and Regan?"

Ben shook his head. "Not yet and I highly doubt we'll get them there. I can see Leith grabbing Regan and taking off, hiding them himself. We can't protect him if he does that."

Caleb looked at the house again, hearing John's Border Collie howling. Sage would need to be taken care of. "Bring Sage to Laycee. She'll look after her. Have you found John's son yet?"

Ben once again shook his head. "No. I have no idea where he is." He stopped at a thought and squinted against the sun. "You know, this bit with the break-ins. That fits David's mentality. I can see him doing that very easily."

"You're right. We need to find him. Send out the alert."

Caleb slowly walked up to the Evans' door. His heart was breaking for his friends. How was he to tell Regan her uncle was gone?

Regan answered and stepped back. "Caleb, don't even start. I'm not going into protective custody."

Caleb held up his hand. "Let's sit, Regan. That's not why I'm here."

Regan searched his face, seeing the sadness. Her hand came to her mouth and she stumbled. Caleb caught her arm and helped her to sit.

"Not my parents. Please, not my parents."

Caleb looked down, praying for the words. "No, not your parents. It's your uncle. I'm sorry, Regan, he's gone."

Tears welled up as she shook her head. "He can't be. He just can't be." Sobs shook her body.

Caleb stood and walked to the kitchen, returning with a glass of water. He waited until her sobs had softened. "Ben is tracking your parents. Do you have any idea where they might be?"

She shook her head. "No. I talked to them three days ago and they were heading home but they weren't sure what route they were going to take. They were having such a great vacation." She stopped speaking, lost in thought. "Where's David? I just know he had something to do with this."

Caleb tilted his head and studied her. "Why do you say that?"

She snorted. "I know him. I know what he's capable of."

Caleb shook his head. "I don't think so."

Regan stood. "I know my cousin. I know exactly what he is capable of. If you want to find out who is breaking into the store, find him." She stood at the window, arms wrapped around her wait. "I need to be alone, Caleb. Please."

He hesitated, then said, "Call someone to stay with you. I'll let you know when the coroner has released the body. In the absence of anyone else, you'll be the one notified."

When she didn't respond, he left, closing the door softly behind him. He stopped, puzzled at her words. Why would she say that about David?

He turned to look at the door and started back, then hesitated. He would send Hannah and Laycee over in a while. They might be able to help.

Caleb headed back to his office. It would be a long night. He had to determine what needed to be done with Leith and Regan as well as trying to track down her parents.

Ben followed him into his office and shut the door. Caleb sank into his chair with a sign of relief and buried his head in his hands. Days like this were just too much.

He looked up as a cup of tea appeared in line of sight and nodded his thanks. Somehow, he was going to have to find time for some food.

Ben sat in silence, nursing his own cup of coffee. He shook his head at his thoughts.

"Any luck, Ben?"

Ben nodded. "I managed to find Joseph and Rebecca. They're about six hours away. Joseph said they had planned to stop for the night but would grab a bite to eat and keep driving. They were worried about Regan. Did you ever find David?"

Caleb shook his head. "I was going to ask you that." He leant back in his chair and steepled his fingers. "Regan said something strange tonight before I left her. She asked if I have found David. She is convinced he had something to do with the break-ins."

Ben studied his hands. Caleb waited him out, knowing he liked to put his thoughts in order before speaking.

Ben spoke. "I haven't said much as I haven't proven it totally yet, but David's fingerprints were in the Bell House and also on a some of the imported tile crates. John said he hadn't worked for him for months and that these crates had come in after David had left. He felt bad saying anything but he was too honest not to."

Caleb ran his hand through his hair. "Well, I guess we won't be able to ask John anything more on that. I wonder if he said anything to Joseph. We'll have to wait on that one. It makes one wonder how well Regan got on with David."

Ben looked at him with a seriousness Caleb seldom saw. "You're about the same age as David. Regan is I think about four years younger. You wouldn't have seen much, being young yourself. David always has had a vicious, mean streak to him. John worried about him. My feeling has always been that Regan took a lot of the brunt of it from David. David was adopted as a young child and never felt he fit in. John did tell me he had had to write him out of ownership of the store; David knew this and handled it very poorly."

"That certainly puts a different light on things, now doesn't it."

A tap came at the door and when asked, Annie entered. She handed Ben some papers and left.

Ben studied them and then handed them to Caleb. Caleb looked and then his eyes shot to Ben. "Five hundred thousand dollars in uncut stones just in that packet. The report says they are almost perfect."

"Five hundred thousand reasons to kill. This just changes the whole game we've been playing."

"That it does. Now we have to figure out if they are meant for someone here or if this was just a drop off site on the way through."

Ben leaned back and looked at the ceiling, his lips moving silently in prayer. He dropped his head back. Caleb was watching him.

"Go home, Ben. Get some sleep. You'll think better then."

Ben nodded and stood. "Follow your own advice, Caleb. This is far from over. You'll need more strength that you know before it is."

Neither knew how prophetic those words would be.

Five days later, the funeral for John Sullivan was over and the will had been read. Regan and her father were now sole owners of the business. There had been no word on David. He had not shown up anywhere.

Regan slowed as she approached the house where she knew she would find Leith. She was torn. Her father had been adamant that he would not need her in the store. He wanted her to follow her dream and if that dream was setting tile, then that was what he was pushing her to do. She needed to talk to Leith. He had been there in the background over the last few days, comforting in his presence but they had not had time to talk.

She shut her truck door and drew in a deep breath. She had no idea how this was going to go. She stepped into the house. It was not a big job, not a renovation like the last one, but there was enough tile work to keep both of them busy. She headed for the kitchen, where she could hear his clear whistle. Stopping in the doorway, she watched him.

Sensing her presence, Leith stopped and then turned. His gaze went to the clear gray eyes he was beginning to learn to love. He said not a word.

Regan stepped forward and stopped, rubbing her hand on the countertop and studying the backsplash he was working on. It was simple, just a few colours, but striking in how he had planned the layout.

She didn't look at him. "Well, Leith, where do we go from here?"

He waited for her to look up and when she didn't ducked his head. "Nothing has changed. If you still want to work for me, then you should. If you want to go work with your Dad, then do that."

She sighed. "I didn't think it would be so hard to make a decision."

"Mom would always ask if we had prayed about our decisions. Don't rush to make one. Spend the time in prayer. Remember that you are not alone in your decisions. Whenever you feel frightened about what you are deciding, run to that strong tower God has provided."

She tilted her head. "How do you always know exactly what to say to me?" She turned. "My kit is in the truck. Where do I start?"

Leith laughed. This was his Regan, back on track.

As they sat at lunch, Leith asked about John's dog.

"I have her. Sage is such a sweetheart but she is grieving. People don't expect dogs to grieve but they do. It will take some time but I'll do my best with her."

****

The ragged clothing on the man denoted his status in society, a lowly of the low. He stumbled through a haze into the abandoned building, looking for shelter. He stopped. What was that stench?

He turned and almost ran from the building. Stumbling through the debris on the building's parking lot, he exited to the street. Coming towards him was a patrol car. He waved at it and then stumbled as he lost his balance.

Eddie opened his door and approached the vagrant. Hearing his words, his eyes shot to the building and then back to the man. Keying up his mike he asked for assistance.

Caleb pulled to a stop behind a cruiser and got out. He was never ready to hear of a body being found. Ben approached him.

"Any identification yet?"

Ben shook his head. "Not that I know of. Eddie's around here somewhere. He's the one old Charlie flagged down."

Caleb took a look around. "Where's Charlie?"

"Eddie sent one of the officers with him to the diner up the street. He thought if he could get some food into him, he might be more alert and answer questions."

Caleb and Ben looked around as footsteps approached them.

"What do you have, Eddie? Any I.D.?"

Eddie shook his head. "It looks as if the body was stripped of anything of value, either before he was killed or after. The coroner thinks six to seven days but he'll know more after the autopsy. This is the only thing he found." Eddie held up a clear evidence bag with a key on a key ring.

Caleb reached for it, then tilted it towards Ben. "Sullivan's."

Eddie nodded, then looked back at the decrepit building. "The body has similarities to John's son. I have a suspicion that's him and that's why we couldn't find him for the funeral."

Caleb stilled. David Sullivan. What was his tie to everything? They already suspected him for the break-ins but what was he looking for? Was it the packets of jewels like they had found?

"Tell the coroner to call me once he's done the preliminary." Caleb motioned for Ben to follow him.

Ben spoke. "What was it we were saying a couple of days ago? If this is David, there could go our link to the gang."

"I don't think we're done. They will want that packet Regan found. I suspect there are still packets in crates at the store. I'll talk to Joseph about having a search done for the shipments from outside the country that we were tracking. Did you ever determine if the packets were inserted on the route or not?"

Ben shook his head. "Can't. Not enough information. Until we crack this, we won't know."

"That's it then. Okay, carry on. Did you get the arrangements made for more patrols and cover for Leith and Regan?"

"Since I can't get them to cooperate, all I can do is send more patrols around their homes and if men are available and willing for overtime, have a car sit outside. It's not the best solution but it's what we have for now."

Caleb nodded, knowing Ben had tried. Things seemed to have settled down, but his gut said otherwise and he had learned to go with his gut feeling.

****

Ben stepped into Caleb's office and shut the door, siting down while he waited for the phone conversation to end. He studied the report in his hand, not liking what he had to tell Caleb.

Caleb's call ended and he stared at Ben, who silently handed the folder to him. Caleb opened and read through the report quickly, then read back through more slowly. He dropped the folder on his desk and buried his head in his hands. Now what?

"It's David Sullivan." At Ben's nod, he drew a deep breath. "Get us a search warrant for John's house and David's place. I'll talk to Joseph and see if David had anything at the store. We may need a search warrant for there."

Ben spoke up. "I don't understand. John loved that boy so much."

Caleb's gaze searched for answers across the room and found none. "I know. Good parents can have bad kids. Once you have the warrants, get started on the search. Keep it to as few as possible. There's still something going on in this town, I can feel it. Somehow, it almost feels as if there'a leak somewhere and I would trust all our people with my life."

"I know that feeling, Caleb. Just keep praying. We'll get it sorted out."

Later that afternoon, Caleb parked outside Joseph and Rebecca's home. He didn't want to make this call, didn't want to make this notification. It was too soon after John.

Rebecca answered the door and after greeting him, invited him back to the kitchen. She put a cup of tea in front of him and went to find Joseph.

Caleb stood and shook Joseph's hand before they were all seated once again.

"I am really sorry about John."

"Thank you, Caleb. He never did tell us how sick he was. I guess that's why he pushed Rebecca and I to go on that trip. But that's not why you're here. It is about Regan?" Joseph's keen eyes searched Caleb's face.

Caleb stared at his tea and then raised his eyes, shaking his head. "No, not that I'm aware of. We're still investigating what's going on with the store. It's David."

He saw Rebecca hand fly to her mouth and Joseph reach for her other hand.

"We found his body early this morning in an abandoned factory on the east side of town. I'm sorry to have to be the one to tell you this."

Joseph's face hardened and tears flowed down Rebecca's face. "What happened?"

Caleb drew in a breath. What he had to say now was the hard part and would be devastating to the family. "It wasn't an accident. David was shot once. The coroner figures it was at least a week ago."

"Before John died." Rebecca whispered and Caleb nodded.

"We have search warrants for David's place and also for John's. It's standard procedure. I know you can give permission for John's but we'll do it by the book."

After speaking with them for a while and calling for their pastor and his wife to come over, Caleb stepped outside. Joseph followed him out.

"What aren't you saying in front of Rebecca?"

Caleb stared at the night sky, amazed at the clarity of it and the number of stars he could see. He needed to remember that God was in control, the Creator of the stars was also the Creator of man, and the Author of a man's life.

"We may need to search the store. It is looking more and more like David was involved in the break-in at the store and the incident at the Bell House."

Joseph too looked at the sky. "What you're saying doesn't surprise me. He was an unhappy child and an even more unhappy man. John and his wife did their best but could never really reach to his heart. He got involved with a rough crowd early in high school. Things would happen. He always denied his involvement." He stopped, then continued, "Talk to Regan. She never liked him, never wanted to even be in the same room as he was. She has never said but I think he had something to do with her moving away for those 10 years. If that's the case, that young man cost us precious time with our daughter." He stopped, laid a hand on Caleb's shoulder, and then headed back into the house to his wife. They had another funeral to plan.

Ben met Caleb as he stepped from his car in front of the rundown shack David called home. "You wouldn't think a son of John's would live is such squalor, would you?"

Caleb shook his head. "I don't think John was able to do anything. Joseph mentioned last night that John didn't seem to have any influence on his son at all. What did you find?"

"The team is just getting started but it looks as if he was into some pretty heavy stealing and has been for some time. It will explain some of the thefts from around town. They'll be looking hard to find out if he has any information on that packet Regan found."

Caleb thought for a minute. "I'm sure you're right. Joseph has given permission for us to search John's house, even though we have a warrant, and also the store. He wants answers." Caleb stopped. "He said something interesting though." Caleb stopped for a minute, watching traffic move by. "He followed me out of the house and we were talking about Regan. He told me Regan had no use for her cousin, wouldn't be around him. He always felt that David had something to do with her leaving town."

Ben thought about that for a few minutes. His keen eyes watched the activity around the shack. "I could see that. Regan has that ability to read people. She has an intuition not many people have. I would trust her instincts any day."

Caleb turned to look at Ben. "Really?"

Ben nodded. "I've known her all her life. Joseph and Rebecca are good friends. She would say something about a person, even as a child, and almost 100% of the time, she would be right on with her comments."

"We need to talk to her and soon."

Eddie approached them with a clear evidence bag in his hand, handing it silently to Caleb. Caleb studied it, then shot a look at Eddie. "Any more like this?"

Eddie shook his head. "We're still looking but this definitely ties him to the incident at the Bell House."

Caleb handed the bag to Ben. In it, the evidence team had placed paper from a tile crate, clearly marked. The mark didn't have anything to do with the type of tile or the manufacturer.

"This is good. Now we know what we are looking for." Ben handed the bag back to Eddie. "Make sure this information doesn't get out. I will personally fire anyone who leaks even a tidbit of news about this."

"I'll make sure."

Ben and Caleb looked at each other. Their thoughts were similar. Now they were making progress.

Three days later, Regan wandered around her parents' home. She really needed to find her own place. Her uncle's dog, Sage, kept pace with her. Regan reached down and patted the silky coat.

The threat from David was gone. She should have spoken up years ago, but God had known where He wanted her. She would be back at work tomorrow, and immersing herself in the pattern and colours of the tiles would help. She loved that part of the work, taking the rough paper pattern and translating it into finished work. She thought, that is just what God does—He takes the roughness of our lives and translates them into His workmanship, His creation.

Leith approached her, watching intently as she stopped. "We need a break, Regan. We need to get away, just like we had planned."

Regan shook her head. "No, I want to work."

Leith stopped her with a hand on her arm. When she wouldn't look at him, he commanded, "Look at me, Regan." Her eyes flew to his. "You need a chance to get away from here, a chance to do something that takes your mind off what has happened."

Regan looked at him and gave a small smile. "Looking out for me again, are you?"

Leith's hand came up and he gently touched her cheek. "I'll pick you up tomorrow morning at 8 and we'll do the town. Wear something casual and comfy shoes." He hesitated. "Thank you, Regan, for doing this."

Regan watched him walk away, her fingers on her cheek where he had touched it. No, she thought, thank you, Leith Bradley. Thank you for caring. You are making me care too much and I just can't do that again.

****

The King turned from his store front window and paced the store. Business was really down and he had no idea why. People weren't buying. He really needed those packets. Now he would never find them, thanks to that fool of a Jester.

204

He would need to deal with him shortly. But first, he needed his Knights to find those two who had interfered and bring them to him. He would deal with them and then the Jester.

After that he would pack up and move, retiring from his store, go overseas to some warm climate.

He motioned forward his one Knight and gave his orders. They would be carried out in a summary manner.

****

Liam watched his brother and sister as they played with Laycee's Sheltie. Defiant certainly seemed to be winning the battle for the ball. He loved this dog. He looked down as he felt something hit his leg and picked up Laycee's tuxedo cat, Terror. She cuddled down in his arms, licked his hand, then sat staring around with her intense green eyes. He still didn't know what to make of a cat that sang and chirped her way through the day.

Laycee came back into the house, shutting the door behind him. Leith had sat on the deck steps and Defiant had crawled into his knee. "We need to get him a dog."

Liam laughed. "Yes, I think we do. Why do I think you have one in mind?"

Laycee smirked. "That's because I do. I know of a trainer whose dog has had puppies. One would be perfect for Leith. Or even for you."

Liam held up his hand. "I don't think so. I'm not a dog person."

"No? Then why is Defiant, my stand-off Sheltie, all over you when he sees you? And for that matter, why is Terror is your arms? You're not a 'cat person' either, you say."

Liam shrugged. "What can I say? It's my magnetic personality."

Laycee swatted her brother. "Please." She turned and looked back at Leith. "He's got it bad, doesn't he?"

Liam broke out in laughter, startling Terror who sprang from his arms and raced through the house. "And you don't?" He hugged his sister. "I am so glad for you. I hated what you went through, but God brought you the mate you needed."

Laycee tilted her head back. "Yes, He did. Joshua is that." She gave him a saucy look. "Now, we need to work on you."

Liam shook his head as she headed for the front of the house. Laycee was Laycee and loved by many.

Leith stepped back into the house, shutting the door as Defiant's plushy tail cleared it. "I'm off. I'll let you stay and hear the wedding talk. I'm glad Laycee's settled."

"Me too, brother." Liam stopped speaking, watching his brother. Leith was tired and worn and it showed in his face. His face was drawn and there were lines that hadn't been there just a few weeks ago. "How are you doing?"

Leith shrugged, not meeting his brother's eyes. Liam moved towards his brother, hands coming up to grip his shoulders.

Leith looked up. "I'm getting there. It's been a tough few weeks."

Liam drew his brother into a bear hug and then released him. "Take some time. You need it."

Leith smirked. "That's what I'm doing tomorrow, taking some time," he shot over his shoulder as he headed for the door and his truck.

Liam shouted with laughter. "And I suppose taking time tomorrow won't include someone by the name of Regan?"

"I'm not telling." He shut the door on Liam's renewed laughter.

"What's he not telling?" Laycee stuck her head back into the kitchen.

"He's off tomorrow with Regan, probably to do one of those wander through a small town days he loves."

Laycee's eyes shone. "Wonderful. Now come, I need you to look at something."

"Not wedding stuff!" Liam groaned.

"Stop it. You're having a ball with this and you know it."

Liam's arm draped over his sister's shoulder. She was so right. He was having a ball and enjoying every moment of her romance she cared to share with him.

Chapter 12

Leith helped Regan into his truck and then moved around to climb behind the wheel. She had taken him at his word and dressed in coloured jeans, a soft green sweater that highlighted her hair so well, and denim jacket. Comfortable leather shoes finished it all off.

"So where are we off to?"

Leith pulled away. Today was going to be wonderful, he thought. "When I take a day off, I like to wander through small towns, just to see what life is like somewhere else. I often get ideas for designs in some of the older homes that are open to the public."

"That's sounds like a fun day. Which town?"

"I thought Elmtown. I haven't been there in a couple of years."

"I haven't been there for many years. It sounds fun."

Conversation drifted through many topics. Leith kept checking his rearview mirror.

"Are we being followed?" Regan's voice broke through his thoughts.

"I'm not sure. I've had the feeling I've been followed for days, but the vehicles seem to change. I thought maybe it was Caleb's doing, but this vehicle is not obvious like an officer would be."

Regan shot a glance out the back window, then at him. "Today, we're not worrying about that.

You promised your 'friend' a day away from work. Now, let's get at it." She laughed.

Leith laughed as well. "You've got it."

Still uncomfortable at the thought of being followed, Leith watched the traffic behind him. He was looking forward to this day and didn't want anything to ruin it.

Leith and Regan spent the day wandering in and out of shops, small stores, and homes open to the public. Regan could see why Leith said he got a lot of ideas. A shared lunch of fresh-cut fries and fresh cider halted their adventure in the middle of the day, although Regan laughingly protested it wasn't a healthy meal. Leith shrugged, told her she was on vacation, and to eat up.

Late in the day, they made their way to the little foot bridge that crossed a small brook in a nearby park. Leith reached for Regan's hand and held on tight when she tugged at it. She finally relaxed and then he felt her hand grip his. She stopped in the middle of the bridge, recovered her hand, and leaned forward to look down.

"This is so peaceful. I could stay here for a long time."

"I could too." Leith agreed, watching her face. He had seen it relaxing over the day. "I'm glad you agreed to come."

She laughed. "Yes, friend. I'm glad too. We needed this." She looked into the distance. "I'm glad." She repeated herself, then turned to look at him.

Leith stood, hip resting again the railing, and facing her. His eyes traced her face.

"Leith," she spoke hesitantly. "I really need to talk to someone. I think you're it."

"About what?" His voice was calm but his heart was racing. Here is comes, he thought, she's about to say she has met someone else.

"About David." She stopped as her eyes flew past him. A figure dressed in black and with a ski mask covering the face was approaching them. "Leith. Behind you."

Leith spun, hands in the air ready to defend them, He heard Regan give a cry behind him and shot a glance over his shoulder. A second figure, clad like the first, stood behind her, arm around her neck and revolver to her head. His eyes danced between the two men. There was no way he could get her away without one of them getting hurt. He kept his hands up but opened the fists in a sign of surrender.

The men shoved them off the bridge away from town. Pushing them through the undergrowth, they came to a black van. The door was opened and they were shoved in. Cloth was tied over their eyes and their hands were roughly brought behind their back and tied.

Regan shifted over as close to Leith as she could get. Her thoughts flew, her mind raced. Who and what? She lifted up prayer after prayer as she tried to keep her balance on the floor of the van.

Leith surged with anger. How did he let this happen? Who were these men? What did they want? He felt Regan close to him and so desperately wanted to hug her to reassure her. He struggled with his bonds but the men were professionals. The bonds were not loosening.

After numerous twists and turns and who knew how long, the vehicle stopped. He could feel the shift in it as the men stepped out. There was a low conversation, then the door of the van opened. Leith was pulled out and he heard a cry from Regan as she was roughly dragged out. He was helpless and he hated that feeling.

They were pushed into a building, he could tell by the change of temperature and light. It smelled old, as if it hadn't been used in years. Up a long flight of stairs they were made to walk and down a hallway. Rasping sounds came as a lock was opened and then the grating of rusty rings as a door was pulled open. They were shoved inside. Leith stumbled, caught his balance and turned.

"What do you want?" he demanded.

"You'll find out. The King will be asking the questions in the future, not you."

Leith's head turned from side to side as he tried to track the voices and the footsteps. He heard a small cry from Regan, then felt a prick on his shoulder. His body grew faint and he collapsed. He couldn't protect her. Lord, save her, he cried as the darkness won.

****

Caleb set his mug of tea on his kitchen counter and caught up his phone. It was Liam. As he listened, his face paled and his heart sank.

"I'm on my way, Liam. Sit tight."

Caleb approached Liam standing on Leith's porch. "Have you been inside?"

"No. I noticed the door was open a bit, pushed it open and called for Leith. He hasn't answered."

"Stay here. I have officers on the way. I'm going in."

Caleb drew his revolver and entered, searching each room as he made his way through the

211

house. Leith was not there, but whoever had been had done a good job on searching. It was a mess.

Caleb came back out and stopped by Liam. "He's not in there that I can see. It's been tossed so someone was looking pretty hard for something. Let the team work through it."

Liam stared back through the door at the damage he could see. He shook his head. "What is happening in our town, Caleb? And why us?"

Caleb watched as the evidence team and responding officers approached and drew Liam off to the side. "I don't know, Liam. I really don't know." He drew him to the side. "Track down Leith and see if you can find him."

Liam glared at Caleb. "I'll try but I have a bad feeling about this." He turned and stormed away.

Caleb watched, then shook his head. He had to agree. Something was going on in their town.

Later, Caleb approached the Evans' home. There was no one home. He then tried the store. Both Regan's parents were adamant she had not come home last night. They knew she had planned to be away the day before but Regan hadn't said with whom. Caleb had a pretty good idea it was Leith but it was not like either one of them not to come home or call if they had had any trouble with a vehicle. Something stank.

****

Leith stirred, his body moving restlessly on the dirty, garbage-strewn floor. His mouth felt so dry and bitter-tasting. He rolled to his side and tried hard to open his eyes. They cracked a bit and then fell shut once again. He was just too tired to try again.

Hours later, he felt hands on his arm and shoulder and a gentle shaking. A soft hand touched

212

his face. "Leith." He knew that voice. Whose was it?

Regan shook Leith again. She just had to get him awake. They needed to get away while they could.

Leith rolled to his back and groaned. Eyes opening, he stared up and then focused on Regan. Her worried face was bent over his.

"Leith, we need to move. We need to get going." She tried to raise him up but he was too heavy and his body wasn't cooperating.

He tried to wet dry lips and croaked, "Give me a minute." He gathered his strength and managed to get upright, head spinning as he did. Her arm came around him to support him.

"How long?"

"I don't know. It's daylight so I think it's the next day." Regan's eyes shot around the room. "We need to get out of here. I don't see any way but the door and it's locked tight. The only windows are those tiny ones up at the top."

Vision clearing, Leith scanned the area. She was right. They didn't have many options. They couldn't even surprise someone coming in—the door opened to the hallway.

"Help me up. I'll see what I can find." Leith staggered to his feet and swayed as he regained his balance.

Gaining strength and balance, Leith felt his way along the walls and then again. He stopped by the door. Yes, he had felt a weak spot.

Beckoning Regan over, he whispered, "See if you can find a piece of metal bar or wood that I can use. It's weak here."

Regan frantically searched the large room, finally finding a piece of metal pipe under the debris. She rushed with it over to Leith. He looked at her and grinned, then surprised her with a quick kiss. He winked and then moved to work on the weakened metal.

Regan's fingers went to her mouth. Leith's actions had surprised her. But it was a good surprise. When they got out of here, she would ask him what he meant by that.

Leith worked as quickly and as quietly as he could. The metal gave bit by bit. Soon, he was able to shove it back enough for Regan to step through. A little more, and he was free. He caught her hand in his and moved towards the stairs, listening as he went. He looked over the railing and leaned over just enough to see. No one seemed to be there. He pulled Regan after him down the stairs. Hesitating for a moment, he headed to the back of the building. Whatever it had been, the equipment had been removed. There were scattered crates and metal but nothing big enough for them to hide behind if they had to. They reached the back door and he shoved. It creaked. He stopped, heart in mouth. If anyone was here, they would have heard it. He shoved again and they were out. There was an area they had to cross that was open but he figured if they were quick, they would be through it and into the woods on the other side before they were seen.

Clasping Regan's hand tighter, he pointed to the woods, and waited until she nodded. Another glance around and the race was on. They had made it. Now he just had to figure out where they were and how to get back home, all the while keeping Regan safe.

They walked as carefully as they could, trying their best not to leave a trail or make a noise. It was hard. The woods had really become overgrown at this point. Finally, Regan tugged on his hand.

"I need to stop, Leith. I need to rest. I can't go on."

He turned. She was right. They did need to rest. "I can hear water over there. If it's clear, we can get some and rest a bit too."

****

The Jester looked around the room where they had hidden Leith and Regan. They were gone, vanished into thin air. He looked at the wall by the door and the opening Leith had created and then down at the metal pipe on the floor. How had they missed that? The two Knights had searched the room.

The King would have his head. His head would roll. The Knights knew they were in trouble too. He could tell by the way they were moving. The blame would fall on him though. He was the one who had found this place and assured the King that those two couldn't get out. How was he ever going to explain this?

He turned, not seeing the hand raised towards him. A single shot and he fell. The Jester's life had come to an inglorious end. No one would ever find him here.

The two Knights looked at one another and then left. They needed to find those two. Searching the grounds, they found no sign of where they had gotten to. Whispered conversation and they turned to stare at the woods. That had to be where they were but how would they find them there? Neither of them wanted to be the one to tell the King the situation as it now stood. They had agreed they needed a search dog and they knew just where to find one. Leith's home town was known for its search and

215

rescue team. One of those dogs would do. The owner wasn't needed.

****

"Leith, I need to stop. I need to rest." Regan gasped.

He looked around. "I can hear water. Over there." He pulled her with him until they reached a small stream. "Wait."

When he was certain, it was okay he led them forward. Regan dropped gratefully to her knees and greedily sucked up water. Leith stopped her.

"Careful. Not too much at once."

He sat back on his heels and scanned the area, hazel eyes searching. "We need to keep moving, but I have no idea where we are."

Regan shook her head as well. "I have no idea either. The way they kept moving, it confused me. Not being able to see didn't help."

"Take another drink. We need to get moving."

They slowed their pace and continued moving away from the stream and the building. Dusk was falling.

"Leith, we need to stop. We can't go on in the dark."

He nodded. "I know. Let's see where we can hole up for the night."

216

Chapter 13

The King stared at his Knights. His rage was palpable.

"What do you mean they have escaped? I thought you had them where they were unable to get out. You're all a bunch of fools." Spittle flew from his mouth as he continued to berate them. He stopped.

"That one. Get rid of him."

The Knights looked at each other and one spoke. "The Jester has been taken care of. We have a plan to find them."

After they left, the King stormed around his office. It was all falling apart. When would it end?

****

Caleb looked up at the commotion at the front of the station and then moved forward. He could see Anna Welch talking with the officer working the front desk. When she saw him, she motioned for him.

"What's up, Anna?"

"It's Betsy, my search and rescue dog. Someone has stolen her from her kennel. I was out for about an hour and came home and she's gone."

"Give us the details and we'll canvas your neighbourhood. No chance of the kennel getting open on its own?"

She shook her head. "I have a lock on it when I'm out. The lock was cut."

Caleb rubbed his neck. Who would want a search and rescue dog? He spun.

"Anna, I think I know why. I can't say right now."

Caleb headed back for his office and motioned Ben in.

"I think Anna's dog, Betsy, was taken to try and find Leith and Regan. They're starting to get desperate."

"No word from them yet?"

Caleb shook his head. "Both the Bradleys and the Evans said they would call if they had heard anything and they haven't. Where are they? Without a clue, we have no idea where to search for them." He looked up at a knock at his door.

Eddie stood there. "Caleb, I just got word Leith's truck has been found in Elmtown. I'm headed over there to speak with the responding officer."

Caleb nodded. "Let them know what's happening here and see if they had any word."

Caleb drew a deep breath. Things were happening, he had no idea what, and he had no idea who or how to respond.

"I'll give Liam a call. He'll want to head that way."

Caleb agreed. "It's not our town but it's just over the area we patrol. Let's hope wherever they are, they are headed this way."

****

The sun rose on a new day. Leith stirred quietly, not wanting to disturb Regan, but he knew they had to get moving. He gently awakened her and they moved off. He hoped he was headed in the right direction.

A noise made his stop. Regan screamed and then her scream was cut off. A black figure stood in front of him. A sudden blow to the abdomen doubled him over and he dropped to his knees, blackness blocking out the slight and sending him gasping for air.

Regan struggled to free herself but the grip was strong. She finally braced her hands on the arm around her waist, stretched herself as far forward as she could. She could feel the breath on the back of her head. She slammed her head backwards and heard bones crunch. She was released and stumbled forward. That was not a good idea. Her head was hurting now. She grabbed a nearby branch and lunged at the man standing over Leith. Before he could turn, she brought it down over his head. With a groan, the man collapsed.

Regan hurried to Leith's side and dropped to her knees. Lifting his face, she said, "We need to go."

Turning from him she grabbed up the knapsacks and guns the men had dropped. She saw a dog standing nearby and went towards it. She knew the dog. It was Betsy, a friend's dog. She caught the leash and came back to Leith. Helping him to his feet, she tucked a shoulder under his arm. They disappeared from sight.

The two Knights staggered to their feet and looked around. They reached for the packs and guns and found them gone. They had other weapons on them. They searched and found the trail. This time, they would not fail. They would find those two and bring them to the King.

Leith stopped. "I need a breather."

Regan looked worriedly behind her. "We can't stop long. They'll be coming."

"I know. Just for a moment, then we'll get moving."

Noise from in front of them stopped them. Sudden blows rained down on them to the barking of the dog and they sank into blackness. They had not made it out.

****

"Caleb." He turned at the voice behind him. "How you found them yet?"

He shook his head. "Not yet, Liam. They were seen around town two days ago but it looks as if they never made it back to his truck. There are just so many places they could be."

Liam's face was drawn. Where was his brother? He looked at his brother's truck and closed his eyes in prayer.

"So what do we know?"

Caleb motioned and led him over to a nearby picnic table.

"We do know that David Sullivan was involved in the break-ins; we have proof. We found his body a few days ago. We also have that packet Leith and Regan found. It contained uncut jewels. We are trying to track the source of them. Somewhere along the delivery route the packets of jewels are being inserted into the crates of tiles. We have some ideas as to who is to receive them but aren't releasing any more information yet."

Liam buried his head in his hands. He was at the point where he felt so helpless. With Laycee, he was able to help. Now, he just didn't know what to do.

"So, where do we go from here?"

Caleb looked at his notes. He was at a loss too. He didn't think they would find anything in or on the truck. It looked like Leith had locked it and walked away.

Ben approached and motioned for him to come.

"I'll be right back, Liam." He stopped, laid his hand on his friend's shoulder. "You're carrying those burdens again, my friend. You know where to lay them."

Ben spoke, "I have someone who saw Leith and Regan taken away."

Caleb's glance shot to Ben's. "Where and when?"

"There's a little park over the way. The witness says he saw them standing on the bridge, then a dark-clothed figure approached from either side. They forced Leith and Regan to go with them."

"Did the witness get a good look?"

Ben shook his head. "It's a younger fellow, in his early teens, but very good at detail. He said they were in black and seemed to have paint on their faces, like they were playing war."

Caleb stilled. "Camouflage paint." He sighed. "Not a lot to go on."

Ben stood and looked into the distance. "I don't like this. This is too organized. Whoever is behind it has big bucks to spend."

"I know. I wonder." Caleb looked back at Liam, then back to Ben. "I have an idea and I need to you run some background information. Dig as deep as you have to." He scrawled a name on a page from his notebook, ripped it out, and handed it to Ben.

Ben took a look at the name and his eyebrows raised. Then, he nodded. "That does make sense. Too much sense. Let me see what I can find out. I have some contacts at the federal level that can help."

Caleb walked back to Liam. "We'll have Leith's truck towed back to our yard and go over it. I doubt we'll find much though."

Liam looked up. "What aren't you telling me?"

Caleb sank down on the bench on the other side of the table. His face was troubled. He glanced at the sky, trying to gather his thoughts and words. "We have an eye witness who saw Leith and Regan abducted the day they were here and forced into the woods. The department here will set up a search, but I think they're back into our area somewhere."

Liam's breath caught in his throat and his eyes slid shut. Please Lord, not that.

Caleb's hand settled on his arm. "We don't know the details. Keep the faith, my friend. God is in control. Leith will figure out a way to get them out of there."

Liam couldn't answer. First Laycee, now Leith. What was happening to his family? All of a sudden, he didn't feel like the brother who should be able to protect them. He felt like a scared little boy who wanted his parents.

Caleb watched the emotions flickering across his friend's face. He sent up prayers for him, for Laycee, for the department to find answers, but even more that Leith and Regan would be kept safe, wherever they were.

It was late and Caleb was back in his own office. Eddie stuck his head in the door.

"We have another body."

Caleb closed his eyes. Please Lord, just please not one of them.

"It's Eric Brand. He was a friend of David Sullivan."

Caleb sat back. "Eric Brand. Now that's a name that has meant trouble in this town. Run with it, Eddie. Let me know what you find."

"Will do."

Caleb looked at the paperwork on his desk and then locked it away. Tomorrow would do. He needed time with his wife and family.

Liam stood behind Laycee, hands on her shoulders. Tears were running down her face and neither Liam or Joshua had been able to help her.

"Caleb's trying, Laycee. He's really trying."

"I know. I just wish they were here. Why didn't we know they weren't back that night?"

"I don't know. Leith has been pretty good about that but he is entitled to his privacy. We don't talk every day, so it wasn't unusual for us not to hear from him."

She nodded, then turned to hug her brother. He wrapped his arms and held on tight. Tears were in his eyes too.

"I want my Mom and Dad," she whispered.

Tears did fall then from Liam's eyes, dropping onto her black hair. "I know, honey. I know. So do I. I miss their prayers."

Joshua stood watching the siblings, devastation in his face. Now he understood how Liam and Leith and Caleb had felt last year when he and Laycee were missing.

Liam released his sister and turned her to Joshua. "Take care of her, Joshua." Unable to articulate another word, he turned and almost ran from her home.

Looking at the sky, his anger burned. How could he find his brother? Then he sobered.

"God, you're in control. Protect them. Bring them home."

Leith stirred, moving restlessly. His abdomen hurt and so did his head. He couldn't remember why. Eyes cracking open, he blinked and then gazed around. Where was he? The room was smaller. There were windows but he couldn't tell if it was night or day. His eyes ran around the room. There was a sectioned-off area in the back. The door looked solid from what he could see. He continued to move his eyes, then the world spun and he dropped back into darkness.

Regan sat beside Leith, watching him. He had been awake and had slipped back into unconsciousness. She felt defeated. Where are you, God? Why didn't You prevent this? Why didn't you let us get away? She reached out and laid her hand on Leith's head. She needed him to wake up. She had no idea how long they had been there or who had taken them. The last thing she remembered was that they were running from those men.

Betsy! She rose to her knees and searched. Betsy wasn't there. Oh, Betsy, please make your way home. Please find us again.

Sounds came at the door and she moved to lay silently where she had awakened. She stilled her breath as much as she could to mimic the unconscious state she had been left in. Her head hurt so she knew she had been hit at some point.

Eyes closed, she heard the lock open and then the door. Boot steps crossed the room, stopping first by Leith and then another set crossed to her. She kept still. Please don't let them touch me, she prayed. A boot toe prodded her. She kept the groan inside. The boots waited and then walked away. She cracked her eyes just a bit and watched. The men stood for a few moments watching them and then walked away.

"How hard did you hit them?" The voice said.

"Not that hard. They shouldn't still be out. I have no idea what the King is going to say. You know how he handles problems."

She knew at least one of those voices. Her memory was fogged but eventually she would remember. Darkness closed in on her again and she slept.

****

Hannah watched her husband in their yard. He was wandering, mug of tea in hand. She listened —the boys were still sleeping. She opened the door and crossed to where he had stopped, staring at the waterfall that would soon be flowing again.

Her arm around him, she leaned on him. He switched his mug to his other hand and wrapped her close to him.

"I know you've been praying, Caleb. So many other people have been too. Our ladies' group is meeting today to spend the day in prayer."

"I know, honey. I just don't get it. I feel like I am missing something."

"God's timing is perfect. He has a plan, you always tell me. So what is His plan? Are we to understand the mind of God? No, we're not. Jeremiah tells us that His ways are not our ways and His thoughts not our thoughts." She paused.

Caleb waited. Over the years, he had learned his wife had a deep understanding of God, far deeper than he did. God had used her many times to provide answers. Would this be another one? She had with Laycee and Joshua.

Hannah looked at the sunrise brightening the eastern sky. This was a favourite time of the day for both of them, both early risers. This is when they knew they would have time for their couple's Bible study. Duties often came in later in the day and prevented that. She was trying to sort out her words. She knew God had spoken when she was reading His word this morning.

"I know you can't say much and never do. You have that integrity of a Godly man, my love. I have watched over the last few weeks. I have seen the struggles and the sorrows you have borne, not just for your friends but for your town." She tilted her head to look up at him. He was staring across the yard, listening intently to her words.

She continued. "I know you. You will find the answers. God has spoken to me, just like you know He does. There is a source in town for the contraband you are dealing with. This is the name God has given." She hesitated and then gave him the name.

Caleb stilled, then had to remember to breath. He closed his eyes and hugged his wife.

"Honey, I wish I had that connection with God you do. You certainly are a tool that He uses. Don't ever change. This name, this name. I don't know that I even would have considered it." They stood for a while longer, then as Hannah heard their boys up and ready for the day, they turned and walked back to the house.

Caleb strode into the office, a new light of determination on his face. Searching the room, he headed for both Ben and Eddie. "Come with me."

The men looked at each other and then at Caleb.

"Gather what you have and meet me in the conference room. I have a new lead."

Ben and Eddie were waiting for him when he entered, a stack of files on the table.

"Okay, before I give what I have, start a chart, Eddie." He tossed him a white-board marker.

Going through the files and sorting through the chain of evidence, a clear picture was emerging. They had one murder now they were sure were linked to the break-ins, possibly the second one.

Caleb stood back and studied the board. "We need to add Eric to that list. I think you'll find he was involved as well. He and David were pretty thick over the years, both into petty theft."

Ben and Eddie looked and then nodded. Eddie added the name.

"Walk me through it, Ben."

Ben walked them through what they had, the evidence they gathered.

"Okay. Now comes the fun part. You both love puzzles, I know. Give me your speculations and guesses and hunches. Eddie, you make a separate list."

They brainstormed for a while. Then Caleb walked to the board, took the marker from Eddie, and wrote one name down. The two men stared at it, stared at Caleb, and then stared at each other.

"It has to be Hannah again," Ben said and watched as Caleb smiled and nodded. "Where does she come up with these names? She was bang on with Laycee and Joshua. You didn't know, Eddie, that Hannah gave us a link to solve that case too."

"I know. It's a God thing she has going." Caleb smiled. "And I hope that God thing never stops.

"Eddie, it's your task to do leg work around town. Be cautious. He's had people killed. I don't want to attend an official police funeral.

"Ben, use your resources. But be as careful as you can. Having been in this town for so many years, who knows who he has in his pocket. Talk to your federal contacts. This will likely become a federal case for the smuggling, but we have murders and kidnappings on our books."

Both men left. Caleb studied the boards, pulled out his phone and snapped pictures of them, and then reached to wipe them clean. It would stay with just the three of them for now.

He stood and stared at the clean boards. "Lord," he prayed, "let this be the answer. Help us to solve this mystery. We need to find those two and soon. There needs to be healing in the families and in the town. With things unsolved, we just can't do that."

He turned. Liam was standing in the doorway behind him. Caleb went towards him and then directed him to the street. He needed time with his friend and his friend definitely needed time with him. Prayer would be the order of the day. The desk officer nodded as he left.

****

Leith stirred once more, eyes slowly opening. He didn't remember being awake before. Once again he studied the room. As his gaze moved around he saw Regan. He rolled to hands and knees, waiting for the spinning to stop, and then crawled over to her. He reached out a hand and breathed a sigh of relief. She was alive.

He sat back down and stared around, his mind working. How were they to get out of there? It looked a lot more solid than the last place. He stood, staggered as he caught his balance and then began a desperate search for an opening to get out. It was a solid room. He would never be able to chip through the wood, even if he had an axe, and he was pretty sure there wouldn't be one in the room. There was no garbage laying around this one. Whoever had set it up had made sure of that this time. The partitioned room had a toilet and sink. Leith stood at the doorway of that room and looked around. There was a fireplace at one end and cabinets on the wall. It looked like a cabin someone had been using over the winter, given the supply of logs stacked there. He searched the cupboards and they had been stripped of everything. He stopped by the windows. They had been boarded up but he just might be able to get one open. He checked. They had been nailed shut.

He heard a soft moan behind him and turned. Regan was stirring. He dropped back down beside her.

Regan moved, her head hurting with that movement. Where was she? It didn't feel like her bed. Her eyes moved and she focused. Leith's face swam into her view. She reached for his hand.

"Oh, thank God. You're awake. I don't know what I thought when I saw you earlier."

Leith studied her. "You were awake earlier?" At her nod, he spoke. "We need to try a find a way out of here. Are you up for that?"

She sat up slowly, finding this time there was no dizziness. "That I am." She thought a moment. "The two men were here. I know one of them but I can't think of his name."

"You know one of them?" At her nod, he looked around. "Okay. First we leave this place. Then we figure out how to get back home. Caleb will be able to help."

Both of them searched the room again. Regan finally stood in the centre and looked helplessly around.

"There is just no way, Leith. No way out. And I'm afraid that they will be back before we can escape."

"I'm going to find away." He stopped and searched the ceiling. Something had caught his eye. He moved towards the end where the sectioned off area was. "See there?" He pointed. "There, up in that corner. That's not a log. That's just plywood. And it looks as if it's been wet many times. That will soften it. I think if I can get it out, the hole will be big enough."

He pointed to the door. "Listen over there. If you hear anything, call."

Regan positioned herself by the door, and then watched, heart in throat, as Leith climbed logs to the area he was interested in.

He pushed and felt the wood give a bit. He looked down at Regan and she shook her head. He pushed again and this time wood fell away. He kept pushing and twisting, hanging on by his one elbow. Then the rest of the wood fell away. He was right.

Regan would have no trouble getting out and he was sure he could get out by twisting and turning.

He dropped back to the floor and motioned Regan over. Whispering to her what he wanted to do, he took another search through the room. Feeling way back into a drawer, his hand touched something. He managed to pull it forward. A kitchen knife. Not real sharp but he was taking it with him.

Leith sent Regan up the wall, watching to make sure she didn't fall. She wiggled her way through and he heard a soft sound as she dropped to the ground. He wasted no time in scaling the wall and then dropping down beside her. The forest was a lot closer this time, just feet away. He grabbed for her hand and pulled her with him. A soft sound came to him and he spun, knife held ready. A dog appeared and he breathed a little easier. It was Betsy. Somehow she had followed and found them. He called her to them and then waited. No other sounds.

Then they heard the sound of a motor approaching. They needed to run but where? Leith grasped Regan's hand and turned into the forest. They were on a path they could follow for a while but they would need to find something else. He wasn't sure what kind of shape either one of them was in to keep running. Betsy followed at their heels, ears turned back and listening. She would warn them of danger. He needed to remember to thank her owner in a tangible way.

****

The King stepped out of the car and stretched. Finally, those two were locked up and he would be able to deal with them. Tonight would be it.

He motioned to the Knight who had been driving and sent him to unlock the door. The door swung open and hit the wall. The King stepped through. It was empty. The Knight followed and stared, mouth falling open. He strode to the bathroom area. Empty. He spun. They had been here six hours ago. Now they were gone.

The King's rage was intense. Not again. Not again. He was out of patience with everyone.

The Knight looked at him. "They were here. The door's locked. There is no way they could have gotten out."

"Well they did. You're responsible. Find them or you too will pay the price." Human lives no longer mattered to him.

The Knight searched the cabin and as his eyes raised, he saw the opening that Leith had created. Admiration for his determination to survive swept through him. He was a worthy opponent but one that would also succumb to his power.

The King swept from the room and back to the vehicle. The Knight closed the door and looked around. He would be back. He would get his gear and be back to track them. This time, they wouldn't make it back alive.

Leith could feel Regan starting to lag.   He looked around for a spot for them to rest.

"Over there."   He pointed.   He led her to a shaded area and helped her down.   "Betsy will watch for us."

Regan rested her head on her knees.   "I can't go on, Leith.   I just don't have enough left to go on."

He was breathing heavy too.   "We'll rest and then go on.   We'll move slower.   I think we're far enough away that we'll be okay.   If it was them, chances are they aren't prepared to come in after us. They will have to go away and come back.   Thing is, I just don't know how long that will take."

Regan raised her head and looked at him. "Still being the hawk, are you?   You're watching for game, just like a hawk."

He smiled.   That seemed to be her word for him.

"Okay.   So what is that I see, Leith?   There." She looked around.   "That looks like it's in the south. Isn't that the tower from town, the one they used to have the bells in."

He squinted, then nodded.   "It looks like it but it's so far away."   He looked around and then pulled her to her feet.   "Come on. We need to keep moving."

She reluctantly moved with him.   "We need to find some water.   There won't be anything to eat out here."

He nodded. "We will. Let's get as far as we can tonight. Maybe we'll be lucky and find someone we know."

Regan hesitated before speaking. "I don't know, Leith. How do we know who to trust? I know that voice. I just can't place it."

"It will come," he reassured her.

****

The Knights returned to the cabin. They had gathered what they needed. With first light, they would be on the search. This time, their prey would not escape. They did have admire their tenacity though, getting out of two locked buildings. But time was now of the essence. The King was very unhappy and he had let them know in no uncertain terms he wanted the situation dealt with. They didn't need to ask but they knew he was rolling up his business in town and getting ready to move on. To move with him, they needed to succeed.

****

Caleb moved quietly around the house, trying not to awaken any of his family. He couldn't sleep. His mind was trying to sort through so much information. He needed to think and couldn't.

He stepped outside and stopped. A dark figure sat on his deck. From the bit of light that was shining, he could see who it was and it was not who he expected.

He moved over and sat in silence. The silence continued but he made no effort to break it.

Finally the figure spoke. "I know where they are. And I know why. Can you help me if I help you?"

235

Caleb studied the figure. "You should have come to me before, Mark. Two of your friends are dead. What do you know?"

Mark Bell's head dropped. "I know. I wasn't here when that happened. Dad had me away at school." Mark's voice continued in a quiet manner as he detailed what he knew. Almost all of it, Caleb knew already.

"You say you know where they are?"

Mark nodded and gave an address.

Caleb stopped him. "No, Mark, that's not right. There is no such address and you know it. I want you to go with the officer standing behind you."

Mark jerked and looked around, a defeated look on his face. The officer helped him to his feet and walked away

Caleb sighed. Now what? This had the feeling of a set-up to get information. They had now brought it directly to his home and he didn't like it.

Morning came, and Caleb headed for Liam's house. He wasn't there and Caleb knew he had gone back to his work. He tracked him down in his office, asked some questions, and then left.

Liam's eyes followed Caleb as he walked away. What was the meaning of those questions?

Laycee appeared in his doorway next. She had come to spend time with him, and her work came with her. She settled down in a corner of his office and was soon engrossed in what she needed to accomplish with the therapy group she had been asked to lead. Joshua, she said, had gone to work as well. All of them felt they were in a holding pattern, a waiting game.

Liam looked down at his work. He needed to concentrate on the detailed drawing he was making and he just couldn't. He reached instead for his Bible.

****

Leith stirred in the dawning light. He listened and heard nothing. He looked at Regan who was still sleeping. He hadn't got much sleep, trying to keep watch, but his eyes had finally closed and he had slept. Betsy had crept between them, her body warmth spreading to both. She lay with her chin on his arm, intelligent brown eyes watching him. She was making him think twice about a dog. Maybe, when this was all over, he would look into one. He loved his sister's, Sheltie, Defiant, but had never really given much thought to a dog of his own. He sat up, thinking through the day They were getting closer to home but he needed to somehow find a food source for them. Water they could find but had nothing to carry it with them.

He reached over Betsy and roused Regan. She rubbed her eyes as she sat up. She was pale and tired and he could see her strength was waning. He needed to take care of her and he had no idea how that was even possible any more.

He grasped her hand and pulled her to her feet. With Betsy in front, they set off down the trail. Leith kept as close an eye as he could around them. He knew the dog would hear something well before he did and that warning he hoped would give them time to react and get to safety.

He looked up and asked for deliverance and safety. He still had no idea why they had been targeted but he hoped that Caleb had sorted it out.

Leith kept Regan moving as best he could, but he knew they couldn't go much further without

237

proper food. He looked around. The area was getting more familiar they more they moved towards the south. If he remembered, there was a cabin near here somewhere, and that cabin was usually stocked with food and unlocked. It belonged to an older gentleman, a friend of his father's. He studied the sky and then veered their steps more to the west. Soon, he thought, they would find the cabin.

He had been right. There it was.

"Regan," he said as he pointed. "There's old man Jones' cabin. We'll find food and water there more than likely if he still stocks it."

Regan looked at the cabin, then her gaze shot around. "How do we know it's safe?"

"Betsy. I'll let her go in ahead of us. She'll alert if anything's around. They won't harm her, if they're there. They'll want her for tracking."

Regan's eyes closed. "Please, let there be no one around. I need some food."

Betsy headed for the cabin at Leith's command. Sniffing around, she circled the cabin, then came back and faced them, tail wagging slowly. It was safe, at least for the moment.

They made their way to the building. Leith tucked Regan behind him and slowly opened the door. Betsy entered, sniffed around and came back out. Leith breathed a sigh of relief. Now, if the cabin was as he remembered it, they could get some food and get away again.

Regan sank down onto the easy chair. It felt good to sit in a chair instead of on the ground. Leith was rummaging in the cupboards and brought her some trail mix he had found.

"Eat this. I don't want to start a fire. It would give us away. I'm going to pack up some stuff to take with us."

Regan dug into her pocket and pulled out some bills. "Here. Leave this somewhere so he'll find it." Leith turned as she spoke. "I always tuck money in my pockets, just in case."

He smiled. "That's good to know. Smart thinking."

They quickly packed up what they needed in a knapsack Leith unearthed. He knew he would be able to return it at some point.

With Betsy in the lead, they once more made their way towards the south. The tower was getting closer. Now that he was in more familiar territory, he would be able to pick the trails that would move them in a quicker manner to town.

Coming to the edge of a road, Leith stopped. He could hear a car coming and drew Regan back. It was a forestry vehicle, moving slowly. Leith ducked his head to see who it was and recognized a friend. He stepped out and waved down the vehicle. A quick explanation, and they were in the vehicle on their way to town and back to their families.

The two Knights halted and watched the vehicle pull away. They had been so close, just like so many times. Another failure. How many would there be before they succeeded?

Eddie tapped at Caleb's office door and entered. Ben was already sitting there, file folders open in front of him.

"So, where do we stand now?" Caleb asked.

Ben spoke, shuffling through the papers. "I'm still waiting for some of the financial information to come back from my contact, but it looks as he's been putting money away for years overseas. It runs into the millions. There is no way he has made that much money with the legitimate business."

Eddie nodded. "That's what I'm finding too. Word is getting around on the street that if you want work, you contact him. And it's not for sweeping and cleaning. He's becoming violent. I don't know how much longer he'll stay controlled enough to be able to enter normal company."

Caleb leaned back and thought. "We need to keep up the pressure. When they searched the homes and store, did they find anything?"

Ben handed over a sheet. "This is a detailed report of what they found. Five crates had that mark and we pulled at low estimate three million just in uncut stones. They would be worth much more than that once cut and set."

Caleb whistled. "I guess that explains why the desperation. Let's keep digging." He paused as his phone rang. He dug it out and glanced at the number. The hospital. His heart sank at the thought it was one of his sons.

"Logan." He answered, a professional tone in his voice to cover his fear. As he listened, his eyes widened and his gaze shot to the two men sitting in front of them. Ben and Eddie both straightened, knowing something was happening. "Thank you. We're on our way."

Caleb returned his phone to his pocket as his eyes slid shut in thanks. Opening them, he gesturing for the two to follow him. Without a word, they locked up the files and then ran for the door.

Once in Caleb's vehicle, he turned. "That was the hospital. Leith and Regan were found about an hour ago by a forestry worker. They're safe. He took them to the hospital."

"They're safe but we still need to arrange protection until we can bring that fellow down," Ben commented. "It's going to be very hard to do that."

Eddie nodded in agreement. "We'll come up with a plan. Thing is, how long do we have and will he try again?"

"You can be sure he'll try again." Caleb pulled into the parking at the hospital and turned off his vehicle. "We need to be ready. Before we go in, let's take a minute. Ben, keep pushing those financials. Eddie, keep working the streets. I'll arrange for protection for them, but I have a feeling Regan's Dad is already taking that step. Our job will be to bring this investigation to as quick a close as we can."

Caleb strode into the Emergency Department followed by Ben and Eddie. Eddie headed for the waiting room where the families had gathered. Right now, he would be the protection they needed. Who knew what the next step would be and he had a bad feeling that the families would become a target.

Caleb stopped and spoke with the clerk and then headed further back. He motioned Ben to where Regan was and he stepped into the room where Leith was laying on the stretcher. He stopped beside his friend and watched his face. Leith's eyes were closed. The trauma of the last few days was written on his face in the mud, the scratches, the bruises. He could see the fatigue in the gauntness of his face, the dark circles under his eyes. He raised his eyes and traced the IV line running to Leith's wrist. Questioning could wait. Leith needed to sleep.

He stepped out of the room and found Ben waiting, two officers standing behind him. Caleb motioned for them to take positions at the doorways and then moved away with Ben.

"How is she?"

"Rough. They had a pretty bad time of it I would say. She didn't say much, but she is angry. I'll question her later on what happened. How's Leith?"

"He's sleeping right now. He's in rough shape I would say. The doctors are keeping them overnight?"

"That's my understanding. You'll want men posted the whole time, I gather."

Caleb nodded. "Absolutely. We'll need to get some answers from them and then work from there. The families are in the waiting room?"

"Yes. Eddie's with them. They may well become a target if these two can't be reached. It's going to be a real fine line we have to tread."

"Don't I know it."

After spending a night in hospital, both Leith and Regan were discharged. Caleb was waiting for them as they came through the lobby, surrounded by their families. He looked up at the ceiling, then back down to them.

"Okay, this is what we're doing." He glanced up, eyes narrowing as he studied a man standing near the coffee shop. Word was out and he knew he had to race against time to protect these two. "You're not going to your home, only long enough for you to collect what you need. These officers will be going with you," as he indicated the officers standing beside them. "Your families will be tucked away somewhere as well. Neither one of you will be safe until this ends and I want it to end well."

Leith started to protest but Caleb cut him off. "I have taken the liberty of speaking with the homeowner. He understands the situation and is adamant that he wants you safe and sound. He told me he couldn't find another two tile setters he would work with." A small smile cracked Caleb's face. "I agree with him."

Regan stood in her bedroom and looked around. She had gathered up what she needed but she wasn't ready to leave. Her mother came up behind her, turned her around and hugged her. The family had been through so much tragedy in the last few weeks. Regan's tears soaked her mother's sweater, then with a final hug, she stepped back.

"I'll be okay, Mom," she whispered. "I'll be okay."

Her mother reached and tucked auburn hair away from Regan's eyes. "I know, baby, I know, but I just want you here. I understand." Her mother then clasped her hands with Regan's and bowed, asking for guidance, wisdom and protection.

"You be safe, Mom, you and Dad. I couldn't bear it if something happened to you."

Regan turned, grabbed her knapsack, and descended the stairs to where her father stood. A quick hug and Ben had whisked her out the door. He studied the area, confident they weren't being watched, tucked Regan in his car, and pulled away. Now to take the next step.

Liam stood and watched his brother's back. Leith looked beat up and tired, but determined. Laycee stood beside him, hand on her mouth and tears in her eyes, Joshua's arm around her.

Leith said not a word, didn't go near his family. This was unusual for him. They were close and never left one another without a word or a hug. As he passed Liam, Liam's hand on his shoulder stopped him. He waited until with a soft grip, Liam's dropped his hand. Laycee's hand reached for his, he clasped it quickly and then walked out to where Caleb was waiting, determination in each step. This had hit at his home and his friends and he would stop at nothing to end it.

Caleb watched Leith walk towards him and noted the change in him. He nodded. His friend was ready to fight, and he would help him. Now to get him to safety.

****

The King glared at the one Knight standing in front of him. "YOU IMBECILE!" he yelled. "How did they get away from you again? Are you that incompetent?"

The Knight stared back, no longer afraid. "No, we are not that incompetent. We have being doing our very best. Someone had to be helping them escape, that is the only explanation."

"If that's the case, then who is it and where is he? Find him and bring him to me." The voice shook crystal on the shelves and rattled vases sitting on display.

The Knight turned and left, this time without being dismissed. Was it really worth it, this job? He hadn't been part of the murders but he would bear a penalty the same. He really had to think this through. He heard the sound of breaking glass from behind the door and was glad he was not in that room.

Regan dropped her bag on the bed in the room she had been assigned and looked around. It was a small room, with a bed, dresser, and easy chair along with the table by the bed. There was a small closet beside her and when she walked over to the door on the opposite wall, it opened up into a small compact bathroom. She laid her head on the door frame. That was such a blessing. She so needed to get clean but first she needed to find Leith, to make sure he was okay. She left the room and headed down the hall to the kitchen.

Caleb and Ben turned as she came in and hesitated.

"Come on in, Regan. Ben's got some soup and sandwiches ready. You need to eat and then get some sleep."

She nodded but made no move to walk forward. "Where's Leith?"

"He's getting settled." Caleb studied her, walked over to her and turned her around. "Food can wait. You're almost asleep on your feet. Go. Get some sleep. We'll talk when you awake."

Caleb watched as she walked back down the hall, one hand out to touch the wall and keep her balanced. He shook his head. He so wanted to find the man responsible for the whole situation. He turned back to kitchen and met Ben's eyes. Both knew that they weren't done and who knew what the next few days would bring.

"I'm going to check on Leith," Ben said as he passed him. "I thought he would be out here by now."

Ben returned. "He's asleep. The best thing for those two. I can't even begin to imagine what they've been through."

Caleb nodded from where he sat at the table. "I know. God protected them for sure." He sighed, then continued, "What do we have? Any closer?"

Ben shook his head. "No. I've pulled everything I have. It's not enough. We don't have enough for a warrant to search the premises, let alone arrest him."

Caleb ran his hand through his hair. "We'll need to come up with something. We have to end this in the next few days. Those two can't take much more."

Ben agreed, then was silent as they ate. They would be there for the duration as well. Their families understood.

It was early evening before Leith finally surfaced. He looked around and then remembered. They were still trapped, trapped at the whim of the maniac after them. Until he was found, they wouldn't be free or safe. He let his head drop back on the bed. He had to come up with a plan to succeed, only he had no idea who he needed to succeed against. He was here, cut off from his family at a time he needed them. He rose, grabbed a quick shower and clean clothes and headed to find something to eat.

Caleb turned from the counter where he had been making a mug of tea. Leith stared at him and then turned to get some coffee.

"There're sandwiches in the fridge. Soup is hot on the stove."

Leith nodded his thanks as he grabbed some food and then sat at the worn table in the kitchen. He had no idea where he was but God did. God provided another tower for them to hide in. Please, God, let this be it. Let this tower protect.

Caleb set his mug on the table across from him and pulling out a chair, sat.

"How's Regan?" Leith asked.

"She's still sleeping. I checked on her a while ago. She may well sleep through the night."

Caleb studied his friend. "What aren't you telling me?"

Leith paused in his chewing and then continued to eat. How could he explain his feelings and his thoughts? They were still so muddled in his mind, they didn't make sense.

"I'm so muddled in my thoughts, Caleb, I don't know where to begin. I gave you my statement but I feel like I'm missing something."

Caleb stood, grabbed a pad of paper and a pen and sat back down. "Start talking. Just talk. I'll write. We can sort through it later. Start with your day away."

Leith began talking and Caleb began writing. Page after page was turned. Finally, Leith stopped, exhausted. He laid his head on his crossed arms and almost sobbed.

"I couldn't stop them. I couldn't protect her."

Caleb watched, sympathy on his face. "We can't always. That's what we are trying to do now. Let me go through what you said here and we'll see what we have that's added to what you first gave us."

"Let me help." A voice from the door caught their attention. Regan stood there, then came and sank down in another chair at the table. Leith arose and found food and coffee for her, placing them in front of her.

"Let me tell what I remember. There will be differences. Maybe combining the two will help."

Caleb again filled page after page of notes. When Regan stopped, he looked up. "Okay. I'm going to find Ben."

Leith reached for Regan's hand and touched it. She drew back. She stood and with her back to him said, "No, Leith. I can't." Sobs in her voice rocked him as he watched her run from the room and heard the sound of her door closing. Hands on the back of his neck, he looked up and then back down. This had to end.

Early the next morning, an exhausted Caleb sat back. He and Ben had spent the night going through the pages they had. It was making sense. It was giving them more and more information that would help them to stop this.

"Do you think Regan will remember who the voice is?" Ben questioned.

"In a way, I hope she does. In a way, I hope she doesn't. That's a dangerous spot for her. If somehow word gets out, that it's done for her. Her family will likely suffer too." Caleb stood and paced. "I just don't know, Ben. I just don't know. Guess I'm getting too tired."

"Go grab some sleep. We have men here to watch."

"Thanks. Wake me in a couple of hours."

Leith grabbed another mug of coffee and sat back down at the table, lost in thought. He startled at a hand on his shoulder and looked up.

Eddie stood there, then moved to grab a mug of his own. He sat back down at the table and watched Leith. He could the exhaustion and strain in his face.

"What's up, Leith?"

Leith shook his head. "Nothing."

Eddie smiled, then spoke, "No, something is up other than why you're here. What is it?"

Leith looked up and then said, "It's Regan. I just don't understand."

Eddie smiled again and said, "She's a woman. You're not meant to understand. Seriously though, she's been through a lot in the last few weeks. Abducted twice, taking on a new job after moving home, losing an uncle and then a cousin. Give her time."

Leith shook his head. "I can but I just don't want to lose her again."

"What do you mean, again?"

"She left 10 years ago as soon as we graduated. I was getting ready to ask her out and then she was gone. Now she's back and more beautiful than ever, not just in looks. She's working for me and I have to be so careful. This isn't how I planned it 10 years ago."

Eddie laughed and Leith looked at him in surprise. "Nothing ever goes as we plan it, you should know that, Leith. God is the author of our days, not us." He paused and studied his hands. "I'm going to tell you a story from long ago. Just listen, okay. One day there was a young man in love with a beautiful young woman. They were friends but he wanted her to be a permanent part of his life. She suddenly left town without saying why. He was hurt. When she returned a couple of years later, he tried to get close and she wouldn't let him. Finally, he was able to break through the barriers she had erected around herself, find out what was going on. Their love grew and they married and started a family. It was not an easy road they chose to walk, but God led them through each twist and turn."

Leith studied Eddie and listened as he spoke. "So what are you saying?"

"Give her time. Be her friend. Treat her with care and respect. Stay within the boundaries she has set up to protect her heart. The day will come when she will talk to you and you to her. You're still young. You've got time." Eddie rose and went to set his mug in the sink. As he walked by Leith, his hand came out and he laid it on Leith's black hair as if in a benediction. "Those two young people I told you about? You know them very well. They were your parents."

Leith spun to stare after Eddie. He had never known that. He wondered if Liam or Laycee did, but doubted it. His parents never spoke of early days. He knew Eddie and his parents had been long time friends but didn't know he had history of them the family had never known. He would need to get to know Eddie better.

Caleb stopped at the department. He needed to get a sense of what else was going on. He stopped and spoke with each officer, finding out where they stood in their duties, and offering words of encouragement.

Entering his office, he sank wearily into his chair and looked at the paperwork his secretary had stacked there for him. He reached for the top folder and dug in to clear as much as he could. He needed sleep but this needed to be done before that.

Hours later he looked up at a tap at his door. Hannah stood there. She walked over to him and into his embrace. Hugging him for a minute, she then leaned back.

"You're tired, Caleb."

He nodded. "I am. I'm also....also...." He stopped, at a loss for words.

Hannah laughed. "It's not often that you can't express yourself. Here, take this. Read it after I'm gone." With a quick kiss, she left.

With a sense of foreboding, Caleb shut his office door and sat down again. He studied the piece of notepaper his wife had handed him. He closed his eyes and opened them again. It was still there. Wishful thinking wouldn't make it disappear.

He slowly unfolded it and read the name she gave him. His eyes closed. Not who he expected. He searched the room, looking for answers or a way to stop the insane ride they all were on. Nothing was there. He reached over to the paper shredder and watched as the paper disappeared. For now, the name remained with him.

He bent back to his paperwork, the name running through his mind. Once he had cleared his desk, he stood. He was headed home for a while and then back to the house where they had stashed Leith and Regan.

****

The King stood once again in front of the window, hands behind his back. His empire was crumbling faster than he thought possible. He had lost underlings and he didn't even know if he could still trust his Knights. His sources on the street were either no longer available to him or could not or would not give him much information. He needed to find those two and eliminate them. But where were they? They had made it back alive and now were hidden. He couldn't get to their families, they too had been hidden away. Somehow, some way, he would succeed.

****

Leith was tired. He was tired of running. He was tired of hiding. He was tired of not knowing who or why. Caleb and Ben weren't saying much and the officers guarding them were tight-lipped. He turned to watch Regan. She was showing the strain but had found a library tucked away in a room and had curled up in a chair to read. The sunlight reflected off her auburn hair and turned highlights to gold. He reached for paper. He might as well put some of his design thoughts down. Had it only been that short a time since they had wandered through that town, laughing and plotting designs? He was soon engrossed in his work.

253

He looked up as he heard the door and Caleb and Ben walked in. The serious look on their faces made his heart rise to his throat and then plummet. His first thought was that something had happened to Liam or Laycee.

"Leith, can you join us here?" Caleb asked.

He sank down on the couch near Laycee's chair. She had lowered her book and was staring at the two. He could see that she was thinking the same as he had.

Caleb stood in front of the fireplace and warmed his hands at the low fire burning. Ben had gone to stand in the kitchen door.

Caleb turned, leaned his arm on the mantle and rested his head for a minute. Raising his head, his eyes searched the two in front of him.

"We have made some progress. Not enough yet to let you go home or for your families to go home. I'm not telling you where they are and they don't know where you are." He paused, drew in a breath before continuing. "I have been given a name and I want to give it to you. Think very carefully before you respond. I will not tell you how I got it. Before you respond to it, again think over your dealings with this person."

He studied them again as he waited. They exchanged puzzled glances and then returned their eyes to him.

"George White."

Leith's eyebrows drew together as he mulled over that name. He remembered him from his high school class but hadn't seen him since graduation. He had no idea if George was still in town.

Regan's gasped, drawing all eyes to her. "That's him." She turned to Leith. "That's the voice

I heard. Oh, no!" Hands flew to her mouth and she paled. "He was friends with David. Did he have something to do with David's death?"

Caleb crouched before her and reached for her hands. "We don't know, Regan. We don't know. We are trying to locate George but he has hidden himself well over the years. We'll find him."

Regan's eyes filled with tears and she reached for some tissue.

"What can you tell about him?" Caleb keen eyes searched her face, taking in the shock that she had just received.

"Sit, Caleb." She motioned for him to sit down. "I have a tale to tell and may be if I had told it earlier nothing would have happened."

She hesitated, then stopped. "I can't, I just can't." She sprang from her chair and ran to her room, shutting the door behind her.

Leith stood as if to go after her, then hesitated. Anguished eyes met Caleb's sympathetic ones.

"Let her go, Leith. She needs time."

"So what are you not telling me?"

"George has always been outside the law, you will agree? For the last five to seven years, we have known contraband has been sliding through our town. George was fingered as one to watch. He has pretty much disappeared and yet the smuggling continues. Small stuff that's easy to hide, but which brings in a lot of money. We know there is someone here is town masterminding it but we don't have the proof we need. We're getting close."

Ben spoke up. "What you two have dug up for us through your adventures has helped. I don't think you realize how much information you two stored away. Impressions, voices, etc."

Leith shook his head. "I don't care about that. I care about her and I want her safe."

"So do we, Leith. So do we. Her family and your family want you both safe and that's what we're trying to do. In the next day or so, we will have to move you both again, just because this may be a compromised site."

Leith looked up at that. "So you're saying you have a mole in your department?"

Caleb shook his head. "No. But there is more traffic than normal coming here. Someone will notice and say something to someone who will say something to someone else, and the snowball starts and doesn't stop."

Ben added, "By tomorrow, we'll have another place ready for you and you'll move. Your families are safe."

Leith leaned back. "I am so tired of it all."

Caleb and Ben had to agree. They would be glad when everything was back to as normal as it ever got.

****

Liam turned from the window he had been looking out and sighed. He wanted his life back, he wanted his family to have their lives back. He watched Laycee as she paced, frustration in her every move.

"When, Liam? When do we get to go home?"

"I don't know, Laycee. Soon I hope. I just pray that Leith and Regan are okay. We're not getting told to protect all of us."

Laycee stopped her pacing and rested her gaze on him. Then her shoulders dropped as she gave into the thought. "I know. I really do know. I just wish…" She let her voice drop away. They both wished for the same thing.

Joshua stood watching them both, hurting for them and in particular for his fiancee. He knew she was really hurting and was learning how to trust God in a whole new way. He was too. He reached for her and gathered her close. His eyes met Liam's over her head and they agreed. Whatever it took, they would do to bring their families back together.

Morning came, and Regan zipped up the backpack, checking to make sure she had everything. Caleb was moving them again and she had no idea where. She was tired and just wanted her own bed. Who knew when that would happen?

She entered the living room and stood, dejection in her manner. Leith's heart broke as he watched her. He so wanted to protect her and sooth her worries, but he couldn't. He just couldn't.

Caleb came in through the door, phone to his ear. Ben stood waiting in the kitchen doorway, Eddie on the porch. Caleb finished his call and then pocketed his phone. His keen eyes searched the group and then turned to watch the outdoors. He didn't feel right about this. Something felt all wrong. He had learned to trust his instincts.

Ben caught his eye and motioned with his head. Caleb and he stood in the kitchen talking. The others couldn't hear what was being said but knew something was up.

Caleb returned to the room.

"This is what we're going to do. Leith and Regan, you're with Ben. Stay tight with him.

"Eddie, we need to clear this place, to return it to what it was. That's your job." Caleb stared at him.

Eddie stared back, then caught on to what Caleb was meaning. He nodded. "No problem."

"Let's go, people."

Leith and Regan slid into Ben's car and he drove away. A couple of miles down the road he turned onto the side road and then continued for just a couple of more miles. He pulled off into a laneway and waited. The car was hidden from view. About 30 minutes later, a black car passed them going in the same direction as they had been headed. Ben pulled back onto the road and returned the way he had come, back to the cabin. Caleb and Eddie were waiting.

Ben rolled down his window. "Black Lexus, this is the plate and year."

Caleb drew a deep breath and looked over the car at Eddie. "You were right. We have a leak somewhere."

Regan and Leith exchanged glances. A leak and who? Where their families safe?

Ben turned in his seat. "Guess you heard, eh? We're down to just us three looking after you two. We'll keep you safe."

Regan spoke. "Get me a gun."

Leith turned to stare at her as did the others.

"Get me a gun. I have a permit to carry but don't have my gun with me. Get me a gun. I'm trained."

"Very interesting, young lady." Ben's tone was amused. "And when were you planning on telling us something we already knew?"

Regan smiled. "I gathered you did. It's not something I like to talk about. Things happened and I needed to break away from that. I'm still not sure I can shoot someone."

"If we need to, we will." Caleb looked around. "For now, we need to get you out of sight. This place has been compromised as well, from what Eddie says."

Eddie held up the bag he was holding. "Bugs and not the kind that bite."

Leith laid his head back on the seat. "I hope you guys know what you're doing because it sure is beginning to feel like you're 10 steps behind."

Caleb leaned down to look through the window. "We do. Ben is taking you down the road to another vehicle and then we're off, just like Dorothy in the Wizard."

Regan shook her head. "Caleb, your age is showing. Are you reading that to your boys or spending time watching it?"

Caleb laughed at her and then hit the roof of the car for Ben to move off. He and Eddie stood watching.

"I have a bad feeling, boss," Eddie commented.

"I know. So do I."

Ben turned into an older home in a part of town they were not familiar with. He hit the remote to open the garage and then closed the door once the car was inside. He turned.

"Being in town brings a few new rules. This place has been closed up looking for years. It has been kept that way, as if the owner is just away on vacation. It is clean inside although the furniture is sparse. We have you on the main floor, just for safety's sake. When we go inside, I will run you through the escape routes we have set up. Learn them. Your life may well depend on them."

Regan's frightened eyes met Leith's. They still weren't safe. Why was God letting this happen? The faith she had depended on for her bedrock of life felt like it was starting to slip.

Leith took her hand as they entered the house, his grip strong and steady. They followed Ben as he took them through what they needed to know. He really hoped they never did need to use them, but somehow someone kept finding them.

For now they would be safe. But for how long?

****

Eddie tapped, then entered Caleb's office, closing the door. Caleb looked up and at Eddie's nod, his eyes slid shut. He had been afraid of this and had hoped it wasn't true. Eddie had confirmed their suspicions.

"All right, Eddie. You know what to do."

Eddie left and then returned with the department's younger secretary, Susan. Caleb studied her and then indicated she should have a seat.

Susan sat and waited. She shifted uncomfortably as the silence grew.

"Why, Susan? Why the betrayal?" Caleb voice was soft and composed, belying the anger that raged inside him.

"Why, what, Chief? I don't know what you're talking about."

Eddie bent over her shoulder from behind and starting laying documents and notes down into her hands. Her face paled as she saw each one, saw that they had tracked her through everything she had done in the last year.

"Why, Susan?"

Her rage exploded. "I never get the credit for my research. I never get acknowledged. This is a dead end job with no room to grow. I want more from life. I want more, just more."

"You knew when you hired on what the job entailed." Caleb stopped and then stood. "We are going to spare you the humiliation of being incarcerated in this jail. Eddie will take you to the conference room. Your purse and jacket are there. From there, officers from Oak City will escort you to their jail. You will be arraigned first on federal charges of smuggling, and then the list of charges will grow."

"You'll never find who you're looking for. He's too well hidden." She spit the words at him.

"We already know, Susan, we already know. Our case is just about built."

She stopped, shocked at the words. Before she could say anything else, Eddie escorted her away in a quiet manner that drew no attention.

Caleb sat back down and rubbed his neck. Eddie came back and shut the door, handing Caleb a mug of tea as he sat down in a chair in front of the desk.

"We'll need a cover story. She can't just disappear without someone asking."

Caleb nodded. "I hate this part of the job, Eddie, finding out one of our own is involved. It leaves a bitter, bitter taste."

"That it does. I just hope she's the only one. It would really hurt if she isn't."

"You've delved into her background?"

"I have. There were no red flags at first until I started more digging. She had been married, divorced and was using her maiden name. Her married name is Brand. Husband was Eric. She had hidden that well. It's almost as if she had help at the court house to do so."

"Now that's a scary thought, Eddie. I don't even want to think about that one."

"Me neither, Chief. Listen I'm headed off the night. Take some time too. Ben will call if he needs us."

"I intend to spend some time at home with Hannah and the boys. Ben will give an update later. Have a good night."

Eddie raised his hand as he left.

Caleb stretched and then closed and locked away the files he had been working on. He didn't need anyone seeing the case until he was ready for them. After Susan's betrayal, his trust level just wasn't there. He turned the light out in his office, caught up his briefcase and made his way out of the department.

Regan stretched and then reached for her Bible. All was quiet in the house. She didn't know how Ben kept going, being the only one. She just so wanted to see her parents and couldn't. Soon, she hoped, and she opened her Bible to read through favourite passage of comfort.

Leith stood at the counter, restlessly tapping his finger as he waited for the coffee. He was getting frustrated at no activity. He wanted to go back to his life. He wanted to see what would happen with Regan, who he wanted as a permanent part of his life.

Ben grabbed the coffee pot from in front of him. "If you snooze, you lose, boy?"

Leith laughed and held out his mug. "Here, you pour. You've got the pot."

Ben laughed as well. "Caleb says he found our leak at the department. They are hopeful that it's only the one."

Leith turned and looked at him, eyes moving over as he saw Regan in the doorway. "Who was it?"

Ben shook his head. "Not telling. You'll find out when we get it all sorted out. In the meanwhile, he's afraid this place has been compromised as well. Drink your coffee and then grab your stuff. He's lining up another place."

Regan turned. "No, no coffee for me. I can't handle it. I can't handle another move."

Leith turned to go after her. Ben's hand on his arm stopped him. "Be patient with her, Leith. She's hurting in ways neither one of us can imagine."

Leith nodded and then followed Regan. He stood at the door watching her pack.

"I'm tired of it too, Regan. I want time with my family. I want my life back, to go back to the quiet tasks of planning and laying tile. We'll get there. We just need…"

She turned and her anger flared. "We just need what, Leith? Just what is it?"

The sound of a breaking door and Ben's surprised yell startled them. Leith grabbed for Regan's hand and pulled her down the hall to the back bedroom. He shut and locked the door, then turned finger on her mouth. "Quiet. We need to get away. Come on." He led her to the closet and then pushed on the panel Ben had shown them. Shoving her through, he slid the panel back into place. It was very dark and he didn't a light. He caught her hand and pulled her down the steps and then along a low damp space. Ben had thought it might have been from smugglers long ago as they were close to the river. He had no idea where it would come out but he wasn't waiting around to find out who was there. He said a quick prayer for Ben that he was all right.

"There are boards, Leith. Is it safe to move them?"

Leith stopped and listened, then carefully pulled one away, then a second one. He pulled her with him. They were in a shed, Leith figured at the back of the property. He cautiously pulled the door open and peeked out. So far, so good. He crept out, Regan right behind him. They followed the wall until they could reach the back fence and then push out the boards Ben had told them would move. They went on as silent feet as they could towards the next street.

Sirens sounded behind them. Help was on the way but they wouldn't go back. They had to move forward. A sound in front of them stopped them and they looked up. A black-garbed man stood in front of them, arm raised, revolver pointed at them. Leith pushed Regan aside and leapt for the gunmen. A muffled sound and Leith fell. Regan screamed and ran towards him. Another sound and she was down.

The gunman walked forward and stood over them, then turned and walked away. The Knight had completed his task. The job was ended and he could go on with his life.

****

Caleb shoved the door to his car open and revolver drawn ran cautiously to the open door of the house, Eddie at his heels. Scanning the area, they moved into the house, officers spreading out to surround it. Caleb's heart sank when he saw Ben's crumpled form. Eddie stooped and then nodded. Ben was alive. They quickly cleared the house. There was no sign of Leith or Regan.

Caleb stared around, then turned to Eddie. "There's an escape route. If I remember, it ends at the shed. Come on."

The two turned and raced for the backyard, praying they were in time. Sudden shouts sounded from the other side of the fence and then gunfire. Their hearts were in their mouths as they pushed through the fence and ran down the road.

Caleb skidded to a stop. Two forms lay close together, almost touching. Raising his eyes, he could see officers handcuffing a man in black. Caleb approached the two bodies. Leith and Regan. "Please Lord, let us be in time."

Eddie has bending over Regan. "She's alive but just barely."

Caleb felt for a pulse. "Leith is alive too. Get the paramedics in here."

Caleb stood back and watched as the paramedics worked on his two friends. Movement beside him made his turn. Ben was standing there, bandage on his head.

"You should be at the hospital, Ben."

Ben shook his head and then grimaced. "Not until they go. Not until then." He squinted against the light. "Eddie says they got the gun man."

Caleb nodded. "George White."

Ben thought about that and then said, "It fits with him. It really does." He stopped as more commotion came from where Leith and Regan lay. Leith had been moved to a stretcher and being wheeled to a waiting ambulance. The paramedics were frantically working on Regan and Caleb's heart fell when he saw the paramedics desperately trying to stop the bleeding. He prayed she made it. He watched as she was loaded onto a stretcher and raced to a waiting ambulance, as the race to save her life continued. He looked around.

Eddie was ahead of him, already in a cruiser ready to lead the rush to the hospital. Ben and Caleb stood watching, hearts in mouths, and prayers on their lips.

"Send some officers to bring their families to the hospital. Just say they've been hurt and they've been taken there. We'll deal with what we have to when we get there. Then get yourself there."

Ben nodded and walked away, shoulders slumped from more than pain. The blow to his head was hard enough to handle but knowing he hadn't be able to save them just added to his burden.

Caleb made his rounds with the investigators and crime scene team. They would be busy for a while. He knew they would get to him with what they had as soon as they could.

He turned and scanned the area, still feeling like he was being watched. It's not over yet, he though, not yet. Eyes lifting to heaven, he once again prayed for his friends.

He slid behind the wheel of his car and inserted the key into the ignition, then sat back. Something was still niggling at the back of his mind. He shrugged. It would come, he supposed, when he least expected it.

Chapter 21

Ben met Caleb outside the hospital. He had had his head examined and besides being told he had a hard head, just that he needed to rest and take his pain medications. He had no concussion. He stared ahead of him as Caleb stopped beside him, fearing the worse.

"The families are in the waiting room at the back. The officers cleared it and set up security there. It's the easier way to watch them."

"How are Leith and Regan?"

"I think they've taken Leith to surgery already. He was hit in shoulder, but they don't think it's done much damage. He's a very fortunate young man. It shouldn't affect his work once he's healed."

"And Regan?"

Ben didn't comment and Caleb's heart sunk again. "I haven't heard much, other than that she's still alive. It was really touch and go on the ride over. They almost lost her a couple of times." He paused, then turned to look at Caleb. "It just isn't fair, Caleb. A beautiful young woman like that, targeted because of some greedy crazy, and she almost dies. The bullet hit her chest, really near the heart. They're taking her to surgery, but they won't know until they get in if the heart has been damaged. She may not come through surgery, may not even make it to the Operating Room."

Caleb didn't speak. His emotions, usually under strong control, were getting the best of him. "We'll pray her through, Ben. Knowing the pastor's wife, she already has the prayer chain working."

Ben nodded towards the door. "The pastor is in there with them."

Caleb took a deep breath and faced the door. His head moved and he looked up at the sky that was starting to darken for night. "Nothing we train for ever really prepares you for this. It's been a long few days. Where's Eddie? "

"He headed back to the department. He said he wanted to make sure everything is by the book."

Caleb nodded and then stepped forward. Nothing ever prepared him for this. He would never ever get used to times like this.

He nodded at the officer at the door to the waiting room and entered, eyes searching. Hannah saw him and rushed to him. He held his wife, drawing from her strength. She didn't have to speak, he could hear what she was saying.

His gaze rose and connected with Liam. Liam headed for him. Hannah moved to one side. Liam stopped in front of Caleb, unable to speak, emotions too high to control. His brown eyes were shiny with tears that he refused to let fall. He reached and drew Caleb into a bear hug.

Liam stood back, hands on Caleb's arm, unable to speak. He clapped his friend's arm and then turned away.

Laycee stood there, Joshua's arm around her. Caleb reached for the two and hugged them. Laycee's face was wet, but there was a peace there. Caleb hoped he could find that peace but he wasn't sure any more that he could.

He then paced to where Regan's parents sat and squatted down in front of her mother. She reached and touched his face.

"I know, Caleb, I know. You're hurting. You feel like you failed. You didn't. You kept them as safe as you could in this evil world. You kept them in a strong tower for as long as you could. You did your best. God led you. He is in control. Let it go."

Caleb bowed his head. He felt unworthy of their words. He felt a hand on his head. Joseph Evans was reaching out too, in the midst of his own grief and worry. He didn't hear the words that were prayed, but a sense of peace began to filter through him.

He stood, eyes clearing and looked around. He walked over to Ben and Eddie. His eyes drifted past them and stopped. How dare he come here and watch? Caleb dropped his eyes again. He murmured something to them and they turned. The man had left.

"See if we can get set up here something to go over what we have. I don't want to leave." Caleb looked around. "I just need to be here with my friends, I need to be myself, a hurting friend, not the chief for a few minutes."

"We look after it," Ben said. "Eddie has brought the files you wanted. We'll come find you."

Caleb stood, lost in thought. There was still something he was missing.

"What are you missing, Caleb?" Liam stood beside him. Caleb's friend knew him well, knew he would puzzle away at the problem like Defiant with his knuckle bone, until he reached the answer.

"I wish I knew, Liam. There's something, and I know Regan has the key. She started to say something once and stopped. She said she couldn't continue. Then she asked for a gun, said she had a permit and that something had happened where she was living. I wish I had been able to get those answers."

"I wish I could help. Even Laycee, who kept in touch, has no idea why she left or what went on. Have you talked to her parents?"

Caleb turned to look at them. "No, but I am going to have to." He reached for the cup of tea Joshua was handing him. "Any more word yet?"

Joshua shook his head. "They said it would be quite a while. We'll be here for hours yet."

"Make sure you all get something to eat. You'll need it."

"You too, brother." Joshua moved away to Laycee.

****

Caleb stood and stretched. They had commandeered a conference room just down from the waiting room and had been at work for hours, putting the bits and pieces together.

"We're missing something," he said. "I wish I knew what."

A tap came to the door. Ben answered it, glanced at Caleb, and then took the note he was handed. He retuned to the table and set it down in front of Caleb.

Caleb looked at it and then up at Ben.

"Hannah's at it again. You might as well read it and then fill us in." Ben's voice had that droll tone to it he had when he was trying not to laugh.

Caleb shook his head and then opened the note. Not again, he thought, not again. He handed the note to Ben and then Eddie. They nodded. Now it was all making sense. They just had to make sure they could follow the trail before it ran cold or the culprits had disappeared.

Another knock at the door, and Ben found Liam standing there. He pulled him in and waited. Caleb stood and faced his friend.

"We have word," Liam stated. "Leith is in recovery. There was some muscle damage and blood vessel damage but they are optimistic that he'll have a full recovery." Liam's voice broke and he staggered. Caleb caught his arm. "Regan is still in surgery. They haven't updated yet, but the last one was pretty grim. The bullet was really close to the heart."

Caleb placed his hand on his friend's shoulder in support. "God has not brought her through what they have gone through to let her die."

Eddie spoke up. "Caleb's right, Liam. Trust and pray."

Liam nodded and then slipped from the room.

Caleb looked at the two left. "Are we ready to roll? Plans are finalized. Can you think of anything we've missed?"

"No, just adding that name to our warrants search teams."

Eddie agreed. "We're ready. Let's go get them."

They gathered up their paperwork and headed back to organize and then execute the raids that were coming. They were winding it up and as far as Caleb was concerned, it was far too long.

Liam and Laycee stood by Leith's bed as he moved restlessly. The pain was evident in his face. Laycee's eyes sparkled with tears as she watched. It hurt to see Leith lying so white and in pain.

Liam's arm came around his sister and his other hand rested on his brother's arm. The surgeon has said it would be a while but he should be awake soon. They would wait, however long it took.

The surgeon had stopped on his way through and spoken with them. They trusted him and trusted God but it still hurt.

Regan's father stood as Regan's surgeon approached, a grim look on his face. They were expecting the worst.   He sat beside them and searched for words. Rebecca's hand reached for her husband.

The surgeon hesitated and then spoke, "She came through surgery. It was not as bad as it seemed. The heart is fine; it wasn't touched. There's certainly damage in the area but we've done the best we can to repair it. Barring any bleeders or set backs, she'll be fine. We'll be monitoring her in Recovery for a while and then sending her to an ICU unit. I'll have a nurse come find you when we move her." He stopped, then looked at them again. "You do know that her heart stopped before she got here and the paramedics kept her alive.   There were a couple of times in the operating room that I thought she was gone but she came back. I could tell that was when your prayers were the strongest."

Neither parent could speak but they nodded at him as he rose and walked away. Their daughter was alive, that's all that mattered.   Caleb was looking after the rest.

Caleb opened the door to the jewelry store and entered, officers coming in behind him and spreading out through the store. Adam Bell, the owner, approached him, an arrogant manner in his walk.

"What is this meaning of this, Chief? Why are you and your men here?" Adam Bell demanded.

Caleb said nothing, just wandered around the store, looking at the display cases. He wondered how many of these had been made with contraband jewels that cost next to nothing, if you didn't count lives lost.

"Well, I'm waiting. It's almost time to close and I have a meeting tonight for the Chamber of Commerce I have to be at in an hour." He pulled his sleeve back and uncovered the solid gold watch he was wearing.

Caleb took note of the jewelled rings on his hands and the jewelled tie pin. Still, he didn't answer, just kept wandering and taking note of the jewelry. As he reached the door where a curtain covered access to the back, he stopped and then motioned two officers through.

"How dare you, Chief Logan! That's a private staff are and workroom that no one is allowed into." The spit almost flew from Adam's mouth, he was so angry.

Caleb turned and made his way to stand three feet in front on him. Arms crossed on his chest, he continued to stare. He could see the sweat beading on Adam's face. Good, he thought. He's rattled. Keep it up, Caleb, he thought, and he'll make a slip.

Caleb continued to watch, not moving. He heard the officers return from the back and slanted his body slightly. At a nod from one, he turned back to Adam.

"That meeting is one you'll be missing, Adam."

"I don't think so. You and your men can leave."

"I don't think so, either, Adam because you see, you are under arrest."

"Under arrest? For what phoney charges?"

Caleb stared him in the eye, then spoke, "Well, let's see. For starters, smuggling jewels. Then we'll add conspiracies for murder, intimidation, break-ins, theft, assault on police officers. I'm sure as we go along we will find more to add. And those are just our charges. The federal authorities are waiting to speak with you too."

"I'll have your badge and the badges of everyone in this room. I want to speak with my lawyer."

"Go ahead." Caleb turned away.

As Adam was being read his rights and handcuffed, Caleb turned back. "Just so you know, you won't be the only Bell in our jail tonight. Mark was arrested a couple of days ago and has been held in Oak City. That department is returning him to town tonight."

Adam howled and lunged at Caleb but was held firmly by the officers. They led him away, cursing and screaming vindictively.

Caleb looked around with sadness. Such a waste, he thought. So many years, so much pleasure Adam had given, all lost to greed.

Ben entered the store, and Caleb turned.

"I take it that didn't go over well."

"Not at all." Caleb sighed. "We'll have to let it work through the courts now. You and Eddie will be busy sorting everything out. You have a team with the warrant at his home?"

Ben nodded. "There are a lot of unhappy campers there, too. Eddie says he has tracked down a storage unit or two that Adam had in another name. We're getting warrants for them as well." Ben paused. "His wife works for the courts. She's the leak there. Hannah was right on again. Sure you can't put her on the payroll some how?"

Caleb smiled at his friend's gentle teasing in the midst of the darkness. "We'll meet with the families in a few days. It will take a while to sort out all the whys and wherefores." Caleb paused and looked at out the evening sky. The sunset was brilliant in its pinks and reds and purples. "I'm going to head back to the hospital."

Ben laid a hand on Caleb's arm and stopped him. "You did well, Caleb. This has been a really hard case to crack. I don't think we could have solved it any sooner. Adam covered his tracks way too well."

Caleb nodded. "That's true, but there's little consolation in the fact that two young men are in jail as well as George and Adam, that two young men are dead, that we lost a really good secretary, and that two friends have ended up fighting more than once for their lives. I don't understand how God lets things like this happen. I can't doubt Him, but there are just times where I wonder."

"I know, Caleb. I'm the same. The only advice I can give is that God really does have a plan, that He knows the ending that will come. Trust is what it's all about."

Chapter 23

Ten days later, the group gathered in the Evans' home. Regan was ensconced on the couch, a quilt draped over her. She was still weak but being home was certainly making her feel better. She would never take home for granted again.

Leith sat beside her on the floor. His shoulder was still healing but he had already talked to Pietro, who had sent one of his grandsons to town to help. Paul loved the area and the work with Leith so much, the 22-year-old was doing his best to talk Leith into hiring him on a full-time basis. Regan and he had talked it over together and with Pietro. Paul would be staying.

The rest of the families had spread themselves out through the room. Eddie and Ben leaned against door frames, knowing what was coming, but relishing the re-telling of the story.

Caleb stood back to the fireplace and gazed around the room, eyes stopping on each one. Each one had been affected in some way or other. Some had been affected more. His glance stopped on Joseph and Rebecca, who had lost a business partner, brother, nephew, almost their reputation and more importantly their daughter. Regan was next. She had her head bent talking with Leith. Those two, he thought, yes those two. They have had an adventure of a life time but had learned so much of God's care. Regan called Leith her Hawk, who watched for game. He had provided for her in so many ways over this hard days. Caleb brought to the mind the verse speaking of the hawk and thought how true it was when Caleb headed them south to town.

Liam was next. He stood alone yet strong. He was the eldest, the protector of the family. What name would suit him best, Caleb wondered? Somewhere someone would find one that just fit him. He had been through a lot with his two siblings in the last six or seven months. He needed a break.

Laycee sat curled up in an easy chair, feet tucked up under her. The sparrow, Caleb thought of her. Little but noisy; noisy but so important to the family. She had been through so much a few months ago. As had his brother, Joshua, who perched on the arm of her chair. He was so thankful everything had worked out for him last year and that he was here today.

Caleb cleared his throat and all eyes fell on him. Where to start he wondered?

"It's hard to know exactly where to start. I guess with George. George was the contact who would find the uncut stones, steal them and then secret them in the cases of tiles. They had been doing this likely for 10 years or so from what he says. He was also one of the Knights as Adam Bell called them.

"Next is David Sullivan. He was called the Innocent. He provided access for George to the store to retrieve the stolen gems.

"Eric Brand was the Jester as he was called. He pretty much was a gopher, working between Adam, David and anyone they hired to do some dirty work. This kept Adam's name and face out of it. I don't think Eric knew who he was working for.

"Mark Bell was really just a courier. He had no idea what his father was up to. He was asked to deliver packets of gems at times and had no idea that they were stolen.

"Susan, our secretary. That's a hard pill to swallow. She had been married to Eric, divorced, and took back her maiden name. Their marriage had been out of the area and didn't show up on her initial check. The check has now been improved.

"Jane Bell, Adam's wife. She worked at the court house and helped to hide information on background checks.

"Adam Bell. Our town jeweller. The one we turned to for so many years for so many jewelry items. We will never know if we have a stolen gem or not. He set himself up as the King of an empire and basically thumbed his nose at us.

"We do know that George is responsible for the murder of Eric. Eric murdered David. Mark was set up to come ask for information by his father, which backfired on them. I doubt he knew exactly why Adam wanted that. George is responsible for the kidnappings. We are still tracking the other Knight but our suspicion is that George took care of him.

"Now I think that's it. It all stemmed around greed and lust for money. Adam had planned in the next couple of years to wind down his store and retire, supposedly to the south but he had bank accounts overseas and was really planning on a name change and a country change."

They sat absorbing Caleb's words.

Ben spoke. "It is ironic, Leith. The Bell House you worked on—it was Adam's grandparents before it was sold. He never forgave his parents for selling it. Part of the vindictiveness directed to you is from that, that you changed how it looked from what he remembered to what the new owner asked for."

Regan hesitated, then spoke. "I have known for years that David was no good. He was always cruel." She looked at her parents with tears in her eyes. "I had to leave. I couldn't stand to be around him. He had threatened friends and hinted at causing you harm. I should have spoken up but I was just so scared."

Her parents were shocked. They knew the two younger people had not gotten on but hadn't realized it was to this extent. This would take time to absorb.

"What about John?" Liam asked. "Was his a natural death?"

"As far as we can determine it was. If there were factors leading up to it, they were not physical. We will never know if he found out about David or not."

Joseph spoke up. "He knew. We had talked. He was trying to find a program that he could get David into but he ran out of time.

They had a lot to absorb and a lot of healing to do.

"Why don't we gather back here in a day or two?" Rebecca asked. "You too, Eddie and Ben, and your wives. Hannah and the boys, too. We'll have had some time to think and if we have more questions, maybe we'll have answers then."

Leith waited for the room to clear, then stood and gathered Regan into his arms and sat back down. She looked at him.

"You're taking a lot of liberty, boy."

Leith laughed. "No, just an armful of woman." He tilted his head to look at her. "How are you really doing?"

"I hurt in ways I never imagined I could, but with God I will get through it." She looked at him. "Now put me down. You need to go home."

He laughed again, dropped a quick kiss on her surprised mouth and then left.

Three months had passed. Leith and Regan had healed physically but they were still working through some issues.

Regan sat on a wicker chair on her apartment deck. She had finally made the move to her own place, content to be back in her home town. Her place overlooked a large park and the river and she loved it.

She heard the door open behind her and knew Leith had come out. A mug of coffee appeared in front of her nose.

"You're taking a lot for granted, aren't you, buster?" She laughed.

"That I am." He leaned in for a quick kiss, then pulled up the wicker chair beside her. They sat in silence watching the sky and the river.

"Leith, I can't tell you how grateful I am for your care over the last few months. When we were going through that awful, awful time, you were there, even hurt, to watch out."

Leith shrugged. "I care very deeply about you." He turned to study her. "We need to do another day away."

"Oh no," Regan stated as he laughed, shaking her head. "One of those days away is enough."

"This time, my darling, it will be different. You're not in danger any more. Life is more sane." He reached for her hand. "Laycee had the right idea. She asked Joshua to go steady. Will you be my girl?"

Regan's head tipped and she studied him. "Well...." He wrapped his hand around her neck, drew her forward and kissed her. "Okay, steady as she goes they say."

He leaned his head on hers and laughed. "I can see a sea voyage in our future. As long as we have the Captain we need, we're set."

Regan's hand touched his face. "Yes, my Hawk. Our Captain never fails."

A noise interrupted them. "What is that?" Leith asked.

Regan giggled and reached down beside her. "Close your eyes." When he had, she handed him a puppy.

Wriggling, the puppy reached to lick Leith's face. His eyes popped open and he laughed. Petting the puppy and trying to get it to lay still, he had to ask. "What kind of dog is this? I don't think I've seen that colouring before."

"I talked to Laycee who had a friend whose Sheltie had had pups. This is what you call a bi-blue. It's the gray, white, black combination." She reached to stroke the puppy's back. "You get to name her."

"A dog, hmm." Leith sat back cradling the puppy. "A girl. Well, I think Abby would be a good name for her."

"That didn't take long," Regan laughed. "I think that's a good name. Now," as she reached down again, "what do we call our calico kitten?" as a kitten made its appearance.

Leith shouted with laughter, startling the two animals. "That name, my darling, is up to you."

"Well, then, I guess she'll be Emmy."

Leith leaned over and kissed the woman he loved. "You, my darling, have made my life complete. We will definitely have a wonderful adventure together."

Regan was silent for a few months, then spoke. "When we were going through all that and I didn't think we would make it through, God really emphasized how He had provided the strong tower for us to run to, to protect us. In some ways, it felt like He hadn't but I know He did. I never want to forget that."

Leith's hand caught her free hand in a strong grip. "We never will, my darling. We never will. He will never let us."

Dear Readers:

Thank you so much for joining me in the next book for the Bradley Family, the story of the youngest, Leith.

Once again, a Bradley sibling is in danger and has to rely on others but more importantly on God. Twists and turns once more dominate. I love a good story where you can't figure out whodunnit until the end and I have tried so hard to incorporate that in the stories.

The story of Laycee was a dream novel - a dream novel in the sense that I have always wanted to put pen to paper, or in modern terms, fingers to keyboard, and create a story. That dream was the last one I shared with my Mother.

In this story, I have tried so hard to show that God is our strong tower. When we need comfort, a place to rest, a place to hide from whatever is betting us, He is that strong tower for us. I have a picture in my mind (and each of us will have a different picture) of a high rough stone building, with some small windows, stone work around the top with openings for weapons and lines of sight, but more importantly, only one door. One door to enter, we don't need more than one.

The story of Leith incorporates my heritage. The name Bradley was given to my Dad by his parents. It was my Grandmother's maiden name. I have teaspoons engraved with the stylized B that she brought from England with her back in 1919. My Dad was a carpenter and worked in that trade until he was 74. He had had to learn more than just wood — he laid foundations, laid blockwork, did drywall, plaster, tiles. The words Leith speaks to Regan about how hard construction is on a woman and the atmosphere that is quite often found on a job site— those were my Dad's to me. I wanted so much to enter a trade. He felt I needed to do other. But that's okay. His example and teaching have lead me to remodel my own house with my own hands, from installing plumbing fixtures to tiling to laying laminate flooring and anything I could find to do inbetween. The very first task I did was to install a new back door, which Dad and I had debated over whether it would fit or not. It fit. He would come up and ask if I had done something, tell me what to do, and then step back. His words when I finished are treasures: You did a wonderful job. He graduated to heaven in 2012 but I know I would be hearing that today if he were here.

So my friends, I don't know what you are facing in your lives right now. None of us know the plans or the plots or the twists and turns that God allows in our lives. He is the Author of Life and knows the ways and means of where He is leading us. Never be afraid to say to Him you don't understand, that you need comfort. Run to the Strong Tower that He is.

Ronna

The Eagle

Under His Wings Trilogy
Book 3

by

Ronna Bacon

Dedication

To my Heavenly Father, who has provided the words I write. He really does give strength to rise and face each and every day.

Isaiah 40:31   They that wait upon the Lord shall renew their strength. They shall mount up with wings like eagles. They shall walk and not faint.   They shall run and not be weary. (KJV)

Table of Contents

The sun was high, brilliant and strong, reflecting back from the river's water. He disliked having to mingle like a commoner, wearing clothes off the rack. He shuddered at how long he had to have them on. He wanted his designer clothes back.

His contact was to have left the information he needed on a flash drive for him and was to meet him here. He had to be somewhere in this mess of rocks along the river. He looked down at his hands and wished he had gloves he could put on.

Only thing - it looked different from the picture he was sent. Something had changed. Something had been moved. Anger rose within him. That fool. He must have sent the wrong picture.

He pulled out his phone and brought up the text with the picture and looked. He was in the right area but the man isn't there. If he wasn't there, that meant his package wouldn't be either, unless he had dropped it and was afraid to tell him.

He would have to come back later when there were fewer people and search again. Once he had that information, then he would be set.

Chapter 1

Liam Bradley stood on the banks of the river and watched the water flowing by. The sun was low in the sky and it was cooling off a bit from the heat of the day. This was a favourite time of day, work was done, he could relax. He raised his eyes and studied the rock formation along the river. He found them an inspiration for his work as a landscaper. Many times, he had worked in some form of his inspiration from here. He had a new contract, a family just moved to the area in the last six months, who wanted a rugged look to their yard and a waterfall. They had had outbuildings erected that he would be working around, but he was up to it.

He moved his line of sight and watched a black and white dog at play in the shallow area. He searched the tree line and spotted its owner, standing back. The form moved forward and Liam saw it was a female but she was too far away for him to identify her. He looked back at the dog. It wasn't one he was familiar with. Tourist season brought a lot of people to the area and many brought their animals as well.

He watched the woman and her dog play, then turned and made his way further along the river bank, to a more rugged area. He needed to watch, it was sometimes slippery if the wind had been blowing the spray from the small area of rapids.

He turned once again and looked behind him and down the river. He never grew tired of watching the water. He turned with his back to the river and ran his eyes along the rocks and bushes. This was what he was trying to envision for the new site. A glint of light caught his eye and he reached forward. Picking up a small plastic container, he turned it over, studying it, and then tucked it into his pocket.

A movement to his right startled him. A sudden yell and he was falling. He felt the water cover him and then his head hit rock. His vision faded. He didn't feel himself tumbling down the river or rising to the surface.

Ashling Downie heard the shout and looked around. Teagan, her Sheltie, stopped, barked and then dove into the water, headed for the other shore. Ashling raced for the water, stopped and then heart in mouth, dove in as well, swimming for the body she saw. She reached it and pulled it up on the riverbank she had just left. It was closest. She felt for a heart beat. He was alive but unconscious. Reaching for the phone she had dropped, she called for help and then waited.

She studied the man's face and frowned. She thought she knew him, had seen him around, but she couldn't place him. Teagan crowded close at the man's side and laid her head on his arm. She then watched Ashling, intelligent brown eyes never wavering.

A sound behind her and she spun. Paramedics were coming towards her, with police officers right behind them. She stood and called Teagan away. Moving further back, she stood and watched as they worked on the unconscious victim and then carried him away.

She breathed a prayer that he would be all right and then turned to walk away. An older gentleman stood near her. Ben Johnson, she knew him from church and as a senior police officer. She sighed, guessed she wouldn't be going anywhere anytime soon to get into dry clothes, and prepared herself to talk to him.

Ben studied the young woman in front of him. He knew she wasn't happy about having to stay but he needed her statement.

"Ashling Downie," Ben spoke. "What happened?"

Ashling looked back at the water, then at Ben, and shrugged. "I really don't know. Teagan and I were playing here at the water. I was doing some training with her. She just alerted and dove into the water. I saw what she was after and went in too." She shrugged. "Isn't that what anyone would do?"

Ben shook his head. "Not always." He looked around. "This is one of Liam's favourite areas of the river. He spends a lot of time here."

"If that's all, I need to go. It's starting to get cold."

Ben looked at her, then down to her dog. "Come on. I'll give you a lift."

As they turned to walk away, Ashling hesitated. She felt eyes on her but could see no one. What was that about?

Caleb Logan, police chief for Riverville, brought his vehicle to a stop near the emergency entrance of the hospital. He hesitated before he got out and said a prayer for his friend. Ben had called him, letting him know that Liam was on his way in by ambulance. He shook his head as he got out. What next for this family: Laycee and his own brother, Joshua, last year, Leith and his now fiancee, six months ago, all targeted for murder and that by upstanding members, or so he thought, of their community.

He stepped inside and looked around, then headed for his brother and his wife. They were newlyweds, just wed about six weeks. Joshua saw him and stood, coming towards him.

"How is he?" Caleb asked.

"They're still working on him. They haven't said much."

Caleb tilted his head to look at Laycee, her long black hair hiding her face. "How's Laycee?"

His brother shrugged. "She's not saying much. I sort of expected that though. She's very vocal with Liam, but with something like this, she can get very quiet."

"Where's Leith and Regan?"

"They were still on a job site and had to finish what they had going. They'll be here as soon as they can."

Caleb laid his hand on his brother's shoulder and then headed back into the exam room area. He wanted answers and he didn't want to wait for them. Something had happened and he wanted to know what. Liam was not one who was careless and lost his footing that easily. He had a bad feeling that once again he would be searching for answers while trying to protect a friend.

He spotted Dr. Young coming from a room and spoke with him, then stepped into the exam room where Liam was lying wrapped in heated blankets, with an IV dripping into his veins. Liam's eyes were closed, his face pale and wan. He had blood on the left side of his head, likely from the fall onto the rocks, Caleb surmised. He stood for a few minutes watching and then turned. Dr. Young had said it would be a while and he had things to do. He would be back, but first he needed to catch up with Ben.

Ashling hesitated at the waiting room door. She had come to see how Liam was but didn't know the family well enough just to walk up to them. If Leith's Regan was here, she would feel more comfortable. She moved to the side to let newcomers move around, then heard someone say her name.

She turned to see Regan Evans beside her.

"Hi, Regan. I just wanted to see how Liam is."

Regan studied her for a moment, then reached out to touch her still damp hair. "You're the one. Eddie said a woman had pulled Liam out. It was you." She reached to hug Ashling, then keeping an arm around her, drew her along with her to the others.

Laycee and Leith turned as Regan approached, eying the newcomer.

"Laycee, Leith, you have met Ashling Downie before. She's the one who pulled Liam out."

Laycee's mouth went into an "O", then she was hugging Ashling. Tears were on her face and she couldn't speak. Ashling's eyes met Leith tear-filled ones. She smiled and nodded at his thank you.

Dr. Young appeared beside them and spoke.

"He's had quite a blow to the head and has the headache to match. No concussion. Lungs are fine. I would like to keep him here for a while just to make sure, but he can go home later. Which one of you will be the one who has to watch him?”

Leith spoke up. “I am.”

“He should be good to go in about two hours. I’ll have the nurse find you.”

Laycee turned to watch him walk away. Joshua studied his wife’s face.

“What’s bugging you, Laycee?”

She shook her head. “I don’t know. There’s just something different about Dr. Young. I can’t put my finger on it. He’s changed.”

As the rest studied Laycee’s face, Ashling stepped back. She had found out what she wanted and now she was going to head home and let them be by themselves. She smiled in greeting as Pastor Paul, their minister, went by her. Good, she thought. That is what they need.

She was crossing the pavement to her car when she once again heard her name. She turned, and Leith stood behind her.

She held up her hand. “No, Leith, don’t say it. No more thanks. No more comments. I was there and so was Teagan. She’s the one who really deserves the thanks. If she hadn’t seen him, I wouldn’t have.”

Leith stood, hands deep in the front pockets of his jeans. He looked to the night sky and then back to the woman front of him, half in the shadows. “I do mean thank you.” He held up his hand as she protested. “No, you don’t understand. He’s my only brother. He’s the one who has held our family together for so many years since we lost our parents. He’s the one who watches and protects us. Without him, our family wouldn’t be the same. It would be damaged in a way that I don’t want to even imagine.” He paused. “What I was going to ask. I know you do dog training. With things the way they are now, I would like to have better training for my Abby and also for Laycee’s Defiant. Let me know what we can work out.” He stopped, started to say something else, and then turned and walked back to the hospital.

Ashling's hand came to her mouth and she hesitated, almost going after him, then turned to her car. She would come up with a plan. She didn't know all the history yet but she would find out what they were so afraid of.

****

He watched from the shadows near the door. He had to find out if they knew anything. He had to find that flash drive. He wanted out of this town. That was the only way he knew how. His occupation didn't let him save what he wanted to save. If they had it, they would pay. He turned and walked back to his tasks. One day, one day very soon, he hoped.

300

Liam moved his head. It hurt. He opened his eyes. That hurt. He could hear someone near him, but it seemed just too much of an effort to wake up.

A hand on his shoulder roused him again. "Liam, come on, buddy. Time to wake up."

Liam squinted at the voice and groaned, "Go away, Leith. This isn't funny."

He heard a small laugh, then Leith spoke again, "No, it's not, Liam, but we need to get you up. You've been discharged and they need your bed for someone who is really sick."

Liam's eyes opened wider and he looked around. He was in a hospital room. How did he get here?

His eyes closed as Leith raised the head of his bed. As things steadied, he reopened them. He stared at his brother, headache pounding behind his eyes.

"Dr. Young has discharged you. You have a choice —my place or Laycee's."

Liam glared at his brother, then sighed. "Yours. Tell me what happened. I don't remember."

Leith perched on the side of the bed, and watched his brother. "You were fished out of the river. Somehow you fell in and hit your head. If Ashling and her dog hadn't been there, you wouldn't be here."

Liam puzzled at this, then shook his head, regretting it instantly. "I don't even remember being near the river."

Leith stood. "It may or may not come back to you. Come on. Let's get you home."

Moving slowly, Liam managed to dress and then make his way to his brother's truck.

"Where's Laycee?"

"Likely waiting for you at my place."

"Great. I don't need that."

"Whether you need it or not, accept it. It's our turn to give back to you."

Liam turned his head to look at Leith. Leith's eyes were straight ahead, not looking at him. "I'm sorry, Leith. I'm grumpy and have a rotten headache. That was uncalled for."

Leith slanted him a look and then a smile. "You have always been one to give, not accept. It's your turn to accept." Leith stopped, then spoke, "God was with you today, Liam. I don't know if I could have handled losing you."

Liam was silent. He didn't feel he could respond. Leith was right. God had protected him. He sighed to himself. Now he just had to get rid of the headache so he could go to work tomorrow, and he already knew Laycee would be on his case.

Liam headed into his office in the morning. He wasn't up to working at any of the job sites his landscaping business had going. Maybe in the afternoon his head would be well enough that he could.

His foreman, Bud Whalen, was waiting for him. Liam went over the work they had on the go, then sent Bud out to the sites.

He sat back in his desk chair. His head was aching, but not like last night. He just couldn't remember what had happened. He tried to work for a while, then in frustration, threw down his pencil, got up and walked out of the office. He kept walking, heading to the river. He needed to see for himself where it happened. He didn't remember being there at all.

Liam stood, watching the peaceful flow of the water. Last night, it had almost taken his life. Today, it was serene. He looked up at the sky. "God, You were there last night. You saved me. Thank you."

When he looked back down, he shuddered at how close it had been last night. He turned to study the ground where he was standing, then walked further along the river bank. How had he slipped? He knew this area so well and was cautious walking it.

Footsteps sounded behind him and he spun. Eddie Brown, a town police officer but also a good friend, stood there, watching him.

"Liam. Good to see you upright and out and about."

Liam reached to shake his hand. "I hear I had quite the adventure."

"That you did. If it hadn't been for that dog, no one would have found you until it was too late." Eddie looked at him and then around. "What I don't understand, Liam, is this. How did you slip? You're way too cautious."

Liam nodded. "That's what I'm trying to figure out." He searched the area, then stopped. "I was about here. Eddie, I wasn't on the rocks that were wet. I was over by this one." He paced over to a larger rock. "I just can't remember why."

Eddie came to stand beside him, studying where Liam had been standing, then turning to look at the riverbank and the river. He paced to the edge of the river and back.

Liam stood silent, watching him, his mind racing at the possibilities.

Eddie sighed. "It's what we were afraid of, Liam. It wasn't an accident."

Liam's eyes shot to Eddie's and then slid shut. "Who?"

Eddie shook his head. "That's what we now have to figure out. Come on, Liam. Let's get out of here." He turned to leave, then stopped. "It's the unknown, not knowing who, that is going to be the problem. You three

Bradleys - you're well liked in the community. Your parents were. Your family goes back to the founding of the town. But please, Laycee and Leith's adventures in the last few months have been enough. We don't need you going on an adventure like that."

Liam stared at him. "You don't think…" His voice trailed away and then he walked past Ben. "As far as I know, I have no enemies. I was just in the wrong place at the wrong time."

Eddie's voice drifted after him. "But who decided you were in the wrong place at the wrong time?"

Ashling headed towards the local cafe. She had discovered it shortly after the family have moved to town. It was Friday, and she knew SueEllen always had freshly made scones on the menu. She planned to pick up some and take back to her parents' pet store for their morning tea.

A voice calling her name stopped her and she turned. It was Laycee Logan.

"Wait up a minute, Ashling." Laycee hurried to catch up. "I can't keep up with you. You're too fast."

Ashling grinned. "That's what I'm told. Always in a rush. It's the running I do. You need to come with me some morning."

Laycee tilted her head and thought. "I certainly do. Now if I could just find the time. What I wanted to ask. Would you be willing to come speak to our therapy group some time? Your choice of topic."

Ashling looked around, then said, "I don't like public speaking. I'm not comfortable in that. One on one is fine. I would really have to pray about that."

Laycee nodded. "Do and then let me know. I don't want to pressure you." She looked past her. "There're Leith and Liam. I need to catch up with them. Please call me." Laycee started away, then turned back. "I would really like to have you as a friend. Let me know when we can get together for coffee or a meal."

A surprised look came across Ashling's face. "As long as it's tea and not coffee, you're on."

As Laycee caught up with her brothers, they looked up. Leith's hand came up in a wave to Ashling. She could feel Liam studying her, puzzling out who she was. Ashling shrugged, then continued on her way. She really wanted those scones for their morning break.

The three Bradly siblings settled into their booth in the cafe and gave their orders. Liam studied his brother and sister. God had spared their lives through kidnappings and murders in the last few month, Laycee because of an accountant involved in financial fraud, Leith because of a jeweller smuggling stolen uncut gems. He listened to their chatter and his mind drifted off to the plans he should be working on.

A hand on his arm brought him out of his reverie. Laycee was watching him.

"You didn't hear what we said," she accused. "You're off in that world of planning again aren't you?"

He nodded. "I guess I was. So what had you asked?"

"Leith and Regan have an idea about their wedding and they want our input. Can you stay with us for a while or should we let the senior toddle off back to his office?"

Liam laughed, caught his sister in a hug, and dropped a kiss on her black curls. "I'm listening, I'm listening." He caught Leith's eyes and stopped. There was a seriousness there that seldom showed, not that deep. He would have to question him with Laycee wasn't around.

Laycee finally stood. "I need to get going. I'll see you all later."

They watched their sister walk away, then Liam turned to Leith. "Ok, give. What are you thinking about?"

Leith studied his almost empty coffee cup. He was finding it hard to put into words what he wanted to say. He knew he wouldn't be able to if he looked at Liam. "It's… It's…"His voice kept dying away.

Liam's voice was laced with amusement as he spoke. "That's not like you. You're never at a loss for words."

Leith tossed a balled up napkin at his brother. "We could have lost you last night, Liam. I'm not ready for that. And I don't think it was an accident." He stopped, looked up, and then at his brother. Liam was shaken at the depths of emotion Leith showed, something he so seldom did. "I think you're being targeted too, just like Laycee and I were. If God had not protected you, you would have died."

Liam leaned forward, arms on the table. "I doubt it. I think I was just a bit clumsy and slipped."

Leith stood. "Think what you will. I don't think that way. Change of subject, come on. I need to get some food for the critters and you need to come help me."

Liam protested. "They're your animals, yours and Regan. Why do I have to help?"

****

The Colonel sat in his office, rage building within him. He needed that flash drive. If only the fool who had it had been smarter. Planning a drop by the river—that was a childish game. Now he was facing ruin. He needed that information, then he could leave this town.

He picked up his phone, made a call, and set in play a plan that would not be stopped. He rested his hand for a minute on the phone, then picked up his pen and began his paperwork. His rage burned but just maybe now he would be safe.

Chapter 3

Leith swung open the door to the Downie's Fur and Feathers pet store, then stepped back to let a customer out. Liam followed him through the door and then stood looking around. He didn't have pets, had no occasion to shop in a pet store, but this place was clean and tidy. He could vaguely remember when it hadn't been under the previous owners.

At the sound of a female voice, his attention to turned to the counter. A young woman was finishing up an order for a customer who he realized was Dr. Young's wife. When she turned to leave, she looked discontented and unhappy.

"We'll have that delivered this afternoon for you, Mrs Young. Either Lorcan or I will bring it by."

A voice could be heard, "Good bye. Good bye. Don't come back." Mrs. Young stopped, then Liam saw the disgust and anger in her face. What was going on?

Leith raised a hand on the way by the counter.

"Morning, Leith. The food you wanted for Abby is on the shelf and Emmy's food is as well."

"Thanks, Ashling."

The woman had not looked up from the paperwork she had moved to. Liam watched in fascination as a small green bird hopped down the counter and then up on her shoulder.

"Sally good."

"No, Sally's not good. Sally's a bad bird."

"Sally good bird. Sally pretty bird."

"Sally is a pretty bad bird."

307

Sally slid along the shoulder and tucked her head close to the woman's face. "Sally good. Sally good."

"No Sally, you're not. You weren't nice to the customer."

"Sally nice."

"Sally, you need to behave. Next time she comes in, you're in your cage."

"Sally good. No cage."

Startling blue eyes raised for a moment and caught Liam's, then dropped. By this time, Leith had set the bags of food on the counter and was grinning. A young man had entered behind the counter, also grinning. Leith assumed it was the woman's brother, their features were so alike.

"Sally, don't argue. You know you were bad. Now to your cage."

"Sally pretty. Sally good. No cage." The bird then let out a chorus of notes.

"Ashling, you know you can't win with her."

"Shut up, Lorcan. It's your fault. You just had to teach a macaw to talk, didn't you?"

By this time, Leith's head was buried in his arms on the counter, body shaking with laughter. Lorcan let out a shout of laughter. This startled Sally, who fluffed her feathers, hopped back to the counter, and looked around. She then spied Liam and headed for him.

"Sally, no. You're not a good girl today. Bad girls go to the cage." Ashling reached under the counter and pulled out some pieces of fruit and a few toys. She tapped a toy and said, "Here, Sally. To your cage."

By this time, Sally was on Liam's shoulder, cuddling into his neck. Liam stood still. He had never had a bird on his shoulder before, let alone one who talked. He shot a look at Leith for help, and saw that obviously no help would be coming from that direction.

"Sally, come. Your cage."

"Sally good. Sally stay."

"No, Sally, you're not good. To your cage."

"Sally love. Sally stay."

A stern note came into Ashling's voice. "Enough, Sally. Here's your treat. To your cage." Without looking up from her paperwork, she pointed to the end of the counter where a cage rested. "If you don't you'll not get out again today."

Sally looked at Liam, looked at her treat, then back at Liam. She finally hopped to the counter towards Ashling. Ashling had gathered up her paperwork, clipped it together and set it aside. The whole conversation with the bird had been done while she was working. Liam assumed this was a longstanding debate between the two.

Sally came forward, took her treat and headed for her cage. Once inside, she dropped her treat. "Sally good. Sally pretty."

This sent Leith and Lorcan into fresh gales of laughter.

"Don't encourage her, you two. Next time, you get to deal with her." Ashling came around the counter. "Just for that, Lorcan, you get to stay and watch the store until Da or Mam come."

Liam watched her walk towards him. She tucked her hand under his elbow and turned him back to the door. "We adults are leaving. You children can stay and play with Sally."

The door opened to fresh gales of laughter as they reached it and Caitlin Downie entered. She took a look at the two at the door and then at the two men at the counter.

"Sally again."

"Yes, Mam, Sally again. She's decided she's in love and has been flirting with the customers."

Caitlin laughed. "Then get him out of here before she decides she needs to flirt again."

Ashling steered Liam out of the store and down the street. Letting go of his arm, she turned. "Now that I've rescued you, I should apologize. Sally's a miniature macaw and Lorcan just had to teach her to talk and sing."

Liam stopped her. He stood staring down at her. Brilliant blue eyes and golden blond hair sparkled in the sun. He was over six feet in height but the top of her head easily reached his chin. "No. It's the other way around. You rescued me last night."

Ashling shook her head. "It was really Teagan." At his puzzled look, she continued, "My dog. She saw you and went after you. If she hadn't, I wouldn't have seen you." She looked around, uncomfortable. "I didn't do anything that someone else would not have done."

"Can I at least buy you a cup of coffee?"

Ashling studied him. "No but a cup of tea will do. I don't know how you can swallow that horrid stuff."

Liam laughed, then looked around. "There." He pointed to a street vendor. "Gail always has a nice selection of teas as well as coffee."

Cradling her cup of tea, Ashling stood and looked at the town around her. It was busy with tourists but she was beginning to recognize a lot of local people. Liam nodded to a park bench that was empty and they headed there.

Liam sat, at a loss for words. This was unusual for him. He watched Ashling as she sat beside him.

"I know you don't think you did much, Ashling. If you hadn't been there." He shuddered at the thought.

She turned to watch his face. "God knew I was needed there. I usually don't go out there at that time of night. I usually have classes." At his look, she continued, "My Teagan and I are competitive, working in agility and herding. I also teach dog classes, obedience, that kind of stuff. Last night, I just had to go. God compelled me to that spot. He knew you would need Teagan."

Liam thought about what she said. Lately, his faith had slipped. Sure he was still in church, still read his Bible, still spent time in prayer, but the spark had faded. He need to re-ignite it but didn't quite know how.

Ashling turned to gaze across the town square. "I'm getting to know your family. Both Laycee and Leith have said you are the eagle in their family. That you have always watched out for them, have protected them. Laycee described you to me as the one who seems tireless, relentless in his search for God." Her eyes turned back to him. "I sense that you are really struggling, that the events of the last months have really tried your faith. God understands when we struggle and doubt. Let Him gather you under His wings and rest for a while, Liam."

Liam stared, astounded that she had read him so well. How was that? He liked the bit of accent he heard peeking through her voice, its cadence sending peace through him. "You have described it well, Ashling. I really do struggle. I haven't said anything to anyone though. How did you know?"

Ashling shrugged. "I just do. Da says it's a gift. Sometimes it feels like a curse. Mam always tells me that intuition should never be ignored but strengthened and followed. It may be the Irish in me, but more likely God." She finished her tea and then stood. "I know you have things you need to get to. My prayers are with you."

Liam watched as she strode away, movements loose and free. She's a runner, he thought. Interesting. I'll have to see if she wants a partner to run with. He then thought about what she said. Yes, she had him pegged. He was struggling. He sighed. I guess I need to speak with Pastor Paul, he thought. A sudden shiver ran through him and he looked around. He could feel eyes on him but couldn't see anyone watching him. Suddenly, he felt very vulnerable in the open, even with people around him. Dropping his cup in the trash, he headed back for his office.

Caleb looked up as Ben tapped at his door. He motioned him in and Ben dropped into a chair in front of the desk.

"I'm getting too old for all these hours. It's wearing me out, some days."

Caleb waited. He knew Ben really didn't feel like that.

Ben eyed him, then continued, "That new K9 program just might take off. Lorcan Downie's training from the other force is really going to pay off. Once he can find the right partner and get the dog trained, it will really add to our department."

Caleb nodded. "It will. You taking on the training on the evidence side is really helping. Our officers are getting much better, and they were good before." Caleb looked down and then back up. "But that's not why you're here."

Ben shook his head. "No. I've been hearing scuttlebutt from the street and so has Eddie. Liam's fall last night, it wasn't an accident. He was pushed."

Caleb stilled, studying Ben. "That's what we thought. It just didn't look right, or sit right with me."

Ben stood. "Now we just have to figure out who and why. I hope we don't have another Laycee or Leith."

Caleb agreed. "No. That was enough."

Ben didn't know how prophetic his words would turn out to be.

Chapter 4

The Colonel watched as Liam walked away from the town square. He was sure he had something of his. He just needed to find it. The Major had said he had two men that would be able to do that very task. If not, then he would see. He just wanted out of this town. He had had enough.

****

Liam's steps lagged as he approached his home. It had been a long day and he was tired. All he wanted to do was take something for his headache and then lie down. Food didn't interest him.

He reached with his key for the lock and stopped. Something wasn't right. He touched the door and it swung open. Not again, he thought. Not someone going through his stuff. It had been bad enough with the other two, now him?

He stepped away, pulled out his phone, and made the call.

Ben and Eddie approached as he leaned against his truck, watching the activity. Eddie handed him a coffee.

Liam took it with a word of thanks. "Don't say it."

Ben smiled, then sobered. "I was hoping it had been an accident last night, Liam. This makes it seem like it's not."

Liam sighed, took a sip of his coffee, shook his head and then regretted it. Squinting, he looked at the two. "Somehow, I thought you would say that."

Ben studied him. "What is it with you three? First Laycee, then Leith. You just couldn't let them get ahead of you, could you? You really didn't have to join them, you know."

Liam smirked. "I know." He glanced up at the darkening sky. "I just wanted to come home, take something for the headache and go to bed."

Eddie took a look at him, stepped away and then returned, holding out something. "Here's your pain medication. The kitchen has been cleared so it's okay. Now take it."

Ben continued to watch his young friend. He could see past the pain, to how tired he really was. The last year or so had put a lot of strain on him and he was beginning to crack. It was subtle unless you knew him well. Ben really didn't know how well Liam would be able to handle what he feared was coming. His eyes met Eddie and he could see Eddie felt the same. How could they protect him when they had no idea from whom or what? It felt like the last year just wasn't going to end any time soon.

Eddie nodded towards the house and Ben turned. The crime team was finished and they could enter the house. Liam pushed himself away from the truck, momentarily staggering. Eddie reached to steady him. Liam shrugged his hand away and moved to his home. He hesitated, took a deep breath and entered. There was not much of a disturbance. He had been afraid it would have been worse. He wandered through his house, taking note of where things had been disturbed.

Ben and Eddie watched as he paused at the stairs. Liam took a breath and then slowly climbed them, the two other men on his heels. Liam went through each of the three bedrooms and their attached baths. Ben noted that his house has been upgraded nicely. It had been pretty run down when Liam purchased it. Both Joshua, a renovator, and Leith, a tile setter, had been involved.

Liam stood at his dresser, staring down at the top, not really seeing anything. "I don't see anything missing. That's so strange. I have nothing anyone would want." He turned, brown eyes showing his fatigue.

Ben nodded. "The team didn't find much. Whoever it was, they were thorough but tidy. That's not your usual snatch and grab thief. They also weren't destructive. That tells me they wanted to get in and out without you knowing."

Eddie stepped away to speak with an officer, then stepped back. "It looks as if you just missed them, Liam. We checked your alarm system. The alarm was turned off about 20 minutes before you got home."

Liam paled and then sank down on his bed, eyes closing. "Who? I don't have any enemies. I don't have competition. Not many people want the hard and dirty work I do."

Ben and Eddie exchanged a glance. "Liam, we need to get your locks changed and that's not happening tonight. We are going to post a patrol here for the night, but you shouldn't be here on your own."

As Liam looked up in protest, Ben continued, "We need to keep you safe. You have a choice: spend the night with Laycee or Leith or spend the night at either Eddie's place or mine or even Caleb's. You're too tired and sore to think straight. Let us help you. Don't protest, either."

Liam looked down in shame. That exactly what he had been about to do. "You're right. I'm not thinking straight." He squinted against the pain. "So, who wins the coin toss?"

Eddie smiled. "Come with me. I'm playing bachelor for a few days while my sweetheart's away with her parents."

Later that evening, Caleb tapped at Eddie's door and then followed Eddie through the beautifully decorated bungalow to the kitchen. Eddie made Caleb his tea and then sat down at the table with a mug of coffee.

"How is he?"

"He's sleeping. Wouldn't eat anything. I checked on him about 10 minutes ago. He is worn to the bone right now, I'd say," Eddie replied. "He wasn't happy about not staying at his place. We didn't give him an option. If he had refused, Ben was ready to lock him up."

Caleb laughed softly. "That sounds like Liam. Did the team find anything?"

Eddie shook his head. "Not that I know of. Whoever it was, they were professional. In, search without disturbing much, then out. It just worries me as to how close it came for Liam actually being there."

Caleb nodded. "I know. I just wish I could figure it out."

The men talked quietly for another thirty minutes or so and then Caleb rose to leave.

"We need to have someone stick close to him and he's not going to like it. Who do we have that likes landscaping?"

Eddie thought for a minute. "I hear he's going to being working at the Downie's starting in the next couple of days. I wonder if Lorcan would like to get his hands dirty."

Caleb thought, then smiled. "Perfect. Protection without it being obvious."

****

Things were definitely not going well, the Major thought. His two men hadn't found what he sent them after and had just missed being spotted. The Colonel would not be happy. Right now, the Major wasn't answering his phone. Until he could speak more thoroughly with the men, he wouldn't. These men were professionals. They knew how to find hidden items and had reported that it wasn't in Liam's house. That meant they now needed to search his office and shop. That was going to be a whole lot trickier.

316

Chapter 5

Liam struggled the next morning. He was more tired and sore than he wanted to admit, but he needed to be on the job. They were headed to the Downie's to start that project. He wanted to be on site for that one as much as he could.

Eddie watched closely as Liam entered the kitchen. He didn't say anything, just handed him a plate of food and a mug of coffee.

"I'll take you to get your truck before heading to the office and check your place out. Ben said Andy would be there early to do your locks and would drop off keys for you at your office." Eddie continued, "I know you feel like we're smothering you, Liam, but something is up and we need to find out what."

Liam sighed. "I know in my head that's why you're doing it. I just can't accept it that I'm a target."

"I know. People who are targets quite often feel that way."

"Thanks, Eddie, for stepping in last night. You and Ben were right. I shouldn't have been on my own."

Eddie smiled and nodded. He knew it was hard for Liam to admit that.

Ashling stood on the back deck and watched the activity in front of her. It was like watching a bunch of ants, she thought, scurrying around, looking as if they didn't have a clue what they were doing, yet accomplishing much. It would be interesting to see Liam's plans come to life.

She turned as the door behind her opened. Her mother came to stand beside her and handed her a cup of tea.

"Thanks, Mam."

"It's going to be a busy few weeks here, my dear. How is that going to affect your classes?"

"Most of them are at night, which will be okay. It's after the men have left for the day. The others, we'll use the work as a distraction test and see how it goes. If we can work in the far building, we should be okay."

"You've thought it through, just as I knew you would. I'm off to the store."

"Don't let Sally flirt with any more customers, Mam."

Caitlin started to laugh. "I would have loved to have seen Liam's face yesterday."

"It was priceless," Ashling agreed, laughing with her Mam. "He really didn't know what to do. And to have that little pest say Sally love must have really floored him. What was Lorcan thinking?"

"You know Lorcan, he finds humour in the most unexpected places."

"That he does."

Liam stood and scanned the area at the end of the day. It was starting to look like just maybe something was going on. It had been a week they had been working here and he was pleased. His body was back to normal and he had been able to put in a good day's work. He turned as he heard Lorcan come up beside him.

"Have you seen where Ashling has her classes?" When Liam shook his head, Lorcan motioned for him to follow. "I thought you had. She's out there now but doesn't have classes tonight. I'll show you."

Liam followed Lorcan to one of the outbuildings. He was surprised when he entered and saw the spacious lay out, the kennels built in along the side, a dog grooming area at one end. Someone had put a lot of thought into the planning.

Ashling turned as she heard them. Liam thought she looked tired. He knew she had been putting in longer hours at the store and also at night.

"Lorcan, did you find out about that lab?"

"I did. Can you spare some time tomorrow or should I pick her up and bring her here?"

Ashling thought. "Either one, though off her home territory may give up a better sense of her personality. See if you can get Suzanne to bring her over sometime tomorrow night. No, that won't work."

Lorcan stared at his sister who stared back. Liam's eyes flew between the two. He knew they were communicating silently but it sure looked like a battle from where he stood. Lorcan's eyes finally dropped.

"You're right. Tomorrow night is booked. I forgot. How about Monday night?"

"That should work. If she can be here around 6."

Lorcan turned to leave, then stopped. He went to say something and then shook his head and left.

Ashling watched him walk away and then turned to Liam. "You've never made it back here. I thought you would have."

Liam gave a gentle smile. "I was never asked. It's your work place. I didn't want to intrude."

Ashling tucked her hand into his arm and led him forward. "Then let's give you a tour. Teagan is around somewhere as well."

Liam had to admit to himself he liked the feel of her hand tucked into his arm. It felt right. Maybe it was time he thought seriously about dating and marriage. He just hadn't before, but now Laycee and Leith were settled. He listened to her soothing voice with just the hint of the Irish accent in her parents' voices describing the training building.

"You've put a lot of thought into this," he said.

"I did. I worked in some great centres and have always had this dream of having my own. It's a lot of work but it's so worth it. I think you understand."

He nodded. "I do." He stopped walking, and turning to her, studied her profile. She had a peaceful look about her, a calmness that flowed and calmed those around her. He started as she began to giggle.

"I'm sorry. I just keep thinking of the look on your face when Sally was on your shoulder."

"You're not sorry." Liam laughed. "She is quite the bird. Did Lorcan really teach her?"

Ashling nodded. "He did. He has such a dry sense of humour at times and teaching Sally just seemed to fit."

"Ashling." Liam hesitated and she turned to look at him. "We haven't know each other a long time." Again he stopped and searched the far end of the building. "Would you be willing to go out for a meal with me?"

Ashling tilted her head to study him, and then turned and walked outside. Liam's heart sank. He had blown it. He followed her. She was standing, arms around her waist.

"I'm sorry. I shouldn't have asked."

Ashling shook her head. "No, it just took me by surprise, that's all. When were you thinking?"

Liam shrugged. "I don't know. I guess I really wasn't."

Ashling started to laugh again and Liam joined in. "Liam, you really should have thought this through, you know?" she teased him. "Okay, so what's your schedule like for the next couple of days? I don't have anything on other than the store and I know Da and Mam will cover. That is except for some specialized training with Teagan, and she could use a day off from that."

Liam thought through his work schedule. Tomorrow would do. He had booked the work time line so that weekends out be free for his men. They put in long hours and he knew having two days off in a row were needed to help refresh them. "How about tomorrow?"

She thought and then nodded. "Okay, just let me know what time."

"How about 11? That way, we can go somewhere for lunch and then maybe a nice walk."

"Oh that's it, is it? First, lunch and then a walk. You drive a hard bargain, Mr. Liam Bradley. I agree."

****

The Major watched from the tree line. He lowered his binoculars and waited. Somehow he was going to have to approach them and find out if they had that information. He wondered if they did now. If they had and the police had it, the Colonel would have been arrested.

He looked behind him at a slight noise and faded back into the trees. He couldn't be seen. He would have to have the Sergeants start following them. That was the only way. If it came to it, then the Sergeants would bring those two to him. He didn't want to report another mission failure.

Liam pulled up to the Downie's home and stopped. He was nervous. It had been so many years since he had asked out a woman on a date. He approached the door and knocked. Lorcan, heading out for work in their store, opened the door, looked him over from head to toe, and then grinned.

"She's ready. Go on back to the kitchen." Lorcan stopped as he walked by Liam and came back. "Be patient with her, Liam. She's been hurt in the past and underneath that strong, calm veneer, she is fragile."

Liam took a look at her brother. "No, she's really not, Lorcan. She's a lot stronger than you think."

Lorcan shook his head. Liam had it bad all right.

Liam followed female voices to the kitchen and found Ashling and Caitlin in a hot debate. His eyes bounced between the two woman. Neither was backing down and it seemed as if neither was the winner.

A hand of his shoulder made his turn. Ashling's father, Lachlan, stood beside him, a grin on his face. Liam could see the strong resemblance to Lorcan.

"They're not mad. It's how they discuss things at time. You'll get used to it."

Liam's eyes flew to Lachlan's, who grinned again. "You have it bad for my daughter, I can see, my boy. We'll talk when the time's right." A quick squeeze and Lachlan headed for his wife and daughter.

"Okay, my girls. Time's up. Liam's here and waiting, Ashling. Go, enjoy your day."

Ashling turned, her face flushing as she realized he had been standing there for a while. He grinned at her in amusement. Another facet of her personality was showing.

Caitlin laughed. "Hello, Liam. Welcome to our more common mode of speaking in the morning. It's not all quiet talk and hugs."

Liam spoke. "I'm used to a lot more than this. Try keeping peace with Laycee and Leith when they get going. My mother used to have to actually put them in separate rooms. Neither would back down."

Ashling turned to her parents, giving each a quick hug and kiss and then headed for him. Tucking her hand under his arm, she turned him, speaking over her shoulder, "We're off. See you later. Just make sure Lorcan doesn't train Sally in any more words." Her parents' laughter spilled out the door behind them.

Liam closed the truck door behind her and then circled the front to his door. He stopped and looked around. Why did it feel like he was being watched? His eyes searched the area and saw nothing. He shrugged and shoved that feeling away from him.

Ashling watched as Liam's stood looking around. Her eyes went from him to the tree line behind their house. She had not said anything but she knew Teagan had alerted to someone there. She had seen an area or two where it looked as if someone had been standing for a while. A shiver ran down her spine. She did not like that feeling.

Once behind the wheel, Liam turned to her, watching her face. "We're off."

"And not to see the wizard, I should hope," Ashling responded.

Liam stared at her, caught her words and shouted with laughter. Her unexpected responses were just too cute. "No, hopefully not to see the wizard. How about Elmtown?"

She nodded and he pulled away. He didn't see the vehicle pull away from the curb and follow them.

"Leith," Laycee's voice came over the phone, a distressed note in it.

He stopped on his walk to the cafe and asked, "What's wrong?"

"Do you feel like someone has been in your house in the last few days, searching through?"

Leith paused. That's what had been bugging him, exactly that. He found items shifted from where he knew he had left them and shrugged them off as being tired, or that maybe Regan had moved something. "You know, I think I do. Have you?"

She gave a sigh and said, "I do. Joshua has the same feeling. He's calling Caleb now to come out and see. You may want to call too."

Leith's fingers came up to squeeze the bridge of his nose. He and Regan had planned to meet for a late breakfast and then head to Oak City for some time away. He guessed that wouldn't be happening now. "I will. Let me know what he says."

Regan headed to him from the direction of the cafe. She stopped in front of him, hands on his arms. "What's up?"

He pulled her into a hug and held tight. "Laycee just called. She thinks someone has been through her home. Joshua was calling Caleb."

Regan tightened her hug on her fiancee. "I know. I thought that about yours. I don't think mine has been but I'm in an apartment and Mr. Jones doesn't let anyone in the door unless he knows them or someone can vouch for them."

Leith looked down at Regan. "They could still find a way in. Ben told Liam it looked as if professionals had been in his place." He gazed towards the cafe and then sighed. "I guess breakfast at SueEllen's isn't happening today, is it?"

She shook her head and turned him back to his truck.

****

The Sergeants were on a mission. They were following Liam and Ashling. They needed to get close to them. The Major was putting the pressure on them. Whatever it was they had of the Colonel's, they needed to

324

find it and fast. The Colonel would not suffer fools gladly, they knew.

They watched as the truck ahead of them turned into the parking lot of a small family-owned diner and the two occupants get out. They looked at each other and shrugged. They might as well go and eat too. They doubted they would be noticed.

****

Liam watched the woman sitting across from him. She had a natural physical beauty, but it was the beauty inside that drew him. She was studying the menu and then looked up to catch his eyes on her. She blushed slightly, set the menu down and propped her chin in her hands and looked back.

"So, this is how it's going to be today—you stare at me and me at you? Or do we get this out of the way now and go on with our day?" A mischievous smile crossed her face.

Liam laughed. "You caught me, I guess. Let's just say, we go on with our day. It's going to be an interesting one, that's for certain, with you, Ashling Downie."

Ashling smiled. She had made her point with humour and Liam had responded the same. Yes, it would be a good day.

They wandered through the small town, almost a village, for a while, and then headed for the nearby lake. The town was noted for having some well-planned walking and riding trails. Both were eager to see them.

Ashling stopped Liam with a hand on his arm and pointed. They stopped to watch the variety of ducks, and then their attention was drawn to some swans.

"I could watch those swans all day," Ashling commented. "They are just so peaceful."

Liam turned to study her. Her eyes were on the swans. He felt the same way about her. She had such a peaceful look on her face. Her eyes flickered to his brown ones and then back to the lake.

325

A small smile crept across her lips. "You really need to stop that, you know."

Liam grinned. "Stop what?"

She swatted his arm and moved away. "You know exactly what I mean. Men!"

Liam gave a shout of laughter and then ran to catch up with her. She tucked her hand into his arm and they continued. He liked the feel of that but would rather have been holding it.

Late that afternoon, they headed home. Both were tired, but the day had been wonderful. Liam's fingers tapped the wheel as he thought. He glanced over at Ashling. She had her head back on the head rest and was staring out the side window. He listened; she was humming slightly, content with herself, her company and the day. Liam smiled. It had been a good day. He had needed a day away from work and from all the stress at home. He needed to do this more, and just maybe, he had found a friend to escape with.

Lights caught his vision from behind. They were coming fast, almost too fast. He looked for somewhere to pull off. There was nowhere he could. Steady hands on the wheel, he kept his speed even. The lights pulled up behind him, way too close for his comfort. Then a second vehicle passed and pulled in front. This vehicle's brake lights came on. What was going on? Ashling looked at him, looked ahead and behind.

"Looks like we have a bit of a situation, doesn't it?"

"It does. Look, we're in our own area. Put in a call. I don't like this. Your door is locked?"

She nodded as she pulled out her phone. She had a really bad feeling about this as Liam was forced to a stop, boxed in front and back. This was not a good way to end their day.

Regan stood with Laycee as she watched both Leith and Joshua talking with Caleb and Ben. There had really been someone through the two homes. It was subtle but it had happened. She shuddered. What if they had been home? Laycee reached for her hand and gripped it, replaying in her mind when her home had been invaded a year ago. At least this time, there was no damage but the feeling of violation was still here. She knew Leith would feel the same.

The two men parted from the Caleb and Ben and headed their way.

"What did they say, Leith?" Regan spoke first.

He shook his head. "There's not much, if any, evidence they can see. Someone was in and out very quickly." He rubbed the back of his neck, then rested his hand on his black head of close-cropped curls. "Caleb figures it was professionals. Ben thinks it's the same ones who went through Liam's."

"Liam's!" Laycee's shocked voice cut through the silence his words had brought. Joshua's arms came around his wife and pulled her to him. "Why? What would we have of Liam's that they would want?"

Joshua rested his chin on his wife's dark head. "That's what we don't know. Someone apparently thinks Liam has something of theirs and because they didn't find it at his place, then maybe we have it. Caleb said he'd up the patrols here for a while."

Leith spoke. "Come on. I really don't feel like going in the house right now. Let's head for the cafe and at least get us a coffee. Maybe if we brainstorm, we might come up with something."

Caleb turned to watch the four drive away. He closed his eyes in a quick prayer for guidance and then turned to look at Leith's home.

Ben studied the area around them, an uncomfortable feeling niggling at him. "I feel like we have eyes on us, but I just can't see anything."

Caleb agreed. "I just don't get it. Liam has given neither one of them anything in the past month, not since before he was hurt. So who thinks he has and what is it?"

"I told you, Caleb. It's that Bradley thing. One can't get ahead of the other." He sobered at a thought. "I guess we'll have to track down Liam and find out what he has remembered. I'm not banking on much though."

Caleb thought about it and agreed. "No, I don't think he will. We searched that area and came up with nothing." He turned to his vehicle. "Let's take this up again in the morning."

Liam reached for Ashling's hand. She hadn't had a chance to finish her call. His calloused hand grasped hers tightly.

"We don't know who they are. Just sit tight."

A light appeared at his window and blinded him. He heard a voice but didn't respond. His eyes moved to Ashling's side of the truck. A dark form was there as well. He shot a quick look at her. She was calm, a concerned look on her face, but not fright. He wished he had her calmness and peace.

Liam waited. He was not getting out of his truck. Glass shattered as the window behind his gave way. He ducked, pulling Ashling down with him. More shattering of glass and his door was pulled open. He turned. A gun was pointed at him and a hand was motioning him out. He hesitated and Ashling's door was yanked open and a gun pointed at her. Her eyes met his, scared but calm. He drew strength from her peace. Seat belts unclicked, they both climbed down.

No words were said as they were pushed towards the vehicles. Liam turned and reached for Ashling's hand, but she was pulled to the vehicle behind them. Prodding from behind forced him to walk to the truck in front, heart in mouth as he pondered what was happening. His thoughts focused on Ashling and her safety, he climbed in the truck. His hands were bound in front of him and then the trucks moved away. As he glanced back, he saw his truck following. There would be no leads, nothing to be followed. How was he to get away, find Ashling and get her to safety? He leaned his head back and closed his eyes in prayer. If this was how he had to get close to God, he would rather have done it a different way. God, where are You? Are you here? Why, God? He felt a whisper of peace envelop him. God was here. God knew where they were.

Ashling kept her gaze steady and calm. Her heart was racing inside her as she contemplated what was happening. Who and why? She didn't know of anything in her past that would have led to this. It had to be something with Liam. Was it from his fall in the river? She had wondered if there was more to it than said, but no one had commented. Her thoughts turned to prayer and she turned her heart to her Father God.

The trucks slowed and then turned into a manufacturing complex. They headed for the very end. Waiting while a gate was unlocked, they then proceeded forward and into one of the buildings, the door shutting behind them. Liam thought it had the look of a garage but he couldn't be sure. Heart racing, he scanned the area, trying to find a way out but the lighting was too dim. He saw nothing. The trucks stopped and then a blindfold was clapped over his eyes. He was roughly pulled from the truck and then shoved forward and then shoved down into a chair. His hands were loosened and then pulled behind him and he was once more bound. He tried to hear Ashling but couldn't. There was just that silence. He hadn't been able to get a glimpse of the men, the lights had been too bright, and he knew they wore masks.

Ashling had been blindfolded as well and then shoved into a room. She stumbled as she was pushed and went down on one knee, her bound hands barely catching her as she fell. Who and what, she wondered again? Is it safe to remove my blindfold? She sank to the floor, head on her knees. The room was cold and felt dirty. She knew Liam was out there but was he safe?

Liam heard foot steps approaching him. The men waited, he couldn't tell how many, but he sensed at least three. Was he to find out why they had been kidnapped?

A hand grasped his head and pulled it back. He winced at the pain.

"You have something that I need. Tell me where it is." The gravelly voice sounded familiar, but he couldn't place it.

Liam shook his head. "I don't know what you want. I don't have it."

A hand slammed across his face and he blinked at the sudden pain, tasting blood on his lip. He shook his head. "I don't have anything you want."

The questioning continued. Liam's body finally sank forward as he lost consciousness. The Major looked at the other men.

"Put him in the room. We'll try again later. Meanwhile, have you searched his truck?"

One of them nodded. "It was clean. So were the houses we searched. What did he do with it?"

The Major stared across at the locked door. "I don't know and we had better find it and soon. The Colonel is getting very angry. You don't want to anger him."

Ashling raised her head at the sound of the lock being opened. She had removed her blindfold and managed to get out of her bonds. She drew a breath as Liam's body was carried through the door and roughly dropped on the floor. The door slammed and locked. Then there was silence.

Caleb raised his head from the never-ending paperwork on his desk at the tap at his door. Both Ben and Eddie were standing there and behind them, Leith and

Joshua. He motioned them in and Ben closed the door behind them.

Keen eyes studied the other four. His heart sank as he realized it wasn't a social call. Something bad had happened and with those two here, it had to be to Liam.

"Liam didn't make it home last night. Ashling's mother called this morning. Ashling didn't either. That is not like them. They had planned to have dinner with her parents. She had waited, thinking they had decided differently or had had truck trouble. We can't reach either one on their phones." Leith's breath caught for a minute and then he stopped.

Caleb's eyes turned to Ben.

Ben responded. "We've put on an alert for them. Nothing yet. Lorcan's on duty and he had a pretty good idea where they were headed. Liam had been doing some digging on what Ashling liked to do on her time off."

Caleb shook his head. One part of him could not believe that the third Bradley sibling was involved in something like this. "Where are Laycee and Regan?"

Joshua spoke up. "They've gone out to the Downie's. They thought if they were together it might be best."

Eddie spoke up. "I'm headed to the town they were going to be at yesterday. I'll ask around and see what I can find." He headed for the door, hesitated and turned back, started to speak, then stopped. He looked at the ceiling and then back at each of the men. "I don't have to tell you, Leith and Joshua, and your girls, we'll do our best. We'll figure it out. Right now, you two need to be in prayer."

Caleb nodded as he left. "He's right. Now you two get back to the Downie's. We've got some planning to do to find them."

Leith stood, stature rigid. "I want to be part of it, Caleb. I won't sit on the sidelines and wait."

Caleb studied his friend. "Didn't think you would. But let us do what we need to do first. We can't go running off half-cocked without knowing where we're running to.

Just be ready to go if we call. It's going to be hard but we need to keep things as normal as possible."

Ben watched as the two younger men walked away, despair and defeat in their demeanour. He turned to Caleb. "I don't know, Caleb. I just don't know. Something is off. I feel it."

Caleb searched for words. "I know, Ben, I know. I..." His words failed. He looked up to the ceiling. "Once again, we are going to have to trust in ways we never have before."

Ben nodded. "Unless Hannah has another one of her moments."

Caleb smiled. "I pray she does and quickly." His wife had been instrumental in providing the names of the ringleaders in both Laycee's and Leith's situations in the last year.

Ashling moved towards Liam's limp body. She reached out, her hand shaking, and felt for a pulse. He was alive. Her eyes closed in a prayer of thanks. The light was dim, the window dirty. She rolled him to his back and tears clouded her eyes as she looked at his battered face. Dear Lord, she prayed, please let him be okay. Please provide a way out for us. She felt him over. His ribs felt tender and when she pressed, he let out a groan. Bruised at least, she thought, if not worse. She tugged him towards the wall and then slid down, cradling his head on her knee. She wanted water to clean his face but there was none. A single tear dripped and fell and she angrily brushed at her eyes. Tears wouldn't help.

What were they after? Whatever it was, Liam had refused to give them. She bent her head over her friend and her thoughts turned to God. God, where are You, she cried? Why are we here? Please, dear Lord, protect us. Heal Liam. Let someone find us quickly. Her head sank back against the wall, strength spent. Her eyes slid closed and she slept.

A noise at the door roused her. It was daylight she could tell. A figure appeared, face masked, and set a paper bag down. Gray eyes met her and then the door was closed and locked. She leaned back and looked up. It hadn't been a dream after all. They really had been abducted.

She looked down at Liam. He was still unconscious. Whoever had questioned him had not spared him at all. Bruises and small cuts covered his face. Carefully sliding his head to the floor, she crept over to the bag and opened it. Water and food. Apparently they were intended to live.

She pulled out one of the water bottles and reach for some of the paper napkins. She would have preferred a cloth but this would do. She returned to Liam and loosening the bottle cap, she dampened the napkins and brushed lightly at his face, removing dirt and blood. She cringed at the sight of his face. She then lifted his head enough to tilt the bottle to his mouth. She needed to get some fluid into him. He swallowed and then groaned, rolling to his side. His eyes flickered and slid shut. Ashling slid back to the floor and leaned against the wall. She had no appetite. Her eyes too slid shut and she slept.

Neither heard the door opening or saw the man standing watching them. He stepped towards them, distaste in his manner at the surroundings. He stood and watched them, then turned away. He would find out the information he needed, even if he had to kill them to do so.

He waited until the door was locked behind him, then turned to the Major. "Find what I want, then kill them." He strode away.

The Major stared after the Colonel, then back to the door. How was he to find out what the Colonel wanted? Liam had said nothing despite the beating. If he didn't talk, then how was he to find it? He had no stomach for hitting a woman. He didn't think the Sergeants did either. He paced, thinking. They had found nothing on their searches. Could it still be on the river bank? Or had it fallen into the river? If so, they would never find it. He had been sure it had been in his pocket and now it was gone.

Eddie tapped at Caleb's door and then entered to find Ben there as well. Closing the door, he sat, exhaustion evident in his movements.

"What did you find, Eddie?" Caleb searched his face, knowing the answer before Eddie spoke.

"Nothing. I really didn't find anyone who remembered them being there. And I should have. Lorcan was adamant it was that town."

Caleb ran his hand through his hair. "We have nothing. No truck. No Liam. No Ashling. No ransom demand."

Ben nodded in agreement. "So what do we really have?"

A knock at his door stopped any further comments. It was Lorcan. He looked spent, and worried.

"Chief, I went back over the route they may have taken. I found this." He held up a bag with some bits of glass, then handed it to Caleb. "It's window glass."

Caleb studied it. "And you think it's from Liam's truck?"

Lorcan nodded. "I do. It's too fresh to have been there long. And I checked. We have had no reports of any vandalism or accidents in that area. It's a remote area, perfect for an ambush."

The three older men exchanged glances, then brought their eyes back to Lorcan. "Lorcan, do you have a dog ready that can track?"

Lorcan's head came up and he nodded. "Teagan. Ashling was working with her, teaching her to track. She wanted to make sure she knew what she was doing when she trained my dog.”

“All right. It’s too dark now but first thing in the morning, go with Eddie and search that area. See if you can find anything.”

The next morning, Lorcan and Teagan searched the area. Caleb and Eddie watched.

“Ashling was here. I can tell by how the dog’s reacting.” Eddie turned to search the area. “I don’t see that anything is disturbed along the road though.”

Caleb turned as well. “No. It’s like the two and Liam’s truck just vanished into thin air.” He sighed. “I’ve had enough of our people vanishing for days on end. Who is doing it this time?”

Eddie’s eyes traced Lorcan’s movements. “He’s hurting. He needs to find his sister to make sure she’s okay and he can’t. The dog’s hurting too. Ashling and that dog have a bond I have never seen before.”

Caleb nodded. “I’m headed back to the office. Let me know if you find anything.”

Lorcan approached Eddie, Teagan at his side but watchful, searching for her mistress.

“They were here, Eddie. They were here.”

The anguished look on Lorcan’s face tugged at Eddie. “I know, Lorcan. Nothing else other than the scent that stops and the bits of glass?”

Lorcan shook his head. “It’s like someone reached down and plucked them away.” He searched the area. “Now what? Where do we search? It could be a small area or a large area.”

Eddie studied him. “You were involved in search in your previous department. Run me through the steps of how you started and if you searched in a wooded area, an urban area, an industrial area. All of those mean a different search pattern. Think it through. We’ll head back to the office and you can be ready to tell me.”

Liam stirred. He hurt all over again. His face was the worse. His hand shaking, he reached to feel. He didn't like what he felt. What had happened? And why was he lying on cold concrete?

He rolled to his back, groaning at the effort. His hand went to cradle his ribs. He couldn't tell if they were fractured or not but they hurt. A whisper of sound came to him. He just couldn't look, couldn't keep his eyes open.

He felt hands on his arms, his face, and then a soft voice.

"Liam."

He knew that voice and struggled to open his eyes again. He blinked to clear his vision and looked up.

Ashling knelt beside him, hand on his head. "Liam, you're awake. Thank goodness."

He blinked again and tried to speak. The hand left his head and then he felt it underneath, raising it up. Water touched his lips and he drank thirstily.

Ashling drew the water back after Liam had had some. She wouldn't let him drink a lot yet, it would make him sick.

"Do you think you can sit up?"

He nodded, then regretted it. "Give me a minute." His voice was raspy, his mouth and throat dry. Finally, he was able to raise himself up, Ashling's arm behind him to support him.

"If you can, slide backwards a bit. There's a wall there you can rest against." She helped him move backwards.

He closed his eyes, it had been such a struggle just to move. He drew in a deep breath, and then he felt her fingers around his, closing them on a bottle.

"Drink, but in sips and slowly only."

"Where are we?"

"In a locked room in that building they brought us to. It's been a day or so I think." Ashling looked around.

"I've tried to find a way out but I can't. We're stuck. They did bring food and water. I won't touch the food but the water bottles seem okay." She slid down to sit beside him, her shoulder touching his.

"We'll get out, somehow." He reached for her hand and gripped it. "Where's your faith?"

Her head hit his shoulder and he thought he felt the dampness of tears. "It's there. It's just a dark spot right now."

There was the sound of the lock being turned and the door slid open. A figure stood there watching them. He stepped forward, face hidden. He motioned for them to stand. Liam groaned as he came upright and Ashling's arm slid around him. She pulled his arm over her shoulder, offering him support.

They were directed out into the large open area. Liam stumbled and almost fell, but caught himself. They watched the man as he motioned them, once again in silence, to the door at the far end of the building. They were motioned through and the sun blinded them for a minute. They stopped and turned. The man watched them, then pointed behind them. They turned. A vehicle sat there.

"Go," he said. "I can't let them kill you. That's what they're planning. Go. Godspeed." He turned and walked back into the building.

Liam stumbled as he turned. Ashling turned as well, studying the area around them.

"Come, Liam, let's go." She pulled him to the vehicle, helped to shove him onto the car seat, and then ran around the front. Keys were in the ignition and it started as soon as she turned the key. Cautiously driving around the building, she headed for the open gate and freedom.

"Please, God, keep us safe." She glanced at Liam. His head was back and eyes closed, pain evident on his battered face. "I don't know where we are, God, but You do. Drive for me. Guide my hands."

God answered. She soon found herself in familiar territory and headed for the hospital at home. Parking near the Emergency entrance, she ran for help. She knew she couldn't get Liam in on her own.

Caleb stood on the river bank, once more studying the area. Something puzzled him. Something had happened here, something that had almost cost a friend his life. He raised his eyes to the sky and prayed once more for wisdom and guidance. His phone ringing cut into his prayer. His eyes slid closed as he listened and then he turned to run for his vehicle. Liam and Ashling were safe.

Ben met him in the parking lot at the hospital, both intent on reaching their friends.

"Any word on what happened?"

Ben shook his head. "Not much. The doctors are with them right now. Eddie's been able to get Ashling's statement. Ashling said briefly that one of the men let them go and gave them a vehicle. She's worried about him. She was able to give Eddie an address. We haven't been able to question Liam yet."

"That's good. Let's hope we find some evidence there."

The waiting room held the family of both Liam and Ashling. Caleb ran his eyes over them and just thanked God that it was a hospital room and not a funeral home they were gathered in. It could have easily been one or the other. He touched Ben's shoulder, murmured a word and then headed back to the exam room. He spoke to the ward clerk and then turned to the room to his right.

Ashling sat on the stretcher, bracing herself with her arms. She looked up when he entered, blue eyes tired and strained. He could see the fatigue in her face.

"How are you, Ashling?"

She shrugged. "Alive. Out of that place. Ready to go home. Take your pick."

Caleb watched her. Her response was not typical for her. She was hurting in a way that he couldn't put a finger on. "Eddie got your statement." At her nod, he asked, "Have you thought of anything else?"

She shook her head. "No. How's Liam?"

"I haven't seen him yet. The doctor was with him."

She nodded, then as the nurse entered the room with her discharge papers, she said, "They hurt him bad, Caleb. I thought he was going to die." She raised her eyes and stared at him. "Find them."

Caleb nodded. "We will do our best."

She slid from the bed, staggered, then caught her balance. "Is your best good enough though?" Walking away from him, she left the room.

Caleb rubbed the back of his neck, having to agree that their best might not be enough. He went to find Liam.

Liam lay in an adjacent exam room, eyes closed, IV once again in his arm, this time with needed fluids and antibiotics. Caleb stopped beside the bed, hand resting on the raised bed side. He watched his friend's face and winced at what he had been through. Caleb doubted he had seen a beating like that for years. Eyes came up and he stared across the room. Liam wasn't ready to talk, but when he was, Caleb would be there. Anger began to burn within him.

Returning to the waiting room, he found Leith and Laycee. He spoke with them for a few minutes and then left. A hand touched his arm as he exited the hospital and he turned in surprise. Lachlan stood there.

"Let us know what we can do to help. We need to be doing something."

Caleb sighed. "Right now, pray. That is what we need."

Lachlan nodded. "That I can do." He walked away to where his wife and daughter stood.

Caleb watched them walk away. He had no idea who he was looking for.

Later that night, he stood at the entrance of the building and looked around. One more abandoned building used for nefarious activities. He turned and studied the outside, then stepped inside. Eddie came to meet him.

"What do we have?"

Eddie shook his head. "Not much. I would swear, if I was a swearing man, that someone knows exactly how to avoid leaving any evidence. We found where Liam was questioned, the room they were held in. Nothing else. Tire tracks aren't there, it's too dry to leave much of anything."

Caleb took a deep breath. "Why do I feel like we are always running behind? Do we have another leak?" He thought about how the secretary had betrayed them a few months ago.

"I hope not. We don't need that."

Chapter 9

Liam struggled to open his eyes. The pain was better and he couldn't figure out why. Then his vision cleared and he looked around. A nurse stood beside him adjusting an IV. He was in the hospital. He really hadn't dreamed it.

At his movement, the nurse looked over and then reached for his wrist. She smiled. "The doctor will be in shortly."

The door opened and a doctor he didn't recognize entered. He stopped by Liam's bed and studied the young man.

"I'm Dr. Adams. How are you feeling today?"

Liam eyes the doctor, who looked to be in his 40s. "I hurt. How am I supposed to feel?"

The doctor smiled. "Yes, you will for a few days. I don't know who did this to you, but they did a good job. Beside the bruises on your face, you've got some ribs there are bruised. Those will take some time to heal. The cuts on your face, I am assuming are from glass."

Liam thought for a moment, then cautiously nodded. "I think I remember the truck windows being broken."

Dr. Adams nodded. "That would explain it. It's mostly the left side of the face. Your clothing protected your neck and back and arm." He studied Liam's chart, then said, "I'm going to release you once the IV's finished and it looks like it almost it. You need to take it easy for a few days." At Liam's snort, he looked at him. "Yes, I know what you do for a living. You have men working for you. Let them do the work. You won't be doing much until those ribs heal anyway. And for the next few days, you'll not be on your own. Someone will need to be with you."

Liam glared at him, and Dr. Adams laughed. "I've met your family. How about your girlfriend's family?"

Liam's eyebrows raised in surprise. "Girlfriend."

Dr. Adams nodded. "Sure. She's been around a few times checking on you. If she wasn't, why would she?"

Liam closed his eyes. Ashling was fine. "Thank you, Dr. Adams. I was worried about her."

"Hold on to her, young man. She's a keeper."

Liam lay and watched the drip in the IV line. He wanted out of here. He wanted to find Ashling and see for himself she was fine.

The door opened again, and Leith and Laycee walked in. Laycee hugged her brother. Leith stopped at the end of the bed and watching Liam closely.

"Don't ask," Liam almost snapped. Both Laycee and Leith stared at him in surprise. That was not Liam. He never snapped at them. "And no, I'm not going to stay with either one of you. So don't even ask. It's not even up for debate."

Laycee looked at Leith, then back to her older brother. "But, Liam, you have to have someone with you."

He shook his head. "Not one of you. I'm a target and I won't put you there."

Laycee's eyes filled with tears as she stared at her brother, then turned and ran from the room. Leith watched her leave, then eyed his brother.

"Not debating it, brother. The only debate is which house, mine or yours."

"Leith, you don't understand. I can't put you at risk. If you're at risk, so is Regan."

Leith shook his head. "So, it's okay for you to pull the big brother card when it involves Laycee or me, but we can't pull the younger brother/sister card. Doesn't work that way. You're stuck with me. Joshua would gladly have you there as well."

"I can't, Leith. They're newlyweds. I won't intrude."

"Then maybe you need to apologize to Laycee and tell her that. She'll understand."

Liam laid his head back. Leith was right. He did need to make things right with Laycee. He just wasn't thinking clearly.

"Go find her. She won't have gone far."

Leith left and found his sister. Liam was right. She was just outside the door. He stood looking at her until she raised tear-filled eyes to him.

"He's worried, Laycee. He's scared that you or I are going to get caught and hurt." He reached for his sister. "Come here." She clung to him as he hugged her.

"I'm so afraid, Leith. All I can think of is that I can't lose him. We almost lost you six months ago. He's been there for us always. When Momma died from her heart disease and Daddy from that work accident, he was there. He set his own grief aside for ours."

Leith felt her tears soaking his T-shirt. He laid his head on his sister's head and his own tears caught in her black curls. "I know, honey, I know. It hurts when he shoves us aside and he doesn't even realize he has. We just have to keep reminding him we're family and we're not going anywhere. We'll talk it out, we always do. Just keep those prayers going."

Laycee nodded, hugged her brother tight once more, and then stepped back. "I gather he sent you to find me?"

Leith stood, eyes on his sister's face, and hands on her shoulders. She looked so much like their mother. What advice would she give? What would their father tell them?

He nudged her towards the door. "Go, make your peace with him. Just remember, he's scared too, just won't show it. We have to let him have that. Just pray, honey, just pray. God is in control. Liam's been struggling since your episode last year. He's still the big brother, wanting to protect both of us."

Laycee nodded, swiped at her eyes, drew in a deep breath, and then pushed open the door to Liam's room. Liam looked up and then reached his hand for his sister. Leith watched through the slowly closing door as Liam caught his sister in his arms, looked up and mouthed his thanks.

Leith leaned back against the wall, emotionally drained. He so wanted to go in there too, but these two needed to work out what had happened between them. He wasn't needed. He looked up as someone stopped in front of him.

Caleb stood watching his friend. His heart hurt for him. The three had been through so much. Now the family was starting to show cracks. He lifted eyes and prayed for them, prayed for healing, for strength. He prayed for wisdom for his officers. They were at an impasse and without any further clues, they would not find out who was after Liam.

"It hurts, Caleb." Leith's soft voice broke into his prayers and his eyes returned to his friend.

"I know, Leith, I know. Come on, let's go get you a coffee and me a tea." He nodded at the door. "Laycee and Liam need this time. Your time with him will come."

****

The Colonel stood and watched, rage building within him. The fools had failed once again. What would it take for them to succeed? He needed that information. Did he have to take matters into his own hands. He glared at the door behind which Liam lay and then turned away to his tasks. Soon, he thought, soon I will have the information and you will be no more.

The Major watched the Colonel as he walked from the hospital and across the parking lot to his car. He knew time was limited for himself and the Sergeants. Which one of them had let them go and provided them a car? The Colonel had been in a rage when he found out. He now had to backtrack, pick up the pieces and make plans to find that information. If he only knew exactly what he was looking for, it would help.

Caleb sank into his desk chair and once again contemplated the files piled up his desk. He thought he had cleared it off last night but it was once again piled down. He sighed. He hoped to be out of here early tonight to spend time with his wife and boys. He wasn't sure if he would be able to.

A few hours later, a tap came at his door, and Ben and Eddie entered. He watched them.

"What do you have?"

Ben and Eddie exchanged a glance, then Ben spoke, "We've had a hit and run out near that industrial complex. The young man fits the description Ashling gave us."

Caleb thought, then nodded. "Of course we do. Another lead to follow. All right, run with it and see how far you get. We need to find these people and find them fast. Things are getting out of hand."

As they turned to leave, Caleb had a thought and stopped them.

"I know we've discussed this in the past. We need to start tracking who is prominent in the town who would have hidden access to what we're finding. There's something there, and no, Hannah has not come through with a name as yet." The two other men laughed and then left.

Caleb leaned back in his chair, deep in thought, pen rolling in his fingers. He nodded and then reached for the phone. He could help in a tangible way and he would.

A few hours later, Liam sat on the side of his hospital bed, trying to gather strength to get dressed. He had been discharged. Caleb had been by an hour or so ago and said he would make sure he had a ride. Strange, Leith hadn't been back. He was to go stay with him. Apparently, from what Leith said, Regan was already planning on

345

mothering him, planning meals to tempt his appetite. Laycee and he had talked through what had happened. She understood he didn't want to intrude on Joshua and her. Leith and Regan was getting married in a couple of weeks and he didn't really want to intrude on their last few weeks as a couple before they married. That time was too precious for them.

A tap at the door brought his head up. Lachlan Downie entered and stood watching him.

Lachlan studied the younger man, taking in the evidence of his recent beating. He watched him, knowing his character. His daughter wouldn't say, but he could read her pretty well. This man, sitting on the bed in front of him, was becoming very important to her. He would do just about anything to keep him safe. His daughter had been hurt in the past and he didn't want to see that happen again.

"Liam." Lachlan spoke, then waited. Liam watched, wondering what was coming. "I've come to take you to our place. No, don't protest. Caitlin used to be a nurse until she retired a few years ago for personal reasons. With Lorcan as police officer, Caleb thinks you'll be fairly safe, about as safe as anywhere right now. You need a mother to look after you right now. You haven't had that in many years, I understand. Sometimes the strong one in the family, the protector, needs to step aside and be ministered too. Let us be your ministers." He looked up and grinned, looking very much like his son. "Besides, I have an added attraction at my house that Leith doesn't."

Liam's puzzled look made him laugh again. "Come on, Liam. Think about it. Ashling doesn't live at Leith's house. She's at mine."

Liam flushed, then laughed. "I guess we're going to have to have a talk at some point, aren't we, Lachlan? You've got a really special girl there."

Lachlan's head tilted and he watched the emotions flickering across his young friend's face. "We shall, my boy, we shall. She's pretty special in my opinion, and she needs someone pretty special in her life. You're that."

Liam looked up in surprise. When had his secret got out?

Lachlan laughed again. "Don't worry. You haven't given yourself away. Caitlin and I have been watching you and really haven't forgotten what young love is like. Now, let's get you ready and on the road."

Ben stood at the side of the road, studying the area where the body had been found. There was't a lot of evidence that they could find. Whoever had done it had stopped and cleaned up after themselves, or else the hit and run had been elsewhere and the body dumped here.

He looked at the picture he had been given. A young man, late teens/early 20s. Someone's son who wouldn't be coming home. Eddie was right. He did match the description given by Ashling. He sighed. He would have to go talk with her and he really didn't want to tell her the young man who saved their lives was dead. It would hurt her, he knew.

He turned as Eddie approached. Eddie had managed to track down a name and address. This was one call they alway hated. They turned and walked to their vehicle. Someone would hurt today in a way they shouldn't have to.

Caleb accepted the cup of tea Caitlin handed him and sat at the table on their deck. Liam was there, drawings in front of him as he worked through projects he had upcoming and proposals he needed to submit. Work was helping, Caleb knew; it helped to keep the mind from thinking of what happened, at least during the day it did.

Lachlan and Caitlin joined them. They knew Caleb was not here in an official capacity but rather as a friend. Talk drifted through the messages they had been listening to at church.

A sudden squeal and then a shouted "Lorcan" startled both Liam and Caleb. They looked up and searched the yard, wondering what was going on. A glance at Lachlan and Caitlin showed smiles on their faces.

"Watch," Lachlan commented. "Lorcan has done something to Ashling. He won't get away with it."

As their gaze returned to the yard, they saw Lorcan running towards the outbuildings, Ashling at his heels. To their surprise, she tackled him and then sat on him, holding him down. Teagan danced around them, black and white fur glinting in the sun, barking. Lorchan's hands came up in surrender and after giving him a smack on the shoulder, Ashling stood. His left hand reached for her foot and she danced away, saying something to him. They heard a shout of laughter and Ashling darted towards the rocks at the back of the yard, Lorcan scrambling to his feet to follow. They could hear the laughter from the two before they settled on a large rock, shoulder to shoulder.

Caitlin laughed. "He never learns. It's been like this all their lives. He will torment her and then take off. He has never yet been able to outrun her."

Lachlan spoke up, laughter still in his voice. "She's taken part in marathons and half marathons. She's always been a runner. There have been few of her friends or teammates who have been able to catch her." He turned to Caleb with a sparkle in his eyes. "I don't know that Lorcan would want it known that his sister can still outrun him and beat him up."

Caleb shook his head. "I'll hold on to this. I may need insurance some day and it would be good to bring this up."

Liam's eyes were still trained on the two at the back of the yard, not saying anything. Caitlin and Lachlan exchanged a glance. He was seeing a different side to the woman they suspected he had come to love and it floored him. Their daughter had many sides to her personality and as she got to know someone, the sides came out.

Lorcan dropped into a chair by his mother and reached for a cup of tea and a scone.

"What did you do this time, Lorcan?"

He grinned. "Me? I didn't do anything."

Lachlan snorted, drawing the attention of the other two men. "Right, tell us that again."

Lorcan laughed. "I got her with the hose."

Caitlin looked at her son, shook her head as she stood. "I'd chase you too if you turned the hose on me." She dropped a kiss on his dark brown head. "Thank you, son. She needed that."

Liam's eyes turned from them to the woman sitting at the end of the yard. At a touch on his shoulder, he looked up. Caitlin stood behind him. "Go," she said softly. "She won't come to you."

Liam studied her, then stood hesitating, then headed for the stairs to the yard and Ashling. She looked up as he approached and then sat on the rock beside her.

Lorcan watched, then commented, "He's got it bad, that he does."

"And you will let her be, my boy." His father watched him until he looked. "Let her be."

Lorcan's face sobered and he nodded. "I'm off. I still have to find that dog for Ashling to look at."

Caleb turned the cup in his hands, his thoughts dark. He looked up to find Lachlan watching him.

"What do you know, Caleb? I know you're here as a friend, but you've moved ahead in the investigation."

Caleb nodded, his eyes once again going towards his friends. "I do. The young man who helped them escape? We found his body early this morning, a hit and run. It's too coincidental to it being an accident."

Lachlan's eyes slid closed. He worried for his daughter, for her friend. "You have identified him, I can tell from what you're not saying. Keep me updated, please."

Caleb stood, looking down at Lachlan. "I will, but keep watch. If either she or Liam remember anything, call me, Ben or Eddie."

Lachlan nodded, then spoke once again. "I find it interesting that you want one of the three of you called, not your dispatch. You are suspecting a leak somewhere. We will be in prayer."

Caleb's thoughts caught at how quickly Lachlan had picked up on that. He nodded. "Thank you."

The watcher in the trees stood so close, he could almost touch them. Thankfully, the dog had moved away or he would not be able to be so close. He watched to reach out and snatch them, take them somewhere he could find the information. As the dog returned, he stepped back and left. Soon, he thought, soon.

Teagan growled softly and faced the trees. Ashling reached down and soothed her, not realizing the danger that had lurked behind her. She turned to Liam.

He was watching her. "Did I really see you tackle your brother and take him down?"

She giggled. "You did. He can never beat me. It's been like since we were kids. He'd try and fail dramatically."

She sighed. "Liam, do you remember anything? I can only remember bits and pieces."

He shook his head. "You likely remember more than I do. But there is something. There was a voice that sounded so familiar, but I can't quite catch it. It's like the voice was out of the normal place I would expect to see him."

"You've lived here all your life. You know a lot of the people. It will come." She stood. "Come, I need to get to work, and you need to go relax. Doctor's orders and the nurse up there is watching for you to come relax."

He sat and watched her walk away, Teagan at her side. Lord, please keep her safe. I can't when I don't know who to protect her from.

He studied the ground around his feet. Something caught his eye and he bent over to pick it up. What was this doing here? And who had dropped it? He turned it over and over in his fingers. He needed to get it to Caleb.

He searched the deck. Caleb had gone. He would call him or else Ben or Eddie.

The watcher in the trees had returned just in time to see Liam pocket something. What had he pocketed? Was it what they were looking for? He would have to find some way to find out. He slipped away. He needed to make plans.

The Colonel stood and watched the Major. He was failing him and he would need to be dealt with. Eyes then wandered to the house and the man walking towards it. Soon. Soon he would have his information and he would be free to leave this place.

Caleb stood at his kitchen sink, fingers absentmindedly tapping. He had been home in time to spend it with his boys. Hannah walked up beside him and wrapped her arms around him. He hugged her back, and they just stood, looking out at the darkening sky.

"You're worried in a way I haven't seen in a long time, Caleb."

"I am. It's this thing with Liam. I just don't get it."

He could feel her nod. "It will come. God will grant that to you."

He smiled. "What, no name yet?"

She slapped him and then moved away. "No, nothing concrete. Just impressions. It's coming." She stopped and turned to watch him. At her silence, he turned. "I think it is going to be another one of those unexpected names. What I am getting is that it is something who is well respected and a long-standing member of our community, once again." She sighed. "I just wish someone else would get these names."

Caleb reached for her and pulled her back into his arms once again. "I know, me too."

She rested her head against her husband and listened to his heart beat. "I just wish I knew now. I have a bad feeling."

Caleb sighed. "I do, too. Time is running and we can't stop it."

Liam helped clear the lunch dishes and then turned. He was at a loss. Ashling had taken Teagan and disappeared earlier that day. He was healing but the ribs still wouldn't let him work out on the job site like he wanted to. He had caught up on his drawings, all the paperwork, and his secretary had told him to leave and go find something to do.

He turned as he heard Teagan and Ashling return. She smiled at him in greeting on the way by.

"Hey, Mam, Liam's bored. Let's send him to see Sally. She'll cheer him."

He heard Caitlin laugh as she headed to answer the front door. "That we should. He can teach her new words too."

Ashling came and stood near him. "If you're tired of holding up the counter, we could go find something to do. I have some puppies you can help socialize."

He eyed her. "They don't talk and flirt, do they?"

Ashling laughed. "No, but they would if they could." She stopped as she heard voices in the hall. She shot away from him towards them, and he heard the joy in her voice.

His heart dropped and he turned and walked outside. Why did he think he had a chance with her? Other than what they had gone through, did they really have anything in common?

During the afternoon, he hung around the outside of the group. He could tell Ashling and the four men around her age were good friends. He searched faces to see if she had an interest in any of them. None that he could tell.

Lorcan stopped beside him. He nodded at the group. "Don't worry. I can see you are. Ashling, Marc, Tim, Eric and Wayne and their wives have been friends since they were kids. They're a really close knit group. You don't recognize them, do you?" When Liam shook his head, he named a group that was popular in the area, singing music from the 50s and 60s. Liam's eyes shot to the group and then back to Lorcan. "You heard me right. I would hazard a guess, seeing as they're singing here at the festival this weekend, they're up to something."

Liam watched as Marc, he thought it was, handed Ashling what looked like a CD. She was shaking her head, laughing. The four men were doing their best to convince her. She turned, sought his eyes, and then turned back, giving a reluctant nod. Marc tucked his arm in hers and she laughed, again shaking her head. One of the others got down on his knees in begging position. She laughed again, pushed him, sending him backwards, and sending the other three into peals of laughter.

Lorcan slapped his shoulder. "Don't worry, brother. There's only one man here she has eyes for."

Liam hesitated, then walked back through the house. It was time he went home, he thought. He headed for his room and then packed his bag. He went to find Caitlin, thanked her and then left. Her eyes followed him, compassion in her gaze. He was hurting in ways that weren't physical.

Later that night, Caitlin tapped at her daughter's bedroom door, then entered. Ashling was curled up on her window seat, turning the CD over in her hands. She didn't look at her mother.

"What happened, Ashling?"

Ashling shrugged, then looked at her mother, tears in her eyes. "I don't know. The guys showed up and things changed. Lorcan said he told Liam that the guys, their wives and I had been friends for so long. When I looked, Liam was gone. I didn't mean to exclude him. You know what those guys are like."

Her mother reached out to stroke her daughter's hair. "I know. You didn't exclude him. Right now, he's unsure how he feels about you or how you feel about him. It's all so new. Besides, you and he have been through a lot in the last few weeks and he feels it is not safe to be around you, if the danger is directed at him. He's torn." Caitlin stopped. "You also need to remember, he lost his parents when he was young, just in his early 20s. He had to grow up fast and be a father figure to Leith and Laycee. He's hurting, honey, and hurting in a way that only God can reach."

Tears sparkled in Ashling's eyes. "I know, Mam. I told him I saw that in him. I only wish I could help." She found herself in her mother's arms and hugged tight. She could feel her mother's lips moving against her hair in prayer.

When she pushed away, she searched her mother's face and nodded. She knew what she had to do, she just didn't know how or when.

"Get some sleep, honey." Her mother dropped a kiss on her head. She too knew what she had to do and tomorrow she would track down a certain young man.

The next morning, Caleb looked up as Eddie tapped at his door. Eddie entered, closed the door, and handed a file to Caleb. Caleb opened it, read the report, and then set the file down.

"Does anyone know beside you?"

Eddie shook his head. "I haven't seen Ben to tell him, but you're the only one.'

Caleb tapped his fingers on the closed file. "Let's follow up and see how his friends are. Someone has to know something about him. Andy Cole, let's see what you have to offer us."

Eddie left and Caleb settled back to his paperwork, then stopped. He knew the Coles, they ran just inside the law. They had never really been able to pin anything on them over the years. If this was the son, when did he cross that line?

He sat back in his chair, the leather creaking. Something was niggling at him, some connection to the Coles. He shook his head. It wasn't coming. He'd leave it sit and work away in the back of his mind. It would come.

****

The Major stood and walked toward the Sargeants. He was angry. He had the Colonel angry at him and the anger flowed through to these two men.

"You are fools. You really are. Did you think killing this young man would help?"

The Sergeants looked at each other. "He knew who we are and who you are. We don't know how he found out but he did. He's the one who let them go. We couldn't let him go to the police."

The Major stopped just short of them, fist raised and then lowered. If that was the case, then they couldn't have let him live. It was a shame. He had been a good source to get information for him. Now he would have to find another.

"Out!" He shouted at them. "Out. Go find that information we need. Do something right for a change."

He paced after they left. The Colonel was really coming down on him and he couldn't right what these two men had done. He stopped, staring into the distance. He had to come up with a plan quickly and fix what had gone wrong. But what?

****

Caitlin rang the door bell at Liam's house and waited. She knew he was at home. When he answered, surprised to see her, she entered.

"What a beautiful home you have." She looked around. "This is nice. You've kept to the period of the house with modern updates and touches."

Liam looked pleased. "I tried. Joshua really did an outstanding job. I haven't told him, but I have entered pictures into a renovation contest. I am hopeful that he wins. Leith worked his magic with the tile work."

357

Caitlin looked at the tile in the entry and nodded. "Both those young men are talented." She looked up at him, tucked her hand in his arm, and nodded. "Show me your kitchen. I understand it is really something to look at. And if you have a spare teabag, a cup of tea would be nice."

Liam looked down at her, then escorted her to his kitchen. She looked around at the off-white cabinetry, the beautiful porcelain tile flooring, the soft yellow, almost cream walls, the mottled brown countertop and colourful backsplash.

"This is really nice, Liam. You feel at home here."

"My mother used to say the kitchen was the heart of the home. Whenever anyone came it, it was the kitchen they came to." He set her cup of tea front of her and then sat beside her as she patted the table. "But you didn't come here to see my kitchen, did you?"

She studied the young man, wisdom gathered over the years teaching her to read him. She shook her head. "No. No, I didn't I guess. I came to see you."

At his surprised look, she nodded. "Right now, you need a mother. You are hurting, you feel lost. You don't know which way to turn or who to turn to. You need either your mother or your father and I am guessing you feel like a little boy lost."

Liam looked down, tears springing to his eyes as his friend read him so accurately. He nodded, unable to speak.

She reached for his hand and grasped it. "There will always be a part of everyone who needs their mother and their father. Fathers give protection, they give wisdom from a man's point of view. If you need that, you have men in your life to provide that—Ben, Eddie, Lachlan, even men in your church. I would hazard a guess and say you really don't have a female in your life that you can talk to." He shook his head, and she continued, "Liam, look at me. Now, please look."

He raised his head and she studied him, then nodded. "I know how you feel about my daughter." Her grasp on his hand tightened. "Don't worry. Not many do. You are very cautious with your dealings with her and I thank you for that. She has a story that only she has the right to share with you and one day the time will be right for that. But for now, please think of me as another mother for you. Talk to me. Let me speak with you and pray with you."

At her words, something in Liam broke, something he had blocked up for many years. His head went down on his arms and he wept. He had been strong for so many years, not letting anyone other than his two siblings close, and even they didn't know all that he kept inside.

Caitlin let him weep, knowing he needed this. The crisis he was in right now was the catalyst to healing in his life. She finally stood and hugged him, her head on his like she would her own son. Her prayers for healing and strength resonated through him. When his tears stopped, she brought back a warm damp cloth and handed it to him. She stayed, talked with him, lead him to passages in the Bible she felt burdened to give him, and then prayed once more for him.

"Thank you, Caitlin. God knew I needed a mom today." He stood staring down at the mother of the woman he loved. He reached and hugged her. "Can I call you Mom?"

She laughed. "Of course. And if my daughter has anything to say, you'll be family." She stopped him. "No, I'm not saying anything else. I know my daughter and I am beginning to know you."

He closed the door after her and leaned on it. His heart felt lighter than it had, almost lighter than it had in years. He thanked God that Caitlin had felt led to come and talk with him. He whistled as he headed for his study. Now maybe he could work on that plan he had festering in the back of his mind.

He sat at his desk and reached for his pencil. His hand stopped and he instead reached for the object he had picked up at the Downie's. Instead of drawing, he rose and headed for his truck. He need to find Caleb or Ben or

Eddie. Maybe they could figure out what this flash drive was all about.

Caleb entered SueEllen's diner and looked for Liam. He raised his hand at SueEllen's gesture with a mug and a piece of pie. She knew what he liked and would bring it to him. He looked around and saw Liam sitting in a booth at the back. Sliding in across from him, he studied him. Something had changed with him but he couldn't say what. He looked more peaceful, maybe. Liam would tell him at some point, he thought.

SueEllen set his tea and pie in front of him, topped up Liam's coffee and then left.

Liam sat, hands around his mug and stared out the window. He finally looked at his friend and saw the fatigue and tired lines in his face.

"You need a vacation."

Caleb snorted. "Like I'm going to get one?" He sipped his tea, then asked, "What's up? You wanted to meet and I don't think it was just for coffee."

Liam hesitated in a manner that was not like him. He finally reached into his shirt pocket for an object. He motioned for Caleb to hold out his hand and dropped it into his open hand.

Caleb looked at it and then peered at Liam. "What's this?"

Liam shrugged. "I don't know what's on it. I figured you'd have computer guys you could take a look at it." He stopped. "I found it near the rock formation I did at the Downie's. There should be no reason for it to be there. It was down into the dirt a bit, as if it was dropped and then stepped on." He paused again, his eyes once more searching the outside of the cafe, looking for what, he couldn't say.

Caleb waited, wondering where Liam was going with this. He knew if Liam suspected the Downie's then it would be very difficult for him to accept that.

"I asked Lorcan if they ever copied anything onto flash drives. He said no. They had a back up they used all the time and burnt copies onto disks. He said sometimes Ashling was given a flash drive by a band she friends with but it's a professional one and not this name. When we were sitting up on the rocks the other night, Teagan alerted to something in the trees behind us. Ashling didn't seem to catch that there was something wrong. I went back later and looked. Someone has been watching their home." His brown eyes bored into Caleb's. "Someone has been watching them and not just recently. There is a spot that is well worn, I would say likely from before we started the work."

Caleb studied the flash drive in his hand, turning it over with his fingers. He nodded. "I'll have it checked out. It may be nothing or the break we've been looking for." He looked up at his friend. "How are you actually doing, Liam? I haven't had a chance to speak with you about all this."

Liam shrugged. "I'll be glad when you find the guys. Then I can go on with my life. Caitlin Downie stopped by today and we had a good talk. She has me pegged in a way only my own mother would."

Caleb nodded. "You need someone like that right now. Stay close to her and Lachlan." He then smirked. "It will give you a chance to stay close to another female in that house."

Liam looked at him and shook his head. "Now that sounds like something Leith would say."

Caleb stood, dropped money for his tea and pie on the tabletop, and hesitated. He laid a hand on his friend's shoulder. "We'll get it figured out, Liam, we'll get there."

Liam nodded and watched his friend walk away. He looked around. He still felt like he was being watched and he didn't like that feeling at all. He searched the faces in the cafe. A lot of them he knew, the others were tourists, he supposed. No one seemed particularly interested in him.

****

The Major watched through the window. Liam had given Caleb something and he wanted to know what it was.

361

He couldn't see. He had a bad feeling things were about to get a lot worse for him.

The Colonel would not be happy if that was what he had been looking for. He had no idea how he would ever retrieve it now.

It was the day of the annual down town festival. Caleb was worried about Liam and Ashling. It would be a perfect day for something to happen. He had spoken with Ben, Eddie, and Lorcan. He would officers patrolling the down town but they always had lots of crowds. It had become a very popular tourist attraction.

Liam headed for the down town. He had hoped to take Ashling but she has asked to meet him there. He searched the crowds, not seeing her but finally seeing Lachlan and Caitlin. He headed for them and stood just behind them.

A popular group had stared playing music from decades ago. He could see some couples and lots of children dancing in the open area in front of the crowds. Strange that there was a roped off area. He wondered why. When he looked up, he recognized the group as the men who had stopped by the Downie's the other day.

He felt someone at his shoulders and looked. Lorcan stood there, scanning the crowds, eyes alert and not missing anything. He was on duty but had been asked to come in street cloths.

Lorcan shot a sidelong look at Liam. Ashling hadn't told him, obviously. He nudged him with his shoulder.

Liam looked at him.

"She really didn't tell you, did she?" At Liam's look, Lorcan laughed. "Well, I'm not about to spoil the surprise. It's coming."

Liam stared at him, then as the music changed beat, looked at the band. Lorcan laughed at again and shook his head.

Marc, if Liam remembered, spoke, "We found out after we were booked for this festival, that good friends had moved to this area. It took some persuading but we managed to convince one of them to join us today on stage or rather in front of the stage. For your pleasure, ladies and gentleman, Teagan and Ashling." He held his hand out and waited. "Um, Teagan and Ashling, you are out there aren't you? Ashling? Teagan?"

The crowds were laughing. Liam got a quick look of concern on Lorcan's face and then Lorcan laughed. Liam followed his gaze and his jaw dropped.

Ashling and Teagan ran out from the side of the stand and stopped. Ashling was dressed for the decade in pedal pushers, red sweater, sheer white kerchief on her neck, and a red sheer kerchief on the high ponytail she had drawn her hair back into. Liam wondered what was coming. Lorcan nudged him again.

"Watch. You'll enjoy this. It's something really different. She hasn't done this for a couple of years, last time with these guys."

He watched as she shook her finger at Marc, who laughed at something she said. She then positioned Teagan and started to walk away. Teagan crept along behind her. Ashling stopped turned, and hands on hips, spoke to Teagan, who crept backwards, head down as if in shame. The crowd shouted with laughter. Every time Ashling moved, Teagan moved. Finally, Ashling turned, Teagan stayed where she was, eyes intent on her mistress.

Marc spoke, "Teagan, are you finally ready?" At Teagan's bark, Ashling shrugged, said something to Marc, who again shouted with laughter. "All right, everyone, sit back and enjoy."

The drums started, then the other instruments. The men in the group broke into a melody of slower and more upbeat songs from decades ago. He could feel Lorcan moving to the music beside him, but his eyes were on Ashling and Teagan. He had never seen a program like that. Both moved to the music, with spins, sideway movements. Teagan would back through the legs as Ashling moved. At one point, Teagan was even on her back legs. He couldn't begin to describe it. It was amazing. The dog was actually dancing? What was with this family? A bird that talked and flirted and now a dog that danced?

Lorcan took a look at Liam's face and nodded. If Ashling hadn't had his heart before, she did now. He knew Ashling wasn't real comfortable out there, but her focus was on her dog and the music.

The music ended and the applause was thunderous. Marc motioned Ashling and Teagan to the stage with them, and standing with an arm around her shoulders, thanked her.

"And people, this lady and her dog live in your community. You have an amazing talent in this dog trainer. She also has an amazing voice. We tried to get her to join our band but she said we had too many years of friendship going for her to ruin our gig." He kissed her cheek and then let her go. Ashling and Teagan disappeared.

Liam's eyes sought for Ashling in the crowd. Then he felt a hand tuck under his arm and looked down. She was standing beside him, not looking at him. He could feel her swaying to the music. He watched until she looked up, and then smiled.

"You do hide a lot behind that beautiful face, don't you?" he asked.

She blushed, then nodded. "I wasn't sure I would be able to get out there, but Marc and the guys insisted. They were right. I've missed that." She looked up at him again. "It's not the first time we've done that as a group. We used to have fun when we were teenagers."

Liam reached and hugged her. She was surprised at first then hugged him back. Liam saw Lachlan and Caitlin watching them, smiling. Lachlan nodded. Caitlin searched his face and eyes and then nodding, let him know she was aware of how he was finding his peace and his way back.

Liam took her hand and led her away from the crowds in the square. They wandered for a while before he led them to a bench in a quiet area. He held out her cup of tea and waited until she sat. They sat in quiet for a while, then Liam spoke.

"That was quite the show, you and Teagan. Where is Teagan anyway?"

"Da and Mam took her home. They weren't staying."

"Your mom is quite the lady. Do you know she paid me a visit the other day?" When Ashling shook her head, he drew her close and left his arm around her shoulder. "She knew I needed my mom and offered to be my mom. She had such words of wisdom for me."

Ashling listened as he spoke about his conversation with her mother. She nodded when he finished. "She does have so much wisdom. So does Da."

She suddenly shivered and looked around. "I don't know, Liam. I feel like someone is watching us."

Liam was searching around them as well. "I feel the same. Come on. Let's go." He reached for her hand, but she tucked it into his arm instead. "Some day, you'll have to explain that to me."

"Explain what?"

"Why you don't let me hold your hand?"

"Oh, that."

"Yes, that."

"That." She tilted her head to look at him. "One day, maybe I will."

He smiled. "I'll hold you to that." He looked up. "That looks like trouble coming."

Eddie and Ben were headed their way, grim looks on their faces. Their eyes were scanning the crowds.

Ben spoke. "We've been looking for you two." He looked around. "We need to get you two away from here."

Liam and Ashling exchanged glances. What was happening?

Eddie spoke. "That flash drive you handed Caleb yesterday? We don't have a name, but it's got some really powerful names and money amounts. Looks like some blackmail going on, at the very least. If the blackmailer thinks you have it, he won't stop at anything to get it."

Liam's steps faltered. Blackmail! That's what this was all about?

"What flash drive?" He could hear Ashling's voice beside him.

"Liam found a flash drive near the rocks at the back of your property and yes, we know it doesn't belong to any one of you." Eddie's hand came up as Ashling went to protest. "Liam already knew that before he asked Lorcan if any of you used that type of flash drive."

Liam could feel her eyes on his and he looked down. A mixture of emotions were in them. He knew he would have to talk with her at some point.

Ben urged them forward. "We need to get you under cover somewhere. I'm afraid that whoever is after you has been here. I enjoyed seeing you and Teagan work this afternoon, Ashling, but it probably wasn't the wisest move."

Ashling stopped and faced Ben. "I refuse to live in fear. I will go on with my life. I know someone could very well have shot me today, but I'm not about to stop what I love to do because of that."

Liam turned his head and watched her. Her Irish temperament was showing. Okay, he thought, there can be sparks.

Ben and Eddie tucked them into Ben's car and they left.

"Where are we headed, Ben?" Liam asked.

"Right now, we're heading to your place for you to pack and then to Ashling's. We're working on a place."

"I hope it's safer than where you had Leith and Regan." When the two men winced, Liam flushed. "I'm sorry. That was uncalled for. I know you did your best but that that leak."

"We'll find somewhere, Liam. We don't want to go through that again."

****

The Major stood at the bench. He had been so close. His sergeants were there too. They had just missed them. How did they always just miss them?

The Colonel was getting anxious and more angry by the day. He was losing patience, and the Major really didn't want to find out what happened when there was no more patience. He drifted away in the crowd. He would have to come up with an idea and fast on how to find them.

****

Ben's eyes constantly watched the traffic around him, searching for a tail, or something that seemed out of the ordinary. Eddie was monitoring the radio chatter.

Liam reached for Ashling's hand. Her fingers curled into his and tightened. He knew she was scared but it didn't show in her outward calm demeanour. He himself was angry, angry towards whoever it was that was stalking them. He had finally got to the point where he could think about his own life now that Laycee and Leith were settled.

His head went back. Leith and Regan—their wedding was in a few days. No matter what, he would be there, even if he had to ditch his guard and walk back from wherever they were headed. He would bring that up with Caleb when he spoke with him and speak with him he would.

Ashling was tired. She rested her head on Liam's arm. She had been fighting and running for a long time and it was time it stopped. Her eyes slid shut and her heart opened up to God. She just longed to rest under His wings and be whole again.

Leith and Laycee stood facing Caleb. He had asked them to meet him at the Downie's. All had gathered in their living room. Regan sat on the couch, watching, eyes moving from one to the other. Joshua stood at the mantle,

368

arms crossed, eyes not wavering from his wife. Lorcan stood beside him, eyes on his parents. Caitlin sat in her favourite armchair, Lachlan perched on the arm, holding his wife.

"Where are they, Caleb?" Leith demanded.

Caleb shook his head. "No, Leith. I won't tell you. It's not safe for them and it's not safe for you. You remember what you and Regan went through just six months ago."

Leith shook his head. "Doesn't matter. I want to be there to help."

Caleb shook his head again, then let his eyes wander the room. He saw the concern, the love on the faces of those gathered. Hannah, he thought, I could really use a name. Please come through, honey, and soon.

"We are keeping it as quiet as we can. We have been given some information and in the process of tracking it down. It's really powerful and damning information. I won't take a chance on anyone's life." He stared around at the group. "Anyone's. Got me?"

They nodded. He then turned back to Leith.

"I know, Leith. He's your brother. You want to be with him, just like he did with you. I also know your wedding is coming up and you want him here to share these next few days with you. I will make arrangements for you to talk. And he will be here for what he needs to be. I know it's not the same, and this time can never be made up again."

Leith took a deep breath, then nodded. Caleb would do his best.

Liam stood and looked around the bedroom of the house he had been taken to. It wasn't much to look at. He knew now how Leith felt last year. Please, God, he prayed. Let this end soon and well. I don't know if I could go through what Leith went through last year with Regan, almost losing her. Please, God, please hear my plea.

A tap at the door had him turning. Ben stood there, watching.

"I'm really sorry, Liam. I really hated to break up your day today."

Liam sighed, then sank to the bed. He motioned Ben to the chair. "I hated to have you do it. I just want to make sure Ashling safe. I hate that something directed at me has been brought to her."

Ben eyed his friend, trying to assess where he was at. Liam had learned to cover his feelings, partly from having had to head up his family so young.

He hesitated, then spoke. "Liam, you have borne a huge burden for the last 10 to 12 years. You have become a real man of God." He held up his hand as Liam went to protest. "You're struggling right now. I can see that. You hide it but those of us who know you see it. You have been the head of the home, the protector, the one who has watched out for your siblings in so many ways. Now, they are settled, Laycee married, Leith about to be, and you feel lost. That phase of your life is over and you really don't know where to turn. You are struggling to trust right now with what is going on. God understands. He is there wherever you turn. I can remember your father talking in a study group we were in not long before God called him home. He was talking about how God spreads His wings to cover us, that He shelters us. He provides a place to rest and refresh. That's where you are now. You need to do that. No matter what is going on for the next few days, that's where God is for you."

Liam looked at the floor, feeling rebuked. Ben was so right in what he said. He nodded.

Ben stood, placed his hand on Liam's head, hesitated as if to say more, then left. He closed the door behind him and rested his head back. Lord, he prayed, we're in that dark place before dawn. Be our light.

Ashling stood in the kitchen, assessing what was available for food. She was hungry and wanted food. She hadn't eaten earlier, being too nervous. She and Liam had planned on finding something at the festival but plans had changed. Now she needed to fix something. There was not a whole lot right now but she could make sandwiches, and checking the cupboard, soup. Not much but it would be filling. As long as there was tea to be had, she would be fine.

She turned. Eddie stood watching her.

"What?"

Eddie smiled. "Won't work, you know. The best have tried and it doesn't work."

"What doesn't work?"

"Wishing it was different. Wanting to leave. Please don't try and run. I can't run fast like you and I don't want to even try."

She studied him, then looked behind him at Ben. "I can't promise that, Eddie. I just can't. I trust you both but if it comes to protecting those I love, I will make the decisions I need to."

Eddied sighed. "Ashling, that's what I'm afraid of, that you'll make a decision and take off. If you do that, I can't protect you."

Ashling watched him, not seeing that Liam had entered the room as well as Ben. "Let me tell you something not many people know, other than my family. You can verify with the police department where we last lived.

"When I was about 18, I had a stalker. It was brutal. I won't go into the details. It was a horrible, horrible time." She stopped, looking at the ceiling, tears shimmering in her eyes. She looked back at Eddie. "The police tried to protect me. It didn't work. I finally had to strike out on my own, away from my family. After about six weeks on the run, they finally tracked him down. He was within 30 minutes of finding me. He had threatened my parents, my brother, my friends. So don't tell what I will or won't do. My life is ultimately in my hands and God's." She brushed by him and headed for her bedroom.

Silence reigned in the kitchen after she left, shocked looks on the men's faces. They had not expected that. Ben spun to look down the hall, then back at Eddie and Liam. Liam sank to a chair, shock vibrating through him.

Ben turned away to take a call. It was Caleb. He stepped into the living room to have some space.

"How are they, Ben?"

"Quiet. Ready to fight us already. Ashling has as much as told us she'll run if she has to. Liam, he's not saying much but I know he's feeling the same. Just whether they run together or not." Ben hesitated, then asked, "Do you know Ashling's history at all?"

"That she had a stalker? I just found that out from her dad."

"I wasn't expecting to hear that." He paused at the window and looked out. "Now where do we stand with the flash drive?"

"I have someone working on it. Unfortunately it's going to take time and digging. I called a contact at the federal level. He's working on it as well since it looks as if there's federal crimes." Caleb stopped. "About Friday and Saturday. We need to get Liam back early on Friday. He needs to be with Leith. The wedding's on Saturday. I've had a number of men come and volunteer to do security. Their wedding is small and they opted to have a small dinner in the church hall. That helps. Makes it easier to control who gets in and out."

"That's good. I am gathering that Liam will want Ashling there. Can we work it out?"

Caleb thought and then agreed, he thought they should be able to.

"I'll call in the morning. Lorcan has already come to me, wanting in on his sister's security. I don't plan on that unless I have to. I don't want both Lachlan's and Caitlin's children in the line of fire."

"No. We don't. Has Hannah come up with a name yet?"

Caleb laughed softly. "No, and I wish she would."

****

The Colonel stood over the body of the one Sargeant. He had failed him. He had tracked him down by following the Major without him knowing. This would be a warning to the Major and the other Sergeant.

The Major stood in shock, watching the Colonel. He had never expected him to appear and then to kill the man. It was up to him now to dispose of the body. He was angry as well. Thanks to the Colonel, he was down to one man and himself. What was he thinking?

The Colonel stared at him, then turned without a word. No word was needed.

****

Leith wrapped his arm around Regan and pulled her close. She could tell he was worried. She had no words for him. He didn't need them. He stared across the room at his sister and her husband. They were just as quiet, lost in their thoughts about their own race to survive.

Joshua looked up and caught Leith's eye. He shook his head slightly and Leith's eyes closed. Caleb wouldn't say where they were. He knew that. He had promised Liam would there on Friday and Saturday. He just wanted him here now. It wasn't fair. Regan's hand tightened on his and he looked down. Her eyes were on his and they had a peace in them he just wasn't feeling. He pulled her to her feet and walked with her to the door. He needed to take her home to her parents. Then he would come back to his place and spend the night in prayer. He would petition the heavens on his brother's behalf and also behalf of the woman he knew his brother loved.

Two days later, Liam stood watching his brother, dressed in suit and tie, rose on his lapel, pace. He felt relief, his brother and sister were settled. His parents would be pleased at the life mates God had provided them. Now to get him through to the dinner and he just might survive.

Leith turned, watching his brother. "Liam."

Liam looked up, studying his brother's face and eyes.

"I just want to thank you. You've put up with a lot but you've stood in Dad's place so many times. I wouldn't be who I was if you hadn't."

Liam caught his brother in a hug, then stepped back. "Things will be different now. Our family has changed, it's grown. Come, let's get you out to your bride."

The wedding was small, just close friends and family. There was still sorrow in Regan's family after the deaths of an uncle and his son. Leith and Regan had not wanted a lot of fuss and bother.

They waved off the newlyweds. Liam sought out Ashling finally, his duties done. He could see Ben and Eddie headed their way. He wanted time with Ashling, time on their own. He held up his hand to the men, asking for five minutes. They stopped and Ben nodded.

He pulled Ashling with him into the chapel. She looked around.

"It was such a beautiful wedding. Regan was lovely."

Liam stood watching her, hands in his pockets. "It was. But she's not as lovely as what I am looking at right now."

Ashling refused to look at him. He moved to stand in front of her and when she wouldn't look up, he cradled her face in his hands and raised it so he could see. Tears sparkled in her eyes. One had escaped. He reached with his thumb and wiped it away.

"Don't cry, Ashling. You are beautiful to me." He pulled her into a hug. "I know we have to go back into hiding but soon, soon we can talk."

She shook her head. "I'm not going back into hiding. I refuse to."

Liam stood still, shocked at her words. "Ashling, please. Don't say that. If you don't, I won't either."

She shook her head again. "No."

He looked past her, Ben and Eddie standing at the doorway waiting. "Come on, precious one. We have to go."

She turned, resigned in the knowledge that she was leaving her family once again. She wasn't ready to, but she had no choice, not at the moment.

Caleb's phone rang as he was hanging up his suit coat. He pulled it out and answered it, a grave look coming across his face. This was not the news he had been hoping to hear. Another body. Another unknown. Another murder. Not in his town. Man in his depravity was wreaking havoc and he wanted it to stop.

"Okay, let me know what you find out."

Hannah stood watching him, compassion on her face. "Not another, Caleb."

He nodded and sank to the edge of the bed. "Another one. I'm so ready for this to be over."

Hannah sat beside him and took his hand, fingers turned to mingle with his. She had stood behind him all these years, supporting him. His sons sometimes complained that they didn't get to see their father as much as other boys did but in their young minds they knew why. He was keeping the town safe. She leaned against him and sighed. "I wish I had a name for you. This time I don't. Just the impressions I gave you before."

Caleb dropped a kiss on his wife's head. "It's okay, Hannah. I don't expect you to every time. It's nice when you do. I know you'll tell me if you do."

"Do you have to go out again tonight?"

"No, I don't think so. Eddie and Ben are covering the security detail. The other officers are working the murder scene. They'll let me know if I do." He looked down at her. "How about a movie night with pizza, popcorn, and my favourite girl?"

She looked up at him and smiled. "Sounds good, favourite fellow." Her smile dropped away and distress filled her eyes. "Oh, Caleb, I just got a name. I don't want to tell you."

He took in the look on her face. "Never be afraid, my dear, to ever tell me anything." He pulled her into a hug. When she whispered the name, his face paled and his eyes closed. Never would he have imagined that name. Now he would have to pull either Ben or Eddie back in to follow it up.

Ben closed his phone and went to find Eddie.

"Caleb called. Hannah gave him a name."

Eddie watched Ben's face. "Did he tell you who?"

"Not yet. He wants one of us back to the office to meet with him."

"You go. I'm fine with staying."

"You sure?" At Eddie's nod, he turned to the door. "I'll see if we can find someone to send out."

Caleb met Ben at the office and then closed the door. He sank wearily into his chair.

"I hate to put this to you this late at night, but I feel like we're running out of time." He studied the paperwork on his desk, hesitant to continue.

Ben watched him. "It must be pretty bad for you to be looking like that."

Caleb sighed. "It is. I can't even imagine the betrayal it's going to cause." He looked at his friend, studying his face. He said the name and Ben's eyes slid shut.

Ben shook his head and then looked at Caleb. "No, I wouldn't have expected that one." He sat for a moment, and then stood, fatigue showing in his movement. "I'll get started tonight and then catch a few hours of sleep. We're going to have to pull someone in to help Eddie."

Caleb nodded. "I know. With this, we can't work with just us three." He rubbed the back of his neck. "I really don't know who though."

"Lorcan."

Caleb shook his head. "He's too close. I'm not sure he could keep his perspective enough. They're really close."

"They are. That may be where the strength will be. But then again, if Lorcan disappears too, then they'll go after their parents."

"Let me think about it. I'll be here. That couch over there can be comfortable at times."

****

The Sergeant stood beside the Major.

"I've found them. I need to call in a favour and I'll have someone who can work with me. I'll bring them in. By this time tomorrow, they'll be in your hands."

"But will we have the information we want?"

He shrugged. "Maybe not, but he'll tell us where it is. You were sure he found something that day."

"If we can find it, then the Colonel will be happy. When he's happy, we're all happy."

Chapter 15

Caleb looked up as Ben entered his office. Ben looked as tired as he felt.

"We have another murder. No, not one of them." Ben sank into one of the chairs. "I just might not leave here. It's Paul Caswell."

"That's not a name I recognize.

Ben shook his head. "I have something digging into his background to see where he fits in."

Caleb sat back in his chair. "We need to end this and soon, Ben. I have a bad feeling."

Ben stood to leave. "I do too, Caleb. We need healing for our town. With this, we won't get that until it's all wrapped and who knows how long that will take."

Liam felt a hand on his arm and then his mouth. A voice in his ear was soft.

"Shh, Liam. Quiet. We need to leave." The hand was removed.

"What's going on?" He asked as he sat up.

"Eddie and Ben are talking. Ben's back. Whoever it is has found this place. They're trying to figure out how to get us out and keep us safe."

Liam's eyes searched the room in the early morning light. "We can't leave."

Ashling shook her head. "We have to. We're putting them at risk." She held up her hand. "I know, it's what they do for a living." She snuck a peek at the door. "I know where we can go. We'll be as safe there as here. Where's your wallet?"

"My wallet?"

"Yes. Take your driver's license out and all your money. Stuff that in your front jeans pocket."

When he hesitated, wondering what she was up to, she repeated it. He looked at her and then his wallet, finally moving to do what she had asked. She took his wallet and stuffed it into his knapsack.

"Ben and Eddie will make sure our stuff gets home."

She grabbed a beaten-up knapsack she had set on the floor by the window. She motioned him to her side as she carefully slid up the window. Once they were out of the room, she slid the window back down and then catching his hand, led the way to the open field at the back of the yard, then to the trees lining it. She stopped, staring back at the house.

Liam stood beside her, watching as well. "Okay. So's what the plan?"

Ashling smiled. "You'll never believe it I told you. Let's watch. Ben and Eddie will know soon and then they'll leave, making the ones after think we have moved to a new house."

Ben walked towards the bedrooms and listened. Silence. He tapped and then opened Ashling's door. The room was empty. A bad feeling came over him and he headed for Liam's. It was empty too.

"Eddie, they're gone."

"They can't be. How?"

Ben picked up a note Ashling had left, read it and then handed it to Eddie.

"That girl is scary." Eddie had to admire her. "It doesn't say where they're headed."

"No, she wouldn't put that down in writing." Ben sighed, then looked at Eddie. "Well, I guess that means we get to break the news to Caleb they're gone. It looks as if she has a plan she hasn't told anyone about. She did ask we make sure we take their stuff."

Caleb looked up at the tap at his door and stared. Ben and Eddie stood there but there was no Liam or Ashling. He beckoned them in. After closing the door behind them, Ben and Eddie sank into the chars in front of him. Caleb kept his eyes on them. Neither looked at him. Finally, Ben handed him a piece of paper.

Caleb took it and read it. He shook his head and re-read it. "You were there, and they still managed to get away?" At his nod, he threw the note on his desk, leaned back, throwing his hands in the air. "How are we to keep them safe when we can't even keep them in protective custody? How do I explain this to the families?"

Ben shook his head. "I don't know, Caleb. I really don't know. Ashling has a plan, I'm sure. She thinks things through, but it would have been nice if she had shared."

Eddie spoke up. "She wouldn't. She's not sure who she can trust right now." At Ben's protest, he held up his hand. "Yes, she knows she can trust us, but she thinks someone is leaking information. Considering no one knew where we were, it seems strange that car showed up just as we were leaving."

"What car?"

"An expensive one, with lots of power. They had covered the plates with mud so we couldn't read them. We didn't want to stay around, we wanted to make it look as if we were on the run."

Caleb just stared at the ceiling. What next, he wondered? God, are You in control and running this? Because I'm sure not.

He looked down at his desk and then at the two across from him. "Guess all we can do now is follow the leads we have and hope we solve this before something else happens."

The two men stood and headed for the door. Ben stopped and then looked back at Caleb. He went to say something, stopped and then headed out the door. Caleb watched him, wondering what he had been about to say. He sighed as the door closed behind them. It felt like everything was spirally quickly out of control. He prayed that not one of his friends ended up as the next statistic.

****

The Sergeant stared around the house, moving from room to room. How had they gotten away again? Who was tipping them off? The Major would not be happy at all and he hated to hear what the Colonel would say. He was glad he had never met him and didn't have to. He was not looking forward to telling the Major those two had slipped through their hands again. Did they have a leak somewhere, had someone talked out of turn?

****

Liam followed Ashling as she made her way towards the down town area. He had no idea what she had in mind, but seeing as she seemed to know where she was going and why, he went along with her. She stopped near a rundown building and looked around.

"Come, Liam. In here." She pulled the door open just enough for them to enter and held it so it didn't slam shut. "Over here." She led the way to an area at the back that was dark and somewhat sheltered.

"I need you to stay here for me," she whispered. "I need to go get us some stuff. You'll be safe her."

Liam protested. "No, I need to come with you."

She shook her head as her fingers covered his mouth. "No. It's not safe if we both are out there. I can get in and out without a problem."

He stared at her, wondering how she knew she could. He studied her clear blue eyes. She was so sure she could. He didn't want to have anything happen to her.

He reached for her and pulled her to him. "I don't want you hurt."

"I won't be. I have friends here."

His hands slid down her arms and he pushed her back. "You have friends here?"

382

She nodded. "Trust me, Liam. I know who I can trust here."

He watched her face, eyes roving over it as if to memorize it. His hand came up to cup her cheek and he felt her lean into it. She shook her head and then moved away.

"Give me about an hour."

Liam sank to the floor and laid his head on his upraised knees. All he could do was pray. Somehow, he questioned if that was even enough right now.

An hour later, he heard a whisper of sound and raised his head. He tilted his head to listen. It didn't sound like Ashling's steps.

He stood and drew back into the shadows as much as he could. A form appeared in his line of sight, and he heard his name called. It was Ashling, but he would never have recognized her.

She had changed into scruffy sweat pants and a torn T-shirt. Dirty sneakers covered her bare feet and he saw there were holes in the shoes. Her face, arms and hands were filthy. But it was her hair that he couldn't believe.

He reached out a hand and touched it. Pink, blue, green and it was teased to look as it is hadn't been brushed in days. He wouldn't have recognized her. She had a pair of cheap sunglasses in her hand.

"What did you do?"

She grinned. "Didn't recognize me, did you?" She handed him some clothes. "These are yours. Go change and bring me back what you're wearing."

He looked at what she had handed him and then at her.

"They're clean. I was at the thrift shop. Don't worry. I wasn't recognized. Hurry, we need to get on the move."

Liam changed, feeling very uncomfortable in his new clothes: worn, holey jeans, stained sweatshirt, ball cap. He gathered up what he had been wearing, making sure to transfer his license and money. When he came back to Ashling was waiting, she studied him and then reached for a container she had.

"Bend down." He felt her rubbing something in his hair and then over his face and neck. He cringed.

"Be good, Liam. I know your mother told you to wash behind your ears. This time, you won't. It will help hide you." She finished running his hands and arms and when he looked all he saw was dirt.

He looked at her and went to say something when she grinned at him. "I found the cleanest dirt I could."

He shook his head and then took the ball cap she handed him. Pulling it down over his eyes, she studied him for a minute and then nodded.

"Okay, here are the rules. First, never look at anyone in the eyes. That's a threat. Next, keep your thoughts off your face and your face as blank as you can. Don't argue with anyone. That's a quick way to end up locked up. We don't want that. Don't stand straight, hunch over as much as you can."

He shook his head again. "Are you sure this will work?"

"It did for me when I ran away at 18. I know most of the people out there. I come here every month or so just to make sure they're okay." She looked around. "We need to go. Bring your clothes and we'll dump them in the box at the thrift store." She grinned at him again. "Sure I can't interest you in some hair colouring?"

"No. And I hope that's not permanent either."

"It's not. A few washings and it will be gone." She led the way to the door and cautiously opened it. "Come on. We'll get rid of this. I want to find Frankie."

"Who's Frankie?"

"He's a friend. I can trust him. He wouldn't squeal on us. He's been down on his luck and trying hard to get back on his feet." She looked around. "It may take us a while but we'll find him. I have word out I'm looking for him."

She stopped, then say, "My street name's Ember. You need to remember that. I need to come up with one for you." She thought for a minute. "Any suggestions?"

Liam studied her. "No. I'm never ever thought about changing my name."

"Trust me. You'll need another name. Your name is not that common. It would be easy to track."

As they walked through the down town area in the graying light, she pondered a name. Finally she looked at him and shook her head. "Nope, that one won't work, nor that one, nor that one."

He snickered. "Is it really that hard to come up with something to call me?"

She pushed him sideways and he stepped off the curb. "Yes, it is. Nicknames mean something here." She shrugged. "I'll come up with something, or else Frankie will."

Lorcan looked up as his mother stopped beside him. He was brushing Teagan, who was looking so forlorn. His mother's hand rested on his head and then she moved past to sit in one of the wicker chairs in the sunroom.

"Do you have any idea at all, Lorcan? Do you know where they are?"

He shook his head. "Ashling can be very wily when she wants to be. She's got street smarts about her that some of the average cops don't have. That's how she survived for those six weeks."

His mother laid her head back on the chair and closed her eyes. "I just wish I knew she was all right. It worries your Da and I."

"I know. Caleb, Ben, and Eddie are working on something, I know. They haven't said much but Caleb did mention that he might need my help."

Caitlin turned her head to study her son. So much like his father, just so much like her. He had a peace about him that she didn't feel herself.

"Did Ashling ever say much to you about those weeks?"

He sat back and thought. "No, she never really did. I know she said she had some good friends there she was concerned about but she lost contact with them. Do you know she goes down there every few weeks to make sure everyone's okay?"

"No, I didn't. It makes sense, though, knowing her."

Lorcan watched his mother. He could see the lines of stress on her face. He wished he knew where his sister was, but he could understand why she ran.

"If it had just been her, she would have stood and fought. She won't when someone else's life is at stake." He stood, crossed to his mother and hugged her. "I need to get going. I'm on duty soon."

It had been three days since Ashling and Liam went on the run. Liam's secretary was doing her best to run his office but things were piling up that only he could answer. Laycee tried to help but she really didn't know a lot about it. Leith was just back from his honeymoon (they had taken a long weekend and planned a longer trip once work had slowed a bit into the winter) and had his own work to look after but stopped by Liam's office to meet with Laycee.

"Liam gave you the power of attorneys, didn't he, Leith?"

Leith nodded. "But I don't think this is what he had in mind when he did that." He stopped. "I just wish I knew where they were."

"Me, too. Joshua and I were talking about that this morning. If we knew for sure they were safe, we'd be okay."

Liam's secretary appeared at the door. "Liam said a while ago that he had wanted to slow down this fall a bit. Did he mention that to you?" When they shook their heads, she hesitated. "I just don't know. Bud keeps pushing for more work, but Liam wasn't budging on increasing the work load. We can't go ahead with new jobs without Liam's input."

Leith watched her. "No, we'll let it go for a week or so and then consider what we need to do. Hopefully by that time, Liam will be home." He stood and looked over to Laycee. "I have an errand to run. Will you be okay here?" At her nod, he left.

Caleb looked up at the knock at his door. Leith and Joshua stood there. He beckoned them in and Joshua closed the door. He sat, just watching and waiting.

Leith spoke. "What's going on, Caleb? Do you know where they are?"

Caleb shook his head. "Wherever they are, they're safe. I haven't seen any reports about them. They both have good heads on their shoulders. I know, I know. They ran from protective custody. They shouldn't have, but they did."

Leith looked down at his hands. "I need to make some decisions about Liam's work. I just don't know what to do."

Caleb spoke slowly. "I would hold out for as long as you can. Liam's got a good reputation; his customers are understanding."

Leith nodded, started to say something, then stopped. He gave a half smile. "I now know how Liam felt. I don't like it." He stood and walked from the room.

Caleb looked after him, then at his own brother. "Stick close to him, Joshua. There are things happening I can't talk about but it is really going to hurt that family and this town."

Liam sank down to the sidewalk. He was exhausted. This was worse than putting in a long heavy day at his work. He leaned his head back against the building. He just wanted to go home, to get clean, and sleep.

Ashling sat down besides him, her head going to his shoulder. She was exhausted as well. She had managed to track down Frankie, a friend on the street, and he was out looking for information for her. Hopefully he would find out something. He said he had bits and pieces but wanted to put it all together.

"Did you think we'd be here this long?" Liam's voice was tired.

He felt her head shake. "No, I thought a day, but Frankie's good. If anyone can find out what we need, he will. He'll pass it on to Ben or Eddie for me." He felt her smile. "How do you like your street name?"

He snorted. "Who in their right mind calls me Eagle?"

"That's what you are, my friend. Frankie sees into people in a way most people don't."

"Why Ember for you?"

She shrugged. "Part was a play on my name. Another part, he said I had a spark about me he didn't see much. He comes up with a lot of the names for his people here." Her voice trailed away, and Liam felt her relax. He wasn't comfortable out here in the open like this, but he didn't think too many of their friends would recognize them.

He watched as she slept, watched those around, watched for those who might come. He knew he was falling in love with this lady and he didn't want harm to come to her.

Frankie dropped down on his other side, then peeked at Ashling. "She's running on nerve. She can't keep going."

"I know. I just want to get her home. She got involved just by being my friend."

"That's not what she tells me. She tells me you got into trouble, she helped out, and now she's stuck with you. I say it goes both way. You're both stuck with one another. Take care of her, Eagle, or you'll answer to me." Frankie stopped talking and just watched. "Tell her I passed the information on like she wanted me to." He got up and left.

Ashling stirred, then looked after Frankie. "I knew he would come through."

Liam let out a quiet laugh. "You were faking it, and Frankie knew it. Hopefully, whatever he passed on will be enough to let us get home."

"I hope so too." Ashling stood, then reached for his hand. "Come on, it's almost time for supper at the shelter. Maybe tonight we'll be able to get some cots and sleep indoors for a change."

Ben went looking for Caleb and found him at the photocopier. He handed him a mug of tea and then waited. Caleb looked up, the fatigue and strain evident in his face.

He nodded and then grabbed the copies he had been making.

Once in Caleb's office, Ben handed him a dirty envelope. Caleb opened it and began to read. His eyes slid shut. Ashling and Liam were safe.

"We were right. She did run to the streets."

Ben nodded. "I know who that is who passed that on. He feels like he owes Ashling. He'll keep her as safe as he can and as long as Liam stays with her, he'll be fine. She has made a real difference in lives down there. I never knew how much until now."

"I didn't know she was down there that much."

"With the information Frankie has found, where do we go?"

"More digging, my friend, more digging. He has really done a lot of leg work for us in such a short time."

"He has." Ben stood. "I'll keep digging from my end. Maybe we'll meet somewhere in the middle."

Caleb blew out a breath and knew he needed to meet with the families for an update. He couldn't share much but at least he could let them know Ashling and Liam were alive and well.

****

The Sergeant stood in the down town area. He had searched so many areas of the town. This was one area he hadn't and he really didn't want to be here. He had no use for the people who lived on the streets. As far as he was concerned, they were losers. He looked around. He had heard rumours that those two were here, but no matter how much of a reward he offered, no one would tell him what he wanted to know. He would keep searching, hoping to find someone desperate enough to want his money.

****

Caleb had met with the families. He could offer little for their comfort, other than the two were alive and safe.   He entered his home, soft lights filling the

390

downstairs. Once again, he was too late to spend time with his boys.

Hannah came into the kitchen as he dropped into a chair. She moved to make him a cup of tea and heat some dinner for him. He felt almost too tired to eat but knew he had to. Talking quietly as he ate, they discussed the day's events in each of their lives, then joining hands, bowed their heads to raise their friends to the Heavenly Father.

Chapter 17

"We've found them."

The Major closed his eyes in relief. Now maybe the Colonel would back off and let them find the information he wanted.

"Where?"

"They're in the down town area somewhere. They keep on the move but someone saw him. There was a girl with him but they couldn't be sure if it was her."

"Find them. We'll deal with them once you have them."

"Give me a day at the most."

****

Liam stood watching the crowds, tense. He had had a feeling all day he was being watched but couldn't pinpoint a face. They had been found, somehow. He turned to find Ashling. He reached for her hand and pulled her with him.

"We need to go."

Her eyes flew to his. "Where are they?"

"I don't know but they're out there. Where can we go?"

Ashling's eyes flew around the area. She knew if she asked, her friends would help, but she didn't want to ask them to risk their lives, and she knew that's what would happen.

"Come, let's head that way. Keep your head down. Wait." She looked around, darted away and then came back. "Here, put this on instead of the ball cap." She handed him a battered straw hat. "If they've seen you in the cap, this might just give us a chance to get ahead of them."

Liam caught her hand and led her slowly through the crowds, head down, but eyes watchful. He tried to shuffle as he had seen those do who really had no hope did.

Ashling searched for somewhere they could hide, but where? Where would they really be safe? Did they go back to Caleb? They couldn't go to their families, that might be their deaths.

God, she cried, where are You? Where do we run?

Liam pulled her hand. They headed down a small alleyway, trying doors. He pulled one open and shoved her inside

"I'm going to try and block it somehow. If I can, we'll try for the other door and leave that way. We need to get away from this area."

Ashling stood and watched as he jammed the door, He grabbed his hand and pulled her forward to the end of the building. He cracked the door. They were safe so far. They ran for the end of the alley, then towards the edge of town.

"There!" Ashling pointed at a derelict building. "In there. I know there are hiding places in there they would never think of." She led him in and away from the doors. How she knew of these places, he wouldn't ask now but one day he would.

The men following them stopped and stared around. Where had they gone? They couldn't have gotten away again.   They looked at each other and then one pointed to a building. Just maybe that one. They took off on a run towards it.

Caleb met Ben and Eddie at the edge of the down town area. They were on a search for Liam and Ashling. It was crucial that they found them and found them today. Word had come from the street that a contract was out to bring them in to the Colonel and it really didn't matter what condition they were in, as long as they could still speak. Caleb had a piece of paper tucked in his pocket. He had been devastated when Hannah handed it to him. After all these years, he still didn't understand the way God worked through her, to provide names for him. He hadn't shared it yet with the two beside him.

Ben and Eddie's eyes scanned the area as well. It was a busy day down town with the local farmer's market and the annual artisan's market. How would they ever find them?

A voice spoke to their right. "Don't look. I know where they are. Head for the old electric building." The voice stopped and the man slid away through the crowd.

"Frankie." Ben was sure that was who it was.

Caleb nodded. "We need to split up and make our way there one at a time. We have enough men around here out of uniform if and when we need them. Ben, find Frankie. He knows more than what he said."

One by one, they disappeared into the crowd. They were leisurely in their walk, not in any hurry to get there. Eyes scanned the crowds for the one man they had confirmed was involved but they couldn't see him. If he was there, the crowds hid him well.

Ben stopped at a bench and sat for a minute. A hunched figure in tattered clothes sat there already. Ben handed over a cup of coffee he had purchased just for that reason.

Frankie peered out from under his hat. "They're hiding. The ones after them? They're getting close. Someone gave them up to him."

Ben didn't acknowledge that Frankie had spoken. It was an unwritten understanding that he didn't. "Do you have names?"

"Yes." Frankie repeated names to Ben.

Ben's eyes slid shut. Caleb was right. It was really going to hurt when they had to make those arrests. He stood and stared down at Frankie. "Go on," he said in a loud voice. "Move on before I arrest you."

Cowering, Frankie moved away, until he was lost in the crowd, then straightened up and headed for the abandoned building at the edge of town. Ashling was a good friend. He needed to help her. Her friend, Liam, he was still not sure about him, but Ashling seemed to like him, and like him a lot. So if she liked him (and he knew she read people very well), then he would help keep him alive.

Liam sank to the floor and tried to catch his breath. He was done running. He wanted his life back. He was ready to go to Caleb again. He paused, thinking of Ashling. She had pushed him back here and then disappeared again. His eyes slid closed as he prayed for her safety.

A small noise reached his ear and he tensed. It was Ashling.

"I think we're okay here for now." Her voice was low as she spoke near his ear. "There's an opening wide enough for us to get out if we have to just behind that tank."

"How do you know all this?" Liam stared at her in the gloom. She was tired, dirty, and unkempt but still very beautiful to him.

She shrugged. "Friends tell me. My friends here on the street? They find these places. There are times when they need to escape and have a whole system of hideouts."

Liam shook his head. "Ashling, what am I do to with you?"

She gave a soft laugh. "If you don't know, then who am I to tell you?" She stopped. "Shhh. There's someone out there. Be prepared to move."

Ben stopped by Caleb. He watched his friend's face. He saw the fatigue and stress in it, but he could see there was more than that.

He spoke. "Frankie came through again."

Caleb nodded and waited for Ben to speak. Ben seemed to be having difficulty with his words. Caleb had a good idea why.

"He gave me a name." Ben looked up at the bright blue sky. "I suspect Hannah has already told you, I can tell." Ben paused. "Why do people have to be like that? Why destroy what you have built up? Why damage people so badly? Who would ever of thought of that name?"

Caleb spoke, "You're right. Hannah did give me that name. It's really going to tear through our community, more so than with the other two." He hesitated, then spoke, "Man's depravity and sin sometimes just overwhelms us. If I didn't have God, I don't know if I could continue in this line of work."

Ben nodded. "Let's go find Eddie and break the news to him."

The two men moved off.

****

The Major followed after his Sargeants. Where were they headed? Had they found them? The Colonel was getting very anxious and angry. He just wished he had never gotten involved with him. Maybe he should just cut his losses and run, but where would he run to? He was in way too deep now to do that. He sighed. It was not what he had envisioned when he was approached by the Colonel.

Ashling drew closer to Liam.   They could hear voices and footsteps in the large open area of the building. Debris was kicked. She grasped his hand tightly, prepared to move. They knew the building was being searched and they could hear the searchers coming closer.   Then the footsteps moved away to another section of the building. Ashling pulled at Liam and motioned to the back of the building. They rose as quietly as they could and made for it.

"You're not going anywhere, my friends." A voice spoke behind them. "You're coming with us."

Liam didn't look around to see if the speaker was in the room where they had hidden. He pushed Ashling ahead of him towards the opening and prayed that they made it safely. A shot pinged off the tank ahead of them and they dropped to the floor.   Steps sounded behind them once again

"On your feet, you two. We've places to go and people to see."

Liam pulled himself to his feet and helped Ashling up. His heart sunk. All this time, they had been safe and now they were once again in the hands of their hunters. He took a quick look at Ashling. Her face was calm, serene, how he wondered. Her eyes were staring at the men, but he could see that she was thinking about how to get away.

They were roughly pulled from that room and then shoved towards the door. The men no longer bothered to cover their faces, as if they knew Liam and Ashling would never live to identify them.   Liam started when he recognized the two who held them. How had they sunk so low?

Another figure appeared in the sunlight streaming towards them. Liam vaguely recognized the man, but his mind refused to believe it was who he thought. He shook his head.

A shove from behind sent Ashling to her knees. Liam spun, ready to fight for the woman he loved, then his hands went up in the air as the revolver pointed at him cocked, ready to fire. He wouldn't be able to help her if he was injured or dead. He reached for her hand once again, in defiance of the men holding them.

The Major spoke. "Well done. Now, let's get out of here before the police get here. The Colonel is waiting."

Liam's head jerked towards the speaker. It was really who he thought, a friend, someone he thought he knew and trusted.

Once outside, they were shoved roughly into the back seat of an SUV. Liam grasped Ashling's hand. She was calm and he wondered how she could be. His eyes darted around, looking for a way out and not seeing one.

A curse came from the driver. "What are they doing?" The horn honked as people started to mingle around the vehicle, keeping it from moving forward.

Hands reached for the doors and pulled them open. The three men were shouting, the driver trying to inch forward.

Liam felt a hand on his arm and he was jerked from the vehicle. Ashling followed, holding tight to his hand. They disappeared in the crowd. They could hear the shouts and curses from the vehicle. Ashling's friends slowly moved away. They had returned her love and friendship to them in such a tangible way, Liam was awestruck.

Frankie appeared and motioned for them to follow him. He led them to another building, this time at the other end of town. When they were safe inside, he stopped and studied them.

"You tried, Ember, you tried. You and the Eagle almost made it."

She nodded. "Now what, Frankie? Where do we go? If they found us once they'll find us again."

He pursed his lips as he thought. "Yes indeed they will. However," he held up a finger, "I might just have a plan. Are you prepared to go back into custody again?"

Liam watched him closely. There was something different about him right now, but he wasn't sure what.

Ashling was shaking her head. "No. I don't trust everyone in the department. I think someone gave us away."

"Someone did. And I know who. Stay here. I'll be back at dark."

Ashling watched him leave, then turned to look around the building. "Liam, I don't like this place. I don't feel safe here. I trust Frankie, but something isn't right."

Liam caught her close in a hug. "I know. Something seems different about Frankie right now. I think we should try to find a place on our own. But where?"

Ashling hugged Liam back. She was filthy, exhausted, hungry, yet Liam made her feel like the most beautiful woman on earth. She could get used to that.

She turned and wandered through the building. She came back to where Liam stood. "I don't like this building. It's unsafe. Do you know what they used to make here?"

Liam had to think. The building had been abandoned for years. "I can't remember off hand, but it was something in the manufacturing field." He spoke as he walked through the building. "It will come, but I think it was…" He shook his head. "No, it's not coming to me right now."

Caleb looked around at the building. "They were here. From the dirt, it looks as if they were taken out and not willingly."

Ben shook his head. "No, they weren't." He took a deep breath. "But where are they? I heard that a large group of people stopped a SUV. Wonder if they got away?"

Caleb gave a brief laugh. "I can bet Frankie had something to do with that. Has Eddie been able to track him down?"

"He was trying to, but you know Frankie. If he doesn't want to be found, he won't be."

Caleb nodded and then was lost in thought. "If you wanted to hide someone, where would you take them?"

Ben pondered that a for a few minutes, then turned and walked out the door. Caleb followed. Ben knew this town, knew where the hiding places were, which buildings were best.

"I've got it. I just hope we're in time." Ben headed off at a run, Caleb at his heels.

Eddie was coming towards them. "I found them, but so have the others. I'm not sure who will get there first, us or them. I put in a call for back up."

"Which building?"

"The old mill."

Fear shot through the three men. They had to get there before the others. Dodging through the crowded streets, they headed for the mill.

Ashling took another walk through the building, studying it. She didn't like it at all.

"Liam, was this a mill, by chance?"

He spun. "It was. I have heard lately that it has been used at times for drugs. I don't like this." He reached for her hand and pulled. "Come on, we're out of here."

Liam reached for the door and then stopped as it opened. Here we go again, he thought.

Ben stood in front of him. "Don't you think it's time you two stopped running? You've certainly led us on a merry chase."

"That's what makes life interesting, Ben." Ashling stood just behind Liam. "Life's boring otherwise."

Ben just stared at her. "Ashling, we don't need this kind of interesting. We know who we're after now. We just need to keep you two safe until we can arrest them.:

Liam could feel Ashling shaking her head. "No, Ben, you can't. There is someone who is leaking information on us. I just haven't figured out who yet."

Caleb spoke as he entered the building. "We do. Steps are being taken to prevent that person from contacting anyone." He studied the two. "I must say, though, you two have been very creative in how you hid."

Liam shook his head. "It wasn't me, it was her."

Caleb closed his eyes, drew in a deep breath, and then said, "Come, let's get out of here."

Eddie shot through the door. "They've found them. I can see them coming."

Caleb sighed. "Somehow, I just knew that would be the case."

Liam spoke up. "I know who they are."

Caleb looked back at him. "I know. So do we and we know who is paying them. We just need to get you out of here."

"Where's the back door?"

"It's blocked. This is the only way out, unless we go up and out the top door, and there's no guarantee the stairs are safe. I was through here a few weeks ago with that drug sweep we had." Eddie looked around.

"We're not trapped." Ashling looked confident.

"Yes, we are." Liam argued. "Didn't you hear what they said?"

"Sure, but they don't know the secrets my friends have shared. Keep watch and I'll be right back."

As she turned, Caleb caught her arm and stopped her. "Eddie or Ben will go with you."

She huffed and then agreed. "Come on, whichever one of you it is. I can show you an opening that we can get out of."

Eddie was on her heels and then came back. "She's right. There's an opening and I don't think they've found it. They know there's only one door that you can get in and out of."

Caleb heard a shout of "There they go" as they ran from the building. He could hear the sound of gunfire behind them. They reached shelter and paused, Caleb staring behind them.

"Ben, we need these two out of here now"

"I know. It looks like they've trapped us though." He slanted a look at Ashling. "Any new ideas?"

She shook her head. "I think you've had them all."

Liam spoke up. "Now what?"

Eddie took a look around. "Over there. If we can make it, we should be able to get away. That gunfire is going to attract a lot of attention." Sirens could be heard nearing the downtown.

Caleb took a look, and then shoved Ashling and Liam. "Go, we'll cover you."

Ashling and Liam took off running, Eddie on their heels, Ben and Caleb staying behind to provide a cover. They turned as they heard a cry and saw Caleb go down and Ben reach and pull him back to cover. Eddie pushed at them.

"Keep moving. Ben'll look after Caleb. They don't want them, it's you two that we need to get to safety."

They ran for the next building and then slid to a halt. One of the men had circled around and stood in front of them.

"Games are over!" He lifted his revolver. "You're coming with us. The Colonel demands your presence and he really doesn't care much the shape you're in, as along as you can still open your mouths and tell he what he wants."

"No, we're not." Ashling yelled. "Game's over, buddy."

"No, it's not, little lady. Come with me. Now."

Liam drew her back behind him. A sound came from behind and they knew they were surrounded. Eddie looked around for his backup. They wouldn't know where they were.

Ashling shoved Liam aside. "No, we're not. Tell your friend behind us to drop his weapon."

The man behind them laughed. "Don't think so."

A sudden sound from above came to their ears. The two men looked up as did Liam and Eddie. Ashling grabbed at the two men with her and pulled. She knew what was coming but despaired of getting out of the way in time. An explosion sounded and threw them off their feet.

Eddie lay still for a moment and then stirred, lifting his head from the pavement. Ashling and Liam lay sprawled beside him. The two men at either end of the alley lay still. He shook his head. What had that been? Did he really want to know? It felt like someone had dropped a bomb on them.

He stood shakily and made his way to Liam and felt for a pulse. He was alive. Ashling was next. He could get a faint pulse from her but he had to really feel for it. A noise came from behind him and Ben and Caleb stood beside him.

"Are you all right, Caleb?" He eyed Caleb's left arm and the blood on it.

"I am. It hurts though. How are Liam and Ashling?" They could hear the sirens behind them, and then the sound of the stretcher wheels as the paramedics rushed in.

Ben went to check the two men at either end of the alley. He came back and shook his head. "They're dead, but it wasn't the explosion. Someone shot them."

Caleb spun around and then caught his balance as Eddie's hand came out to steady him. "Who?"

"I doubt we'll know. It wasn't one of us. I would think it was likely some of Ashling's friends from the streets. They protect their own."

Caleb nodded as he watched the paramedics working on his friends. Liam had been placed on a stretcher and was being wheeled away. They were still working on Ashling. She has been placed on a backboard and had neck support but the three watching saw that it was a lot more serious than they had thought. Sudden movement showed them intubating her and then starting CPR. She was rushed away.

Caleb's eyes slid shut in prayer. "Please, Lord, please. Don't let her die. Not when we're this close."

Ben's hand on his arm startled him. "We need to get you to the hospital too. You need that arm looked at."

Caleb started to refuse, then nodded. "You're right. You two can look after this scene. Find out what that explosion was though. I don't want a repeat of it any time soon."

****

The Colonel stood at his office window, waiting. He had been promised those two would be here today and they weren't. Why? Had something happened?

He turned with a sense of foreboding. He looked around. He would need to leave soon, leave without the information that would secure his life and source for money.

****

Leith and Regan ran for the Emergency Department. Laycee and Joshua were there waiting.

"Any word yet?" Leith hugged his sister, searching her face.

"No, no yet." Laycee clung to her brother. "I'm scared, Leith."

Leith's eyes met Joshua's over her head. "We'll pray, Laycee, we'll pray."

405

Joshua spoke, his voice raw with emotion. "That's what we can and will do. Caleb was shot today, too."

Regan spoke up. "Oh no, Joshua. How is he?"

Joshua shrugged. "He's still upright. He says it's nothing, Hannah says differently. She's back with him now, making sure he does what he's supposed to."

The four found seats and huddled together, heads bowed in prayer. They didn't look up as their pastor and others from their church family joined them.

Caleb looked over at Hannah. She stood just behind the doctor who was bandaging his arm. He had had to have stitches and knew that in a while, it was really going to hurt. But he wasn't done for the day, not for a while. Hannah's face was white and strained. Once the doctor had finished and left, he drew her to him and into a hug.

"Shhh. Hannah. Shhh. I'm fine. I'm coming home to you and the boys."

She clung to him. "I was so scared when Eddie called me. I thought it was worse."

Caleb felt his wife's tears and a few fell on her hair as he laid his head on her head. "God was watching."

He set her back and with hands on her arms, looked at her. "We need to find out how Liam and Ashling are. Have you heard anything?"

She shook her head. "I haven't but Eddie said they were still working on Ashling. Liam was going for X-Rays or a CT scan or something." Her hand came to her mouth. "What about Ashling's parents and brother? Are they here?"

Caleb's eyes slid closed. "I need to get out there. I need to talk to them." He staggered a bit as he slid down from the stretcher. He caught his wife's hand. "Come, let's go find them."

Caleb found Lachlan, Caitlin and Lorcan surrounded by the church family as were the other four. He stopped and spoke with each one of them. Joshua caught his brother in a hug and the two stood for a few minutes. No words needed to be spoken.

A sound behind them and they turned.

"I'm looking for Liam Bradley's family." The physician searched faces. The four went towards him and he drew them aside for some quiet conversation.

"Liam's pretty beat up, as you can imagine. Lots of bruises, scrapes but no broken bones. No internal injuries that we can see. He does have a concussion. He's still unconscious right now. We're going to be sending him up to a room shortly. If you want, two of you can go back with him for a few minutes." He watched as Laycee and Leith headed for the exam room where their brother lay.

Joshua spoke up. "Thank you, Doctor. That has put their minds at rest." He turned slightly to watch Ashling's family. "If you have news on Ashling Downie, her family's here."

The doctor drew a deep breath. "I'm not the physician that has her care. I'll see what I can find out for you. That's her family over there?"

Regan nodded. "Her parents and her brother."

He nodded and turned, hesitating. He knew the fight that was going on right now to save Ashling's life. Selfishly, he was glad he wasn't her physician.

About thirty minutes another physician entered the waiting room and headed for Ashling's family. Lachlan and Lorcan stood, grim looks on their faces, as they watched him approach them. They tried to read his face, but they couldn't.

He drew up a chair. "I'm Dr. Forrester. I've been working on your daughter." He hesitated and Caitlin's hand came to her mouth. He reached for her hand. "She's alive. We almost lost her a couple of times. We're taking her up to surgery right now. There's internal bleeding that we need to get under control." He looked up at her father and brother. "I need to tell you, she may not make it. We will do our best."

Caitlin gripped his hand. "She is in God's hands. If He wills she goes home today, that it what will happen. Please, our prayers are with you and the medical team."

He bowed his head and then looked at them. "Yes, that she is. I'll make sure you get regular updates."

Hours passed, and finally he returned. "She's in recovery. It was touch and go but your daughter is strong. I'll have someone come find you when we move her to an ICU room."

Caitlin's face was covered in her tears. She reached out to hug the doctor. "Thank you. God used you today."

Lachlan and then Lorcan reached to shake the physician's hand and thanked him. Lachlan then drew his wife and son into a hug and led them in prayer for his daughter's healing, for Liam and for Caleb, for wisdom of all concerned.

Caleb stood at his desk and studied the paperwork in his hands. Warrants were issued and they were headed out shortly to serve them. It was not something he was looking forward to.

Ben knocked on his door and watched his friend. Caleb looked up and shook his head.

"I still don't understand. Do you?"

Ben shook his head. "No and I don't think I ever will."

Caleb and Ben and two officers entered Liam's office. His secretary looked up with a surprised look on her face.

"Where can we find Bud?" Caleb asked, regret in his voice.

"He is the lunch room, right down that hall." She stood and watched as the four made their way down the hall.

Caleb stood and watched Bud for a minute. "Bud."

As Bud turned and saw them, his face paled. "I guess this is it, isn't it?"

Caleb nodded. Ben read Bud his rights and then slipped the handcuffs on him.

"What I don't understand, Bud, is why?"

Bud shook his head. "Until you make another arrest, I'm not saying anything."

****

The Colonel stood watching out his window. He saw the cruisers that pulled up, saw Eddie climb out of one and stand looking at his house, then shake his head and move to follow the winding flagstone path to his front door. He heard his wife answer, heard her exclamation of surprise, a few quiet words spoken, and then a tap at the door.

It swung open and Eddie stood there, officers behind him. He studied the man in front of him.

"Dr. Young, you are under arrest for conspiracy to kidnap, murder, extortion, blackmail. I am sure we will find a few more charges to add to those." He nodded to one of the officers who slipped handcuffs on the once respected doctor. "I don't understand why."

"No, I don't suppose you would. I'm not saying anything without a lawyer." Still haughty, the physician was led from his home, his wife, in tears, left standing the hall.

Eddie stopped beside her, feeling sorry for a woman who had not always been kind, who quite often treated others in a way that belittled them. "He'll be in jail until his bail is made. Then he'll be going to trial. Do you have someone who can stay with you?"

Mrs. Young looked at him, and then she broke down. "I never knew. I'm sorry. I haven't treated people fairly or how I should have. Power and money, I guess, got to me. Now I have no one to turn to, not even my children."

"I'll speak with the pastor. He and his wife will come."

Eddie walked away from the house, shoulders slumped. It had been a bad day all around. His friend and boss had been shot and wounded, two other friends were in hospital, one that he wasn't sure was even going to make it, and now a prominent citizen had been arrested. But what bothered him the most was the betrayal directed at Liam. How Liam would deal with that, Eddie had no idea.

A voice spoke at his shoulder. "You found them, did you?"

"We did, Frankie, we did. Thank you for helping."

"How are Ashling and Liam?"

"Liam's got a concussion, lots of bruising. Ashling." Eddie's voice stopped. He swallowed hard. "She may not make it. She was in surgery a while ago."

Frankie's head dropped. "I'm sorry. I didn't know they were going to drop what they did. I still haven't figured out what it was, but I will. Ashling has many friends down there." He sighed and looked at the sky, then at Eddie. "I'm getting too old for this. I think I need to come back in and drop the street name, go back to being a regular cop."

Eddie laid a hand on his shoulder. "Yes, Frankie, you do need to. What was your real name anyway?"

Frankie gave a short bark of laughter. "You know it well, Eddie, you know it well. Tell Caleb I'll be in touch."

Leith and Laycee stood at their brother's bedside. They knew he was still unconscious but they refused to leave until they knew he would be all right. The nurses had been in and out. Joshua and Regan were in the waiting room down the hall, spending the time in prayer.

Leith drew his sister close to him. She laid her head on her brother's shoulder.

"I am so glad he's alive." She said through her tears.

"I know. I know." Leith stopped, he couldn't continue.

"Have you heard yet how Ashling is?"

"Regan was going to see if she could find out."

"It will kill him slowly if she doesn't make it."

"I know. Come on, Laycee. We need to go and get some sleep. We don't have to leave the hospital. We can wait just down the hall."

Laycee reluctantly followed her brother from the room.

Lachlan and Caitlin stood at their daughter's bedside. Caitlin reached for Ashling's hand. The hiss and click of machines and monitors sounded through the room,

IV dripped into her arm. Lorcan studied the equipment and then his sister. His eyes closed in prayer. Please, Lord, please heal her.

Dr. Forrester entered, chart in hand. "She's a fighter, your daughter is. I really didn't expect us to be standing here."

Lachlan spoke, the lump in his throat making it difficult. "She always had been, Doctor. She's been through stuff I can't imagine."

He finished his examination and then turned to them. "We were able to get the internal bleeding stopped. The spleen was removed, so we'll address that issue with her later. We'll gradually wean her off the pain medications we have her on and off all the equipment. I don't foresee any problems in doing that, barring any unexpected complications." His eyes turned to each one of them. "But with the prayer that is going up for her, I doubt we'll have any of those." He turned and walked away.

Ashling's family were allowed to stay for a while longer and then sent down the hall to the waiting room. It would be a long few days for them. Friends had picked up duties at their store, so they had no worries. Lorcan would be in and out as he was on duty.

A week had passed. Liam had been discharged and had been working to sort out the problems at his work. He felt so betrayed by Bud, his foreman, someone who he thought had had his respect and liking. He still needed to confront him but that would come later.

He made his way back to the hospital. Ashling had been awake on and off for the last day or so and he wanted to spend some time with her. He stopped at her open door. A clean-cut man stood at her bedside, with short brown hair, dressed in a T-shirt, jeans and sneakers. Liam watched as he bent and dropped a kiss of Ashling's head and then turned.

The man walked towards Liam. Liam felt he knew him, but couldn't place him.

"She'll be fine, Eagle. Take care of her." A hand dropped on his shoulder and Frankie was gone.

Liam stared.   That was Frankie?   What had happened?

He drew up a chair to the bedside and sat. He reached for Ashling's hand, cradling it in his. They were really going to have to have a serious talk when she was well enough.

Ashling's fingers moved, and his eyes went to her face. She had turned to face him, a small smile showing. They needed no words right now. Those would come.

Hannah stood on the Downie's deck and watched her husband and sons playing in the yard, Teagan bouncing around them. Caleb could finally put aside work for a day or two and spend time with his boys. Caitlin stopped beside her.

"It's good you could come today, Hannah. We needed to have you here. We can't thank you and Caleb enough."

Hannah shrugged. "It wasn't us, Caitlin, it was God."

Caitlin stopped her before she could continue. "God used you and Caleb." She turned to look over her deck at the people gathered. Their friends and family were there.

Ashling sat wrapped up in a warm blanket and snuggled down in a chair. Liam stood behind her, hands on her shoulders. One day soon, they would talk. This was one lady he would not let get away.

Finally, as they had finished their meal, Lachlan turned to Caleb. "Tell us, Caleb. Tell us what you can."

Caleb looked around. This time, it had really hurt their community. It would take time to heal.

He shook his head. "I'm not sure if I even have all the facts. It's still an active investigation."

He continued. "Dr. Young had been involved blackmail and extortion for years, almost back to when he set up practice. I can't and won't give names. He had been putting money away in accounts under alternate names.

"The flash drive you found, Liam, that contained a list of those victims. Somehow, Bud found it and was doing some blackmailing of his own. We think when he did some work for Dr. Young, he did some snooping and helped himself to it. How he knew, he's not saying. He lost it when he was doing the work here. Not a real smart move to carry it on him all the time.

"Dr. Young thought Bud had lost it one day on the river bank where they were to meet and when you stooped to pick up something, he thought you had found it. He is the one who pushed you into the river."

Caleb paused and studied the sky. "The two men they hired. One was Mrs. Young's nephew, the other a nephew of Dr. Young's. He was the one that was murdered after the hit and run killed the Coles' boy. The other was from out of town. They may have had others involved and we think they did. The young Coles boy - his parents are adamant they don't know what he was up to. I can't prove otherwise. They have lost a son. We still haven't found out who shot the two men. No one will say, but Frankie thinks it was ones from the street, protecting Ember and her Eagle.

"Frankie has not been able to find out exactly what was dropped and there was only trace evidence. Our team thinks an explosive device but they don't have enough left to work with to determine exactly what and the quantities.

"We did find our leak once again in the department. It was a file clerk."

They sat in stunned silence at what Caleb had revealed.

Lachlan finally spoke. "I can't say that it amazes me the level people go to in the depravity. God will judge them." He stood, started to say something, then walked down the steps and away from them.

Ben and Eddie and their wives left not too long after. Life would go on and they would too. They needed time to heal.

Leith, Regan, Laycee, and Joshua all left next. Liam watched his family walk away and nodded. Yes, they would be fine. Each had found the mate God had for them and they would be stronger now then they had been.

Caleb and Hannah stood in front on the two.

Ashling looked up at Caleb. "Frankie - what will he do now?"

Caleb shook his head. "I'm not sure. He's resigned from the department. He hasn't said if he'll stay in town or not." Caleb's eyes met Liam's over Ashling's head and in Liam's, Caleb read the knowledge. Liam knew that Frankie had been in love with Ashling and now that she had made a choice that didn't include him, Frankie wasn't sure he could stay in the same town as she lived.

Hannah hugged Ashling and then the four Logans left, the two boys waving and asking if they could come back and play with Teagan.

Liam stood studying Ashling, then gathered her into his arms. She leaned her head back and studied him.

"You, my precious." Liam stopped. He dropped down into the chair she had been in. "I almost lost you. My heart couldn't take it if I had."

A hand came up and touched his face. "God knows, Liam, my eagle, my strong protector. Leave it with him." She turned to watch the sunset.

Liam caught up with Ashling as she walked the river bank three months later. The wind was chilly and clouds covered the sun. He wrapped an arm around her and stopped her.

She stood beside him, watching the water lapping at the river's edge.

"I never thought all those months ago that we would have such an adventure"

"Me either." He turned her to face him. "Ashling, my precious, do you know what you do to my heart? When I thought I had lost you, I didn't know how I could ever go on?"

She dropped her eyes and laid her head on his chest. "Liam, don't. Don't go there. We've talked about it so many times, I just want to forget."

He hugged her tighter.

"So, my precious, this is where Laycee would be asking to go steady, Leith to get engaged." He could feel Ashling starting to laugh. "I think we should just skip that step, the step of being engaged, and just get married. We can beat them at their own game."

She pushed away from him and stared. "What! No way, buster!. I have dreamed of years of being engaged and all that goes with it! You're not depriving me of that."

He stared in the sparkling blue eyes before him and laughed at her nonsense.

"Ashling, my precious, you are the one I love. Will you marry me?"

Ashling turned and Liam's heart fell. He had blown it big time.

Ashling giggled. Liam's eyebrows rose. She had giggled. He started to laugh.

"Ok, missy, turn around and look at me."

She did and nodded.

"Now, you just have to get past my Da and brother."

He smirked. "I already did. Your father gave his permission four months ago."

Her mouth dropped open. "Four months!"

He nodded. "He knew. Come on, my precious." He took her hand and led her towards the road and the way home.

"By the way, will you ever tell me why now I can hold your hand and before I couldn't?"

She slipped her hand from his and tucked it into his arm. "Because when my hand is tucked here, I am safe. I am close to you. Holding hands - it means you care. Like this, it means you are my protector. You have me close to your heart."

"I have been finding my way back to God and to peace. He has set my priorities straight once again." Liam looked down at her. "He has used you in a big way, my precious."

She drew him to a stop and then said, "The verse that has gone through my mind through all this has been the one about waiting on the Lord and renewing our strength, rising like an eagle. Frankie named you right. You really are an eagle."

He drew her close and then led her to the car, tucking her inside. He stopped, kissed her, and then said, "Eagles mate for life. You, my precious, are my mate for life."

Dear Readers

The third story in the Under His Wings trilogy is complete. It has been quite the ride, characters entering, demanding to be heard, fear, happiness. Through the series, I have attempted to show how much man's sin and depravity can affect those around them, but that with God, we can rise above what is around us. He provides us with wisdom, with strength, with honour, with trust, with truth. It has been my prayer throughout these books that you will turn and seek God in a richer, fuller way. Like Liam, we too can go through the motions of our Christian life, coasting along. This is not how God has intended that we walk with Him and in writing these books, particularly Liam's, I have been speaking to myself in a big way.

Characters changed their names and their occupations in my books. Plot lines changed. Dr. Young, the villain in The Eagle, was to be the villain in The Sparrow and refused to cooperate with me.

My dear friend and sister in Christ, Faye Silvestro Kubassek, has once again taken on the task and proofread the story and made some suggestions to the story flow. Thank you, my dear friend. I really didn't mean to make you cry with this story. We have laughed and cried together so many times and sharing the occupation of medical secretaries has made our friendship so much deeper.

My parents have graduated to heaven. I miss them so much, particularly now when I have decisions to make about my books. I just want to sit down with them and hear their advice. They never steered me wrong. My father would shrug and tell me it was my decision but he always talked to me. My mother was the one who would be bold and blunt and tell me what she thought, and she was usually right. I miss their prayers, the joy they would have shared with me, my mother's smile of I knew you can do it, my father's you did a wonderful job. My first ever published novel, The Sparrow, was written on a challenge from my Mother. The Hawk and The Eagle flowed out of that book.

As I look to the future, characters in The Eagle are demanding their stories. I look forward to seeing what they will be up to. But rest assured, their lives will be centred on God.

God bless each one of you who have picked up one of my books and read it. I pray that you were blessed, challenged, and had a little bit of fun with trying to figure out who really did it before you got to the end. I enjoy a good mystery and have endeavoured to bring that in my stories.

My life verse is the one this book is based on: Isaiah 40:31: They that wait upon the Lord shall renew their strength, they shall mount up with wings as eagles, they shall run and not be weary, they shall walk and not faint.

Find your verse. God has one just for you.

With God's blessings and my thanks and love,

Ronna